The Enchanted Cup

THE ENCHANTED CUP

BY

Dorothy James Roberts

Appleton-Century-Crofts, Inc.
New York

W

TO

Kay Smallzried
and
Carolina and Robert Donaldson

Acknowledgments

I wish to thank Dr. Joseph E. Tucker of the Department of French and Italian of the University of Wisconsin, Miss Esther Vinson of the English Department of Illinois State Normal University, Miss Patricia Schartle of the Editorial Department of Appleton-Century-Crofts, Mr. Alasdair Spens-Thomson, and particularly Miss Kay Smallzried, who willingly searched bookshops and libraries, for help in collecting some of the materials for this book. To Dr. Julian Harris, Chairman of the Department of French and Italian of the University of Wisconsin, I owe my first interest in the story, and the first collection of materials.

Miss Elizabeth Paschal gave me other assistance for which I wish to express my gratitude. And Miss Bettina Brown rendered valuable service in the preparation of the manuscript.

The story of Tristram and Isoud as here set down has been based, at least loosely, upon the version found in the *Morte Darthur* by Sir Thomas Malory. When Malory wrote his book in 1485 the legend of the lovers was already old and had suffered many changes, corruptions, and additions. But because Malory wrote in English prose, and especially because he wrote with strength and beauty, his book has had more appeal to the present storyteller than earlier, purer versions. Malory's spelling of proper names has been used throughout with one or two minor exceptions adopted for clarity.

Malory concluded his masterwork with these words: "I pray you all gentlemen and gentlewomen that read this book . . . from the beginning to the ending, pray for me while I am on live that God send me good deliverance, and when I am dead, I pray you all pray for my soul." As his story is echoed here, let the prayer of Sir Thomas be echoed too, and all gentle people pray for the soul of him who enlarged the legend that none of us whose tongue is English can outgrow or forget while we are "on live."

Dorothy James Roberts

Mamaroneck, New York

The Enchanted Cup

Part I

Chapter One

O^N a summer morning when the gardens at Tintagel were blooming with fuchsia and foxglove, King Mark of Cornwall emerged from the castle and walked toward a little green sheltered by yew trees. He was still a young man, and handsome, and in his plum-colored kilts and short sword he had an air of elegance becoming to his slender, rather short figure. His hair was dark, and his eyes were dark, and he wore a neat, small beard which set off the lean hollows of his face. A chain of silver links hung breast-length over his shirt of soft leather and supported a medallion given him by his seneschal, who had found it in the ruins of an ancient Roman town. This medallion bore the portrait of a governor or an emperor, some Roman dignitary whose name Mark did not know, and an inscription he was unable to read. But he had no very serious wish to know, being satisfied to find the ornament weighty and shining and different from the native medallions patterned with spirals and interlacings of gilt or bronze. He fingered the silver disc sometimes, glad to think his forefathers had driven these dead, almost forgotten tyrants from Cornwall and from every shore of Britain.

Five or six ladies were sitting on stone benches under the yew trees. Sea winds always blowing from the west over Tintagel head had twisted the trunks of the yews into cablelike shapes and wrenched their branches all in one direction. These trees, grey and scaly and old, and the sound of surf hurling itself against the foot of Tintagel cliff, gave the ladies a look of youth and impermanence

3

(though, except for one, they were not young) like flowers which bloom a little while and are blown away. Mark had nothing fanciful in his temperament and did not think of this, but he was pleased to see the ladies attractively dressed and well-employed with needlework, as suited women of breeding and high calling. They were the attendants of his sister Elizabeth, princess of Cornwall. Elizabeth sat with them, and on the bench beside her, his hands tucked into his pleated cuffs, was Magan, her priest.

"Good morning, my lady," Mark said.

Elizabeth rose. "Good morning, my lord." She was dark, as he was, delicately made, and would have seemed a child except for the full, finely pleated skirt she wore, and the draped tunic, which was fastened at the shoulders with great gilt brooches. The dress was too heavy and muffling for her slight curves. And the amber and amethyst necklace and bracelets of bronze set with jet and coral overweighed her beauty too, and gave her the appearance of a girl masquerading in women's clothes. She did not care for these massive pieces, and only wore them to satisfy her brother and to reflect his ability to adorn her. At sixteen she had been mistress of Tintagel castle for a year, and realized she had resigned her right to please herself when she assumed her office.

She stood before the king unsmiling, her eyes lowered. The ladies, who had been laughing at something Magan was telling them, fell silent.

"I have come to inform you," Mark said, "that a runner arrived a while ago with news that knights from Lyonesse will be at the castle by sundown."

"Thank you," Elizabeth said. "I shall prepare for them, my lord. Did the runner tell you how many knights are expected?"

"Two. Meliodas always sends two. And so he lets us know he still has in Lyonesse two men young and healthy enough to stand up under the weight of arms." He showed his teeth in a laugh, and the ladies all hastily laughed with him, like so many small bells pulled by the same string. Elizabeth could not laugh, only blush under her brother's eyes at this banter which she had a reason to feel was cruel.

4

"I have promised to inspect the north port this morning," Mark went on, "and so I must ride. I shall be back about the hour of nones, I expect, in good time before the knights reach us. If I am delayed, you will receive them." He turned to Magan. "Be present if I am not here, Magan."

"Certainly, my lord." Magan seemed to smile. But age had given his face long, humorous lines, and it was hard to know whether he smiled or whether he only reflected a habit of smiling.

"God go with you, my lady, and all," Mark said.

"God go with you," they murmured.

When the king had left them their ease returned, and the ladies began to talk of the coming guests and to wonder what errand they had.

"Wait for us here," Elizabeth told them. "I would like to speak with you, Magan. Shall we walk to the church?"

They moved away from the yew trees, and the wind caught them and blew Elizabeth's skirts and worried the long habit of the priest. Magan was the only man, except Mark, of whom the princess had any knowledge, but he hardly counted as a man, being old and womanish and, like herself, patient. He had been her priest since she was five and had taught her her prayers, the calendar, and the holy hours. He taught her to read too, using his own books which he loved more than he loved his life. One or two of them he had copied himself when he was a young man, setting them onto parchment in the beautiful script he had learned as a student and ornamenting the capital letters with curved designs and interlaced ribbons of color. These were pious works. But Magan owned as well a few profane stories, French tales in which mirth was mixed with prowess, and wit sometimes proved stronger than swords and spears. He taught Elizabeth to read in French and to speak the language a little, both of them understanding without words that this was a secret which needn't be told to the king.

Magan had been educated in Ireland, and wore the Irish tonsure. His habit, with a pleated cape and square, pleated cuffs, fell to the instep of his soft-soled skin boots. From his girdle on the left side hung a knotted cord to help him when he wished to count his

5

prayers, and on the right, a knife in a sheath half as long as his thigh. When Elizabeth was a little girl she asked him why he wore a knife so much larger than he needed to eat with, and he had told her the devil sometimes tempted priests, though usually young priests. Had the devil sometimes tempted him? she wanted to know. At least he had never used the knife on the devil, he said, but because he had carried it so long he was used to its weight, and would feel unhabited without it.

At Cornwall Magan resigned himself to being out of the world. Here he had no companion to sit late with and talk learned matters; and here he heard only such news as travellers and wandering knights and begging holy men brought to Tintagel. Once he had hoped to be a historian, but now, when he was near the end of his life and realized he would die a woman's priest in the shabby court of Cornwall, he contented himself with displaying for his pupil the faded cargoes with which his mind had once been stored.

"I cannot skip along the rocks of Tintagel head like a lady of sixteen," he said, puffing. "What do you have to talk about that hurries us so?"

"I'm sorry, Magan." Elizabeth slowed her step to his. "I was thinking what I must do to prepare for the barons from Lyonesse. I've wasted time this morning. I still have many things to look to." As though to remind herself of her duties, she passed her hand across the objects hanging from her girdle: keys, a purse of small coins, a needle case, and a box for flint and tinder. These, the signs of her office, seemed heavy to her, and when she was tempted to run or be lazy or neglect her appearance, reminded her they hung from chains.

The princess had a household to watch over, supplies of meat, ale, fish, meal, and honey to tally, a sewing room to manage where clothing of wool and linen was made for all under her care at Tintagel, and orders to conclude with the potters and workers in wood and metal who were purveyors to the castle kitchens. She served the drink at meals, carrying the cup among guests and strangers. With her ladies she medicined the household knights

6

when they were wounded or ill. And she was learning to weave and embroider from a woman who had been sent for from Britany to teach her.

She was young to handle so many duties, and from time to time she forgot one, but not as often as she might had her brother been less exacting. Now she was embarrassed because the king had found her idling outdoors when she might have been overseeing the weighing of the threshed barley. Yet there was time to weigh the barley. She was determined to use a little of the freedom the king's absence allowed her and speak with Magan about a matter which had been burdening her.

"I didn't mean to hurry you," she said. "Only when I am thinking I forget."

"Why are we going to the church?"

"We don't have to go to the church. I was tired of the tattle of my women. They talk so, and their silly smiles never change. I said the church to get away from them."

"Let us go to our chairs, then."

Their chairs were not real chairs but rocks on the cliff Elizabeth had discovered long ago, and to which she had coaxed Magan times without number when, childlike, she had important secrets to tell him. And as she grew older she used the sheltered coign as a place of escape from life at court. Here she could lie and look down on the sea and think such thoughts as the helpless think, how love was somewhere this side of heaven, and how she could be happy if God were good enough to remember her happiness.

They turned toward the sound of surf and made their way a few steps down the sloping head of the cliff and stopped on a wide ledge from which they could see westward to the blue edge of the world. Below them the water crashed upon the slate sides of Tintagel head and boomed into caves and crevasses and tumbled back upon itself in rumbling, confused falls and spouting jets of spray. They could not see this tumult below them, or the streaming rocks which took their colors from the sea, deep earth-purples and rose. They saw only the limitless ocean itself, all

7

violet and jewel-blue and sun-gilded green. Landward, behind them, the castle, standing above the narrow neck across which anyone leaving Tintagel reached the mainland, was hidden too. But they felt its presence, and knew its grey walls shimmered in the morning light like an encrusted seashell still tinted with pink and pearl.

Elizabeth helped the old priest sit down. "Tintagel *is* beautiful on days like this," she said, as though she were persuading herself of a truth hard to keep in mind. "If only—"

"If only what?" Magan found the wind chilling, and wrapped his arms in the folds of his cape.

"If only my brother were satisfied."

This was a matter on which Magan had no business to hold an opinion. But he thought of Mark, and wondered whether there was not something in all kingship to make the men who bore it restless and fretful. Mark was better situated than some kings of Britain, Meliodas of Lyonesse, for example, whose land was even smaller and less prosperous than Cornwall. Mark at least owned the largest and strongest castle in the west, built as it was on a promontory shouldering into the sea, and on the east protected by steeps so rugged they were almost beyond attack. And as Elizabeth said, his land was beautiful. Cornwall had seasons when wild laurel and golden furze and slopes and glens of oak and hazelnut trees made it as lovely as the ocean whose breakers had forged its coast. But for all its cliffs and rainbow colors Mark quarrelled with it, or with the destiny which had flung him down in a country of farmers and fishermen and countrified knights who were laughed at by King Arthur's men. It was remote from Camelot and the ports of the east where merchants and warriors and foreign princes landed with news of the world. No, Magan thought, Cornwall was not the land for an ambitious man.

"If I were king in Tintagel I should not think about the rest of Britain at all," Elizabeth said.

"If I cared to speak as your schoolmaster, I might say," Magan told her with a dry smile, "that even as princess you have been known to resist thinking about the rest of Britain."

8

"Oh, Magan, was I a bad pupil?"

"Lazy when the sun shone and you had errands only little girls understood, perhaps. But not wickedly lazy. Not ever a bad pupil," he murmured, remembering her in a way she could not remember herself.

"If I was lazy it was your fault, dear Magan. You used to make my lessons seem all play."

"Yes, yes, we've talked over many an adventure of our country's past sitting in these very chairs, haven't we?"

They were silent, each overwhelmed by memories of their life together. To the girl life seemed long and vivid, to Magan as short as the span of a day and a night, blurred in detail. And to Magan his brief happiness as Elizabeth's priest seemed full of the usual human errors of accident and omission. Had he fulfilled his duty to this lady who was soon to leave his governance? Had he given her the disciplined mind and the pure spirit it was his office to impart? Of her spirit he had no doubt. It was clean and kindly and devout. But her mind? He excused his failures as preceptor and guide by reminding himself that no mind is ever formed and disciplined in sixteen short years.

"Perhaps it was I who was a bad teacher," he said, "an idle old man too willing to turn lessons into play."

"But I did learn about Britain, didn't I? I can tell you all about the Romans, and how they built temples and roads and theatres, and how their legions ruled us until they—they—" She gave him a doubtful look.

He laughed ruefully. "Until they what? Why did the Roman legions stop ruling us?"

"Because," the princess of Cornwall said, "because King Arthur made them go home to the east and leave us in peace?"

The priest was silent.

"King Arthur did make them go home, I'm sure. You have said so often enough."

"I suppose it happened that way. Only there were other reasons too, remember? The Romans grew quarrelsome among themselves, and fell into dishonesty and corruption, the way old nations do.

And when that happened, our own people had a chance to throw off their tyranny and put themselves under the hand of a true son of this island."

"King Arthur."

"Yes, King Arthur. When the time came."

"Did you know the Romans, Magan?"

"I am a very old man," he said, making his eyes round to tease her, "and I know a great many things, and I have seen all the men in the world save a trifling few. But even I did not know the Romans. Not Merlin himself knew the Romans. And when I was born Merlin was older than I am now."

"Merlin! You said Merlin was an elf, a dream! I asked you whether Merlin built Camelot, don't you recall, and you told me Merlin was no more than a wise man people chose to believe had powers God does not give men. You confuse me," the princess complained. "I never know whether you are telling me true things, or lies to amuse yourself."

"I have been a frivolous instructor," Magan said with a sigh. "I have talked to you so much of the old gods who lived in our land before the Romans came, and of men with unholy gifts, and of foolish, forgotten tales, that now, when you need to know more than ever the great facts of Britain's past, you know nothing but moonshine."

Elizabeth was troubled. "Do you mean what you say, father? Am I ignorant and ill-bred? Do I shame my brother and Cornwall?"

"No, no," Magan retracted hastily, seeing where his playful self-accusations had led them. "You are a royal lady, a pretty and charming one too. I meant nothing more than that we have talked some nonsense together, you and I."

"I didn't know we were talking nonsense. I believed everything you told me."

"Everything!" Magan crossed himself hastily. "Everything?"

"Did you tell me nonsense about King Arthur? But I have seen King Arthur myself. I know he is a true king and a true knight. He is a better knight than Sir Launcelot, and Sir Launcelot is the best knight in Britain."

"That is not nonsense, at least."

"I know something about King Arthur you didn't tell me, Magan."

"What?"

"My brother does not love him."

"Now that *is* nonsense," Magan said. "And it is dangerous nonsense, and you must never say it again, or think it, either."

"But my brother—"

"King Mark is Arthur's liege man and has sworn faith to him on the Cross. If he seems at times to be restless, it is only because human creatures are independent, and must learn to suit themselves to masters, even good masters. Remember what I tell you, my daughter. If any man but me heard you say what you have just said, you would find yourself in trouble. Even," he said with force, "in peril."

"But everybody knows that my brother—"

"Hush," the priest said. "Let us not speak of this any longer."

They were silent, each recalling how Mark had sworn upon the hilt of his sword to love Arthur and to give him fealty, and who did love him, perhaps, but who found room in his love for anger and jealousy too. It would be hard for any man, any Briton at least, to fail in love of Arthur who had been chosen Britain's king under such moving portents. Arthur had driven from its land the yellow-haired Saxons, and chased the Picts once more north of the Humber River, and marched all the way to Rome to tell the Emperor to his beard that Britain would pay no more truage. Besides, he had given Britain a capital at Camelot, and built towers with windows of glass, and gathered there the noblest men alive, and chosen one hundred and forty of them to sit at the Round Table. Arthur was a better knight than even young Launcelot himself who was stronger, more skilled, gentler, more generous than any knight except Arthur. Yes, Arthur must be loved, even by King Mark.

Only, Elizabeth told herself, Mark did have his side. If he was willing to be Arthur's liege man and fight for him, and keep him as a guest at Tintagel two or three times each year and feed his

11

visiting household, and breed hawks and horses for him, and pay the farm tax, couldn't Arthur feel some gratitude? True, Arthur addressed him as his dear brother and gave him a counsel seat, and rewarded him with war spoils and swore to love him. But he let his knights sneer unreproved at Cornish manners, and belittle Cornish courage. Arthur held every kingdom of Britain, North and South Wales and Scotland and Ireland as well as Cornwall and little Lyonesse. But he had allowed his seneschal, Kay, to laugh at Mark before his own household for having no fief except Lyonesse. Lyonesse, stretching away to the south, was a kingdom of rushes and salt marsh, and even Cornish knights referred to its fighting men with contempt. But it was Mark's fief, just the same, and Mark was entitled to be respected as a king to whom the allegiance of a lesser king was sworn.

It came over Elizabeth that the world beyond Cornwall, the world in which kings like Arthur and her brother and Meliodas lived and treated together, was large and complex and difficult beyond her power to comprehend. Even Magan, usually so safe and known, seemed strange today with his talk of lessons which had been nonsense, and men who were men at one time and elves at another. She was frightened to think that soon she must deal with the world herself, she who had hardly ventured beyond Tintagel where even her loneliness had the reassurance of being familiar. With a shiver she drew close to her old teacher and said, "I don't know what I shall do."

"About what?"

"About the knights from Lyonesse."

"Prepare for them as you always prepare for guests."

"Yes," she said, "but these knights are not ordinary guests. Are they, Magan?"

"You must not ask me something I have no concern with," he reminded her.

"But I haven't anyone to talk to but you. You want to help me, don't you?"

"Always, if I can."

12

She gave him a pleading, uncertain smile. "Please, dear Magan, tell me if you know why the knights are coming from Lyonesse."

Magan pushed his hands into his sleeves. "I am a priest and a foreigner in Cornwall, my daughter. How can I tell you anything of court matters?"

"But you know. I know you know. I have no friend but you, and if you refuse to help me I have no friend at all."

Moved, Magan longed to comfort her, to hold her hand as a father might. He had loved and guided her since she was a little thing, all serious eyes and soft kindness and eagerness to please him. But she had grown beyond that time when he could ease her trouble by laying a hand on her head in blessing. She was a woman now, a princess, past his love in all things except the love he could give her as God's minister.

While he hesitated, trying to find words for her, she said, "In the spring when my brother went up to Camelot with King Meliodas to keep the feast of Pentecost, I know they talked about me, and I wanted to ask you then. It was settled then, wasn't it?"

"My lady—" Magan begged her helplessly.

The princess pressed her face into her hands and wept.

"If anything was settled," he said, distracted, "I suppose it was settled at Pentecost."

"I knew it, I could feel it when they came back!" She caught her lip between her teeth, unable to hold it steady.

"Don't weep, little daughter." Magan wished God had given him the skill to make doubtful matters seem hopeful, even adventurous. "This is strange to you, and seems more difficult than it will turn out to be."

Obediently she tried to hold back her tears. "When is it to be? Will they send me to Lyonesse with the knights?"

"No, no, the knights are only coming, I expect, to bring gifts and letters from King Meliodas asking your brother to give you to him. These things are done with ceremony." He smiled into her frightened eyes. "There will be time."

"Will they let you go with me?"

"Yes," he said, still smiling. "Without you, I have no church. You are my church, my lady."

"I saw King Meliodas at Pentecost. He is big, and has a red beard."

"He is a good man."

"My brother doesn't care whether he is a good man or a wicked one," she burst out. "He has only one liege man, and that is all he thinks of. King Meliodas has paid less barley than he owes, and hunted in our forest, and I am to be married to him so he will have to keep his duties and pay the tax."

"Marriages are always made for a reason, but that doesn't keep them from having kindness in them, and loving faith. And if I didn't believe you will someday be glad this has been chosen for you, I wouldn't try to persuade you to accept it as God's wish. King Meliodas is brave, isn't he? And handsome? Many ladies have to marry with less from their husbands than he is ready to offer you."

Elizabeth wiped her eyes. "I know. I could see he is brave. And he liked me a little when I gave him his cup, because he talked more boldly and boasted of Lyonesse and looked sideways to be sure I heard. It is only," she said, weeping this time less from fear than from all the loneliness and confusion of her brief life, "that I am made to go. Why may I never choose?"

"Who chooses?" Magan said with a sigh.

A long silence fell between them. At last she said, "I shall go into Lyonesse because I have to, Magan. And you shall go with me. I would die if I had to be a stranger among strangers."

"You won't be strange. In a little while it will seem to you that you have never lived anywhere except in Meliodas' house."

She rose, and Magan looked up at her and saw behind her slight figure God's sky, and the blue mystery of the sea. She was a small lady to be venturing so soon upon a large world! Oh, if there was a way in human affairs to stretch old love and faith to a young life's end!

"Now bless me," she said. "I must call my women and go in. Give me your blessing, Magan."

They stood together against the cliff. Time gathered itself and hung like a drop which does not fall, enclosing neither past nor future but only this moment in which they heard the turbulent sea below them, and in the air the long, mournful cry of the gulls. Then slowly, as old men move, Magan made before her forehead and breast the sign of the cross.

Chapter Two

MELIODAS of Lyonesse was not a man to care whether his kingdom was great or small. He was clever enough to appoint able officers, and willingly turned over to his seneschal, his butler, his wardens and reeves the duties of court management and domestic order. Himself, he liked good companions who would spend time out of doors with him hunting or fowling or playing war games. Lyonesse, having a coast of marshes, was full of birds, and Meliodas bragged that his hawks were the best in all the west of Britain. He found enough high ground for forests, and on cool, dry days he rode out with his dogs and hunters in the hope of bringing home a hart. He even fished with the men in the pilchard boats, which was a scandal, since fishing was the work of churls.

He looked less the Briton than his countrymen of Lyonesse, showing, perhaps, a strain of mixed blood which made him burly and fair. Under the summer sun of the south his skin burned red, and the copper hue of his hair bleached out in streaks of yellow. He had a taste for ornament, and when he was unarmed wore above his elbows broad bronze bracelets and narrower bands of the same metal around his ankles. Since the summers in Lyonesse were long and warm, he pleased himself by abandoning the wool kilts and tunic of his rank, and often appeared in the coarse brown linen which was the household dress of his yeomen. Sometimes when drink had made him boisterous his knights called him The Heathen because, in spite of his flax shortclothes, he resembled a little the blond warriors from across the sea who had swept down upon Britain, Saxons who wore white helms and worshipped a lady named Frea.

He was a king who, when he laughed, desired others to laugh with him, as though laughter, and more laughter, would stand as a wall between himself and such things as were strange and terrible. One day he would be merry, and would sit late drinking with his hall companions and helping a belated traveller enlarge a boast or a tale, or sing rude songs. But the next day he might see some portent to make him shake with the fear of evil spirits. Then he groaned and prayed to all the gods, to Jesus whose Cross was engraved on a tall stone in the castle church, and to the others, the old ones, whose vengeance he was afraid to tempt. And though his priest objected, he maintained a small oak altar to these gods right in the church, but at a decent distance from the Cross.

This was the man, this broad, sunburned fellow called The Heathen, to whom Elizabeth of Cornwall was married. He sent his seneschal and chamberlain into Tintagel to join the guard of knights with whom Mark provided her, and met the party on his own borders, armed with his round shield and iron-headed spear. There he greeted the princess with a heartiness already assuming the intimacy of marriage, kissing her and assuring her with a laugh that in Lyonesse they would feed her better than they had in Cornwall, and thicken her up to a queen's proper size. And he ran his eye over the baggage train as though he might be counting the pack animals and wondering what goods his wife brought to increase the luxury of his household.

They made their first evening stop at a castle from whose baron Meliodas could claim hospitality. After they had eaten, the king left the hall and came to Elizabeth's chamber where she sat with Magan and the two Cornish women going with her into Lyonesse. Meliodas asked after her comfort, and then seemed to have run out of talk, only hanging about and staring at her from eyes gleaming blue and bright against the hot color in his face. The women, flustered, rose and withdrew, but Magan tucked his hands into his sleeves and appeared to doze.

17

Elizabeth was afraid of Meliodas. Yet after he left she was sorry, and spoke crossly to Magan, complaining of the nearest grievance at hand, which happened to be Lyonesse. This was what they called a castle in Lyonesse, was it, with dogs all over the place, and wooden supper bowls, and all those misshapen buckets and bottles of animal hide? In Cornwall people knew enough to set the table with good earthenware and to provide bronze and copper bowls and ewers. And silver cups. Had Magan seen a single silver object at dinner? What sort of place was this they had got into?

Magan opened an eye. Didn't Elizabeth think at least that the men of Lyonesse compared favorably with those of Tintagel?

"I'm sure I haven't noticed," Elizabeth said.

"We shall make an early start tomorrow," Magan said, "and so we had better say our prayers and go to bed." He heard her prayers, and those of her women, and said they must call him in the night if they were afraid. He would be outside the door on a pallet, he told them. He went off, smiling at something half-sad, sighing too, and staggering as he walked because his old bones complained of the hours he had spent on horseback.

Within two days Meliodas led Elizabeth home. On the third morning they were married. Before they went to the church the king brought her a gift. It was a stalk of reaped barley.

"It is for luck," he said. "In Lyonesse we give grain to bless a marriage and make it prosper."

"I shall take it to the church with me," she said.

"Well, you needn't make a noise about it. Here." He lifted the purse at her belt and opened it and thrust in a sprig. "Keep it until spring. When the new barley is sown we put this old stalk on the fire. It's for luck," he repeated, "though if you tell Magan, he'll think the way we do things here is old-fashioned."

She was pleased with the gift because it was to be a secret between them. As they were married, kneeling before the Cross, she thought of it and touched the purse where it lay. Afterwards Meliodas gave her an ivory comb and a pair of bronze bracelets, and fastened onto her girdle the ring from which hung the keys

18

of her office. In this way Elizabeth became a wife and queen of
Lyonesse, and entered upon the life for which she had been
trained in her brother's court.

She was lonely at first because she knew nothing of love except
that it had overwhelmed her. Meliodas was a fact, a truth around
which she could hardly stretch the small lore of her girlhood, its
dreams and delicacies, its wordless pleasures of sun and sea and
baby animals and budding flowers. And beyond him was Lyonesse,
a strange, flat land as unlike the high coast and salt winds of Cornwall as her husband was unlike Mark. The wild marshes and the
water fowl rising in great, torn flocks were foreign to her eyes,
and the moist air was thick and heavy to breathe. Meliodas'
presence somehow occasioned this difference, and all other differences too, so that she associated with him the loud, dog-ridden
meals in the great hall, and the fact that the hall was not really
a hall at all, only clay-and-timber walls around a floor. Clay!
Tintagel was all stone, cool in summer, lofty, sweetened with
western airs. And wasn't it because Meliodas stood across her
world like a giant that she had to take a flambeau at night and go
outside and ascend a flight of wooden stairs and open a door in
order to enter the gallery around the great hall where the women
and children of the household slept? Wasn't he the source and
father of all that was strange, all that was southern and outlandish
in Lyonesse?

Yes, it was frightening to be in the hand of a man about whom
was always a tumult of haste and huge oaths and noise. But it
was exciting too, and it stirred a new courage in the queen of
Lyonesse. After only a little time had passed, only weeks, Elizabeth realized Magan had been right; and it seemed to her as
though she had never lived anywhere save in the broad shadow
of her husband.

This knowledge made her shy with Magan, and she sought his
company less than she had in those days when she was a girl in
her brother's court. Besides, Magan now seemed to her old beyond
belief, and a touch foolish too, mumbling out stories of the old
Britons. He, not herself, was the stranger in Lyonesse, with his

Cornish-Irish accent and his slow shuffle up and down the chapel garden, pacing like an animal the length of its chain and back. Yet she did not like to hear him laughed at, and defended him when her ladies, glad to have a victim to maul, asked him to tell them about his travels in the world.

But a time came when she needed Magan, when she flew to him not as to a quavering old man but as to a father. This time fell three months after she learned she was with child.

"I must go home to Tintagel," she said.

She had made her confession, and they were emerging from the priest's chapel into the garden planted in savory, parsley, and saffron, along whose paths Magan had walked away so many hours of his exile in this southern land.

"Let us sit down," Magan said, and led her to a wooden bench against the wall.

"I hate sitting down in a hole in the world and seeing nothing but a handful of grass! In Tintagel wherever you sit you can see water and sky."

"One place is a good deal like another." Magan's head always nodded a little whether he spoke or was silent, and a tear stood in the corner of one eye.

"No," she said, "one place isn't like another. No place is like Lyonesse, as flat as a hearthstone, and steaming with mist, and all the streams black with the bog under them. No place is as ugly as this."

"What is your trouble?" Magan asked her.

"Nothing," she said, angry. "I have no trouble. Is it a trouble to hate bad manners? And people that carry the spoons they eat with all the time as though they were always prowling for food? And earth that sinks under your feet? And sun and flies everywhere?"

He gave her a reproachful smile. "You're asking me to say what your trouble is so you can blame me for putting the name on it."

"Magan," Elizabeth said, "there are witches in this place."

"Where? Here?" He pointed to her forehead.

"No, no. I'm not imagining it. At least—I think—"

20

"Have you met a witch?"

"No, but—"

"Or heard a spell being cast? Or seen a witch fire? Perhaps someone has brought you a bewitched child to cure."

"You told me yourself," she reminded him, "that the old gods still lived."

"But witches don't come from the old gods, or from our God either. Witches are children of the devil. So talk no more about them, but tell me what you wish to say."

Elizabeth stared at the parched grass by the path. "Something is wrong with Meliodas, and whether you laugh or not, I think he has been bewitched."

"I see."

"If he needed my life I would give it to him. I have dreamed that he did need my life, and that I gave it to him. And it was a lovely dream."

"Is it because he doesn't ask you to die for him that you think he has been bewitched?"

"And he would have given his life for me too," she said, a blush rising under her dusky skin, "for he told me so. I was never loved until my husband loved me."

"Yes," the priest said, "that is the happiness the young have for the young—to talk of dying when living is their business."

"Only now," she said, and wagged her head as though to shake it clear of pain, "he has forgotten he would die for me."

"Are you complaining, my daughter, because he doesn't die for you?"

"He used to stay with me," she said. "He didn't leave me for anything. They would send him word his horse needed to be exercised, and he would tell them he'd ride tomorrow. Only tomorrow he didn't ride. He stayed, and we talked and talked."

"But talk is a pleasure, and too much of it is tiresome, like too much of any pleasure."

Elizabeth was not listening. "He talked to me about everything he had done in Lyonesse since he was a child. He told me about going to South Wales to learn to be a knight. And he showed me

21

armor and trophies and all kinds of things he loved, and said where he got them and why he would never part with them."

"And brought you his sword," Magan murmured, "and fastened the baldric around your waist, and laughed because you were so small and the sword was so large."

"How do you know!"

"And now he is restless, and he feels left behind when the hunters ride away in the mornings."

"Now he leaves me, but I knew he would in time. I know what men have to do. And I wouldn't mind, even if I am lonely all day and have no company but my women. I wouldn't mind when he leaves me, except—now—he goes to another woman."

"Oh!"

"And she's a witch," the queen said.

"Why are you so sure?"

"Because, if she weren't a witch, he wouldn't go to her."

Magan coughed to give himself time. "Are you guessing this, my daughter, from hints, or the gossip of your women?"

"I know it. I sent my page Gouvernail to follow him when he said he was going hunting, and Gouvernail saw him leave his knights and ride to this woman's hall." She had been trying to speak calmly so as to prove to Magan her anxiety was only for her husband. But her voice trembled and she drew big breaths. "Everybody in court knew it before I did."

"Wait a little, until you've given yourself a chance to think." And Magan attempted to tell her how brave men like Meliodas felt ashamed before their fellows when they lingered too long indoors living women's lives, and how a day came when they needed to silence the whisper that they had been captured by love and become soft.

"That may be true of other men," she said, "but not of my husband. You're only excusing him, Magan. I can excuse him, too, for leaving me, but God will punish him for running after this wicked witch. And I am so frightened I can't eat or sleep."

"Who is this woman?"

"A foreigner," Elizabeth said, venom in her voice. "Her hus-

22

band comes from Britany. He's a baron, Meliodas' liege man. And he has brought a witch into Lyonesse and spoiled our peace."

Magan tucked his hands into his sleeves, a gesture he often used when he needed to search his soul for counsel. And he asked God hurriedly to make him wise, and to show him a way to mend the happiness of this lady whose content was his only business on earth. He was troubled with his own guilt in the matter of the witch from Britany, understanding that in the days when he had sought to amuse her with stories of old lore, of giants and elves and half gods, he had planted a seed in the mind of the queen which might be flowering in this unwholesome belief she held now.

"She is a witch, isn't she, Magan?"

"Whether she is, or whether she isn't," he said, choosing his words, "she is God's to judge. And you must trust God to remember you, and to hold your care in His hand. He has given you a child, and He intends you to be happy with your child, and to—"

"Yes," she said, "but *you* think she is a witch, don't you?"

He looked about wretchedly as though he hoped some door would open through which he might escape. "Well—as for me— I know—that witches have tempted men—in times past."

"Oh, poor Meliodas! Poor, poor Meliodas! We must help him! What can we do for him, Magan?"

For once in his life the old priest felt God had deserted him. Shamed and confused, he said, "I know only one cure for trouble. Prayer."

"I shall go back into the church this minute and pray." Elizabeth rose and looked down on her confessor with a frightened smile. "Maybe it is wrong of me to think so, but I feel better to know Meliodas has been misled by nothing worse than a witch. If it had been a woman, someone like myself, not even prayers would have helped."

This comes, Magan told himself, of wagging my foolish tongue to please myself. I was trusted to educate her, and I did it by filling her up with frivolous tattle amusing to me because I knew

23

its value, but truth to her. Now here she is, grown, married, with child, and nothing in her head but ignorance. I'll go do penance, for I feel in my bones this matter of witches hasn't reached its end.

He did penance, and added long fasts to the regime he kept, and prayed day and night. But all his efforts did not stop the course of things, or mend it. Elizabeth hugged the notion that Meliodas had been abused by a witch. She wore herself hollow-eyed with petitions to God, and to reinforce her devotions she used the small arts her women told her would neutralize the power of evil spirits. She secreted leaves of beneficent herbs in her husband's clothing, and rubbed the oils of this or that healing plant onto his meat. She even hid a knife under his bed in order to cut the bonds that bound him. And when the months were passed and her child was to be born, she believed nothing so much in this world as that Meliodas' neglect was chargeable to a female fiend out of Britany.

At the last, when the talk of the women was endlessly of the baby and how beautiful it was to be and what it was to be named, when any bird flying across the porch was said to be a portent, and when every trifling object was thought to have the power to help or hinder pains, Meliodas felt suffocated and of no importance. Morning after morning he called his huntsmen and rode into the forest. One day after mass Elizabeth sent a woman to him with a message.

"The queen asks you to stay at home today, my lord."

"Why? Is her time come?"

"Not that we know."

"I have word there's game to the north," Meliodas answered her shortly. "And when there is game we must go after it."

He suffered some dissatisfaction in the matter of Anna of Britany, understanding that all the court knew of his infatuation, and that the women and pages and priests judged his conduct and found it unworthy. As he rode along he was angrily defending himself.

Let the women talk. They were women. And whether they admitted it or not, most of them were willing to share a little illegal

24

pleasure themselves provided it could be kept from the common cry. And when was he, a king, subject to the squeals of beardless boys and priests? All such folk bit spitefully at their betters, and found evil in things they were not men enough to enjoy themselves.

Arguments of this sort made him bold, and in a little while he could perceive no reason why he should not at least ride in the direction of the castle where he was looked for and welcomed like a king. He waved his men toward the path he had chosen.

After they had ridden a quarter of an hour a hart leaped right up before them so close Melodias could see its eyes. The dogs began to bay and run, and Meliodas spurred his horse and galloped off in the lead before the hunters had formed. It was a wild chase, and the king's knights lost sight of him. As long as they could hear the dogs, they followed, and even after they missed the cry they rode back and forth among the trees hoping to find a short way across the circle in which they supposed the hart would run. When noon had overtaken them and the sun began to lie toward the west, they returned to each other and as if by agreement headed their horses home. They rode without haste in order that the king might join them if he chose, but they were alone when they reached the village bridge below the castle of Lyonesse.

They were met in the courtyard by a woman of Elizabeth's jabbering the king's name. Where was Meliodas? The queen was ill and afraid and was calling him.

What could they say? Not any words of theirs could conceal a truth which was the daily gossip of the cooks and stable boys. The woman understood what no knight would tell her and, foolish with panic, ran back into the castle and into Elizabeth's chamber.

"Oh, my lady," she said, "the king has stayed in the forest with the witch from Britany!"

Elizabeth took her by the shoulder. "Have they said so?"

"Yes, yes, my lady. I asked them, and they said so."

"Then," Elizabeth said, "I shall go there too and fetch him

25

home, for I will not have my child while my husband is the prisoner of a witch."

No one tried to stop her. Afterwards, when her flight had become a legend and the women who attended her told it for the thousandth time to the young ones who had not seen it, they said, "Some people think she saw the king in a dream. And some think her poor mind was gone, and she didn't know what she was doing. Whatever it was, nobody could move to hold her back."

Yet they followed her through the courtyard, beyond the wall, across the bridge, even a little way into the forest. But it was late, almost the hour of compline, and before the trees among whose branches the heavy dark was falling their hearts refused to urge them. As they huddled together one woman braver and more loving than the rest ran forward calling the queen's name.

She caught Elizabeth by the sleeve. "My dear lady, you will be lost! What if your pains begin?"

"My pains have begun. Help me. Give me your arm."

They pushed ahead, feeling with their feet for treacherous roots, and fending off branches that pulled their clothes and caught them by the hair. They could not find a path, and neither knew any sort of landmark to provide them a direction.

After an hour of groping and stumbling Elizabeth said, "I must stop in this place, whatever this place is." As the woman eased her onto the earth the queen began to say the name of her husband, and to foretell that she would never live to kiss him a last kiss.

In this way far in the forest Elizabeth of Cornwall travailed with her child. Her woman, strengthened against terror by the need to do what must be done, gave her such aid as was possible, and when the child wept at last, wrapped him in her own cloak.

"You have had a son, my lady," she said.

"Give him to me." Elizabeth summoned the will left her to hold the baby in her arms and to speak to him softly and to praise his beauty which in the dark she could only guess. And she wept, longing to live to see him grown. "Little son, you have been your mother's death."

With endearments the woman tried to comfort her.

26

"Watch over us until morning," Elizabeth said, "and take my son to King Meliodas, and say I have named him Tristram." She went on speaking weakly, and the woman realized she believed Magan was with her and that she was talking to him in the tongue he had taught her, French, saying, "You will understand the name of Tristram, Magan. It is a secret way of calling him *triste homme,* because he has been his mother's sorrow."

"Tomorrow," the woman babbled, "King Meliodas will carry you home."

"Tell him," Elizabeth murmured, but the woman could not be sure whether she was sending the message to Meliodas, or to Magan, or to Tristram when he grew old enough to comprehend it, "to be a friend to my soul as I hoped to be a friend to his."

And that was the last word she said in this world.

Chapter Three

WITH a new life and one that was finished to protect against the cold ooze and night-hunting animals of the forest, the woman wrapped Elizabeth's body in the furred cloak which had been her wedding gift from King Arthur and, cradling Tristram close, sat down to wait for morning. She had no time to weep, and little time for prayers, because the baby wailed and shook his small fists at the darkness, and seemed to be demanding of her why he had come so rudely and without welcome into the world. His cries comforted her, for they were human, and rendered less oppressive the ghostly whispering among the trees. Though she could not see him she could feel that he was strong and big. She moved her hand lightly over his head and touched soft hair and firm, clear features. And she marvelled to think how, even in the blind blackness, the signs of comeliness and vigor could be read on Elizabeth's child.

At dawn a search party of knights leading a horse litter found her. She was glad to discharge upon them the panic she had suffered, and the misery and sorrow.

"You that come late to do big things," she said, "see what has happened to Lyonesse because you lacked the spirit to pluck the king back from wrong. Here is your queen dead in the forest while you winked at his running after witches." And she ordered them about, rubbing the salt of her anger into their consciences, reminding them how she alone of all the household had given the poor queen help.

Some, she decreed, must form a guard to accompany the queen's litter to the castle. The others must ride on to await the king's emergence from the hall of Anna of Britany. This errand was not relished by the knights to whom its performance fell, yet no one was brave enough to propose that Meliodas be allowed to come home alone and learn what must be learned in his own hall, before the knights and yeomen of his household.

They advanced a little way into the forest and then, safe from the woman's tongue, paused to seek advice from each other. An old knight who remembered his youth said, "I undertake to carry the news to King Meliodas. And you, my lords, turn back and wait for us at the bridge."

"Deal fairly with us," a young knight said, "and remember that no blame falls on one of us heavier than on all."

"If we wear girl's faces and talk foolishly of blame," the old man answered him, "we shall find we have a king who doesn't love us."

He chose to ride toward a spring near the wall of the castle of Anna of Britany. If he were the king, he thought, he would go to this spring, for nothing was so pleasant in the early morning, after the delights Meliodas had been enjoying, as to be alone in the earth's silence and to bathe in cool water under a colored sunrise. It was a moment when life was at its freshest, when the soul was cleansed of guilt, or if not quite cleansed, satisfied to suffer some small pang in payment for wrongs committed by an impetuous heart heedless that payment was to be asked.

The old knight reined in his horse and slowly approached the spring. When he saw the kneeling figure of the king he smiled, less because he was amused than that he understood much. He waited until Meliodas plunged his arms into the water and splashed handfuls over his head. I would give a gift, he thought, to be kneeling there for the same reason as is the king of Lyonesse.

When Meliodas had bathed and mounted his horse, the knight

29

rode forward and met him as though by accident. "My lord," he said, "we lost you when you followed the hart yesterday."

"And I lost the hart," the king said. "I was belated," he added, unable to resist too much explanation.

"My lord," said the knight, "I was present when you were crowned by King Mark at Tintagel, and before that I served your father."

"And so you think you're entitled to let a hart outrun you," the king said with a laugh, "after so much service."

"I think I have loved you longer than any knight in Lyonesse."

The king looked at him. "What ails you, man?"

"I am sent to tell you that yesterday about compline Queen Elizabeth went into the forest to search for you, and was overtaken by her pains, and bore you a son."

"In the forest!"

"Her woman was with her. The child lives and is well."

The king shook his head as though he could refuse to hear what must be heard.

"And I am to tell you," the knight said, "that the queen died."

"Now—" said Meliodas, "by heaven," he said, "I shall—I shall—" and he said nothing more. He clenched his hand around the bridle of his horse, his face growing hot with the blood pumped upward from his heart. In all his life Meliodas had never before seen the past, and how it persists into the future, so that on this morning when he beheld his past he was struck down the way a traveller is struck down from ambush.

In this numbness he rode back to the castle. As though he were walking under water he approached the body of Elizabeth, and knelt, and said the prayers. And in the time that followed, as he ordained the burial and the masses and the christening of his son Tristram, as he distributed the funeral money among the poor and sent messengers to King Mark and King Arthur, he moved in this strange, unliving life which had locked his understanding at the spring when he had seen his past plain.

In these days he had no appetite for the life he lived, and he would wonder a whole morning without making up his mind

30

whether to ride with his hounds or to visit countryside farms and forges or to go out inspecting his roads and bridges. Yet he could not mope and dream and waste himself unoccupied. He fell to hanging about the castle shops, watching his harness makers, or the spinners twisting cord for the pilchard nets, or the netmakers themselves in whose hands the awkward, paddle-shaped tool of their craft became an instrument of skill.

For the first time he saw in these artisans men subject to the pain of existence, yet living in something like health and joy. He began to elbow them away from their benches and take their work into his own hands. He liked best of all the boatbuilders who worked on the beach under a canopy of thatch. These men were completing a vessel to be used in trade between Lyonesse and Britany. It was big, a good hundred and thirty hands long, and strong, and maneuverable enough to outrun the Scottish pirates who hid their light, skin-covered curraghs in coastal coves and fell upon the merchantmen in well-disciplined fleets. The boats of Lyonesse were wooden, high in stern and prow, rowed by sixteen oars, and carrying a tall mast. As Meliodas watched the ship-wrights working a bumper of rope below the gunwales, he asked them how they learned to build boats. They could not tell him. In a sea-girt land where fish were each day's meat, where trade brought them what they knew of the world, boats, they seemed to feel, were a part of nature, and men were born knowing how to build them. Meliodas was amused, and laughed, and heard himself laughing, and felt he had been given a gift.

So time proved to be the medicine for the king of Lyonesse, time that swallows trouble into itself and transmutes it as the earth transmutes the festering bodies of all perished things. A day came when Meliodas felt running along his nerves a sensation he recognized, the sensation of being himself. And as he became aware of himself, he became aware of his household again, and how among the women and pages and lesser folk the talk still flew of Elizabeth's journey into the forest the night Tristram was born. He understood that he was hotly blamed in the matter of Anna of Britany, and he was angry. Why should he be blamed who had

31

done all things innocently? God could look into his heart and see he had intended no evil. His sin was only to snatch a little pleasure from a world in which pleasure was scarce.

It was Elizabeth's women, he told himself, who would force this guilt upon him if they could, with their everlasting crying in corners and their eyes always staring at him and, above all, their exhaustless clatter of Tristram, poor little lad, born like a calf in the dark under a tree. Wherever the women gathered, the buzz was Tristram this, Tristram that, his foreign name hissing among them like an ugly whisper. Why must the child bear a name whose only purpose was to chafe his father with remembrance? I will not have them around me, he thought, either the women or the child. And he ordered them to keep their quarters, and come before him only when they were sent for.

As the months passed, and the years, forgetfulness veiled the king's memory of Elizabeth and delivered his dreams of her wan, accusing figure. Though he seldom asked to have Tristram brought into the hall he did sometimes call for the child, noting that he grew well and was handsome and lively. He was relieved to see his son was large and fair like himself, not a little, dusky Cornishman resembling his mother's people. Yet he could not feel a clean joy in Tristram, seeing always beyond him the guilt of which, when the boy was absent, he was free.

For all that, he watched his son's education, and removed him from the women's guidance when the time arrived, and put him into the hand of the page Gouvernail. When Tristram was four years old Gouvernail came of age and was made a squire, and on that day he was given to Tristram to be his man as long as he should live. Gouvernail's own education in men's business was ordained too, so that he should be a worthy companion and perform all things mannerly, as was suitable to the squire of a prince.

Though Magan dwindled each year, and shortened his walks across the chapel garden by a little and a little more until he no longer walked at all but only sat on the bench when the sun shone, he attended Tristram too, and taught him to speak his own tongue

32

purely and to use the French language. But of the old Britons he told the child nothing, nor of the stories with which he had once amused Elizabeth. Now his subject was piety, and how God loved right doing and clean speaking, and how He protected good men who believed in the Cross.

On a fair morning in the spring before Tristram's seventh birthday Magan emerged from his cell by the chapel and shuffled slowly across the courtyard. He was on his way to the hall, and because the walk seemed long he stopped at the round horse trough to rest. He sat in the sun listening to the water as it bubbled into the hollowed, cup-shaped rock and flowed through wooden conduits to fill the trough. Life had come outdoors this day, and women were sitting in the shade of the wall watching their lazy house dogs sniffing the breeze, and children running back and forth across the flags. Magan wondered whether the children still remembered the queen who had lived among them such a short time. The priest stirred restlessly as his own memory of her, so fresh and poignant, moved him. He recalled the day he had read over her young body the words of Christ Who promised everlasting life, and how Meliodas had knelt at the grave and sprinkled into it the pagan meal and wine, and how the king had thrown into it too a little bronze bell because, from time out of mind in Lyonesse, a bell was given to departing spirits with which to summon the ferryman who was to take them across the last river. Who has truth, Magan wondered, feeling he was near enough God's answer to ask the question without blaspheming.

Not since the queen's death had he come before Meliodas except when the whole household assembled, and now he approached the king somewhat timidly. On his side, Meliodas had no hankering to confront this relic of his wife's short life. He had considered many times sending the priest back to Cornwall, but he knew King Mark held a sullen grudge in the matter of his sister's death, and that like enough he would make Magan suffer for a fault he laid at Meliodas' door. And Meliodas lacked heart to expose a man so ruined and helpless, and so innocent too, as this ancient who served God faithfully and offended nobody. So as Magan

33

stood before him Meliodas said, striving for a show of courtesy, "Well, old father, what brings you from your cell today?"

"I have come to ask a favor," Magan said, and pushed his hands into his sleeves to conceal from Meliodas how they trembled.

"It is granted, for I know you don't ask favors an honest man can't say yes to."

"I thank you. I have come to ask to travel under your protection as far as Tintagel when you go up to Camelot at Pentecost."

"I'll take you and welcome," the king said. "Tell me what errand you have in Tintagel."

Magan seemed to gather his strength to answer. "I shall rest a while, and bid good-by to friends I had in Cornwall. And when a ship leaves for Ireland I hope to leave aboard it and return to the land where I spent my youth and became a priest."

"So you think your work is done, Magan?"

"Nobody can say when his work is done. But if God permits me to reach Ireland it will seem He thinks my work is done."

The king nodded. "Make ready then, old father. You know when we set out."

"There is one more thing."

"It is granted too," Meliodas said, expecting the priest to ask for money to help him on his journey.

"It is about the prince," Magan told him. "Tristram."

"Ah!"

"I have instructed him a little, and besides what I have been able to teach him he has learned manners from the women, and from Gouvernail he has come to know the nature of horses and hawks and dogs, and what weapons are. Yet," the priest went on slowly, "there is more."

"You think the court of Lyonesse isn't a fit school for him, do you?" Meliodas began to frown. "You think he ought to go into Ireland with you and learn to ring bells and say his prayers?"

Magan could not forbear a smile. "Ireland is a place for poets, and men who meditate mysteries, and people whose souls are held by a light thread, my lord. Princes are better educated somewhere else. I don't ask to take Tristram to Ireland with me."

34

Meliodas was ready to retort that he was the man to decide where his son was to be educated. But he held back. It occurred to him that Magan might suggest some disposal of Tristram he himself would be blamed for proposing. He gestured to the old man to go on.

"You have seen him grow as I have," Magan said, "and you know he has gifts little lads of seven do not always possess."

"He does well enough."

"If it pleases you, you might send him into a country where he would meet men of many kinds, lords from the east and south whose lands are crossed by travellers' routes, and where scholars and men of war gather. You might send him to France."

"*I* was schooled in Britain! *I* didn't go running after foreigners to teach me how to hold a spear! This soil was good enough for me, and I learned at the court of South Wales all I needed to know to be a knight and a king too!" Meliodas' face grew red with anger.

Magan chose his words. "Britain lacks nothing its sons need," he said soothingly. "But strangers trade in our ports, and we in theirs, and the day will come when the prince has the most advantage who understands the language and arts of men beyond his own borders. Besides," he went on with a touch of his old blandness, "not all France is foreign to us. In Britany people of our blood live much as we do, except they traffic more with men of German and Roman breeding, and with the travellers and soldiers from the north. *These* men may be foreign, but the men of Britany are our brothers."

"Well," said Meliodas, still ruffled with this talk of foreigners and foreign education, "I thank you for your good counsel, Magan, and I shall think of it." Yet, in the most secret place of his heart, he knew the matter was settled, and that Tristram should be sent into Britany. Though the land across the Narrow Seas be never so outlandish and strange, it had one thing in its favor. It was a long, long mile from Lyonesse.

Chapter Four

KING HOËL of Britany received Tristram into his court family for his father's sake, and for his own as well. Anyone could see he was a talented boy who would do honor to his upbringing, being fair and well-formed, and already endowed with knightly ambition.

In this household on a foreign shore Tristram found situations new to his experience. It was larger than that of Meliodas, and its order depended upon a stricter observance of social and physical boundaries. In Lyonesse life was concentrated in the hall, a noisy common ground where masters, servants and animals shared the day's necessities; and in the court bustling with ducks and hens and dogs, with pushcarts and ox-drawn wains, with the comings and goings of mounted knights. Tristram missed the loud and compact life at Lyonesse, and for a while he was fiercely homesick. Hoël lived in a different way. His house was stone, divided into rooms. The court around it seemed no court at all, being so small that by afternoon the shadow of the wall fell halfway across it. Outside was a ditch, and beyond the ditch breastworks of earth. Thatched plaster houses one room large lay below it, and it was in this village, withdrawn from the life of the castle, that the work of the shops was carried on. A vast wall encircled village, earth mound, ditch, castle and all, its four corners marked by squat, cone-shaped towers. A guard of foot soldiers, changed each morning and evening, patrolled the wall and kept in order the stone-throwers along its top.

At home Tristram had been surrounded through most of his years by women. Learning as soon as he could say his name that women liked to be preferred one above another, he exerted a childish tyranny over the court ladies which, for their own reasons, they encouraged. Since Meliodas paid them small or no attention, they spoiled Tristram, hoping to stretch their influence through him into the hall.

But this domestic pulling and hauling existed in Britany, if it existed at all, only as the queen permitted it. Tristram discovered in the shortest possible time that this lady could not be coaxed or bullied, partly because of her own good-humored firmness, but mostly because there was no rival to set against her. None of her women dreamed of disputing her, and even the king accepted her as an equal with himself, yielding in matters which were her concern and willingly hearing her advice in his own affairs. It was plain that something lay between her and King Hoël which Tristram had never seen before between a man and a woman, something he was too young to assess. In his seven wise years the prince of Lyonesse had not yet lived in an air of trustful, warm, and abundant love.

He discovered this when he was made a page of the queen's and began to use upon her the little wiles with which he had subjugated the court ladies at home. Nothing moved her cheerful purpose, neither his charm nor his sulks and fits of anger. She behaved to him exactly as she behaved to Yseut, her own daughter, who was nearly Tristram's age. When he could not force her to prefer him he was lonely and resentful and withdrew into silence. These tactics embarrassed nobody but himself, for the queen had a knack of overlooking rude conduct as she might have overlooked an accident he hadn't intended. After a bewildered while he began to feel the effects of her impartial affection, and to know himself a member of something new and valuable. Though he could not have put a name on it, his heart recognized that he had been taken into a family. This was good, this was not to be lost. So Tristram, in whom Magan had perceived manly qualities beyond his years, bent himself to please the queen and to earn her praise.

Her duty to her page was to accustom him to society, to teach him to be helpful to the weak and courteous to all conditions of men, to practice piety, and to be useful in the house. She had charge of his book-learning, and provided him with masters in music and French. Magan's soft Irish accent had to be rubbed out of his speech, and the roughness of life in Lyonesse cleared from his manners. Yseut, a naturally modest and biddable child, was a help to her mother in these aims. The queen encouraged the two to become friends and to aid each other in the small daily matters by means of which their characters would form. But she watched this friendship with particular care. Since Tristram's flaw was to assert himself impetuously, the queen's ambition for him was that he learn to be a leader without also becoming a tyrant. And she had no mind to see her daughter sacrificed to this needed lesson.

So she guided him with a loving wisdom protecting Yseut as well as himself against his shortcomings. It required diligence to shape his manners and to hold him to regular study. But it required nothing except opportunity to teach him music. He had an inborn gift for singing, and advanced rapidly on the harp, able after a little while to make his own harmonies. Until his voice changed he sang before King Hoël in the hall after dinner, accompanying himself so movingly that even the cooks and grooms crept close to listen. Yseut sat on a low chair between her parents hearkening to these songs, and loving the singer as children love, with a pure simplicity which found him flawless.

Tristram grew in a way to make the queen proud of her labors. She schooled him for seven years. When he was fourteen and she turned him over to the king, she could say (weeping a tear or two because her work was done), "If we had had a son, I would have wished him to be like Tristram."

With other boys his age in the household he became a squire to Hoël. Now he studied the arts of hunting, of war, and of history. He rode with Hoël on civil visits to towns and ports, inspected farms and highways, and attended the audiences of reeves and sheriffs who came to court on tax business and matters of justice. He was present when strangers were received, welcoming them in

38

the name of the king, ordaining the necessary hospitality, and learning to draw from them the news of places and people beyond the limits of Britany. He gave his lineage courteously when he was asked, and spoke of Lyonesse in a way to uphold its honor but avoid sentimentality and boasting.

After his fifteenth birthday he went through a border skirmish with Hoël, and returned to court desiring nothing so much as to be older than he was and to bear field arms. He described the action to Yseut, lining up cups and spoons to show her how the men had been placed and what the terrain was.

"When I go back to Lyonesse and become a knight," he said, "I shall ask my father to let me go to war."

"If you go to Lyonesse I shall go too," Yseut said.

"You will? Why?"

"I shall tell my mother she must let me go."

"Lyonesse is across the sea," he said. "It is a long way for girls to go."

"I know it is across the sea as well as you do. I know all about it." And she told Tristram what he had many times told her, how the coast marshes were full of birds, and what a fowler King Meliodas was, and how Arthur was the greatest lord in the world, and how the knights of the Round Table returned once a year to Camelot and held a great meeting, one hundred and forty of them, and paid their duty to King Arthur.

"I shall sit at the Round Table some day," Tristram said.

"I shall go there too, and see you sitting at the Round Table."

Tristram laughed. "You're going wherever I go. Is that it, Yseut?"

"Yes," she said.

"What if I went to the bottom of the sea?"

"I should go to the bottom of the sea."

"What if I went into a mountain?"

"I should go into a mountain."

"And what if I went to Ireland and became a priest?"

"I should go to Ireland," Yseut said stoutly, "and become a priest too."

Tristram caught her by the hair and pretended he was cutting off her curls in the shape of a tonsure. And he teased her in front of the women and the young squires, saying how she would be a priest in Ireland for his sake. Though Tristram understood much of war and government and music, he did not understand Yseut, and how she had run ahead of him to love.

Because he had grown up with her he did not see she was no longer a child. He couldn't have said whether she was pretty, or how big she was, or whether her hands were brown or white. He did know this much, that she was a good sister and a pleasant play-fellow, willing to follow him to the shore when he was watching for a ship from Lyonesse, and willing to share his disappointment when the sailors brought no letters from his father. She would defend him when he was in trouble, concealing his misdeeds if she could, and if she could not, taking them upon herself. She was his partisan. He knew that much, and was thankful.

But from long habit the queen was more noticing than Tristram. She meditated Yseut's future, half inclined to let matters run on as they were going. Tristram was graceful, strong, and generous. One day before they knew it he would be a man and a prince, if not rich, at least not landless, prepared to take an honorable place in the world. More, he had been her intimate study and she knew his mind as she knew her own. In him was no cruelty to be feared, nothing mean or cowardly. Wasn't it possible God had sent him to Britany intending him to love Yseut when his time came to love, and she him?

Yet the queen was not sure. Lyonesse was so small and so far away, rude too, its court many years without a queen. Besides, Meliodas' attitude to his son puzzled her. Although he provided the things Tristram needed, and twice each year sent Gouvernail with letters to Hoël touching his progress, he did not write of the boy's return. What if he had no will to see a rival near him? What if Tristram's presence in Britany had been, in all truth, an exile?

A day came when she spoke her uncertainties to Hoël. "Tristram is sixteen now," she said, "and we should begin to think of sending him home."

"Why? He's welcome with you, isn't he?"

"Of course he's welcome with me. But we have to consider Meliodas. In another year or two he'll be old enough to become a knight, and who should make him a knight if not his father?"

The king gave her a long, meditative look. "What worries you about Tristram?"

"Worry?" She was open-eyed.

"Come," he said, "speak it out. What has he done?"

"Well," she said, "since you ask me, he has grown up to be handsome. He sings like an angel. And," she said, as though this answered everything, "he has hair the color of a gold bracelet."

Hoël was amused. "I see. All your women are in love with him."

"Not all my women. Only one. Yseut."

"Yseut! Yseut is a child!"

"She is fifteen," the queen said with a sigh.

"But fifteen—" said King Hoël. "Fifteen—" he said.

"I was married when I was fifteen."

Hoël had been walking about the chamber, and now he sat and thought for a time in silence.

"And," said the queen, and paused, looking deeply within her own mind.

"And what?"

"I don't know—something it is hard to find words for. It isn't that I'm not fond of Tristram. I've loved him, and if he had been born to us I would feel God had blessed us. But hasn't it ever seemed to you that he—I don't know—that he exceeds what is moderate in everything he does?"

"No," said Hoël, "he doesn't seem immoderate to me. Is he greedy? Or covetous?"

"Oh, no, no." The queen shook off the idea with a sweeping gesture. "I don't mean his nature is evil. I mean that something holds the rest of us at an everyday level, whatever it is. And this thing is thin in Tristram. Always there is something about to break through."

The king gave her a helpless smile. "I don't understand you, I'm afraid."

"Look," she said urgently. "He does everything more than other

41

boys do it. If he is exercising with the spear, he risks his life. And if he is hit, he isn't just bruised or knocked breathless. He is wounded, and bleeds. When he runs he leaps off the earth as though he is flying too. And when he sets out to win a person to his side, that person wants to die for him."

"Oh," Hoël said, pleased. "Now I see. Our Tristram is larger than life."

"Perhaps." She was doubtful. "But this largeness may turn out to be his weakness as well as his strength."

"You worry too much. His trouble, if you want to call it a trouble, is that he is grown and ready for men's business, and still has to lead the life of a squire. Give him some seasons in camp before you judge him. He only needs to harden his new skin. He's tender yet, like a snake that has sloughed its scales in the spring."

The queen considered it. "I am willing to wait," she said slowly. "Let him go back to Lyonesse and stay two years. Yseut is not so old that two years will turn her into a spinster. Let Tristram go home and undergo this seasoning you speak of, and then when he comes back to us—if he comes back—" She spread her hands.

"Fair enough." The king nodded, satisfied. "I agree, but it should have one condition. Tristram is to go home only if he wishes to go. Even if Lyonesse is no addition to Britany we have nourished him and watched him come on from childhood, and I know, and you do too, my lady, that such men as Tristram aren't often born into this world. Lyonesse aside, I could not wish a nobler husband for Yseut."

"I could not wish a nobler husband for her either," the queen said, "but not for two years."

"You expect him to choose to go home?"

"Yes. He's lived with us nine years, and in nine years he has never forgotten how the birds fly in Lyonesse. And never once in nine years has a ship from his coast come into our harbor but he has gone down to talk to the sailors and to ask for a message from his father."

"Perhaps he hasn't thought about leaving Yseut. And perhaps when he does think of it Lyonesse won't seem so desirable."

"He will weep when he tells her good-by," the queen said sadly, "but before his ship's sails are full he will have forgotten that he wept."

As she had been so often right in matters touching Tristram, Hoël's wife was right in this too. Tristram did weep when he parted from them, from her and from the king, as well as from Yseut. Tears filled his eyes as he knelt and asked their blessing, and thanked them for the love and care they had shown him, and for all he owed them in skill and health. And tears lay on his cheeks as he rose and promised them his duty, and vowed that all the might of Lyonesse should be theirs if ever they needed it for relief or pleasure. When he kissed them, one after another, the three of them standing before him, his kiss tasted of salt.

Yet while his ship was still making its way across the quiet water near shore they heard him shouting to the sailors, his clear voice floating back in a peal of golden mirth which seemed sped from the blue above them, from heaven itself.

Now it was Yseut who wept.

Chapter Five

TRISTRAM watched his own land appear, seeing first the islands at its western end harden slowly in the mist and become low headlands; and next the curve of the marshes which seemed to float between water and sky; and then the reeds rippling in the wind; and at last the birds rising and wheeling and drifting down again, hunching their wings as brakes against the updraughts of air. He wanted to remember Lyonesse and to feel he was coming home to known ground, but his memory was founded less upon the coast marks unfolding before him than upon a pleasant, painless nostalgia for all he had dreamed and imagined of his birthplace during his years in Britany.

Gouvernail met him with the seneschal and two wardens, no great company but enough to satisfy the courtesy due a returning prince. A small troop of mounted yeomen had been brought to convey and protect the baggage. Because Tristram had seen his squire twice each year on month-long visits Gouvernail seemed natural enough. Of the other men most were strange, and the few he had known when he was a child appeared to have withered and grown old. This surprised Tristram, for in his mind nothing about Lyonesse had altered. Yet it was only the first of many shifts and decays in the fabric which had hung for nine years before his memory like the stuff of truth.

They rode up from the coast onto higher ground. Tristram saw again the tiny huts of clay and wattle, and the racks in each farmyard where the flesh of puffin and pilchard was drying, and smelled the smoke of oak fires, and tasted over all these sights and smells the taste which was the essence of Lyonesse: salt on his mouth. Churls working in the fields straightened to watch the riders pass, men dressed in coarse brown kilts and skin boots, their arms and chests bare to the sun which had darkened them until they resembled the Moorish sailors who traded in the ports of Britany. Now and then he saw naked children running about the huts. At every crossroad they came upon a pole or a crude open box set upon a stake to which charms of bone or hair or dried grasses had been nailed, nameless offerings to the forces of weather, and to the malign spirits who brought illness and trouble upon men. At a few junctions they found stones upon which crosses were engraved in neighborly nearness to the shrines. Oh, this was Lyonesse, where the surface of life was humble and without show, but where under the surface the passions of men struggled with mysteries which made mere show insignificant. People had no time to be rich here, only to ask the true God, and all gods, day and night for the one vast good of survival.

Tristram tried to tell Gouvernail how in Britany people were less narrowly concentrated on the secrets veiled by nature, and had an easier care for manners, for neatness and pleasant order and spry humor. But he fumbled, hardly knowing what he would say. As he began one sentence after another with "In Britany," or "In King Hoël's house," Gouvernail said, "Most men here have not been abroad as recently as you, my lord, and it might be better if you spoke of Britany more to me than to others."

"But," Tristram protested, "in Britany I—matters there were— and I have been—" and he fell silent. He who had longed to come home to his own land was discovering the matter of homecoming is not so simple as it seems.

A little before sundown they approached the castle of Lyonesse. Now Tristram's heart beat faster as he thought of the meeting with his father. He remembered how big he was, bigger than any other man, and how strong, and how kingly. He wore splendid jewels on his arms and ankles, and a great medal on a chain which rose and fell with the motion of his breast as he breathed. He would come riding down to the bridge on his grey hunter, with the household knights behind him, unarmed since they had nothing to fear, wearing kilts of grey and black, with hawk feathers in their bonnets, and at their sides their short swords whose hilts were ornamented with carved animal heads. And Tristram would dismount and kneel to be blessed, and King Meliodas would dismount too, and embrace him, and they would all ride up through the village, the yeomen and churls waving and cheering, and enter the courtyard where the bright thatched roofs of the shops would be catching the evening sun, and the church bell ringing, and the soft-eared hounds leaping around them at the mounting stand. I am home, Tristram thought, and swallowed back the tears constricting his throat.

But there was nobody at the bridge. In the village, children driving goats and geese to shelter stared, too unsettled by their curiosity to mind their animals milling about in the road.

Tristram and the others ascended the slope to the courtyard wall.

The gate was open and two men stood within it. One was a yeoman. The other might have been a yeoman too, since he was bareheaded and wore the same brown kilts. Yet Tristram knew this was his father, the king of Lyonesse. As he dismounted and approached he felt himself a stranger beyond help. For in the drawing of a breath all he had dreamed of his father, the beauty and power with which he had endowed him, were torn away. Now he stood face to face with a man shorter by half a head than himself, a man faded and ebbed, his eyes dull and restless under ragged brows, his breast medallion riding on a ridge of soft flesh.

"My lord," Tristram faltered.

"Well," Meliodas said, and took him by the shoulders and looked into his face, "you've grown since you went into Britany."

"The queen says I made a work of growing, my lord." He was moved with a pathos so swift and overwhelming for this diminished man that he felt himself tremble. He remembered he was to kneel, but he could not in decency wrench himself free of his father's hands even for blessing. And so the two stood in intimate touch,

46

neither knowing how to extricate himself from a moment which both had expected would take a different direction.

Meliodas stepped back and motioned for the yeomen to lead away Tristram's horse. They walked into the courtyard in silence, each digesting the shock of the change which nine years had accomplished in the other. Now Tristram was gulping down another sore truth, that the strangeness in familiar things is the bitterest strangeness of all. The great court around the castle of Lyonesse had narrowed, and the shops dwindled, and the horse trough, the church, Magan's garden, even the hall itself settled and shrunk as things do under a minimizing glass.

And where was Magan? Tristram had not thought of him half a dozen times in as many years. But here the old priest's memory consumed him, every small and large detail exact: his white hair standing in a fluff around his tonsure, the long, humorous wrinkles from his nose to the corners of his mouth, his thin, almost transparent hands which it was his habit to tuck into his pleated cuffs. Lyonesse without Magan was a falsehood. For in Magan, despite his Irish breeding, every quality unique to Lyonesse was manifest: its age, its isolation, its unworldliness, its piety, its wild, half-understood poetry. Now all Tristram had hoped for and not found, expressed itself in the priest's loss. As the young prince stood in the courtyard beside Meliodas, the Lyonesse which had never existed except as a bright illusion beyond the coast of Britany rose in a tide around him, and washed over him, and left his spirit stranded.

"Have you heard from Magan?" he asked.

"Yes. He died in Ireland a month after he reached it. A member of his house brought the news."

"Gouvernail might have told me."

Meliodas stared at him. "Why? Who would think you'd remember old Magan?" He waited for an answer, and when Tristram made none they moved on into the hall.

The hall had contracted too. But the walk from the gate had taught Tristram so large a lesson that the lies his memory had raised about his home could no longer stagger him. The hall was dark, and gave up its eternal odors of wood smoke and a thousand past meals and human and animal bodies and dried floor rushes into which had been ground the scraps and discards of much living. If it was not as he remembered it, if it resembled in nothing the cool stone house in Britany, it was at least what it was this evening, an old common room which was to be his dwelling.

He asked for water and stripped to the waist and bathed, watched by Meliodas, by the knights who were assembling to welcome him, by the women leaning over the gallery rail and whispering among themselves of his return, by the dogs too which, being kicked away from the fire, stretched and yawned and came to sniff his boots. Then ale was handed around, and by the time meat was served Tristram had begun to recover from the cold drench of his homecoming.

After they had eaten he asked his father whether he would like to hear a song. Meliodas was something of a singer himself. The songs he knew were camp tunes, ballads of bravery and violent death. And when he was a little drunk he would rumble out rough catches, stressing the bawdy parts in a way to make everybody see and relish the joke. Now he meant to add his voice to Tristram's, and expected that in a little while all would be singing, the evening ending in a tumult of laughter and noise and one last round of ale from which they would go roaring off to bed.

Tristram called for his harp and tuned it and began to give them melodies he had learned in Britany, plaintive, melancholy-gay. Meliodas had never heard such songs as his son sang, or such singing either. He had never been moved by music before except as he was stirred to boldness or laughter. Tristram touched feelings he had forgotten he ever felt, tenderness, innocence, aspiration, clean joy. In the smoky lamplight the prince of Lyonesse seemed to Meliodas to share something with that race of men who deal in dreams and intimations beyond the known. How, if his skill were earthly, could he summon back lost youth and lost love, how could he strip from a man his aging body and his burdened mind, and set into his hand again the sword of his first day of knighthood, and lead into his arms the fresh beauty of Elizabeth of Cornwall? Oh,

Elizabeth! He had loved her more than men love women. What evil infection in his soul had allowed him to betray her!

Meliodas pushed himself heavily out of his chair and stood before Tristram. "That's what they taught you in Britany, is it! Women's tunes!" He reached for the harp, and being unbalanced by the ale he had swallowed, stumbled.

Tristram caught him. "King Meliodas—"

"We'll see what Lyonesse can teach you." He struggled away from Tristram's supporting hands. "Tomorrow we'll see what lessons we can set you at home." And before Tristram or any man could move, he ordered the fire covered and the lamps put out and the house prepared for bed.

Meliodas was drunk. He lay awake, or swam between half-wakefulness and half-sleep, living over old grievances and muttering intentions which would not quite form into plans. Before dawn he rose and went into the courtyard and bathed his head and arms in the horse trough. Then, driven by a need to rid himself of fears or dreams or ghostly things, all the crowd of spectres of the mind a man could never quite see, never quite outrun, he went into the church and knelt before the oaken altar of the old gods. Let me go, he prayed, let me be free!

The morning light mended him a little, and restored to him the habit of kingship within which he could defend himself. Meliodas had one help in trouble: silence. He let the day go by, and many days thereafter, without speaking to Tristram of any matters save the matters their lives made common. And because Tristram followed his father's lead, demanding no room for his own thoughts, this silence in time provided an endurable relation between them. They learned to deal together with reasonable comfort, sharing the necessary intimacies of king and prince, and avoiding all others. They rode on state business, hunted, visited the ports. Yet always Meliodas' mind was restless, twisting this way and that, and reaching no point where it could abide.

On a certain day almost a year after Tristram's return a runner came with news that messengers from Cornwall were within an hour's ride of the castle. Andret and a knight named Dinadan were asking Meliodas for hospitality and an audience on the business of King Mark, his sovereign lord.

Meliodas sent for Tristram. "King Mark's seneschal, Andret, with a companion, will be here today probably bringing writs," he said. "Since they come from your uncle, you might like to receive them."

"Thank you," Tristram said. "I shall try to do you honor, my lord."

"Order meat and beds," Meliodas said, "and take two knights and ride back with their runner to welcome them. Tell your knights to arm."

"I shall tell them."

"One of these days," his father said, "we'll have to see about arms for you, Tristram."

Tristram, who had not dared to hope his father would arm him before he was eighteen, could hardly forbear a plea to be allowed to ride today under Meliodas' own shield. It was on his tongue to tell how he had born a blank shield and spear once in battle with King Hoël, but he had learned long since not to boast of his deeds in Britany. He could only ride off burning with joy because the subject of arms had been mentioned.

He met his uncle's messengers and delivered Meliodas' promise of protection and hospitality in Lyonesse, remembering the decorum he had learned from King Hoël, and proud to acquit himself mannerly for his father's sake. As Hoël had taught him, he rode between the guests, drawing them out with questions about their own country, and learning what he could of their minds so that he could judge how to bear himself with them when their business was in hand.

"I am a cousin of King Mark's," Andret told him. "You and I are of the same blood."

This was the first time Tristram had ever met any man except his father who was of his blood, and he studied Andret closely, wishing to see in him some subtle family mark. Andret seemed to him as little like himself and Meliodas as a man could be. He was dark and heavily built, with legs and arms so short he appeared ridicu-

50

lous, sitting his horse like a stout child. But he had a shrewd face and his black eyes were intelligent.

"And are you of my blood, my lord?" Tristram asked Dinadan.

"It keeps me hard-breathed enough to be of my own blood," Dinadan said. He was small too, though not as small as Andret. He was built as though he had begun life as a big man, and been filed down, his proportions still graceful and strong. "I make no secret of the fact that I am attached to my blood and hate to see it spilled. And I think twice before I claim for cousins big fellows like you who go about the world asking to have their heads broken." He gave Tristram such a merry look, a look so exaggerated and absurd that Tristram loved him and wished that it had been he, and not Andret, who was his cousin.

"Dinadan would rather eat than quarrel," Andret said in good-natured contempt, "and rather sleep than do either."

"And I shall live to be a hundred years old," Dinadan said, "and spend the last fifty years of my life in a monastery saying masses for your soul."

The ride was so pleasant that Tristram was sorry when they reached the castle courtyard. There he dismounted his guests, ordered water for them to wash themselves, offered them ale, and brought them to Meliodas.

The king was acquainted with them, and asked them what their news was since he had seen them last. In the course of the talk Tristram learned that Dinadan was a member of the Round Table. In all his life nothing surprised him more than this. As king of Lyonesse Meliodas had a seat in the fellowship of King Arthur, but after he made his annual journey to Camelot in the season of Pentecost he took no part in its affairs. Save for Meliodas Tristram had never met a knight of the Round Table. He had believed them all to be great, tall heroes as unlike little Dinadan as a hawk was to a hen. And hadn't Dinadan said he had no taste for fighting? There is more in him than he wants men to see, Tristram decided, and began to pay attention to Dinadan with especial care.

"What is Mark's business with me?" Meliodas asked them when the requirements of friendly meeting were satisfied.

51

"We bring you writs touching his matter with Ireland," Andret said. "You know, my lords, that Cornwall has had fishing rights off the Irish banks for thirty years and more. But for the past seven years King Anguissh of Ireland has collected truage from Cornwall on the plea that we owe him a fishing tax."

"I know," Meliodas said. "I advised Mark not to pay."

"He has paid, not because the tax is just, but because Anguissh is strong and can raise the north against him. The Scots will ally with him, for as you have cause to know yourselves, Anguissh buys their friendship by looking the other way when Scottish pirates hide in Irish coves."

"We must clean those pirates out," Meliodas said.

"This spring at Easter," Andret went on, "King Anguissh sent his warden for the tax, but Cornwall couldn't yield it. After the grain failure last year our people starved in the winter and needed much help, and we have no one from whom to collect the truage. So King Mark sent word to Anguissh that if he wanted the tax he could come and wring it out of the cliff of Tintagel."

Meliodas wagged his head in admiration. "What a message to send Anguissh!"

"When you have nothing to be robbed of, my lord," Dinadan said, spreading his hands, "you can invite any man to rob you."

"What did Anguissh answer?"

"A great plenty of words carried to us by a man with a red beard," Dinadan said.

"He sent six ships," Andret said, "to wring whatever is to be wrung out of the cliff of Tintagel."

Excitedly Meliodas got to his feet. "Is it war?"

"Not yet. The Irish fleet is standing off Tintagel under the lea of the island. King Anguissh's brother-in-law commands it, the one they call The Marhaus. And every day The Marhaus sends ashore two men in a curragh who climb up to the castle under a flag of truce and stand before the gate and read a writ saying Ireland has provided a champion to prove upon Mark, body for body, their right to collect the truage."

"God's green hills!" Meliodas said. "Why doesn't Mark meet The Marhaus and send the writ back stuck in his skull!"

"It would seem simple, wouldn't it?" Dinadan said dryly.

"Who is this Marhaus?" Tristram asked.

"First, he is knight of the Round Table," Dinadan told him. "Second, he is twenty-five years old—fifteen years younger than King Mark. Third, he himself admits he is the greatest champion in Christendom which means, once you have translated it out of Irish, that he is a good man with the spear and sword. Fourth, he is a hand taller than Mark, and a hand and a half thicker. Fifth—"

"Never mind your fifth," Meliodas said. "Mark has the right to offer a man in his place if he doesn't care to take the fight himself."

"We have thought of that," said Dinadan. "But Cornwall is a small country where champions greater than the greatest champion in Christendom do not grow on trees. Besides, our best men are members of the Round Table too, and I needn't remind you," he said irritably, "that these brave fellows will not fight each other except under some wonderful conditions of their own."

"You're a member of the Round Table," Meliodas reminded him, "and so am I."

"Yes, of course. And we could fight The Marhaus—if we cared to—by disguising our shields and refusing to tell our lineage. Do you care to?"

"Well—" Meliodas sat down again. "He's twenty-five, you say?"

"Exactly."

"My lord," said Tristram.

"What will Mark do?" Meliodas said.

"He sends us to Lyonesse to ask you whether you have a champion who is young and willing to fight under his own shield with the mightiest man in Christendom."

"My lords," said Tristram. Now he was on his feet, and the color was up in his face. "Let me have this fight."

They stared at him as though they would take in his words through their mouths and eyes.

"I can fight under any shield," Tristram said.

"What shield!" his father answered. "Until you are knighted—"

53

he broke off, looking hard into his son's face. "Until you are knighted," he said in a different voice, "you have no shield at all."

"A pity," said Andret with a sigh.

"Father," said Tristram, "you can make me a knight. For a year I have wanted to ask it. Let me go and win honor for Lyonesse and our blood in this quarrel of my uncle's."

Meliodas was silent.

"Well," said Andret.

"He is too young," Meliodas said. "Seventeen. He has never been out before. He—"

"I fought in Britany with the household knights," Tristram said, "and unhorsed a man who was attacking King Hoël, and made him yield."

Dinadan rose and took Tristram by the elbows and looked up into his eyes which were shining like agates. "The Marhaus is a terrible fighter, Irish or not. You may be asking for your death."

"Yes," said Tristram, "but in a fight one man is always asking for his death. And one man lives."

Dinadan turned to the king. "If he were my son, I would be glad. Knight him, Meliodas. He must go out some time for his first battle, and there aren't any easy ones."

The king of Lyonesse sat before them through a long pause. Tristram watched him, trying to pluck from his appearance some hint of his answer, seeing his heavy, hunched shoulders, and his sunburned arms encircled with the bronze bracelets, and his head bent forward, with the streaked hair falling across his brow. Was there an appeal to move him, any word to make him look up, proud and believing, with consent in his eyes?

"I'll think of it," Meliodas said. "I'll decide it in the morning."

I shall fight The Marhaus, Tristram told himself. My father will knight me tomorrow after mass.

Chapter Six

BUT the conscience of Meliodas paralyzed him. He could neither knight Tristram nor refuse to knight him. Just as he had longed to be free of his son years ago when he sent him into Britany, the king longed to be free of him now. For around Tristram's figure still clung the guilt and darkness which tortured the mind of his father. When Tristram was absent the king could master his misery and live in peace, but when he was present, Meliodas faced it again every morning, and went to bed with it each night.

His fervid desire was to give Tristram arms and send him away from Lyonesse into a battle which might settle, once for all, the doubt and suffering under which he lived. But he dared not. He knew God would punish him if he connived in Tristram's death, and, bad as life was, he could not face the threat of divine vengeance when life was over.

After a night of wretchedness in which he was tossed from one bitter alternative to the other, he rose in an evil temper and sent for Andret and Dinadan.

"I have considered my answer to your lord," he said. "It is this. I wash my hands of his quarrel."

"The king will receive that as an unfriendly message," Andret warned him.

"I know I owe King Mark my duty when he needs relief," Meliodas said, "but only in just causes. This matter between himself and Ireland is one in which the truth may well lie on Anguissh's side. The time for loud talk of outrage was when the demand was first made."

"He sent for you at that time, did he not, my lord?" Andret asked.

"Yes, and I advised him to resist."

"But did you not agree resistance was hopeless?"

"That may be," Meliodas said shortly. "The fact remains he didn't resist."

"And we are to understand also, aren't we," Dinadan said, "that you are unwilling to give Tristram arms and send him to Cornwall to defend his uncle?"

"Whether he is armed or not has nothing to do with it," the king said, "so long as Lyonesse has no reason to judge the lawfulness of the truage."

Andret and Dinadan withdrew to consider what the issue would be if, in King Mark's name, they threatened Meliodas with a war-like enforcement of his obligation.

"We talked away our chance to threaten him last night," Dinadan said, "when we gossiped about the famine and our poverty and the fact that we can't raise so much as one champion, let alone a fighting force."

"I'm not happy with the thought of going home and informing King Mark of the success we've had," Andret said. "Perhaps we should ride to Camelot and ask help from Launcelot."

Dinadan pondered it. "No. For one thing, The Marhaus isn't going to sit at anchor in the cove forever while we ride around Britain looking for champions. For another," he said slowly, "we haven't asked Tristram what he thinks of his father's decision."

"You're convinced Tristram can give this fellow in the fleet some truage to remember, aren't you? Myself, I'm not so sure. These big men with fair skins break open when they're hit."

"Let us at least talk to him," said Dinadan.

They found Tristram at the chapel where he had gone to wait for mass, and to pray to God to make him a good knight and to bless his first battle. As had his father, he had spent a restless night, lying awake in the dark with a premonition that when he left Lyonesse he would never return to it. And though he was young, he was old enough to remember many past things, and to live over his early years when he was Magan's charge and had as friends only his mother's women, and the old priest, and Gouvernail. All the same, for a reason he could not explain, Lyonesse was dear to him, and now that he was to go from its soil forever, he wondered whether his heart could learn to love another land so much.

These thoughts drifted at the edge of his mind, for the first business of his life was his battle with The Marhaus. He had seen tournament fighting in Britany between champions, but never conflict, body for body, to the uttermost. I am younger than The Marhaus, he thought, and I shall be strong at the beginning, but he will be strong at the end. I must do what I can early, and keep him off balance and without breath, and not allow him to delay and wait for me to spend myself. It is a fair quarrel and God will be on my side, he told himself. Yet God's supporting arm seemed less real to him than his own skill.

As he lay in the common room, hearing the snores of the household knights, and the creak of the embers, and the wet salt wind of Lyonesse humming across the thatch, as he listened for some sound to tell him Meliodas was awake and mindful of the morrow, he fought The Marhaus carefully, blow for blow. After he had unhorsed him, and approached him on foot with the sword, after he had advanced and withdrawn, covering himself craftily and drawing his opponent on to unguard himself, he grew too hot and restless to endure the darkness and the smother of his bed. He rose softly and pulled on his boots and kilts. The king did not move. Tristram heard a hound yawn and lick its velvety dewlaps, and in a moment felt its nose in his hand. It trotted along beside him, keeping close to his knee.

Holding the dog by the soft skin of its neck, Tristram emerged into the starlit court. There was no sound save the murmurs of any warm, moonless night: an owl crying, and the wind fingering the walls, and the plash of the horse-trough spring into its stone bowl. He could smell the dewy thatch, and the fragrance of Magan's herb

57

garden, and the damp, mossy stones near the horse trough. With his hand on the dog's head he stood still, wondering whether things he could not see were looking at him and counting the beat of his heart.

The dog shook itself and made a muted, inquiring sound.

"Come on, then," Tristram said, "if you want to say your prayers."

They walked to the church and went in. "Good dog," Tristram said. "Lie down and be quiet. Lie down! Wait for me."

Complaining a little, the dog settled onto its haunches, and Tristram felt his way forward to the altar above which stood the Cross. The church was as black as blindness itself, but Tristram knew its narrow length and its peaked thatched roof with the fullness of sight. It was old, older than the hall, older than any man could remember. Its walls had been standing when the court came to Lyonesse, and fragments of plaster still clung to their inside surface of stone. Some of these fragments were traced with color, brown-orange, and green, and slate-black. When Tristram was a child Magan had told him that long ago these color patches had been parts of pictures, but to Tristram's question what the pictures represented, the old priest sighed and shook his head. These pictures told a story little lads like Tristram could only wonder at.

As he knelt in the rushes strawing the floor of the narrow room, Tristram thought of the ruined pictures he could not see. He peered toward one place where his childish fancy had discerned a horse and rider, only not such a rider as any he knew in Lyonesse. This man seemed to be naked, his head in profile but his shoulders turned front on, and one slender leg and tapering foot visible across the ribs of his horse. Perhaps it was a flaw in the plaster which gave the horse the appearance of having hindquarters resembling the tail of a giant fish. Tristram had wondered when he was a boy what unimaginable errand this pair was riding on who were so different from earthly creatures. But now as he bent toward the place where the colors might be, he had a comprehending feeling of sympathy, as though he himself was a brother to the strong and graceful rider of the sea horse, and to all men who toiled forward through loneli-

58

ness and mystery to some unknown end. He knew the naked man would prevail, whatever he rode to face. And I shall prevail too, Tristram thought, though I am friendless.

He prayed to God for the strength to prevail always in every just cause, and as he prayed, more than his own hopes filled his mind: sorrow, and the darkness through which every soul must find its way, and the incredible bravery of men.

The dog grew impatient and thumped its tail against the floor. Tristram finished his prayers and rose and called it, and they came out of the church. It was not yet dawn, but a new stillness in the air foretold that morning was being prepared. Reluctant to return to the hall Tristram kept the dog close and began to wander along the wall. This boundary of the court of Lyonesse was the circle through which he was about to break, and almost as if in a dream he walked its whole length and returned once more to the church. Now the sky was high and pale, and a few sleepy churls were making their way across the flags to the cookhouse. Tristram called one of them and asked him to take the dog. Then he bathed at the horse trough and returned to the church, seeing its mildewed walls the more vividly because he was soon to see them no more. He sat down on the worn threshold stone whose curved traceries were blackened with moss. As he waited for his father and the priest who would say the mass of his knighthood, Dinadan and Andret found him.

"So you lay awake fighting The Marhaus," Dinadan said.

"I hope to fight him as well when I meet him as I did in the dark, my lord."

"Well said, Tristram. Amen to that."

"Are your arms prepared?" Andret asked.

"Yes. When I came home from Britany King Hoël gave me arms as a gift."

"What will you do if your father doesn't knight you?" Andret said.

"Have you seen the king, my lord?"

"Yes," Dinadan said, "we have seen him. He thinks the duty of Lyonesse isn't involved in the matter of the fishing tax. And it may not be, since King Mark has certainly paid it for seven years. It may not be a quarrel in which Lyonesse is bound to act."

"King Mark is of our blood," Tristram said.

"That rope won't take a knot," Andret said.

"What do you mean to imply, my lord?"

"He means," Dinadan said, "that King Mark is of your blood, perhaps, but not of your father's."

Tristram was angry, but Hoël had taught him anger must serve a man's purpose, not defeat it. He said, "Since I am to fight The Marhaus, it is of no concern whether my father is of King Mark's blood or whether he is not. And if it isn't his intention to knight me, I shall go into Cornwall and ask my uncle to give me my arms."

"If you do," Dinadan said, and offered him an unmirthful smile, "you may find the road back to Lyonesse a long one to travel."

"It may be I shall have no need to travel it for a while, my lord Dinadan."

Dinadan laughed. "You have more answers than I have questions for, Tristram. We've talked enough. It's time we went in and said some prayers."

They entered the church. After Tristram received communion he returned to the hall and sought his father. Meliodas sat with his head leaning on his hand as his son told him what he had decided.

"I ask you, my lord," Tristram finished, "to give me your permission to go to Cornwall and receive my knighthood from my uncle."

"You must do as your courage requires you," Meliodas said.

Now Tristram tried to summon King Hoël's teaching, and to render his father the thanks due him for life and care, and to form a courteous and loving farewell. But a lump filled his throat and he couldn't speak.

"You must do what your courage tells you to do," Meliodas repeated in a heavy voice. "Take what men and horses you need, and purveyance to bring you into Cornwall with honor. God defend you, Tristram."

Tristram desired something more, if it was only to kneel and ask his father's blessing. But as he stood before the king of Lyonesse it came over him that the time had passed when he might ask a blessing or a gift or a privilege of any man in this world unless it was a man of God.

He sent for Gouvernail and told him how they were to leave his homeland. They could not depart at once, as Tristram hoped, for food and gifts must be prepared, and a troop summoned and made ready. It was not until the next morning that they rode out of the courtyard, himself and Gouvernail and the two knights of Cornwall.

They reached Tintagel about noon of the third day, having come up the high ground of the coast. The rainbow colors of the sea and the deeper hues of the cliffs reminded Tristram of Britany, and he wished that, by some means, King Hoël could know he was about to go into his first battle. He was glad when he saw the castle rising like giant steps of stone against the green cliff, for it resembled Hoël's house, only it was larger and more splendid.

Perhaps home was here, he thought, although it had once seemed to him that home lay in the sunburned beaches and bird marshes of Lyonesse. Perhaps he had left Lyonesse, as he had left Britany, in order to come home.

Part II

Chapter Seven

THEY approached the castle over a narrow natural causeway which, lying behind Tintagel head, was protected from the wind. This causeway was all barren rock, tumbled boulders and blocks of slate paved with chips which rattled under the feet of their horses. On both sides of the treacherous bridge the sea raced inland and flung itself in massive crests against the cliff, the spray whistling into the air, and the rumble of the torn water so loud it seemed the causeway must tremble. Above them the castle stood right against blue sky. Only when their horses had struggled up to the crest of the headland did Tristram see how it was surrounded by lawns and bright gardens. Yew trees grew here, and firs clung along the seaward rim, wrenched and tattered by storms foaming in from the west. Wind was blowing now. But in spite of its fierceness before which every pliable thing streamed backward from the sea, high Tintagel seemed to Tristram a place of peace. And for a moment he could not realize that he had come to this lofty spot for one warlike errand only, and not to grow on sturdy roots, like the yews, for life.

The horses were lathered and panting from the ascent, and stood with their heads down, shifting their weight in order to rest their legs. As yeomen in grey kilts dismounted the riders, Mark's steward and butler with a party of household knights emerged from the castle to welcome Dinadan and Andret, and to greet the strangers in the king's name. Tristram thought these men alert and schooled in good manners, like the nobles he had known in Britany, and he could not help contrasting them with the rough companions of his father.

They went into the castle. Though Tristram's mind was running ahead to his meeting with his uncle, he had time to notice the wall draperies of printed linen, and the carved chairs, and the great bronze lamp bowl hanging on three chains from the ceiling. They were brought water and ale. Tristram washed, but refused the ale, since on this day he was fasting. Then Dinadan and Andret led him into the hall where Mark, with his chamberlain and priest, awaited them.

In the king of Cornwall Tristram saw a man who was still handsome and slender in the hips like a young knight. He wore a short, dark beard, and his black hair curled a little. He was dressed in a soft leather shirt and pleated wool kilts of dark blue, gilt rings in his ears, and a gilt chain around his neck from which hung a medallion of heavy silver. Against his swarthy skin the jewels gleamed.

"My lord," Andret said, "we have come back from Lyonesse with a champion to defend Cornwall against The Marhaus."

Mark rose and took Tristram by the shoulders in greeting. He was not a tall man, but he looked up at Tristram with so much assurance that his stature was hardly a thing to notice. "Welcome to Tintagel, and may God strengthen you," he said. "Tell me your lineage, my lord."

"Willingly," Tristram said, as Hoël had taught him. "I am the son of King Meliodas of Lyonesse, and of your sister, Elizabeth of Cornwall. My mother bore me in the forest, my lord, and gave me the name of Tristram."

"Oh!" Mark said. "So you are my nephew, Elizabeth's son!" He peered into Tristram's face as though he were assessing what part of himself he might find there. "Well, though I can't say you take after your Cornish blood, I am glad to see you, nephew Tristram." And he stretched himself to kiss him.

"Thank you, my lord."

Mark sat down again, and took time to look Tristram over thoroughly. "Your father knows how to get sons," he went on with a

66

smile. "But as I reckon your age you are seventeen, aren't you? Young to be a knight."

"I am not a knight."

"But it is a flaw we can remedy," Dinadan said.

"We've brought him in the expectation that you will arm him, my lord," Andret said.

"I have fasted today," Tristram said, "so that I may hear mass and receive my arms."

"This very day!" Mark said, something amused and mocking in his tone. "You're in a hurry to fight champions who have been handling spears for half as many years as you've been alive!"

Dinadan was not pleased. "Tristram has come to relieve Cornwall, my lord."

If King Mark felt rebuked he did not show it. With a frank gesture he motioned Tristram to sit beside him. He was a man who liked to surround what he did with talk, and he talked well, demanding the news of Meliodas and of Lyonesse, heeding Tristram's answers attentively. But in a little while he was speaking of himself, and of the injustice done his country by Ireland. He was not passionate about this injustice, treating it rather as one of the ordinary mishaps of government, and managing to create the impression that though he was grateful for help, impetuous champions were a matter Cornwall disposed of handily every week or so.

As Tristram listened, the sense of homecoming with which he had entered Tintagel began to dim. Though he wished with all his heart to find in Mark a leader worthy of the combat he was about to undertake, he could not fail to notice that the king of Cornwall covered his true feelings, whatever they were, using in place of open truth a sort of bland worldliness which he had learned as he might have learned a foreign tongue. Tristram looked at Gouvernail to see what thoughts his squire might be thinking, but Gouvernail stood aside quietly, his eyes expressing nothing.

"Anyway," Mark finished, "these Irish love so much to boast and threaten and make a thing of what they mean to do that I have had time to fetch you out of Lyonesse, Tristram, while The Marhaus besieged us with nothing worse than writs. Now, if you're ready, we'll send for a clerk and get on with our end of the affair."

"A clerk!"

"Yes. We must get into this battle of writs ourselves. We shall send word to The Marhaus where and when you will meet him."

"Oh." The king was right. The formalities must be observed. But Tristram's head was light from hunger, and he was so fiercely anxious to receive his arms that, for the moment, writs and ceremonies seemed to him irrelevant. He must rule himself and be patient while clerks were summoned and words chosen. But his surprise and disappointment with his uncle, and the delay, and the talk, welled up in him as anger. After all, it was he, not King Mark, who was to encounter the Irish champion. He said, "First, my lord, ordain a mass and make me a knight. After we have eaten, tell me how this island is formed where the Irish fleet lies, and what the best ground is. And then we can call for clerks and send writs."

Mark rose and laughed and appealed to Andret and Dinadan. "Here's a dangerous fellow! He fights with his head, my nephew Tristram of Lyonesse!"

Nobody answered him, but Mark seemed to expect no answer. He turned to the priest. "Go on to the church and prepare the mass, father. We'll follow you."

Tristram spoke with Gouvernail, asking him to unpack Hoël's gift of armor and carry the pieces into the chapel, and to make ready the money to be distributed to the poor after the service.

Mark led his nephew and the household knights into the church, which was different from any Tristram had ever seen. With the priest's cell beside it, it stood in its own little green, its walls partly veiled by the yew trees, symbols of everlasting life. It was square, built of flat stones trued up one upon another without mortar, its only opening a narrow door above which was a slablike lintel stone engraved with a cross. In the dusky interior Tristram could make out an altar, one great, level stone, upon which stood a bronze box ornamented with medallions of silver and yellow glass. Within the box was the mass bread.

King Mark and the knights waited outside while Tristram made his confession. Then they crowded into the church, and heard mass, and saw him receive communion. As he knelt before the altar Mark presented Hoël's sword, hilt first. Tristram held it before him like a cross.

"I swear," Tristram said, "to be a true and faithful knight, to defend the helpless, to take upon myself just quarrels, to do all things with honor in the Name of our Lord, Jesus Christ. May God defend my knighthood while I live, and receive my soul when I die."

He laid the sword upon the altar stone where Mark placed his shield and helm. These weapons were blessed by the priest. Then Tristram rose, trembling with such a joy as almost burst his sides. King Mark fastened around his waist a baldric of leather worked with silver bosses, and hooked on the sword, and set the shield upon his shoulder. "I, Mark of Cornwall, and knight of King Arthur of Britain, make you a knight, my lord Tristram."

They all knelt for benediction. Now Tristram longed for the family in Britany who had schooled and loved him. As they left the church he drew close to Gouvernail who had known King Hoël and the queen and little Yseut, wishing for a word which might reach beyond Cornwall and tie him once more to his friends. He could see that his squire was moved, for his eyes spoke a proud tenderness, but Gouvernail was not a man to wear his feelings like a cockade. So Tristram hesitated, and finally did not seek the comprehension which would have bridged the distance between Cornwall and Britany.

The word ran swiftly through Tintagel that a knight was being made. The king's party found the lawns about the castle full of men and women who hoped for a gift of money: beggars and poor travellers and all the hungry and homeless to whom one gold coin meant fortune. Gouvernail distributed the French pieces Meliodas had sent, defending himself from the snatching hands, and the shouted blessings, and the cries of misery and hopelessness which rose around them.

Within the castle food and drink were prepared, and as they ate,

Tristram heard from Mark his account of the Irish truage, and what manner of men King Anguissh and his brother-in-law, The Marhaus, were. And though Mark belittled the Irish, Tristram could see under his words a restless envy of his neighbors to the north, who were rich, and lived well, and attracted men of learning. He discovered that Anguissh was married, and that his wife was of the same blood as King Hoël's queen. This troubled him, and he wondered whether, in his first battle, he was about to do the family of King Hoël a shame.

Later they walked along the path by the cliff, and Mark pointed out the narrow island in whose lea cove they could see the Irish ships as small from this height as floating leaves. The island's western edge was protected by a ring of low rocks, but its eastern side seemed to be flat and barren.

"I think I had better fight on the level ground of the east," Tristram said. "Now, uncle, you can send for your clerk and write this message: that I will meet The Marhaus in the morning an hour after sunrise, body for body, to the uttermost. Say I shall come to the island. And tell him the ground I have chosen."

For a moment Mark was silent. Then he said, "Tristram, this Marhaus is one of the great fighters of our time."

"Andret told me."

"Besides," Mark murmured, staring down at the island, "the Irish have arts we don't practice. I mean they deal in evil spells and potions—such things."

"Perhaps they need them," Tristram said, "to make them feel big."

"It's fine to be brave, but you'll do well to be warned."

"I am warned."

Mark let a silence stretch between them. Then he spread his hands as though his argument was done. "I'll provide you with clothing to wear with your armor. What purveyance do you need?"

"I shall want a flatboat or barge heavy enough to take my horse and gear. And men to row me."

"Nothing more?"

"A spear," Tristram said, "with an oak shaft. And a trustworthy

70

fighting saddle with good iron stirrups. Let them carry my arms aboard before I enter the ship."

"Well," the king said, and, having left off his banter, he seemed embarrassed, even frightened. "God keep you, nephew Tristram."

Once in Lyonesse, in a time which seemed long ago to him now, Tristram had lain awake as he considered his fight with The Marhaus. But on this night he slept, and awoke to find the sky behind Tintagel turning white. He laid a hand on Gouvernail's shoulder and felt him waken. "It's time," he said.

They gathered the clothing Mark had provided, and moved quietly out of the chamber where the king and his body knights still slept. In the cold gloom of the foyer Gouvernail dressed him in a shirt of heavy oxhide whose breast and shoulders were strengthened by thin plates of iron. There were leather breeches with shin-pieces too, and hide boots. But after he had tried them Tristram took them off, being unused to such encumbrances. "I'll fight in the breastplate and my kilts," he said. "If I need cooking pots on my legs it'll be because I have been defeated anyway."

They went into the dark church and said their prayers. As they emerged Tristram could discern a little color in the flowers of the castle garden, and knew that before the dew was dry on their petals he would have put his life in hazard for his uncle, and for this clean world of Tintagel. The hazard must be worth accepting, else why had God given men hearts desiring—he could not put a name on the nameless things his heart desired: love, and grace, and something to defend upon whose essence God's beauty stood forth, unanswerable.

"Now we have come to it," he said.

"We have come to it," Gouvernail repeated. "I prayed for your knighthood, Tristram."

They descended the steep road, then turned south until they came to a low gap through which a path brought them onto the shore. There they found the barge, and waiting on the sand four oarsmen who guarded a fresh horse and Tristram's armor, already aboard as he asked. He saw that Mark had provided a Cornish spear, a round oak shaft with a flared head of heavy iron.

71

The tide had begun to ebb, and the water was quiet. They could hear the wind high above them, yet here they were in the center of a silence only the lap and gurgle of the water disturbed. The shadow of the cliff followed them, though ahead they could see the western rocks of the island catch the first light, and turn pink, and then gold.

"When you have landed me," Tristram said to Gouvernail, "go back to the boat and have them row you ashore."

"I would rather stay with you, Tristram."

"No. You must return to Tintagel. Commend me to King Mark, and say if I am killed in this battle he is to recover my body and bury it with as much honor as seems best to him. Tell him," Tristram said, "I will never yield through fear, but if I yield for any reason I do not want Christian burial."

"I'll tell him."

"Now," Tristram said, "arm me, and mount me, and put me ashore. And upon your life, Gouvernail, do not come near this island until you see me prevail, or until you see me defeated and slain."

In that high moment of parting tears came into their eyes. Then Tristram mounted his horse and leaped out of the boat and rode up the sand beach into the sun where the light fell onto his helm and broke into a dazzle. The Marhaus waited at the top of the rise.

Tristram had never seen such a knight as this, armed in a shirt of chain and wearing a bright helm from which rose two polished bull's horns. A leather visor covered his nose, and leather gauntlets upon whose fingers silver strips were sewn protected his hands. His shield was worked with three gilt spirals around high gilt bosses, and this same pattern of spirals was repeated in the cloth covering his horse's back and falling as far as the knees. On each cheek of the horse bridle a button of scarlet enamel blazed like fire in the morning light.

"Young knight," the Irish champion said, "you have courage. I have been tried at the hands of the best knights of this land,

and been the victor, and I counsel you to return to your boat and leave this battle to seasoned men."

"For your sake I have been made a knight," Tristram said, feeling a large and joyful lightness run through him, "and I am of a mind to try what my hands will do to relieve Cornwall of the truage your king collects without law."

"King Arthur himself made me a knight," The Marhaus said, "and gave me a seat at the Round Table."

"Then you have brothers," Tristram said, "to take up your quarrel when you have done with fighting."

"We'll see whether you're as brave with the spear as you are with words. Give me your lineage. I am a king's son, and unless you are of the blood of kings I will not encounter you."

Tristram repeated his birth, and his relationship to King Mark, and said once more why he had taken this quarrel. "Now," he finished, "if you are satisfied, my lord, ride back, and let us turn and begin."

They agreed on a level stretch of hard ground above the sand, drew up their horses nose to nose, then turned and rode back, each to an accepted line. As Tristram brought his horse around for the charge he set his spear in its rest on the saddle and gripped it, holding it near his side. I must hit him almost in the center of the shield, he remembered, but not quite, because a center hit will shatter my spear, but one too wide of center will tip his shield and let him come in on me.

A blow struck him and drove his arm into his body. As his horse stopped with a jolt that threw him backward over the croup, he sprang clear of the stirrups and came down on his feet. He had shattered his spear after all, and was holding only its pommel in his hand. He had been knocked out of the saddle shamefully with the first blow. He hurled the splintered shaft into the grass and drew his sword. Then as his senses cleared, he saw that The Marhaus had been unhorsed too, and had fallen, and was now rising, his sword already unsheathed. Fall for fall! Tristram laughed and heard his laughter without knowing it was his.

Something had happened to his side, grazed perhaps, for he

73

felt it, not as pain, but as an awareness when he slung his shield forward on his arm. His wits were cool. He pressed in, driving The Marhaus back, maneuvering him onto rough ground and over rocks, seeking always the chance that would throw him off balance and make him fling out his arm. But his enemy moved with the grace of a cat, suiting his body to every treachery of the course, fighting so steadily that the horns on his helm seemed fixed against the sky. Tristram tried him on the right side and on the left, but always his blade fell against the blade of The Marhaus. This Irish knight could not be circled or made to open his defense.

He did not know how long they had fought, whether minutes or hours. The sun beat down on them, and sweat ran into Tristram's eyes. He could feel his breath hammering inside his chest, and knew he was winded. Now was the time to give a little ground, to collect his strength and husband himself while his lungs eased. But his whole body seemed to be packed around his heart. The sword of The Marhaus cut blinding patterns in the sun, sweeping in narrow arcs faster than it had moved at first until it seemed to be everywhere at once, and Tristram had all he could do to shift his arm to parry it. Besides, his arm had grown heavy, so that he lifted it with an effort which he had to drag up through his body from his very heels.

He moved backward, hoping to spare himself the brunt of The Marhaus's lunges. He kept his eyes on his enemy's sword, feeling his head grow light as the bright blade whistled before him. This was not the fight he had meant to fight, this blind stumble across broken earth, his breath crammed within him and his heart crashing in his ears like thunder. Something was wrong with his side, a pain clutching it and refusing to loosen. I mustn't think ahead, he told himself. I have only to fight one blow at a time.

The Marhaus was trying to turn him to the sea to gain the advantage of the slope of the beach. But Tristram knew the soft sand would trap him, and that to fight on the lower side was more than he could manage now. So, still moving backwards, he ascended step by step away from the waterside, leaping clear when The Marhaus would force him. His foot struck something, a

74

boulder or a ledge, and he knew he had retreated as far as he could. He must stand. He could see nothing except the dazzling rushes of The Marhaus's sword.

His enemy bore in against him until he had pushed Tristram back against whatever it was that pinned him. And then he felt that nothing touched him above the calf of his legs, and he realized this rock which had betrayed him was not a wall. He could see The Marhaus's open mouth, and his beard clotted with dirt and sweat, and understood that the knight had come in close and lowered his shield because Tristram no longer had room enough to strike at his head.

"Now God give me wings," Tristram said, and bent his knees and leaped straight up, twisting in the air like a fish so as to hurl himself backward. He came down on the sloping edge of the rock against which he had been imprisoned, gripped it with his feet for balance, leaped onto the shoulders of The Marhaus, and bore him to the ground. Into his lungs a draught of cool air poured, and sweet, fresh strength ran along his limbs.

The Marhaus had lost his sword, and for a moment Tristram hesitated, remembering that an adversary without a sword should be allowed to yield. But The Marhaus caught him by the legs and threw him onto the sand. Tristram rolled and scrambled up, and saw that the Irish knight had risen too, and regained his sword. For a moment the world seemed to lie perfectly still, and all things hang motionless, The Marhaus, and the beach, and the grasses growing on the beach, like a scene under glass. In this second of unearthly clarity Tristram knew he had prevailed. He let go the leather grips of his shield, raised his sword in both hands, and brought it down cleanly between the horns on the helm of The Marhaus who seemed to stand paralyzed, waiting for it.

For a breath the knight went on standing, as though he shared the suspended clarity revealed to Tristram. His helm was sheared in two, and the pieces slid over his shoulder with awful slowness, trailing blood. A bubble of blood formed at his mouth and broke. With a cry he flung away his sword and shield and turned and dropped onto his knees. He writhed to his feet and staggered drunkenly up the beach, falling sometimes, and scratching forward with a mad singleness of purpose on his hands and knees. He gained the western rim of rock, clawed his way over it, and passed from Tristram's sight.

Tristram picked up the Irish champion's sword and shield and followed him toward the rocks. But he seemed to be divorced from his feet which were taking high, floating steps round and round in a circle. And something was wrong with his side, a hot agony clutched there to suck away his new strength. As he struggled forward the sky rolled over him in a soft billow of light, and pushed him gently onto the sand.

Chapter Eight

WHEN Tristram became aware of his life again he was being carried along through darkness over a rough, ascending trail. He heard horses behind and in front of him, and men's voices, and he decided he was riding in a horse litter, and that Gouvernail was somewhere about, and that he was probably being taken up to Tintagel by the landward road. He had no way of knowing what hour it was, only that it was night. Apparently much time had passed since his battle with The Marhaus, and now he could not be sure whether he had followed the Irish champion and killed him, or whether his enemy had escaped.

He would have called Gouvernail, except at the first sound he made a pain caught him under the ribs like the blow of an iron fist. He said only, "Ho!", surprised to hear his voice weak and hoarse.

"Tristram!" Gouvernail said, so near Tristram realized he was walking beside the litter. "How are you now?"

"I don't know. Where are we?"

"Almost at the neck to Tintagel head, as well as I can judge in this blackness. Shall I stop the horses?"

"No, go on."

"Is your wound bleeding?"

"No," Tristram said, surprised to learn he had a wound, and not able to tell whether it was bleeding. But he was too weary to explain. He would like to have inquired of Gouvernail whether

77

he had killed The Marhaus, and why he was wounded, and how he came to lie in this horse litter, only his teeth chattered in the cold, and he could not keep his mind on what it was he wished to ask. It was plain that nobody could sleep in a horse litter jolting up a mountain trail, yet sleep was what he longed for, and it would be better to close his eyes and rest, at least until they reached whatever destination they sought and he could be put down and laid into a bed.

When he awoke again he was in a bed. It was still dark, though not so dark as it had been, for now a lighted wick was floating in a stone dish of oil on a table near him, and he could see tall shadows behind it jumping on the wall. He turned his head and beheld Gouvernail and Dinadan standing together with a priest and a woman in a long linen skirt which she had turned up over her undergarments and pinned around her waist.

"Give me some water," he said.

The woman brought him a cup and raised his head in her arms.

"Ah!" Tristram said. "I think my horse kicked my ribs in when I fell."

"You are wounded in the side, Tristram," Gouvernail said. "And you have lost blood and caught cold. Your uncle has sent for leeches and wise women to cleanse your wound and cure you."

"I remember," Tristram said. "I felt it happen, though I didn't know what it was. But I beat him, didn't I, Gouvernail?"

"Yes, you beat him. We found his shield and sword under you. You gave him a stroke that broke a wedge out of your sword."

Dinadan told him how King Mark and the household had watched the battle from a barge anchored in the strait between the island and Tintagel, and how they had seen Tristram leap backwards onto the rock and bear The Marhaus down, and how the Irish champion had run mad when the blow cut off his helm, and how his brother knights had carried him into their ship and sailed away.

"When did I fight?"

"Yesterday."

"Did I fight all day?"

Dinadan laughed. "Not even Launcelot fights all day, Tristram! You fought a little more than two hours."

"That was two hours I'll remember," Tristram said, and closed his eyes, then opened them again. "Cornwall is delivered of the tax, isn't it?"

"Yes," Gouvernail and Dinadan answered together.

The woman bustled between him and the others, and drew back the bedcover, and laid cloths freshly dipped in herbal water onto his wound. The cold poultice wrung him, but he was ashamed to show the pain of such a little thing as a wet cloth when he had withstood through two hours the worst buffets The Marhaus could give him.

He slept, and dreamed of his battle, and woke, and slept again. The hours ran by, but he took no account of them, aware only that sometimes daylight stood in the window, and at other times, dark. Always Gouvernail was near, or Dinadan. And now and then he realized King Mark was speaking to him, or one or another of the household knights. He was comfortable when he lay still, but when he tried to move from his bed the pain snatched at his lungs and drove the breath from his body.

A time came when the fever in his side lessened, and his head cleared. "How long have I been pinned down here, Gouvernail?" he asked.

"Twenty-six days."

"Twenty-six days! God's green hills! How could it be twenty-six days!" He looked at his squire and saw the man haggard and pale, as though it were he who had been ill. A surge of terror knocked Tristram's heart upward in his breast, for he knew from Gouvernail's shattered face that he was to die. "Help me," he said. "I must get up and go outdoors. Help me, Gouvernail!"

"Oh, Tristram, you will catch your death!"

"I have caught my death, man. They say I've caught my death, don't they?"

"They say," Gouvernail faltered, "—they say—"

"What do they say?"

"That the spear of The Marhaus was poisoned."

79

Tristram lay back on his pillow, trying to gulp back the wild alarm of his heart. I am to die. If I am to die, God's wisdom is in my death. If I am to die! He was too young to believe in his death, or that God willed it. Anger and panic boiled within him, and he pushed himself onto his hands and thrust his legs over the side of the bed. "Dress me," he said, "and send for men to carry me into the garden."

Gouvernail helped him into his clothes. Then he summoned Dinadan. They took Tristram's arms over their shoulders and supported him as far as the castle garden. Mild sun was shining on the purple tubes of the fuchsias, and gilding with silver the spotted foxgloves. They settled him onto a bench where he could lean against the castle wall and look down on the sea. Because they hovered over him like frightened women Tristram sent them away.

They will bury me if they can, he thought, feeling sweat start out on his body. Oh, God does not love me! His mind swung like an unlatched door, crowds of memories milling through it, unchosen: of King Hoël, and of Magan, and of the pilchard fishers of Lyonesse, and of the wind running across the bird marshes, and of the hound who had gone with him into the church to pray. But around his laboring spirit lay the peace of Tintagel, bluebells swaying under the weight of bees, and fishing gulls flying upward on peaked wings to drop clams onto the rocks, and the echo of the purple sea whose rushing surf reared and broke against Tintagel cliff. In this peace his torment began to lessen, not because he understood it, rather because he did not.

After a little while Mark came through the garden and settled onto the bench beside him. "I was never so glad in my life to see any man sitting here as I am you, nephew Tristram," he said with the false heartiness accorded the hopeless. And he went on talking rapidly about how ill Tristram had been. "When you're on your feet we'll put out banners at Tintagel, and call a meeting of all our barons, and have a mass of thanksgiving said on the castle green. You may ask me for whatever reward you wish then, Tristram, and I'll give it to you."

Tristram leaned back, hearing blended with his uncle's voice the cry of the gulls, and the heavy speech of the sea.

"And," Mark rushed on, driven Tristram did not know by what, remorse, or conscience, "you will live at Tintagel and be made the prince of Cornwall. You are of my blood, Tristram, closer to me than any man."

"Thank you, my lord. But these plans are too large for me, I'm afraid. I am poisoned, and near my death."

"Ah, Tristram!" Mark clenched his hands in a desperate gesture. "I have had every skilled man and woman in this land brought to Tintagel to heal you. And they say nothing can purify the poison except the cure ordained for it. The spear was envenomed in Ireland, and the remedy for it is in Ireland. But how can I send you into Ireland where Anguissh wants nothing so much as to be revenged on you!"

Tristram was silent, thinking of the king of Ireland's revenge. At last he said, "The fever I took of my wound has left me. Nothing ails me now except my side won't heal. If I am to die anyway, give me a boat and let me go with Gouvernail. I shall come ashore safely if God means for me to live."

"I can't," the king said. "Your death will be held against me as long as men remember your fight."

"What difference does it make," Tristram asked him wearily, "whether I die in Cornwall or in Ireland?"

"You put the burden on me!"

"Uncle," he said, "I am beyond talk. Let me go. I ask this as my reward."

Mark, protesting still as though to emphasize his guiltlessness, agreed to let Tristram sail into the country of his enemy to seek the last hope for his life. The king gave orders to his shipwrights, and in three days they built a boat, working on the shore by the water. First, they cut green poles and stuck each end into the sand in the shape of a boat's skeleton ribs. Next, they lashed to these ribs eight layers of dressed oxhide, fastening the skins cunningly to keep out the sea. Then they cut the poles loose and turned the boat over. Now they reinforced the ribs, joined the hides at prow and stern, worked the gunwales with rope, and set thole pins for the steering oar. At last they seated the mast and hung from its arm a square sail of thin, pliable leather. This was the good Cornish coastal boat, light, keelless, fast before the wind, eighty hands long, which the fishermen of Tintagel trusted as a rider trusts a schooled horse.

Mark provisioned it with food, ale, and water, and with warm furs to turn night damps and bad weather. And as Tristram requested, the king sent his harp aboard too, and the sword with which he had fought The Marhaus. The harp had come with him from Britany; and he cherished the sword because, though one edge of it had splintered, it had won him his first battle. These things seemed to him his only earthly possessions.

One sunny morning they lifted Tristram into the boat and laid him on a pallet of skins. In the prow Gouvernail made fast a line passed up by oarsmen in a scaffie who were to tow the vessel around the island and into the northeast current. Mark and Dinadan stood on the shore waving farewell, and Andret waited a little distance from them, his short legs planted, and his hands on his hips. He bent his head, peering from under his brows, as his cousin from Lyonesse left the land in which he had won honor and the favor of King Mark.

"I think Andret doesn't love me much," Tristram said.

"Why?" Gouvernail asked.

"A feeling. He never came about me after the fight with The Marhaus, did he?"

"No, not often."

"And he was against sending me to Ireland in this boat. I think he would have been happier if I had died in my bed at Tintagel. How have I gotten him and what he wants, Gouvernail?"

"Well," Gouvernail said, "until you came into Cornwall Andret was closest in blood to King Mark of any man. And since the king is not married and has no sons, I suppose Andret expects to be king himself some day."

"But now he thinks I might manage to be king of Cornwall."

"Perhaps."

Tristram laughed. "If I live, Gouvernail, I shall never wear a harness that galls me as poor Andret is galled. Give me my harp, and I'll play us a tune to sail by."

When the wind caught them, the men in the scaffie cast off and shouted good-by. Tristram's boat ran gracefully before the breeze, the sea all blue and white around her, and overhead a sky soft with good-weather clouds. Gulls flew with them so close Tristram could see their round, astonished eyes, and watch the lift and tilt of their wings as they trimmed their weight to the turbulent air.

The sea will heal me, Tristram thought, whether or not I reach Ireland.

Three clear days and three starry nights passed over them as their boat drove northward. Tristram began to feel health return to his limbs, and the doubts lighten which had burdened his heart. He found his voice again, and sang the songs of Britany, pleasing himself by telling Gouvernail how he had learned each song, and what the French words meant. At night he lay and listened to the water rustling under the boat, and comforted his loneliness with the faith that God's benign hand smoothed his way into Ireland.

On the morning of the fourth day they saw mist ahead which presently thickened into a purple, rising horizon. As they sailed toward it this purple dissolved into pale headlands and green turf. By afternoon they were running along a coast above which low hills swelled under a velvety sward. In some places the hills rose right out of the water, their faces worn to rock upon whose ledges flocks of seafowl crowded together as white as new snow. Once or twice they saw round stone houses shaped like beehives on these cliffs, and asked each other what kind of men would seek such barren ground, so near the sky, for their dwellings. In other places coves and inlets wound back from the shore, opening views of fields and patches of forest. Boats of many sizes were anchored in the quiet water, and on one level beach they could make out cradles of reeds upon which fish nets were spread to dry.

"I have a feeling there's a harbor of some sort beyond the headland," Tristram said. "The gulls turn and fly inland there, anyway."

"I saw it," Gouvernail said, "but if we go into a harbor we'll find a village or even a castle. And that may mean trouble."

Tristram did not answer, knowing it was Gouvernail's nature to worry and foresee misfortune. The headland was low and broad at the crest, and in its crevices Tristram could discern the tints of yellow and purple wild flowers. Gulls rode up its face on lifting air currents, wheeling against the blue and coasting down again, far out, as though they followed this ascent and leisurely return for pleasure. When their boat had passed the full curve of the cliff Tristram saw a little saucer-shaped harbor, and many curraghs at anchor, and a few ships with tall masts, the sails now furled.

"This means a village," Gouvernail said. With the steering oar he turned the boat into the sheltered water and threaded it among the curraghs. On the shore they discovered nets and open canopies of thatch, and above them curious huts, only sod walls over which fishing boats had been turned to form roofs. Farther inland Tristram could make out a house or two as well, and men moving against a near horizon.

Gouvernail took in the leather sail.

This was a strange land, Tristram thought, where pastures ran right down to the sea, and herdsmen built their cottages within sight of the salt. Here was a harbor of neither rock nor marsh, undefended by anything save green farms and tiny houses of sod, or clay and thatch.

"We've been seen," Gouvernail said.

A woman was walking down the slope. Her full skirt of scarlet fell halfway between her knee and ankle, and her feet were bare. She wore a round-necked blouse of thin, white stuff, and her hair, the color of melted amber, blew around her shoulders in soft curls. Tristram thought he had never beheld such a beautiful woman as this one who walked like a queen on small, naked feet in the jewel-tinted grass. His heart was so light he felt he could leap over the water separating them, and run up the slope and overtake her. But before he could hail her she turned and skimmed away. They heard her voice calling to the cottages at the top of the slope, and then she was gone.

84

Men and women began to come out of their houses, doubtfully at first, moving toward the water in little rushes as though they were divided between curiosity and caution. These were plainly herdsmen or fisherfolk, some barefoot like the woman, but unlike her in every other way. The men wore knee-length tunics of coarse, colored linen belted at the waist. The women were clothed in the same kind of tunics, only longer. The colors of their dress, green, red, purple, blue, yellow, stood out gaily against the slope. Stuff of such hues was rare and costly in Cornwall where only rich men could dispense with brown linen or the dull grey wool of the churl. Tristram stared, enchanted by these fresh-faced foreigners whose childlike pleasure he could feel in his own spirit. He wanted to make the moment memorable, to fix for them and for himself a meeting which his faith told him was friendly.

With the steering oar Gouvernail was poling the boat toward shore. Tristram raised himself against a thwart and took his harp and began to play and sing, choosing merry tunes to speak his heart to the strangers from whom he was seeking welcome. He sang in his own tongue, putting laughter into his cadences, drawing the listeners down the slope to him, until, when the boat nosed onto the shingle, they stood at the water's edge, and even waded into the harbor, saying their names in soft, eager voices, and asking him his.

"No such songs as these are sung in Ireland," a man in a tunic of black and yellow said. "Tell us what land you come from in this boat without oarsmen."

Tristram could not, with courtesy, refuse to inform them of his lineage. Yet he was afraid to speak his name to men who might hate him. He said, "Bring me to your lord, and I will give him my lineage, and my country, and say how I have come to Ireland."

"My lord is wounded and can't walk," Gouvernail explained. "If your master's castle is near the shore, we appeal to his charity to send a litter and bearers to carry this knight to his hall."

"We'll carry him ourselves, and welcome," the man in black and yellow said. He ran up the slope to a round house and returned with a sleeping pallet made of wattles woven between two

85

side poles. He and three of his fellows covered it with skins from the boat, and lifted Tristram onto it, and bore him slowly up the ascent.

Beyond the hill the land opened into a wide green valley in which squares of woodland alternated with fields of oats and wheat and onions. Mulberry trees grew in farmyards, and everywhere great, star-shaped fuchsias, and yellow furze.

Tristram could not resist a surprised inquiry when he saw that the hall to which they were carrying him was built on low ground. "Why does your lord settle in the valley and leave his heights unfortified?"

"We're not much troubled by raiders," the man said, "except for a few pirates now and then. Even they don't bother us beyond what we can bear, because they know if they treat us fairly, we'll treat them fairly in return. Besides," he said, hunching his end of the litter as he made an unconscious gesture, "God formed Ireland in the shape of a bowl, high coasts, low inland. So if we don't see raiders from the shore, it does us no good to see them at all."

"A woman was standing above the beach when we came in," Tristram said. "She wore a scarlet skirt. Do you know who she is?"

"No I don't, my lord," said the bearer, suddenly formal.

You've asked the wrong question, Tristram admonished himself. He was content anyway to look at the peaceful countryside and remember the girl whose hair had blown so sweetly in the salt wind. His eyes had never told him any woman was beautiful. And now that they had taught him so much, he felt the world was cleansed of doubtful causes and truth half made of lies. In this world it might be possible, after all, for a man to come home.

Chapter Nine

WHEN they reached the court and gardens around the hall Tristram said, "I would like to come before your lord walking, my friends."

"Remember your wound," Gouvernail said.

Tristram laughed with the joy beginning to flower in him. "The air of Ireland has a cure in it, I think. And I need to try this ground that wants me to be well."

Gouvernail supported him on one side, and on the other the herdsman in the black and yellow tunic gave him his shoulder. In this way they passed slowly over the cobbles. Tristram had heard in Cornwall that life in Ireland was larger and less arduous than the struggle for existence in most of western Britain, and so he was surprised to find this lord's seat humble. The hall was built of wattles plastered with clay, the roof thatched as the seaside cottages were. But it was much more ample than the round huts, designed in a long, low oval, with windows closed by wooden slats down each side.

Below it toward the sea stood a stone church built as Mark's was without mortar, with a hive-shaped roof and a lintelled door. Small cells of the same construction stood near it, and in the center of this cluster a great stone slab was raised on lesser stones. On the face of a monolith as tall as Tristram a cross enclosed in a circle was engraved, and under the cross ran a simple pattern of lines and spirals so lightly cut that only the shadows in the grooves made them visible. A few priests were moving about in this religious ground.

The courtyard itself reminded Tristram of his father's home in Lyonesse, for it was spacious and full of life. A child was leading two lambs, and hens and ducks fluttered out of the way. There were dogs too, but more beautiful than the dogs of Lyonesse. They were thin-bodied, with soft red coats and graceful heads, aristocrats, Tristram could see, most carefully bred. If this Irish baron did not care to make a luxury of his hall, he at least let the world know his quality with his dogs.

"What is your master's name?" Tristram asked.

"Anguissh, my lord, king of South Ireland."

"Ah!" Tristram stopped short, and so did Gouvernail.

The herdsman looked at them, surprised. "Shall we carry you again, my lord?"

"No. Let us go on."

What could they do but go on? As they entered, Tristram had an impulse to tell the truth to this king who lived so kindly with his people. But even enchanted as he was by the open courtesy of his friends on the shore, and by the sweet air, and by the smiling countryside, he knew the truth might destroy them. It would surely destroy them if The Marhaus had died For then, though Anguissh might have a mind to peace, he was bound by the strongest of earth's ties to avenge his brother-in-law, the tie of blood. More, he would be a king whose first knight had been killed in a foreign land by the sword of an enemy. And for that ill done him he was again obliged to take vengeance.

But Tristram went on into the hall as he might have moved in a dream. The herdsman left them at the door, giving them in charge to a member of the household, a man who wore a light wool tunic, violet-colored, belted with a leather baldric set with bosses of gold and green enamel. This man welcomed them in Anguissh's name and led them to the king.

"My lord," Tristram said, "I am wounded and have come into Ireland to ask hospitality and cure."

"God give you health, wounded knight," Anguissh said. "Since

you come for a peaceful reason, think Ireland is your homeland."
He told Tristram his name and his birth. "Now let us hear your
country and your lineage, my lord, and how," he finished with a
smile, "you swam to us without oars."

Tristram was trembling because his new strength was spent,
and because Anguissh was the noblest man he had ever seen, large
and fair and excellently made, kingly in a scarlet tunic and orna-
ments of gold. But most of all he trembled because the woman
who had run before their boat was standing with the ladies behind
the king's chair. Only now she had changed into a long, slender
gown of green stuff on which a thread of gold traced a pattern of
spirals. But the thread was dulled by the color of her hair.

"My name," he said, "is—is Tramtris, and I was bred in—in
—Britany in the house of King Hoël. And," he said, leaning on
Gouvernail so that he should not fall, "I got my wound in Britain
in a just quarrel. When it wouldn't heal I asked advice from a
leech who told me to come to Ireland for help. I prayed God to
give me good weather and a favorable wind if He meant for me
to find friends here. And that is all my story, my lord."

A woman stepped forward and stood beside the king. She was
neither young nor old, being a lady upon whom time had worked
some signs, but lightly and with grace. She was small, her color
between dark and blond, and under the fading beauty of her face
lay a certain sharp intelligence, as though she had seen much, and
had judged promptly whether what she saw held an advantage or
a disadvantage.

"King Hoël's wife is of my blood," she said, "and if you come
from Britany as well as from God, you are twice welcome, Lord
Tramtris. And I think somebody had better bring you a chair
before your knees give way."

"This is the queen, Tramtris. And this," Anguissh said, rising
and taking the girl in green by the hand, "is our daughter, the
princess Isoud. The queen and princess are skilled in cures, and
they will care for you."

Tristram looked into Isoud's face, and she into his. Though in
Britany he had learned to bear himself mannerly with ladies, and

89

to offer his service when hospitality was given him, he could not find any word at all to say to Isoud of Ireland. His silence did not seem to trouble her, rather to reach her as a greeting, and to meet a welcome in her own. Now Tristram felt as he had felt only once before in his life, that time paused for him, and made a moment which held neither future nor past, but a clear present in whose joy all meanings stood plain.

The queen, her efficiency affronted by people who stood and stared, began to rustle about and give orders for Tristram's care. She swept Gouvernail into her plans, telling him all that must be done, and how Tristram—or Tramtris as he had chosen to be called—must have healing baths, and sturdy foods, and enough rest, but not so much that he neglected regular exercise. Before Tristram could summon the will to follow her, he had been gently seized by servants who bore him off to bed. And for the next while he was so bathed, so dosed, so rubbed, so combed, so fed, so commanded to lie quiet and sleep, that he had no energy to do anything except what he was told.

All this determined medicining soothed his fatigue and made him drowsy. While faces still bent over him, he felt himself falling before the paralyzing drug of sleep. He slept without waking from dusk until sunrise. When he opened his eyes he saw he was in a round and windowless room of stone, and that pale daylight crept through the narrow door. For a little while, as his dreams moved in confusion, running before his growing wakefulness, he could not think where he was, or whether the long journey over the sea had been an illusion of his sleep. He heard himself laugh as he roused, and knew he had laughed with a merry heart because of the princess Isoud. Yet now he could not be certain whether she was a living woman, or part of the mystery of his dreams. But as his assurance strengthened, the whole sobering truth of his presence in Ireland came over him, and he sat up thinking of The Marhaus.

"Gouvernail!"

His squire lay near him on a woven pallet. Gouvernail was not a man to waken lightly, full of glad faith that the world is the best place upon which to open one's eyes. But the part of him which was Tristram's heard, and started up. "What is it? Are you worse?"

"No, no, I haven't any wound this morning. Only I don't remember this place. Where have they put us?"

"In a priest's cell, so you wouldn't be disturbed by the noise in the hall." He rubbed his hands over his hair. "I was sleeping in this priest's cell as though I'd been hit with a club!"

"Gouvernail, I dreamed about The Marhaus! Did you question anyone yesterday to find out whether he lived to get back to Ireland? Is he here? Will he betray us?"

"I didn't see him, though I made a business of looking, believe me! All the time you were talking to the king my backbone kept feeling him breathe behind me." He hunched his shoulders in a shuddering gesture. "Ugh! We have lived through one more night, but if we walk out of here into The Marhaus's arms—"

Tristram could not resist a laugh. "Poor Gouvernail! You see enough miseries for a lifetime when you open your eyes! If we haven't walked into his arms yet, we can hope we won't, can't we? I seem to remember," said the prince of Lyonesse happily, "that when I parted from The Marhaus he had a pain in his head."

"Well," Gouvernail said, "I suppose now we're going to hunt for him, and ask him how his headache improves."

"One thing at a time," Tristram said. "First we'll dress and hear mass."

He felt as though he could leap from his bed, but he found himself still lame and shaken. Yet he knew his health had begun to return, not only here, but on the sea before they came ashore. And he was impatient to hurry his cure, and to be strong again, seeing himself finding deeds to do in Ireland to prove to Isoud how Cornish knights were the equal of Arthur's own men.

When they left the cell they discovered the priests already gathered before the altar slab near the church. Six or eight of them were kneeling on the cobbles, and one stood behind the stone upon which were placed the articles of the mass. Tristram looked at these objects with awe, for they were splendid beyond anything he had seen in King Hoël's house. The silver sacrament box was large, its sloping lid and sides set with panels of enamel under

91

whose glaze hundreds of tiny flowers seemed to bloom. The book was held in a case bound with straps of bronze patterned with gilt interlacings. The cup was polished silver, plain except for two heads with enamelled eyes forming its handles. The first sunlight caught these precious things and burned upward from them in soft beams.

With Gouvernail's help Tristram walked around the church and knelt with the praying priests. And though he felt his own reason to be devout, and to give God thanks for his deliverance from death, he had trouble keeping his mind on his prayers in this strange and beautiful place where mass was said under a sky all tints and pearl with morning. He wondered if these holy men were Magan's brothers, the ones he had returned to from Lyonesse to die. They were not habited as he remembered Magan's habit, with pleated cuffs and cape. They wore long, plain, linen shifts falling without belts from their shoulders to their bare feet. But their tonsure was like Magan's.

It was cold on the cobbles, and when Tristram had received communion and the service was finished he was trembling and too feeble to lift himself from his knees. Two priests supported him to the church where he sat down on the threshold stone. They had rosy, childlike faces, and curiosity shone in their eyes. As he spoke with them he learned that this mass was a celebration of their own to mark a special day of their house, and that the king's family would have a separate service in the church. But they would not hear his apology, assuring him in their mellow Irish voices it was a blessing from God when strangers knelt with them.

And, since God had sent him, they insisted he must share their food too, and tell them his story.

"He is wounded and ill," Gouvernail objected.

"No," Tristram said, "Ireland has made me well." He was speaking the truth of his feelings, for all that was strong in his youth, all that sought companionship, all that desired the recognition by men of his manhood went out in health to meet the welcome the priests gave him. On this morning in Ireland he found himself among friends. And though he did not think of it save as he knew himself happy, this was the first time in his life he had tasted the sensation of equal friendship. He had been loved in Britany as a child is loved. He had been unwelcome in Lyonesse, and doubted in Cornwall. But in Ireland these holy men spoke to him as to a brother.

Leaning on the shoulders of two of his hosts he accompanied them to the cell where they ate, and received their cakes of oatmeal, and a broth of barley sweetened with honey. Then they asked him to tell his story. He repeated briefly what he had told King Anguissh, calling himself Tramtris of Britany.

"And how did you take your wound?" a priest asked him.

"In a fair quarrel."

"Every man who fights, my lord, fights in a fair quarrel if he loves God," the priest said. "What was your quarrel?"

It was one thing to tell these kind priests a half-truth about his name and lineage. But it was another to tell them an open lie. Tristram could not bring himself to deceive them, and remained silent. As the pause lengthened he could see Gouvernail sweating in a misery of apprehension.

An old priest spoke in reproof to the young father who had asked the question. "What would his quarrel be more than the quarrels of any right man? Let it be enough for you that Lord Tramtris fought in his king's cause, or because his honor was shortened, or because his lady asked him to fight."

"It is enough for me," the young priest said, "only a fair fight makes a fine story."

Tristram laughed. "There is no story in me, friends. But if I'm dull, I'll make it up to you by singing you a war song when I'm man enough again to stand and play my harp."

He turned the talk back to them, saying Ireland was a beautiful land, and a strange one. He was curious about Anguissh who lived so like a farmer, and who was still the most kingly of men. He asked the priests how Anguissh dared sit like a pigeon on the shore inviting predatory barons to take what he had.

"He's a prompt man," the old priest said. "If raiders come up from the bogs to steal his herds he is on them like a high tide.

And he follows them home and burns their houses to remind them king's cattle are beyond theft." He went on to relate how Anguissh had built round towers throughout southern Ireland, and how he had brought order by keeping his garrisons sharp-set for counter raids more terrible than anything rebellious men could do to him, and how a few destroyed villages and women stolen for ransom had subdued the taste of bog-country barons for trying the temper of their king. "Our king believes a little war is better than a great war," the priest said, "and that is the reason he goes into the field like God's fist at a time when the cause is still small."

Tristram absorbed all he heard, trying to fit himself and his future to the knowledge his new friends gave him. The old priest was telling him God had cherished Ireland enough to put seas around it too wide for invaders to cross. "Strangers have to come to us in peace," he said, "because if they are practical men their wits shake at the thought of preparing battle fleets with boatloads of troops and weapons and food and water enough to camp on our shores while they harden their plans to bend us. And so Ireland rides like a gull on blue water looking into heaven for truth." He laughed in a voice so gentle and merry it touched Tristram the way a song might have touched him. "We have sat here too far across our moat for the Romans to swallow us down, and too far for the barbarians to swallow us down. And though pirates nibble us, they nibble us as dogs do that are willing to be friends, not as wolves. Ah," he said, "Ireland is the land!"

"Its priests are happy men, at least," Tristram said.

They were eager to speak of themselves. They showed him books they were copying, and how they made dyes for the illuminations from the flowers of fuchsia and furze, and from green moss. And they said how they and their brothers all over Ireland were carrying Christ's message to the barbarous warriors in the valley of the Rhine, and how they sailed west to explore the far islands lying toward the sunset, and to follow the flocks of sea-fowl whose dried flesh was their food.

Because they spoke like poets with something plaintive and wild as bird notes in their words, Tristram listened as he might

94

have listened to magic spells. Always a memory of Magan haunted their voices and filled his heart with a longing to know and love this land, and to be taken into its warmth. Yet he understood well enough that Ireland would never adopt him if the king discovered his battle with The Marhaus. And as he thought of The Marhaus he was reminded that he needed to know more than his hosts had told him.

"In Britany we received Irish priests," he said, "and gave them hospitality. But I never met an Irish knight in Britany."

"Our barons have enough to do at home, like enough."

"All the same," Tristram said, "I heard in Britany that the greatest champions in all Christendom came from Ireland."

"It would be natural," the priest agreed.

"Who is your first champion?"

"King Anguissh himself, of course."

"And second to King Anguissh was his knight, the queen's brother," the young priest broke in, "until he was murdered."

"He was not murdered," the first priest said. "At least he wasn't killed by treachery from ambush. But he lost his life."

"Who was he?" Tristram asked. "And how did he lose his life?"

"His father was a strong lord," the priest said, "out of the north. He belonged to the family of the Marhaus, and he was called The Marhaus in our court. He went into Cornwall on the king's justice and fought a Cornish champion in an island. And since it was a fair cause he fought for, some of our sailors say he was beaten because the island was bewitched ground."

"He took a head wound," the young priest said, "and died on the sea coming back to Ireland. I myself saw them carry his body from the ship. And I saw a piece of the sword that killed him still standing out of his skull like a great comb." The priest jumped to his feet and recited the whole adventure of The Marhaus, praising his beauty and valor, and the righteousness with which he had taken up a just quarrel, and lamenting the bedevilled field on which he had to fight, and saying how Ireland had mourned his death with days of prayers, and with a song made in his honor.

For a moment Tristram was tempted to deny this lying gossip

that he had met The Marhaus on enchanted ground, and to remind them their champion had helped himself with a poisoned spear. But it came over him that these were matters haunted with the mind's mysteries, with the will to believe in God's goodness, and the fear of deserving less than God's care. He was confused, and looked at Gouvernail for some hint to help him. But Gouvernail was drawing long breaths of relief, all but saying aloud, "Well, The Marhaus is one threat less to us."

Tristram felt no relief, only a bewildered regret for the knight who had been so beautiful and so brave, and who had given his life in a cause upon whose justice, the priest said with tears in his eyes, lay the holy light of truth.

Chapter Ten

NOW days began different for Tristram from all other days of the world. This was a little because his knighthood, which still seemed to himself so recent and surprising, was taken as a quiet fact in the court. Here he was not the new knight, or the young knight, but simply the knight who is our guest. On this green shore he had become what he was to be from now until the last day he drew breath: Tristram, the knight. Or as the household spoke of him, Tramtris, for he had not risked telling the king his true lineage.

But mostly his days were different because he spent them with Isoud. Though he was the queen's charge as much as hers, Isoud quickly became his nurse, explaining as she dressed his wound that her mother had the hall to see to, or visitors to greet, or pages to discipline. As long as he remained in the priest's cell she came each morning with the servants who carried him water and food. And after she had medicined him she walked with him, if the day was fine, as far as the church, and sat beside him on the threshold stone, and talked to him about Ireland, and about the cattle raids of her father which had made him first a great lord, and then king of the south. When he was stronger she led him slowly around the courtyard, showing him the sheep barn and the threshing floor and the granary and the thatched houses of the shepherds and swineherds. They visited the hawk mews, and Tristram saw the gyrfalcon which was the king's own bird, and stared into its round hangman's eye until it screamed with rage.

"Hawks don't like to be looked at," Isoud told him.

"How do you know so much about hawks?"

"How does anybody know anything? It's just a fact. Hawks don't like to be looked at."

"I shall look at you," Tristram said.

"I can endure it better," she said, "because I don't have murders on my conscience the way hawks do."

"Hawks have to kill. It is their business."

"Perhaps," she said indifferently. And she led him on to something else, and Tristram did not understand until they had left the mews how lightly she took the soiled consciences of hawks, and how easily she had turned aside his longing to speak to her of herself.

They spent sunny afternoons in the little garden reserved for her mother's use and her own. This was a tiny green enclosed with thorn bushes, a single ash tree growing in its center. They sat in the dappled shade of the ash and Tristram played his harp and sang for her the best songs he had learned in Britany, those whose subtleties escaped listeners not trained in music. But Isoud understood them and smiled with the delight of her understanding at the very places where he watched most anxiously to see whether she would smile. Tristram thought he had never met a lady with such warm and tender comprehension. When she asked him to teach her to play the harp and to sing in French, when she bent over the strings to touch them unsurely, her hair slipping forward against her cheek and her soft mouth forming the foreign syllables, he thought no man could understand happiness who hadn't a pupil to instruct as lovely and willing as this princess.

One day the queen entered the garden while Tristram was singing. She stood between the thorns at the gate listening, her shrewd eyes veiled by her lids, and her lips set together in a close line.

"That was a beautiful song, Tramtris," she said.

"Thank you, my lady."

"One of these evenings you must sing in the hall," she said. "In

98

fact, Tramtris, I have been thinking you'll be more comfortable if you leave the cell, now you're strong again, and live in the hall with the household."

"If the king will receive me I shall try to do his household honor."

"I'll see to your move," the queen said, "today."

"Gouvernail will arrange it, my lady."

"We needn't trouble Gouvernail," she said. "I'll see to it myself."

Tristram knew enough to understand that he was being moved for Isoud's sake, and that the queen was not pleased with their morning meetings, and this harping in the soft shade of the ash tree. But he could not tell himself whether the queen had discovered in her daughter some close-held secret, a sigh for himself, perhaps, a look to say she thought of him. Did she think of him? Tristram picked up his harp and moved his fingers across the strings, gazing at Isoud. She was leaning on her hand, her head bent a little sideways, sunlight running over her hair in golden touches as the breeze moved it. But Tristram could not read her as well as the queen was able to do. And though he wished to ask her what thoughts she was thinking, he dared not.

Before the day was out the queen's servants carried into the hall the small baggage he had brought from Cornwall: his shield, still blank, and the sword Hoël had given him in its scabbard, and the furs with which Mark had furnished the boat. These things were placed near the pallet upon which he would sleep among the household knights. And with their transfer Tristram became King Anguissh's man.

Now Gouvernail attended the princess when she came to medicine his wound. Though he awoke each morning lonely for Isoud's voice at the door of the cell, he was happy to be in the hall, and to sit with the knights at the king's table, and to speak with them of war and the news reaching Ireland from the world. The house of King Anguissh might appear humble from without. Within it owned a luxury surpassing even King Hoël's. The king's cloth-makers furnished him hangings in clear, delicate colors, so that the half-daylight of the long, oval room muted their tints into richness.

Irish mines produced gold for plates and ewers, and these objects shone when the lamp bowls were lit, and reflected in their sides the hues of enamelled bosses on drinking cups of horn and on the clasps and bracelets men wore who had deserved such gifts from the king. Tristram dressed in the Irish tunic of the others, and the wide baldric of leather and silver, and thought that someday, when he had performed fitting service for King Anguissh, he would be given a silver chain and a medallion, and that then he would appear as though he had been born among these men who were to be his brothers, and that whoever saw him would know Ireland was his true home.

The hall interested him, but not so much as the men he met there. The barons who sat nearest the king were Irish, either lords who had been conquered by Anguissh and elected to serve with him, or heads of families of the king's blood. Below these were lesser knights and men who seemed foreign to Tristram because of some distinguishing mark, a dark skin, or speech echoing another tongue, or hair and beards of outlandish cut. One among them was certainly foreign, he who was called the Saracen. His hair was black and shining like the hair of a cat, and he had only a little tuft of beard. But what he lacked in beard he made up in moustaches which he wore thin and pointed and so long the ends reached almost to his shoulders. His eyes were black too, quick and hot, peering around the table from one man to another in a passion whose meaning Tristram could not read. He reminded Tristram of the gyrfalcon shrieking with fury when it was looked at. And whenever his eyes met the fiery stare of the Saracen he expected foolishly that this angry, dark-skinned man would shriek too, in the curse of the Saracens, whatever that curse might be. Yet he was handsome and strong, and bore himself like a prince.

Outside the hall the household knights were slow to make friends with Tristram. He realized this was because he was still thought of as disabled, a man not yet fit to ride or use weapons. He missed their companionship, and yet he was reluctant to run forward in his cure, fearing that on the day he joined the king's party as they rode out to hunt or visit a garrison he would lose his long hours with Isoud. But he was restless when he saw the horses led into the courtyard, and heard the horns blow, and the dogs yelp and squeal with excitement as they jumped against their leashes.

On a certain day he and Isoud were sitting in her garden under the ash tree. They had been laughing much over matters which seemed worth their laughter. And Tristram had been looking at the curve of Isoud's neck where it disappeared under her hair. He fell silent. A long pause went by.

"This is the day," Isoud said.

"What day?"

"The day you begin to think of things you don't wish to talk of."

"I was thinking of you, Isoud."

"No," she said, "you were thinking of the tournament."

"Why should I not wish to talk of the tournament?"

"Because," she said, "you make plans to ride, and you know you are not strong enough, and you will have to go against objections. And you do not want to hurt anybody's feelings by going against their objections."

Tristram could feel himself blush. "I was thinking those things, Isoud. But—"

"My mother says your side isn't strong enough for you to ride in the king's games."

"How did the queen know I meant to ride!"

"She is wise," Isoud said.

"You want me to ride, don't you?"

"Yes," she said, "someday, when you are healed. But the games are a week away, Tramtris, and today we don't have to talk of war and tournaments."

"Your father's Saracen knight tells everybody he will win the prize in the tournament," Tristram said.

"Oh," Isoud said, and she rose and stood by the ash tree, and the wind moved her hair and smoothed her dress against her slim body, "he is a truly big and a truly brave man, but he is always afraid he won't win the prize. He doubts himself among Christian knights, though everybody wishes to be his friend."

"You are his friend," Tristram said.

101

Isoud nodded. "He is my father's liege man. Now let us not talk of Palamides, but—"

"You think of so many things we aren't to talk of," Tristram complained, smiling. "But I am curious about this foreign Palamides, and how your father happens to have a Saracen knight as a liege man, and why he—"

"Now," Isoud said, "if you don't come with me, I am going to walk by myself."

"Where will you walk?"

"To the goldsmith's," she said, "to see him work the mass vessel."

"Help me, then." Tristram held up his hands.

"No, Tramtris, you play at needing help." And she laughed and began to walk lightly through the garden, looking back at him over her shoulder.

How beautiful she was, moving with the grace of a sea bird, pushing aside the flowering branches of the thorn trees which seemed to lean toward her as she passed! Tristram sprang up and followed her, and caught her by the shoulders. "Tell me Palamides' story, or I shall hold you and not let you go to the goldsmith's."

"If you hold me I shall never tell you anything." She moved her shoulders with a swift turn and shook free of him.

"You're angry. It isn't like you to be angry, Isoud."

"How do you know what is like me, and what isn't? Because I have washed your wound you think I am yours to lay hands on, my lord."

" 'My lord'!"

"But," Isoud said, looking hotly into his eyes, "though I have nursed you I am not one of those women who see in all men only little children who must be pampered when they cry for what they want. Don't mistake me, Tramtris. You are not a child, and I am not a child either."

She was more beautiful than he had ever beheld her, her face warmed with resentment and with a kind of defiance, all that was soft in her suddenly firmed into proud authority. Because she had dared him Tristram felt a will to seize her that went stinging along his arms, through all his body. But when he moved toward her he stopped after one step. They looked at each other without words, each striving to prevail.

"I'll come with you to the goldsmith's," he said.

They walked across the green, past the church and the row of cells. Isoud was smiling. "Palamides journied to Ireland because he heard of it from our priests," she said.

"Did he?" Tristram had forgotten the foreign knight.

"Our priests go everywhere, Tramtris. They are travellers and mariners before they are priests."

"They must speak well of Ireland to bring it Saracens from beyond Rome."

"Ireland has many things to speak of."

"If I were voyaging from Ireland I would make a song about you and sing it wherever I went."

"Sometimes," she said carelessly, "our priests set out on the sea when they are young men, and make such a journey they are old men when they sail home."

"Palamides—" Tristram said.

"He came to Ireland. I've told you. Many foreigners come to Ireland. This very day we have holy men from Rome and Africa and Spain in our court. What is so wonderful about Palamides?"

"He wishes to win the tournament for you," Tristram said.

"He wishes to win it for me because he is courteous, and thinks of pleasing my father."

"I shall fight in the tournament," Tristram said, "and win it for you, because I think of pleasing you."

"Unless you show more interest in the goldsmith," Isoud said, "I shan't believe you think of pleasing me."

"I've heard them say you mean to turn Palamides into a Christian knight, Isoud."

"We should want any man who bears arms to be a Christian knight, shouldn't we?"

"In a land where God's ministers are sitting under every thorn bush," Tristram said, "you can leave such works to men whose business is souls."

103

"I will not hear you blaspheme, Tramtris."

"I am not blaspheming, but——"

"Now," she said, "good-by. I am tired of talk. And I am going to run to the goldsmith's, but you must walk, since you need help to find your feet and to limp over the ground."

"Oh, Isoud, you will listen to Saracens, and to all manner of men, but you won't listen to me!"

She ran before him, swift and slender, every curve of her body yielding into movement. Tristram drew even, and kept pace over the cobbles of the courtyard, past the threshing floor and the granary and the sheep barn. His heart beat fast with a desire to be strong before her, to win back the ground he had lost. When they reached the king's shops his breath was thick in his throat, yet not because he had run.

"I've watched the smith working the vessel since the day the gold came from the mines," Isoud said. "It will be the most beautiful vessel ever made in Ireland."

Tristram longed to tell her he would have a more beautiful vessel made for her, that he would travel east and west, beyond any land the Irish priests knew, and bring home finer gold, and clearer gems, yet even then no vessel would be as beautiful as she. But he could not say these things because she was so calm, breathing as gently as a child, thinking of nothing save her wish to see the goldsmith at work.

They reached a round hut before which stood a forge of small size and a cooling trough. The forge was not fired today. They could hear a voice in the hut, and they went through the low door and found the smith at his bench. He had been talking to himself, or perhaps to the work in his hands.

He was one of those men whose craft mark them. His shoulders were padded with fat, and his chest was sunken into a flabby roll of flesh. But his short legs were all bone and scrawny sinew, withered by days and years of sitting. A hundred fine wrinkles netted his brow and the skin around his eyes, which had the alertness of a man used to teaching himself the appearance of things. As he rose to greet them Tristram saw he was wearing close-fitting breeches and a leather tunic falling only a few inches below his waist. A little ruff of white hair gave him the look of an old baby.

"I have brought our guest to see the vessel," Isoud said.

"You won't notice much changed since yesterday, my lady. The ornamentation is slow work."

He explained his design. The vessel was silver, standing on a wide foot, all its pure curves polished and glowing. Below the lip he was laying a band of filigree made of gold wire drawn to an incredible thinness. The interlacings were so fine Tristram thought they could be blown away by a breath, yet the smith ran his thumb firmly over the finished pattern, showing the involutions and the terminals, which swelled into miniscule animal heads. To give the lacings depth, he told them, three layers of the golden thread were used, one upon another. At intervals along the band he was setting enamelled bosses of blue and red in whose shining hearts he had implanted, as if by magic, stars or crossed grills of the gold wire. The handles would be broad, their outer surface paved with fitted checks of filigree, each tiny block forming a design distinct from the others.

"If I live long enough," he finished with a smile.

Tristram stood before the vessel as before a miracle. He had never dreamed that any man, with only the ten blunt fingers God had given him, could accomplish anything so delicate, so without flaw. In the dim house the vessel appeared to gleam with its own immaculate light as he had heard the Grail gleamed. He looked from it to the strange little man who had made it. The smith seemed more like an animal than a man, like some puff-breasted bird bedraggled by storms, in whose eyes a passion less than human glistened.

"Do you have such vessels in Britany?" Isoud said.

"No. I've never seen such a vessel as this anywhere."

"What do you have in Britany that is like Ireland?" She turned to the smith and said, "God bless your work, and I'll be back tomorrow." Then she stooped and passed out of the house through the low door.

"Will you make a ring for me?" Tristram asked the smith.

"Yes, my lord."

"I want a small one formed of twisted strands of the gold wire."

"That will be easy enough."

"Let it be a secret," Tristram said.

"I have to account for my gold."

"I'll send you the gold, enough to make the ring and pay your labor."

"My labor is free," the smith said. "I am a slave, my lord."

"A slave!"

"When I was ten years old I was sold to the court by my father who could not feed me. I learned my trade in this house from the master smith. And now I am the master smith."

"But you could buy your freedom," Tristram said, touched by the wrong that so perfect an artist should be a slave.

The old man nodded. "I could, but I do not want my freedom now. For what should I do if I weren't making this?" He laid his hand on the vessel. "It is your business to love freedom, my lord. It is my business to love this."

Tristram could not answer. He came out into the sunshine consumed by what he had seen, forgetful of Ireland and of his reason for being in the court of King Anguissh. Yet he had not forgotten Isoud.

"You didn't tell me," she said, "what you have in Britany that is like Ireland."

"Oh," he said. "I remember. In Britany I knew a lady who had your name, except she spoke hers in French."

"What is my name in French?"

"Yseut."

"How old was this lady Yseut of Britany?"

"Your age, I think."

"Was she pretty?"

"Yes," Tristram said, "she was as beautiful as a flower."

"I do not understand what men mean when they say women are as beautiful as flowers," Isoud complained. "Flowers are thin and cold, and they die after they have lived a day in the sun."

"They mean," Tristram said as though she had asked for instruc-

106

tion, "that women have faces all white and rose, and skin as delicate as a petal, and that their hair is fragrant, as a flower is. They mean—"

"Was Yseut of Britany all white and rose?"

"Of course," Tristram said. "What a day this is! Do you want to run as far as the threshing floor?"

"No," Isoud said.

"I only suggested it to show you I am well again and can run faster than you."

Isoud walked along gravely, looking at the ground. "Was Yseut fair or dark?"

"Between fair and dark."

"You said she was white and rose."

"I meant—I—only meant—"

She laughed. "Let us walk down to the sea, Tramtris. Did you know I was on the shore when your boat came into harbor, and that I saw you before you saw me?"

"You were wearing a scarlet dress that day."

"Green."

"Green later. You were wearing scarlet when I saw you first."

"I told my father you had come without oars."

"I told Gouvernail you were a queen."

"Why did you think I was a queen?"

"Because," Tristram said, and he had had enough of play and of this light talk which was at once a delight and a smother over true things, "a man knows when he has met his sovereign, Isoud."

"Was Yseut a queen?"

He did not answer. They had reached the top of the slope now, and stood together looking over the harbor and the fishermen's boats and the nets drying on the cradles of rushes.

"It is low tide," Isoud said.

"Yes."

"Some morning when the tide is high you and Gouvernail will come down to the beach and get into your boat and go away. To Britany."

"Not if you tell me I am to stay," he said.

107

Chapter Eleven

THE morning after this the queen came to medicine Tristram's side, and the next morning as well. Tristram did not see Isoud except in the hall at meat when she took the cup from her father and carried it among the guests. She passed near him without looking at him. But Tristram knew from the way she walked, straight and tall-stretched, and from the way she caught her lower lip against her teeth, that she felt their nearness, whether or not as he felt it. For him she was alone in the hall, the others no more than the circumstance which kept their eyes from meeting.

He was bored and wretched, and seemed to himself to suffer a return of his illness. He walked to Isoud's garden and lay in the grass under the ash tree and listened for her footfall. When she did not come he wandered about the courtyard, telling over each day she had spent with him there, and how she had shown him the familiar things among which her short life had passed. In the beginning when he was weak enough to long for her care, he had delighted in the glimpses she gave him of her childhood as she led him slowly from barn to tool shed to mill. Then she had seemed all innocence, all loving warmth for small and helpless things. But on the day they visited the goldsmith he had learned that though innocence and tenderness were a part of her spirit they were its lesser part, a veil half-concealing what he desired above all things to touch, her proud, passionate soul. Why had she withdrawn herself when she had stood so nearly revealed? He was buffeted by the memory of her saying, "Don't mistake me," by the fire of her beauty then, by her absence now.

Who was as beautiful as Isoud? Tristram had heard songs, and sung them himself many times, in whose rhymes the fairness of this or that woman, Alys, or Coustance, or Enide, was said to exceed the fairness of any lady alive. And he had amused himself by thinking these rhymes absurd, though they were pleasant to sing. For surely no woman lived who could be said by an honest mind to be more beautiful than every other. What made a woman beautiful? Yellow hair, or hair as black as night? A red mouth? Skin of white and rose? Every lady had hair of some hue, and colors in her face too.

So he had thought as he harped and sang of Alys and Coustance. But now he understood that the makers of these songs were struggling with a fact so huge and overwhelming words could not catch it with the sound of truth. The fact was this: One woman alone was, in sober justice, more beautiful than all the women who lived. The song makers had known so much only by intimation, and had invented their Enides and Alyses in the hope of seeing, in a blessed moment of imagination, the lady incomparable among ladies. Yet it remained for Tristram to see the real lady, the one the poets dreamed of. And he was astonished almost beyond his power to believe, and humble too, to think he was the man who had discovered her, and walked and spoken with her, and seen her bright hair blow in the wind, and felt the heartbeat in her hands.

He moved about the courtyard thinking whether he could tell Isoud what he understood about her, and whether she would acknowledge this surpassing truth. Oh, if she would come to him! Then time would run ahead gaily again, and his weakness would end, and he could go from her (foreseeing his return) to the field beyond the castle where the king's men practiced with the spear. But when she was absent he dared not seek any pleasure, or mingle in companionship with the knights of King Anguissh, for more would be lost than could be made up if she looked for him and found him gone.

He remembered she visited the goldsmith each day to watch

109

the work on the mass vessel. He had an errand there himself, to carry the smith enough gold coins to replace the metal used for the ring he had ordered. But Isoud was not at the smithy. She was nowhere. Tristram returned to the courtyard well and sat down on its curb. He meditated the making of a song to say in true words the reality of Isoud's fairness, but he was ill and in turmoil, and he could not think coolly as one must if one creates a song.

In a little while Palamides, the Saracen knight, spoke to him. Tristram, blind to a world which did not hold Isoud, had not seen him approach.

"Well, wounded knight," Palamides said.

"Good day, my lord."

"You've changed your cure this morning."

"I am healed," Tristram said, hearing himself, so ill and lonely, assert pathetically that he was strong.

Palamides looked down on him. His moustaches glistened like swallow's wings, and the light in his fierce eyes was tightened into two points. He was wearing a shirt of fine chain and the wrapped trousers of the Scythian horsemen, and he carried his sword. "I am glad to hear it," Palamides said. "I had begun to think some softness in this northern air makes healing slow."

Tristram rose. "What do you say, my lord?"

"I say," the Saracen repeated, his words distorted by the fact that he was speaking a tongue not his own, "in my country broken men find their strength more quickly than they do here in the salt winds of Ireland."

"Have you armed," Tristram said, "in order to tell me this and be safe?"

"Am I armed?" Palamides glanced down at his sword as if in surprise. "I am so used to the feel of clothes such as these that I arm merely to be dressed."

"You find fault with my tunic, perhaps."

"It is an excellent tunic," Palamides said, "for a man who cannot wear a sword."

Angry answers crowded into Tristram's throat. He could play at the game of insulting talk too, and remind Palamides that, however healthy the climate of his homeland might be, it did nothing salubrious for Saracen manners. He stood there trembling with rage, without advantage, unable to choose among the offenses he might give this violent heathen who wished to quarrel.

"My lord," he said, "it is easy to speak loud. I am willing to listen to your words thirty days from today on whatever field you like."

Palamides was grinning, his teeth gleaming white against his dark skin. And he was breathing with such noisy passion his moustaches shook. Tristram thought his contorted face looked like some evil caricature, something that lived in wild places, less than man, but larger and more dangerous than man. Now a feeling began in Tristram, big and free, a will to subdue Palamides the savage and hear him yield.

"In my country," the Saracen said, "when we have business, we do not put it off for thirty days." Before Tristram could answer him he turned and walked away.

Tristram watched him hurry across the court. In his cloth trousers, narrow in the leg and bulging in womanish pads at the hips, he looked ridiculous, but not with the harmless absurdity of a clown. His was the menacing outlandishness of the lunatic. How did I get in that animal's way, Tristram asked himself. He was too excited to sit down, and walked a double turn around the well as he considered what had happened. He gave himself one reason after another why Palamides should want to pick a quarrel with him, but these were self-deceiving speculations. He knew why he and the Saracen had crashed together. Each man desired Isoud.

Was it only half an hour ago he had been thinking of Isoud in terms of poetry? Isoud, rose and white, slender as a lily, holy beyond all imperfect reaching? She was these, but he had already proved she was more. She was the goal, and the prize. She was the reward as well as the reason for manhood. And she was not to be attained by any means less than the means of manhood. It was well enough to walk with her, and look at the newborn lambs, and catch a downy duckling for her to gentle, it was well enough to sit in the garden and sing songs, and marvel at the wonder of her soft

111

mouth speaking French. It would even serve to make a song about her, and praise her beauty humbly as he might praise the beauty of an angel. But this was dalliance and ended with each hour's end. Beyond it lay the gaunt truth that nothing is purchased with nothing, that a man's desire must be earned, if need be, with his life.

He wanted to run, to leap clean over the well. He whistled a dog to him, a half-renegade named Pickpocket, and walked down the cobbles as far as the wall. It was time he opened this gate and went outside the drowsy domestic life of Anguissh's courtyard. Servants were moving toward the tournament ground with bundles on their backs. A two-wheeled cart drawn by an ox was laboring up the grassy slope, loaded, as nearly as Tristram could tell, with tent cloth. The preparation for the games had begun.

Walking beside the cart he came over the rise and saw the course below him. It was a green plain bounded on the east by the sea and on the west by low earth in the form of a natural amphitheatre. With colored posts the workmen had staked out two riding fields, and now at the south end of the ground they were building temporary withdrawing places in the shape of lean-tos, four poles roofed with green branches. Each competing knight would be assigned one of these for rest, and to attend to the wants of his horse. On the landward slope ranks of the same roofed poles would be set in a long line, and over all cloth would be spread to protect the king and the ladies and such visitors as came to see the games.

On one field knights were charging at dummy shields to improve their aim, and a few squires were exercising horses already chosen for the jousts. Around the other a fence of brush had been stuck into the earth, for this was the ground on which the bouts would be ridden, and its turf must not be cut or damaged before the day of the games.

"We didn't have such a course in Britany," Tristram said to the man leading the ox.

"Did you ride on a grass field?"

"Yes, but not grass so thick and fine as this."

112

The man looked pleased. "It is tended like a child, my lord, mowed at the right time of the moon, and raked once a week from spring to winter. This field," he said, "is the son of King Anguissh."

"They say salt fog makes the best turf in the world."

"Salt Irish fog," the man corrected him courteously. "On the eastern side of Ireland our fog is as kind as mother's milk, being born on quiet water."

"You do not speak like an outdoor servant," Tristram said.

"I am in the house, that is true. But I have the duty of seeing that the king's shelter is well covered, and the cloth for it is my charge." He nodded toward the loaded cart.

"Aren't you afraid the wind will get at it if you put it up so long before the games?"

"I'll only order it stowed today. When the games begin there's enough to do without having to carry cloth." And he went on to describe how casks of ale must be carted out, and cakes and cold meats and cheese and fruit. Weapons and horse gear must be transported too, and banners of colored linen set by the knights' pavilions and at appropriate places along the course. "For a few hours' sport many hours of hauling and hammering go ahead, my lord."

"Thanks to stout fellows like you," Tristram said. "As it happens, I have a use for just such a stout fellow as you."

The man glanced away, covering some feeling or other with a look toward the sea. Tristram smiled to see this sign of experience, knowing well that a servant in any king's house was asked to do favors he oughtn't to do, and that men old and clever in usage had habits for turning aside the awkward demands of their superiors. Tristram produced a coin, gold. He saw the man see it, though he still gazed off at the horizon, only now with a sort of unctuous innocence.

"I am in need of a horse," Tristram said, "and blank arms."

"Are you riding in the games, my lord?"

"I have been wounded, and am still under the queen's charge. And my lady does not think me fit to ride."

The man waited to hear more.

"My wound healed long ago, but I do not wish to raise a jangle with the queen. All the same, I can't sit in the grass while my brothers ride against each other for prizes. So if there were a man who would bring me a schooled horse, a good gelding, an hour before dawn on the morning of the games, and a shield without escutcheon, and a helm, and a strong oak spear, I could find some reward for him. Especially if he could put me out of the court by a back gate."

"And what about your squire? Will you fight without a pavilion?"

"I won't need a squire or a pavilion."

The man made no answer. In a moment he shortened the strap with which he had been leading the ox, and pulled up the animal's head, and called for it to go on. "Good-by, my lord. God ride with you on the day."

"Here's something to remember me by." Tristram gave him the coin. Canny fellow, he thought, he doesn't say a word too many. For a while he sat on the high ground and watched the work going forward on the field. The dog raced back and forth between him and the men below as though he had been deputized to report each side's thoughts to the other. He was an excellent red hound with coaxing eyes set well in his narrow head, and a long, pointed plume of tail. But he was a little too heavy for sharp hunting, for he had been petted by the children in the court, and had developed a swaggering sort of personality, busy, curious, and whimsical, which could tease the last morsel out of the hand of a starving man. He should be my friend Dinadan's dog, Tristram thought, and wondered with a feeling of looking back long years on his life how Dinadan was, and whether at King Mark's court anyone except that little knight thought of his cure in Ireland.

"Come on, Pickpocket," he said to the dog. "We have one more piece of business today."

They struck down over the end of the rise and walked back along the beach. It was an hour short of noon, and the tide had just turned and begun to ebb. Rollers washed in with a murmur and rustle, spreading thin fans of water onto the sand, and lacing rocks at the tide line with delicate ruffs of foam. Small birds ran madly

114

down the beach after the retreating water, and flew up just high enough to let the returning wave pass under them, bits of feathers whose whole lives seemed to be this furious rush after the salt. The sea left bladderweed behind it, and Tristram stepped onto the translucent bubbles so much like pearls, and felt them burst under his feet. Was it this same peaceful blue, not loud enough to cover the pop of bladderweed, which roared and beat with such a sound of torment against Tintagel? Am I homesick? Tristram wondered. Yes—no. Ireland was Isoud's land, and he would not leave it. Yet he had fought for Cornwall, and made one friend there. And his uncle's castle lay near the sky.

When they reached the harbor he saw a few large boats shipping out on the tide. They sat low in the water, their sails hardly full yet, and the oarsmen were pulling slowly, counting or singing in a rhythm he could still hear. One, he knew, was a merchant ship from London. It had brought grain, and was returning with dyed cloth. As he watched, an uproar began on the shore, and Pickpocket rushed off, carrying his tail like a feathered arrow, and leaving on the sand the marks of long leaps. Three men were walking down toward a Spanish boat which was still beached. Each of them was pulled along by four or five dogs of Pickpocket's breed on leashes. Tristram remembered that the Spaniards had come especially to buy these red Irish hunting hounds whose sale added sums each year to the treasury of King Anguissh. And what a cargo they were! So many disorders overwhelmed them at sea, fear and cramped quarters and, as Anguissh explained, homesickness for Irish air, that the king had learned not to ship them without an Irish master to soothe their hearts. The dogs were dragged aboard, squealing and crying, and somehow tied there. But as the boat moved slowly into deep water they leaped against their leads, barking wildly. Pickpocket stood ashore screaming a farewell after them, or an encouragement, more probably. It would be like Pickpocket to say, "Courage, brothers," when he was standing free on the shore of home.

I wish Isoud had come down to see the Spanish ship sail, Tristram thought. This would have been a day to remember, the day

115

we watched the dogs leave. But she had seen red hunters shipped out many times, he remembered, and had told him how, when she was a child, she used to weep for the beautiful Irish souls of the dogs departing into foreign lands. The ship had gone far enough now so that the pleas of the hounds came back as music, plaintive and haunting. Pickpocket raced up and down the water's edge looking after his friends with desperate eyes, and plunging into the foam as though to tell them he had been left behind gainst his wish. But Pickpocket probably didn't mean to lie, Tristram considered. His emotions were easily touched.

Tristram called him away from his agonized good-by and walked with him back to the hall. In the courtyard he looked for Isoud, but he was willing enough not to find her there. He had an errand needing privacy.

He left the dog at the sheep barn and went on alone. In the hall he looked for the king's herald and did not see him. Would he be in the armory? He might be, since he had duties in the games, and would need to memorize the escutcheons of any strangers who were riding. The armory was a round house built against the end of the hall and opened to it by the simple means of a knocked-down wall. It was without windows, though Tristram discerned a light within, and smelled the odor of an oil-dish lamp. The herald was squatting on the floor before a plank upon which he had stretched a greatly soiled leaf of parchment. In the flickering light he was drawing rapid notes on the sheepskin with a brush.

"Good day, my lord," Tristram said.

"God go with you, wounded knight."

"Not the wounded knight now," Tristram said, and knelt to see what the herald was doing. "I am almost as good an artist as you," he said.

"This work isn't done to please." The herald sat back on his heels and rubbed his eyes. "I'm teaching myself the escutcheons of the Saracen knight and our two guests from France. And I'm copying them for my pages who will make a confusion of the games if they aren't drilled."

"Has the order of the courses been set?" Tristram asked, lean-

116

ing over as if he were only interested in the drawing on the parchment.

"Yes."

"And who rides first?"

"The young knights. They ride three courses, for one fall each. And the two best ride the fourth course, one fall."

Tristram was amused to think how, in justice, he should be riding with the young knights, since he had never, except as a squire, taken part in a tournament. But the king did not know that, or the herald either. And only he himself knew he had fought The Marhaus.

"And then?"

"Then we come to the two French knights, and the Saracen, who fight as guests."

"How do you manage when you have only three?" Tristram picked up the parchment and studied it closely. "I have never seen sheepskin cured in this way," he said. "Would you, my lord, give me a little square of it?"

The herald raised his eyebrows in astonishment. "How is it different from parchment you know? It is only scraped and dried and softened—surely that's a simple way to cure sheepskin."

Tristram was confused. He cared not at all about the cure of animal hide, and knew nothing of it. He had a use for one small square, however; and besides, he did not care to let the herald see he was interested in the order of the course Palamides would ride. "I may be mistaken, but the surface of this skin seems more pliable and better grained than ours in Britany."

The herald smiled as though the vagaries of foreign men had no limit. "This is dirty enough, my lord Tramtris, and it has been used I don't know how many times. But if you like it, here it is." He drew his short knife from its sheath on his baldric and hacked off a piece of the tough parchment.

"Thank you," Tristram said. "I'll remember your courtesy. You were telling me about the courses the guest knights will ride."

"Oh, yes. When we have three, they draw lots, and the two fight whose lots match. The winner fights the third. But I suppose it is

117

the usage in your country too, isn't it, that any strange knight who arrives at the games and asks to ride may enter? If that happens, the stranger knight will ride a course against our third man who lacks an opponent."

"I see. And do stranger knights often enter?"

"Sometimes. When The Marhaus was our champion the best riders from Camelot liked to come to try him. But this year," he said, shaking his head, "we haven't many men except Palamides to give the games the old glory. And Palamides' name has hardly spread to Britain."

Tristram knew all he needed to know. But he enjoyed this talk of the war games, and lingered to hear more.

"After the guests," the herald told him, "we come to the men of our own muscle." And he named off the names and rank of the Irish barons who served with King Anguissh, allowing Tristram to sample a little beforehand the style with which he would cry the bouts on the great day.

It was good to be at men's business again, Tristram thought. It was even better to know his meeting with Palamides was secure. In a matter of days he would prove upon that dark and passionate man what must be proved for Isoud's sake, she who was the most beautiful among all the women in the world.

Chapter Twelve

O N the morning of the day before the games Tristram received from the goldsmith the ring he had ordered. At first he was disappointed in it, for it seemed small and plain. But as he stood with it in the palm of his hand, studying its plan, he saw it possessed the mysterious beauty of a precious thing simply made. The smith had used braided strands of gold wire to form a delicate relief of interlacings upon a circlet of silver. That was all. Yet it had been done with such imaginative grace that it contained within its small crossings and recrossings a design as flawless as it was fine. Tristram looked up from it with a sigh.

"It speaks softly, my lord," the smith said, "but it speaks."

"It is beyond what I hoped for," Tristram said. "I would like to reward you."

"I am rewarded. I made it."

"If I had worked this ring," Tristram said, "I would want to be sure its owner understood it and would keep it safe for a lifetime. And I can at least promise you that much."

The smith shrugged so that his head seemed to be withdrawn into his round shoulders as a turtle's head hunches toward its shell. "The future is as it may be, isn't it? I suppose people come and go in all lands as they do in Ireland, and that luck is good or bad, and that some souls may love a little gold ring, and some may think it a toy."

"I promise you," Tristram said.

"But there is this," the smith said, turning back to his bench. "If it is lost, it will live like a glowworm under a sod or a thorn bush, and its light will not go out as ours will, my lord."

"We have been taught God will not let our light go out," Tristram reminded him, and smiled, so as to avoid the sound of reproof.

The smith gestured toward the walls of his round hut. "I live in a small space, with not much room for large thoughts. It may be the gods come and go as people do. But the ring will wait."

"Aren't you afraid of the priests when you say things they would hold blasphemous?"

The artist only laughed, not with bitterness or bravado, but as men laugh musingly at a strange idea.

Tristram wished to say something more, a sentence to express the feeling the ring gave him of seeing plain for a moment meanings beyond his comprehension. But matters such as this were hard to think of, and twice hard to speak. He had to content himself with thanking the misshapen little man and wishing him well.

As he was returning across the court with the ring held tight in his hand he met Isoud.

"Good morning, Tramtris," she said as though they had parted the evening before. "Have you been to the beach?"

"No, to the goldsmith's. I've gone every day."

"How is the vessel?"

"Haven't you seen it?"

"I've been busy," she said. "Before the games we have work to do in the hall."

There was a silence.

"You'll sit with the king and queen to see the games, won't you, Tramtris?"

"No," he said, "I've been thinking I would get up at daylight tomorrow, and go with the men in the salmon boats if they'll give me a place."

"If you don't come, you'll make the queen feel she has been cruel. She has only tried to do what was best for you."

"I know," he said, "and I owe her more thanks than I can ever

120

repay for her care." He heard himself speaking stiltedly, as though he were reading from a manual of conduct, and he wished to free himself. But Isoud's air of casual friendliness drove back his longing to tell her the thoughts which had kept him in confusion, even the reproaches he had rehearsed in the nights when he awoke and remembered her absence from the places he had begun to think of as theirs.

"I saw the Spaniards ship out with the dogs yesterday, Isoud."

"I heard the poor beasts being led away."

"Isoud! Why haven't you come to the ash tree?"

She stood before him without any gesture, her eyes untroubled, self-contained and quiet as a flower at sunrise. He could see the shadow of her eyelashes against her cheek, and the chain she wore lift as she breathed. She was his! If she was not his, everything had been a lie, Magan, and King Hoël, and the two hours on the island when he fought The Marhaus and prevailed.

"You do not answer me," he said.

"That is true, Tramtris. I have no answer for you."

"You knew I would wait. I have waited there each day."

Her lips parted in a smile. "If you like I shall send my woman Bragwain to the garden to sit with you. Bragwain thinks you are the handsomest of all my father's knights."

"I shall be happy to sit with Bragwain," Tristram said, anger bursting into his throat like salt. "I have seen her. She is courteous and gentle-hearted."

"She has excellent qualities," the princess agreed.

"You laugh at me."

"Walk with me to the mill and tell me you will see the games tomorrow."

"I have told you. I am going with the fishermen."

"Poor Tramtris, you will spend a weary day in the salmon boats and miss the tournament because I haven't come to the ash tree!"

"If you had wanted to come as much as I wanted to see you—"

"At this moment," she said, "I want to go to the mill."

He was shaken with a desire to hold her, to demand answers, to

121

destroy her peace as she had destroyed his. If her cool poise could be shattered only by taking her into his arms, he would take her. But he remembered the ring closed in his hand.

"Good-by, Tramtris," she said. "I shall hope to see you tomorrow."

"I watched games for sport," he said, "when I was a squire." As he stood looking after her walking over the cobbles toward the mill—who walked as Isoud did, so light and swift!—he was ashamed of his sullen answer. It was stupid and wrong to wish to quarrel with her. It was wrong to talk at all until he had done what could be done tomorrow.

But because they had met and talked, and because he had won nothing from Isoud to ease or hearten him, he could not feel the sober resolve he felt before he fought The Marhaus. He spent a restless day and a restless night, and arose before dawn with a dry mouth and hands trembling as he fastened on his clothes.

He crept from the hall, praying he would not stumble over something in the dark that would crash and rouse the household. When he reached the courtyard he discovered the moon had set, and the stars were high and pale. A dog laid its cold nose into his hand and startled his heart into his throat.

"Pickpocket?" he whispered.

The dog leaped upon him with a squeal of delight.

"Be quiet, Pickpocket! Here! Be still!"

Pickpocket could be counted on to resist a command, but he had once been a well-trained hound, and when he was convinced Tristram meant what he said he followed along silently enough. They moved down the side of the king's hall like a pair of shadows, rounded the corner, passed the armory, and reached the yard behind the house. Now, Tristram thought, if I've judged my friend the ox driver right, I'll find him at the postern gate.

He felt his way across the unfamiliar ground, keeping the direction in which he knew the postern to stand. Pickpocket had trotted ahead and lost himself in the dark, and Tristram's neck tingled as he expected each moment to hear the dog's glad cries of greeting to the servant. But some unnatural discretion prompted Pickpocket

122

to be quiet. When Tristram reached the postern the dog crowded against his legs all but saying, "You kept us waiting."

"My lord?" a low voice spoke to him.

"I was never so glad to meet anyone as I am you," Tristram said.

"It will soon be daylight," the servant said. "A horse is tied outside the wall. Will you arm here or there?"

"Where the horse is."

"I'll open the gate." Tristram could hear him grunt as he moved the heavy timbers. "Now then. We must hurry."

"Where is the dog?"

"I'll bring him back with me. Come on, my lord, or the dawn will surprise us."

They passed through the gate, Tristram following the servant who sped up the rise into a little grove of trees. There he could discern against the lesser dark of the sky the head of a horse, its ears pricked forward, and he smelled its warmth, and heard the slap of its tail against its sides. He laid his hand on its nose. The horse reared its head, wishing to take its own time in the matter of making friends.

"Will you arm me?" Tristram asked.

"I cannot," the servant said. "I am a slave."

"Then I'll be armed by a good man. If I win today I'll buy your freedom, and no one can say I was armed by a slave."

"My lord!"

"Save your thanks until I've won," Tristram said, feeling a sympathy with the servant in whose cry, "My lord!" he heard more than men reveal to each other if they can defend themselves. This Ireland! It was a land where every man had a soul, and where the soul lay close to the skin. He wanted to ask the servant whether he, like the smith, had been born free and sold for the sake of food and shelter, but time was against them, and his own matters nagged at his mind. "What have you brought me?" he asked.

"A spear. It is leaning in the fork of the tree. A shield. I hung it over a branch. A chain shirt, and a helm and leather visor. I have them in my bundle, with breeches and spurs."

Tristram put off his own clothing and stepped into the borrowed

123

gear. Or stolen gear, like enough. Where could the servant have come by them if not in the armory of King Anguissh? But Tristram did not consider this a fortunate moment to ask.

"If things go badly with me," he said, "find Gouvernail, my squire. You know him?"

"Yes, my lord."

"Tell him all you and I have done together. Tell him it is my desire that he protect you if you are blamed in any way, and that he restore these arms, and that he give you gold enough to buy yourself. Now put me up, friend."

"My life is yours, my lord."

"Your own soon, I hope. Put me up!"

The servant mounted him.

"Now God keep you for an honest man," Tristram said. "Good-by. See that Pickpocket goes home."

While the servant blessed him, he brought the horse around. He could feel it was big and high-strung, responsive, though with a will of its own. As it moved under him and his body yielded to its gait, his wretchedness fell away, and he forgot the pain which was the reason for his being here, and knew only that he had plans to follow, and that the plans were well and carefully made.

He had laid out his scheme during the last two days when he covered the ground on foot between the hall and the tournament field. He walked the horse along the outside of the wall, over the low, grassy hill, down the slope, and onto the beach. The tide was out. The light of a clear dawn lay on the water, grey and cool still, though the deep blue horizon was dyed with pale tints of pink and gold. He smelled peat smoke, and knew the herdsmen were up. In the harbor the fishing boats were gone. This day of the tournament meant nothing to men whose lives it was to rise before the sun and wrest from the earth of Ireland and the sea around it the riches nature defended with so many wiles.

Tristram rode along the hard sand, walking the horse which sidled and stepped high, wishing to run. But there was time to spend in this silence by blue water, and the horse must be saved for heavier work. When he reached the upper arm of the harbor he turned inland and followed a hill path. He was well above the tournament field now, and knew it was safe to ride back toward it, seeking a wooded place where he could dismount and say his prayers and wait for his hour.

He could not keep his mind on his prayers easily here under the vast blue, with the waking sea curving away over the horizon, and seafowl trying their morning wings. He needed God's help, and wished to ask it, and to ask too to be knightly in all things, and to win fairly, and to fulfill his promise to the slave who had armed him. But the memory of Isoud came into his prayers, how she had stood so still yesterday, her lashes lying on her cheek, and her soft breath lifting her necklace. She was beautiful! If he could, he would not change so much as one light tendril of her hair! I love her, he said aloud, and remembered he was praying, and began again, asking God to make him knightly in all things for Isoud's sake.

He tied his horse, stowing his spear and helm and shield under a brake of thorn bushes. He walked south until he reached an oak tree whose branches were low and spread in a wide skirt over a knob of high ground. He could see the tournament field from here, and he lay down and propped his chin on his hands to watch.

The plain was bright with people and horses. The spectators' pavilions were already crowded, and he saw that the king and queen had arrived, and that Isoud and her ladies had found their places. Oxcarts, their casks and bowls unloaded in the kitchen shelter, were lumbering back, empty, toward the hall. He could see his friend the herald sitting his horse before the knights' pavilions, with his two pages on hackneys beside him. And for a moment Tristram's heart was with the pages more than with anyone else on the field, for he remembered how he had ridden to his first tournament on just such a hackney as theirs, his blood beating with mad excitement, and a fear in his throat that he would blow a cracked trumpet note and shame his training. Oh, yes, he remembered the big fighting horses stamping and shaking their heads, and the smell of trampled earth and bruised grass, and the thunder of the charge, and that moment which seemed an

125

eternity when you waited to see whether your favorite had been unhorsed or whether he had left his opponent on the field; and the master of the tournament riding out to thrust his sword between the combatants and to say which had won; and King Hoël rising to give the winner the prize, while the loser rode off, or was carried off, and came past the pages with blood on him, and sweat streaking his face, weeping with rage and disappointment; and the horses panting and nickering and pawing the earth because the thrill had been so great and so short, and because they were jealous when the fresh horses paraded by.

The pages were blowing the first course. Ah, there was the cracked note! The herald cried the names of the young knights, and their rank, his voice rising to Tristram mellowed with distance, sweet the way a hound's voice is sweet when you hear it across a valley. The young knights rode to their charge, praying, perhaps, perhaps thinking of a lady, or perhaps thinking of nothing, but only carried forward by the skill which had been growing in them since they were ten years old. Tristram picked a favorite, seeing even at this distance how one knight sat better and moved with more decision than the other. When his favorite unhorsed his opponent he leaped from the grass and cheered. For a moment he forgot he had business on the same field, and that it was not his fortune to perch here under the oak like some forest spirit and watch the curious play of men.

When the young knights had completed their courses, and the herald was crying the names of the French guests, Tristram returned to his horse, and put on the helm and visor. He led the animal down the slope, timing himself to arrive just as the Frenchmen rode the last of their three falls. He entered the field from the north. Holding his shield so as to cover the lower part of his face, he approached the herald. "I wish to ride in your games, my lord, if your custom allows it," he said.

"Welcome," the herald said. "Any knight of lineage may ride. Give me your name and your birth, my lord."

"I can't give you my name, though my reason for keeping it secret is just and truthful. But I am a king's son, and will ride under a blank shield. I have come to challenge the Saracen knight Palamides."

A page was sent to inform Palamides, and to fetch his acceptance. Tristram, peering out from the visor, which he found awkward, could see a stir among the king and his guests as they stretched to stare at the stranger knight and to speculate on who he might be. Isoud was gazing at him too, and Tristram felt she must see through his shield and visor and discover him, the two of them looking into each other's eyes across the crowd as though they were alone. Her heart must know him, and how it was for her sake he was here.

He was given a squire who inspected his spear and shield. If my weapons did come from the king's armory, Tristram thought, this unlucky fellow will recognize them and denounce me. Why didn't I think of that this morning? But the squire seemed to be interested only in his duty to see that the weapons were fair and sound and without weaknesses. He mounted Tristram and led his horse onto the field.

The spectators raised a cheer, and for a moment Tristram was puzzled, thinking the shouts were for him. Then he saw Palamides. He had ridden onto the field and was walking his horse down the line of banners at the side. His mount was black, a splendid animal groomed and shining like jet. Its neck arched and its tail stood out in a silky, shimmering fall. The Saracen knight sat the prancing horse as though he had been made for it, and it for him. Today he wore scarlet trousers and carried a shield jewelled with enamelled bosses and gilt. His chain shirt was so fine and so well fitted that it showed his supple body and gave him the look of a man clothed in some precious cloth of silver. With a flourish he saluted the king and the queen. But when he reached the ground before Isoud, he bowed in his saddle and laid his hand over his heart.

"That is the knight you must encounter, my lord," Tristram's squire said, trying to subdue the pride he felt in the favorite.

"If red trousers make a champion," Tristram said, "your ladies have a champion today."

127

The squire, not catching the angry jealousy in Tristram's voice, nodded. "The lady he is bowing to is the princess Isoud. They say he has promised her to become a Christian if he wins this tournament."

"He is wearing a sword," Tristram said.

"Yes, he always rides with his sword. But he is sworn not to use it."

"Why does he ride with it, then?"

"I don't know, my lord, unless it is the Saracen custom."

Keep your mind on the sword, Tristram told himself, for whether it is a Saracen custom or not, it has edges, and it is hanging from the baldric of a madman. Then he had no time to think of anything. With a "God ride with you, my lord," the squire handed up his reins and ran from the field. The course was blown.

Tristram and Palamides cantered to the center of the jousting ground, their horses facing, then turned and galloped back to the starting line and wheeled for the charge. Hit him almost in the center of the shield, Tristram remembered, only this time keep your eye on his point too. They flew together in a collision that lifted Tristram in the saddle, but he hugged his mount fiercely with his legs and kept his stirrups. He did not know what had happened to the Saracen until he checked his horse and brought him around. Palamides was seated still, but his spear had shattered and he held only its pommel in his hand.

Tristram's head was cool, with the fine calmness that stretches like a wire against something leaping to be free, a wild joy. He knew he should have unhorsed Palamides, and hadn't. He could tell himself his arm was stuffed with rag today, that he had missed one third of his chance to win, since the order was three falls. Yet his purpose promised him he would defeat the foreign knight who dared to desire Isoud. And as he waited for the squire to bring Palamides a new spear, he was correcting the error of the first charge, and laying the scheme for the second. He had meant to look toward Isoud after each fall, but he had forgotten her, for-

128

gotten anyone was on the field save himself and Palamides, forgotten everything except the happiness, and the plan to win.

On the second charge he saw the Saracen coming, and for a moment he seemed to be coming slowly as a rider might approach in a dream. Tristram had time to notice the folds of his scarlet trousers, and the wings of his moustaches sweeping back from his leather visor, and the tight tuft of black beard, and the mouth, open, red as blood. He saw these things as he and the Saracen hurtled toward each other, and saw Palamides raise his shield when his point was almost into its center. Then his own shield was driven against him, and he was knocked blind, and the hill behind Palamides tilted upward, and Tristram was hit by the rising earth with a blow that seemed to tear off his head.

As he lay stunned he saw feet running toward him, and understood that his squire was coming to help him up. By the time the man reached him he was on his legs. Where was Palamides? Unhorsed too, as God loves me!

"Are you hurt, my lord?"

"No. Mount me."

"You have one more fall," the squire said.

One more. Two thirds of his chance gone. But two thirds of Palamides' chance was gone as well, and now it was as if they were riding for their first fall. God, Tristram prayed, it is for Isoud!

His head was ringing from the brutal jolt he had taken, but somewhere within the loud tumult of his blood lay an idea. It was this, that Palamides carried his shield low until the last second of the charge, and then raised and tilted it to offer a glancing target to the spear. I must aim above the boss by two inches, Tristram thought, but I must come in close and straight or my point will scratch off, and he will get in under my guard.

As he brought his horse around for the charge he seated his spear in the saddle rest and held the grip lightly so as to be free to maneuver. He had learned in two rushes that his mount was a veteran of tournament fighting, not brilliant, but solid and fear-

129

less. If the animal could be made to understand what was wanted, it could be ridden so close to Palamides that nothing thicker than parchment could be laid between them. "Come over, son of a good mother," he asked the beast, and pressed it to the right with his knee.

The horse, its ears laid flat to its head, gathered speed. "Come over! Come over!" Tristram entreated. The horse ran as though it followed a drawn line. "Cow!" Tristram cursed it. He fixed his eyes on Palamides' shield and watched it fly forward and enlarge as he might have watched a shooting star. When it was so big he could see the very dust on its boss, his horse curved in to the right, precise and workmanlike, leaning exactly as Tristram leaned. Now, two inches above the boss! His point went in clean. It was a heavy hit; first, momentum violently checked, then lightness, as the horse recovered with a spring from the blow it had sustained on crouched haunches, and ran forward, losing speed. The horse knew what had happened.

When they reached the end of the field the beast was cantering, and Tristram was calling it brother. He made a sweeping turn for the pure pleasure of showing the horse, and of showing himself, and of riding back to the king's line like a victor. He saw Palamides getting up from the grass as a man might climb a ladder, clawing the air and heaving himself onto his legs in stiff jerks. Tristram trotted toward him intending to ask him with a perfect, an absolute courtesy whether he was hurt. It was fitting and princely, oh, it was a delight as large as heaven itself, to show mercy to a fallen foe!

The Saracen knight was on his feet and waiting. When Tristram was within a spear's length of him he snatched off his helm and threw it away, and drew his sword. With a scream he lunged forward and slashed his blade into the shoulder of Tristram's horse, and cut a wound so deep and long the flesh curled back, and the blood burst out of the severed veins and hissed over the arm and the chain shirt of Palamides. With this dripping, shapeless arm the beaten knight struck at Tristram. Tristram's horse leaped wildly, and screamed almost as Palamides had screamed.

The bloodied sword missed Tristram's body and skimmed along his shin.

Crying one appalling cry upon another, the Saracen knight ran from the field. Tristram could not control his horse. The brute was bleeding to death, but before its death it hurled itself blindly against the posts from which the banners floated, against the squires who had run out to catch it, thrashing its head and biting at its own body. Tristram was thrown. Now he did not try to rise. He sat on the sun-warmed grass of the field with his head in his hands, sickened by what he had seen.

Chapter Thirteen

THE tournament master and the herald, responsible for the order of the field, ran to him and lifted him to his feet. His leg had been laid open by a shallow wound. As they helped him toward shelter King Anguissh overtook them and laid his hands on Tristram's shoulders.

"My lord," the king said, "I will make good what has happened here. And as I hope for God's face, I ask you not to judge Ireland's hospitality by what you have witnessed."

"Thank you, my lord, but nothing needs to be made good."

"I will pay two horses for the horse you have lost, and whatever else you ask."

"I am satisfied."

"A litter will bring you to my hall," Anguissh went on. "The queen of Ireland will medicine your hurt."

Tristram began to feel faint from loss of blood. He wanted nothing except to escape from the king's urgent generosity, to leave the field behind him, and to find Gouvernail. But he had won over their champion, and he had been treacherously wounded. More, his name was a mystery, and already through the crowd the rumor was running that the stranger knight was no less a hero than Launcelot of Britain. All these things made him so conspicuous that, before he had reached the pavilions, he was surrounded by squires and barons and half a hundred other curious men who desired to see him, or speak with him, or explain away the shame they felt Palamides had forced upon them all.

He summoned his strength to stand and listen and return their clamoring courtesy. The noon sun was beating down on the field, adding to the misery of his wound and his thirst. He had not eaten since the evening before. "My lords," he said, "I am in need of nothing save—save—" He could not think what it was he was in need of. As he struggled to find the word, he felt his legs turn soft under him, and he drew breath and fell forward into the arms of the king.

He was thinking he had been here before. I am the knight who travels in a horse litter. Knight of the Horse Litter. Did I prevail against The Marhaus? He lay still, realizing he was confused. The question of The Marhaus had been settled, and this horse litter, whichever one it was, was new. His drunken senses began to settle, and as he revived he remembered with a shudder the scream of his dying horse. He raised his hands to his ears to shut the sound away, and felt that he had been unhelmed.

"Tramtris," King Anguissh said.

Tristram opened his eyes. It was not a horse litter after all, but a pallet of branches borne on the shoulders of four men. He was being carried over the grassy slope at the end of the tournament field. The king was walking beside him, looking into his face with a gaze so grave and sad that Tristram was ashamed of his weakness and wished to reassure him.

"I have got my breath again, my lord."

"I would rather have you fight under my shield than any man I've met in a year, Tramtris," the king said. "I had not forgotten your future. And when the day came, I would have thought of you."

Tristram felt the justice of the king's reproof. When he had been planning to enter the war games as a stranger it had not seemed to him a matter touching anything beyond his own will to escape from the queen's well-meant tyranny and secure a victory to offer Isoud. Now he could see that Anguissh had reason to feel he had been hoodwinked by a guest who had received from him

133

only candor and open dealing. The desire came over him to tell the king his whole story, why he was in Ireland, and why he had gone into the field nameless against Palamides. For hadn't he realized from the first that Anguissh was a leader fit to trust and follow, a prince who comprehended the strangeness of life, and the mixed necessities driving a man to tell half-lies and hide under a deceiving name? But he was worn and dizzy, and could not find in himself a way to explain his first untruth in Ireland, or his second. At least these lies need not breed a third. He made no answer.

"We will speak of this later," Anguissh said. And then he laughed with a cheer which assured Tristram he was not hugging a grudge. "Now, if we can, we must explain your new wound to the queen. And that will be work for the wits of us both."

As he walked along he began to tell Tristram about the war games of other years, and what strangers came to challenge the Irish knights, and how they fared. Presently he was speaking of The Marhaus, reciting the triumphs he had won, and saying how his fame had spread before he met his death in Cornwall. "He was the best man I ever had," Anguissh said. "You are not too unlike him, Tramtris."

I wish I could give him back The Marhaus, Tristram thought, if it would buy an end of this talk about him. Did Anguissh truly believe it was fair to collect an unlawful tax? If he did, he was different from what he seemed to be, a king whose honor and wisdom entitled him to stand above other men.

Anguissh went on speaking as though to himself, and his words blended in Tristram's head with the slow rhythm of their progress toward the hall. "The first concern of any king is men," he said. "Whoever takes a king's place at the head of a table develops an eye to look down his board and see what is sitting there."

The Marhaus died because his cause was unrighteous, Tristram thought.

"You see courage often enough," Anguissh said, "and the will to deal justly too. Courage and justice are to be valued. But once in a while brave and faithful men are gifted with something that

134

has no name. Once in a while you see a man who thinks like himself, and acts like himself, and can never be mistaken for anyone else."

He is about to tell me The Marhaus was such a man, Tristram thought.

But the king did not mention The Marhaus again, or say anything more at all. Whatever he was thinking had become his own preoccupation, and he was brooding on it, his face made distant by his meditation.

As they entered the courtyard Tristram remembered the day he had been carried here from the ship. On that day he had been near death, or so Gouvernail believed, at least. But whether or not he was near death, he had crossed the cobbles on his own feet, and come before the king walking. "Let them put me down," he said. "I am strong enough."

Anguissh shook his head, his eyes showing inward laughter. "Strategy before war, Tramtris. Now we have to fight our campaign with the women, and we have a better chance to prevail if we attack on their weak side. They love a fallen man. So you must ride your course on this pallet."

"Isn't the queen watching the games? She should see the rest of the sport."

"The games are over for today."

This piece of news, trivial as it was, offered Tristram's self-dissatisfaction a target. He was annoyed with the king, and with the queen, and with all the men of Ireland who would spoil a day of pleasure for a ridiculous reason. "Surely," he said, "your knights are not so unused to the sight of a trickle of blood that you give up your games for a scratch like this!"

"No," the king said good-humoredly, "my knights, and my lady too, bear the sight of blood with middling courage."

Tristram floundered on the pallet.

"I stopped the games so that I could send the barons who were armed for their jousts and had horses at hand after Palamides. It seemed to me needful to overtake him and arrest him and bring him back to the hall."

135

Tristram was ashamed of his outburst. "Where did he go?"

"I hope my men will find out where he went. He rode north, and he may be able to take cover in the forest."

"What will you do with Palamides, my lord?"

"Catch him first. If you wish, I'll put him in your hands. But we can consider that when the time comes. Now," he said, "you have answers to think of, man. The queen is a lady who loves to be told why her wisdom has been questioned, so if you have strength to spare, spend it on a well-reasoned story."

Tristram would not accept the king's mirthful cynicism. He had hoped to come before Isoud a victor. To be lugged into her presence like a hobbledehoy who had stumbled over a stone offended the dream he had been dreaming for seven days past. Was winning always to be accompanied by a humiliating aftermath? Knight of the Litter! Why was his flesh so untrustworthy when his spirit believed triumph was possible, true and whole?

He was carried into the hall and brought to his own quarters where Isoud and her mother had prepared his bed.

"It was not friendly of you to deceive me, Tramtris," the queen said.

"I did not intend any deceit, my lady."

"Nevertheless," she said, "you might have undone all that has been done for you. My wisdom is poor and small," she said with a throb in her voice, "but I use it, with God's help, to discern what is best for sick and wilful men, if I can. And I would be glad if you will tell me, Tramtris, why you did not ask me whether you were fit to ride against bullies like Palamides when the skin has hardly knit over your side."

Tristram closed his eyes, appreciating the reason in the king's advice.

"His side hasn't suffered, my lady," Isoud said gently. "His leg is bleeding."

Does she remember I defeated Palamides, he asked himself, and if she remembers, does she let herself think I did it for her sake? Can she imagine how I planned to take my prize, and dismount before her, and vow the victory was hers? If she had smiled I would have taken off my helm then, and said I was Tramtris of Britany, and that I owed my strength to Ireland. And the king would have accepted it as an honor, and the queen would have told them all how I was the product of her loving care. But I am wounded, and so I am pulled, and hauled, and thrown without willing it into bed! Isoud, Isoud! I did win against Palamides! Doesn't your heart bid you say a word of recognition?

"He needs a bath, and rest, and nourishing food, and regular exercise," the queen was saying, "if he will be guided—this time." And having discharged her spleen in a sort of awful, hurt patience of voice and bearing, she set about with her usual efficiency to begin Tristram's second cure.

A bath was made ready, and Gouvernail instructed how to lift Tristram into the water and cleanse his wound. "I shall wait here," the queen said, "and dress his leg myself. Now be quick, Gouvernail, or the water will chill him and give him a fever."

When Tristram was alone in the bathing chamber with his squire he said, "I suppose you're out of humor with me too, Gouvernail."

"I would have armed and attended you," Gouvernail said.

"You would have been recognized, and I wished to fight as a stranger."

"Why?"

Tristram did not answer.

"Because of the lady Isoud?"

"Because of Palamides."

"Palamides would have fought you twice as willingly," Gouvernail said with a gloomy laugh, "if he had known who you were, Tristram."

"There is a winning that doesn't end this way," Tristram said angrily. "I beat Palamides. But all they think of is how I deceived them, and spoiled their care of me by getting another wound. But I beat him fairly on the field. Why doesn't the princess see that?"

"She sees it."

"She sees nothing but the wound."

Gouvernail scrubbed him purposefully.

"I shall leave Ireland," Tristram said.

"You have never tried to understand a woman before, Tristram. Women are not like men."

"Wonderful!"

"Don't thresh about so," the squire said. "I am only trying to tell you it is not a woman's way to roar out compliments, and thump a man on the back when he has won for her. If she happens to be young, and—come, Tristram, I'm not enjoying this bath any more than you are—I say, if she happens to be young and fresh of spirit—" he broke off. "Would you like to bathe yourself, then?"

"Go ahead, go ahead!"

"A young and innocent gentlewoman," Gouvernail said, standing away from Tristram and looking down on him, "has not yet been taught by the world that her beauty entitles her to everything she can grasp. And when a man has risked his life for her, and spilled blood, she takes it as a marvel. Who besides you, Tristram, has asked to die for the princess of Ireland?"

"Palamides."

"Well—yes. Palamides. All the same, until this very morning, the lady Isoud probably never guessed any man would wish to die for her, except as all ladies dream of such things in secret. And now that she has learned it she feels more emotion than one proud voice can say. What did you expect, Tristram? That she would come prancing up to you like a witch, with—"

"I expected that—that—she would—"

"Call the pages, perhaps, and have it blown over the field that her heart is yours?"

"If I could believe she noticed me—"

"You have muscles in your head like leather thongs," Gouvernail said with a sigh. "I must get you out of this water, or we shall both answer to the queen."

At that moment they heard a brutal cry. And before they could ask each other what it was, the queen flung open the door of the bathing chamber and rushed into the room. With her two hands she was gripping the hilt of Tristram's sword, and as she ran

138

toward Tristram she raised it before her. She was sobbing the word "Traitor!" and she brought the sword down upon Tristram's head, but she was awkward and shaking, and she struck him with the flat side.

Gouvernail caught her wrists and twisted the sword from her. She dragged against her imprisoned hands, hurling herself from side to side, and crying so that they were too stupefied to ask themselves what was the cause.

"Traitor! Traitor!"

In the door behind the struggling figures Tristram saw Isoud. She gave him one look, her eyes staring from her face which had gone as white as the face of death. And then she turned and ran.

"Let me go or I'll have you hanged!" the queen shrilled.

Gouvernail, who had managed to find Tristram's sword with his foot, and was standing on it, released her hands. When the queen saw she could not regain the weapon, she fled from the chamber.

"What in God's name, Gouvernail!"

"I don't know, but get out of there and put on clothes," the squire said. "She has gone to fetch help."

Gouvernail hauled him out of the water, and together they fumbled and delayed each other trying to hurry him into the torn, unfamiliar fighting garments he had worn on the field. Tristram's sword still lay on the floor, its blade with the broken edge ringing as they stumbled over it.

"We must run for it," Gouvernail said. "Can you run? Can you make the beach?"

"What are we running from?"

"I don't know, and we won't stay to ask. Come on, Tristram, for God's sake!"

Tristram picked up the sword. "Get to safety, Gouvernail. I'll abide. If I have to answer them, I'll answer with this."

"No, Tristram! You saw her! She's gone to get men to murder you!"

"All the same."

"You can't stand them off! You're wounded. You've fasted for

139

a day and a night. You'll be one against ten, or twenty. You're mewed up in a room that hardly gives you room to bend your arms. Your life is done if you stand."

"It is too late," Tristram said. Behind Gouvernail Anguissh of Ireland stood in the door.

The king was unarmed, clothed still in the purple tunic and jewelled baldric he had worn at the war games. With a hand on either side of the door, and his head bent so that he looked at Tristram from under the great red ruffs of his brows, he filled the narrow opening with an awful silence.

Tristram lowered the point of his sword until it rested on the floor. "What am I accused of, my lord?"

"What is your name, Tramtris?"

"I am Tristram of Lyonesse." Now the moment had come, he spoke his name proudly. "I am the son of King Meliodas, and the nephew of King Mark of Cornwall."

Anguissh opened his right hand and held it before him. On its palm lay a glittering wedge of metal. Tristram did not need to be told what it was. Too often he had looked at the gap in the blade of his sword from which this fragment had been wrenched to mistake its shape.

A stillness lay all about his heart, something calm and re-solved, something which moved toward the man in the door with love. Though they might be enemies at last, they were equals. He took the splinter and fitted it to his broken sword. "I lost this, my lord, when I fought for Cornwall against the fishing tax."

"You know The Marhaus was the queen's brother."

"Yes."

"You know she plucked this metal shard from his head and swore vengeance on it."

"I know it, my lord."

"You came to us and asked for care."

"King Anguissh," Tristram said, "for the sake of The Marhaus I was made a knight. I never fought with any man until I fought with him. I was not seeking spoils, or honor, or anything except to relieve my uncle, King Mark, and the land of Cornwall from a tax unjustly collected. I prayed God to give me a righteous cause, and to help me to fight as a knight should."

"Ah, Tramtris!"

"Was the tax just?"

Anguissh did not give him an answer. For a moment they looked at each other across Tristram's broken sword, each seeing in the other what was to be cherished in manhood, what was to be hoped for, what was not to be reached, and claimed, and adhered to while life lasted.

"By law, the queen's vengeance is my vengeance," Anguissh said. "If you stay in Ireland and I fail to hunt you down, the queen will allow me no peace, and my barons will rise against me."

"Give me leave to go with honor." Tristram held himself steady against the grief he felt at the king's silence. Was the tax just? If it had been, Anguissh must have said so.

"Go with honor, Tramtris. I will purvey you a ship."

"Give me leave to bid your barons good-by, and the lady Isoud."

"You have leave."

"My dear lord," Tristram said, "I thank you for the friendship I have had with you here, and the goodness of my ladies the queen and the princess. I am ready to do you service in Britain or anywhere you ask it, and to be my lady Isoud's knight in every right cause, or," he said, his grief swelling into his throat, "in a wrong cause if need be."

"God go with you, Tramtris."

"God go with you, my lord."

"I will keep the splinter," Anguissh said, and took it from Tristram's hand, and turned, and left them.

Tristram's eyes filled with tears.

"He is a great man," Gouvernail said. "I wish that misbegotten splinter had been left on the island."

"Whatever has to be done before we sail," Tristram said, "see to it, Gouvernail. Do you know one of the king's house servants who is about so tall, and has a beard all around his face, like a wreath?"

"A hall servant?"

"Yes."

"I've seen him."

"Give him money enough to buy himself out of slavery," Tristram said. "I owe him a good turn."

"Where shall we meet?"

"And Gouvernail. If Isoud will speak to me, will you ask her to wait by the ash tree?"

"Which ash tree?"

"She knows," Tristram said. "Now do what you must. I'll follow you."

"Where shall we meet?"

"On the beach, in an hour."

Tristram went into the hall. There he found the nobles of the king's household gathered together in groups, and heard them fall silent as they saw him. The news had flown through the dwelling of the king like a cold wind.

"My lords," Tristram said, "I have come to say good-by. I am forbidden the land of Ireland from this day." And he told them his true name, and his lineage, and how he had been made a knight for The Marhaus's sake, and how he had fought in the island to deliver Cornwall from the truage. But whether the truage was just or unjust he did not say. "If I have offended any man, or if any has a grievance against me, let him tell me, and I will make amends."

They regarded him in silence, for some of them were of the blood of The Marhaus, and some found it an outrage that he had prevailed against Palamides. Besides, though they had tolerated him willingly enough, they had thought of him until this morning as a man looked after by women, spending his days in idleness. He stood before them feeling their indifference or their hostility. In Ireland, he thought, I have made two friends, both slaves.

As he left the hall he was moved to seek the priests who had been hospitable to him on his first morning in Ireland. But, though he would have liked to say farewell to them, and thank them for that morning's happiness, he decided against it. They were God's

142

ministers, looking up from earth to heaven for truth. His was a sorrow with which their loyalties should not be troubled. But for a moment he stood and gazed at the church, and thought of them, and of Magan, and of how high hope and the will to do all things knightly went awry.

He found Isoud in the garden under whose ash tree he had taught her to play the harp. She was pale, and she had been weeping.

"I was afraid you wouldn't come, Isoud."

"My father said you asked—"

"Isoud," he said, "you must believe I fought in a just cause as God let me see it."

"He was my uncle," she said, "and our champion."

"I was Cornwall's champion. Would you have wanted me to refuse?"

"It is past. It is too late to decide what I would have wanted."

"It is too late for the others but not for us, Isoud. Ask your heart whether you would have wanted me to be less than a knight."

She turned away from him wringing her hands. "You deceived us, Tramtris!"

"Did I? I said I came to Ireland in peace, and I have lived here in peace, haven't I?"

"I cannot listen to you," she said.

"If you listen, you will believe me."

She moved away from him and walked swiftly to the passage between the thorns.

"Isoud!" He caught her and turned her. "Don't be afraid to believe me, my only love!"

Blindly she came into his arms. But, though Tristram had desired this moment more than he desired life, he knew enough not to seize her beauty, to hold her as a man holds a woman. He kissed her eyes. "I have something for you, Isoud."

"Have you?"

"This." He withdrew the goldsmith's ring which he had worn, folded in the square parchment he had begged from the herald, on

143

a chain around his neck. "I took it to the tournament today, and when I had won, I meant to give it to you."

"I can't wear it, Tramtris."

"Keep it, anyway. And if you ever need a knight—if you ever need me—send it to me, and I shall come."

"I'll keep it always."

"God go with you, Isoud."

"Oh, Tramtris," she said, "if God is good, we shall meet again!"

Part III

Chapter Fourteen

GOUVERNAIL was waiting on the beach above the harbor. "The seneschal has been here," he said.

Tristram made no answer.

"He brought money from the king to pay for the horse you lost."

"It was the king's horse. And even if it weren't, we couldn't accept payment."

"I supposed we couldn't, so I told the seneschal to carry it back and give it to the priests."

"Good! Now," Tristram said, "we have no business except to leave."

"The seneschal offered us a boat and four oarsmen, but—"

"God's green hills!" Tristram cried. "Does the king think we walked to Ireland? We'll find our own boat!"

"It is easier to ride the wind and sea currents into Ireland than to ride them away, Tristram. Our boat is no good to us now."

"Then we'll swim to Cornwall," Tristram said between his teeth.

"I have taken us passage in a boat shipping out for Britany. They'll put us ashore on the coast near Tintagel. It's a merchant ship carrying hides, and going for earthenware." Gouvernail managed an unmirthful smile. "It smells of long life and much stinking cargo, Tristram."

"We can hold our noses, if we must."

The tide was ebbing, and the merchantman lay in the roads. They were ferried out in a fisherman's curragh, and boarded her, and stowed their small goods as they were instructed by a sailor. The boat looked awkward enough, flatter in the keel and wider than Irish boats. But something familiar in the lines of the heavy oak timbers and the high prows told Tristram she was not to be judged on her appearance. He was sure he knew this boat, that he had seen her come into harbor in Britany many times when he had run down to the shore to watch for ships from Lyonesse. He searched among the sailors who were weighing anchor and hoisting the leather sail, and found a man he recognized.

He took him by the shoulders. "Do you remember me, brother?"

"I do, my lord. I saw you come over the side." The sailor spoke in the tongue of Britany. "And him too." He nodded toward Gouvernail, grinning. "I fetched him from Lyonesse more than once to visit you when you were in King Hoël's service."

"How has the sea treated you since I saw you last?"

"As she always does—like a whore."

Tristram clapped him on the back. "I'll hear your news by and by when you can be spared." The sight of this face from Britany and the sound of French speech added homesickness to his sense of loss. As the boat came around and moved into the wind he stood by the mast and thought of Hoël, and of the days when he had been a page and a squire, and of the queen, and of young Yseut. "I'll go into Ireland too, and become a priest for your sake," Yseut had told him long ago. What a dark, pretty little thing she was, the small sister who would follow him anywhere!

He went forward. Bales of hides were stacked under the gunwales leaving room only for the oarsmen and a narrow passage in the ship's center. Tristram sat down and leaned against a thwart and listened to the chant of the oarsmen finding their stroke, and to the creak and groan of the timbers, and to the water rustling away in a wake from the dipping blades. If only he could go back to Britany! If he could return to a time before he had taken this scalding wretchedness of love—if he could! But if he might be free again, and whole, as he was before he saw Isoud springing along the grass on naked feet, would he be free? He knew he would not. If he never saw her again in this life he would die thanking God he had seen her then, and that he had loved her, and would love her while warmth was in his body.

"How are you, Tristram?" Gouvernail stood over him holding a fur cloak in his hands.

"Sit down, old woman. I am still breathing."

"Your leg will stiffen in the cold."

"It has stiffened," Tristram said, "and my boot is full of blood, and I am starved and dead tired. I could use a drink of ale. Is there bread on this sea porpoise, do you think?"

"I'll find you food."

"No, sit down," Tristram said. "I've lived a night and a day with no meat, and I'm beginning to like the sensation of being an angel without a stomach. Sit down, man! This is a pleasure voyage!"

Gouvernail sat down. "You're a madman, Tristram."

"Did you know our boat is from Britany? I've been thinking about Britany."

"Yes," his squire said, "I saw you thinking about it."

"What if we returned to Britany?"

Gouvernail was silent.

"You don't favor it?"

"I think you can't decide until you've eaten and slept."

"Oh, go and fetch meat, then!"

With a sigh Gouvernail rose and moved aft. He's cursing me as the most contrary creature of God's hand, Tristram thought. And I curse him back for having too much long-suffering virtue for one thick-skulled Briton. So we shall crucify each other. Tristram pulled the fur cloak over his face. His grief came upon him with a wild throb. He was weeping.

Gouvernail returned with ale and black bread and goat's milk cheese. Tristram was exhausted and wished to refuse the food, but sullen patience had followed his passion, and he took the meal and swallowed it down. There was no talk left in him, not even a protest when Gouvernail washed his wounded leg with sea water, and spread the furs over him, and commanded him to sleep.

When he wakened, sunrise was dazzling across the eastern water, and no land was in sight anywhere. He raised himself onto the forward bench and looked down the length of the boat at the tumbling white wake which the moving sea took into its own pattern. They were running before a good wind, the brown sail all one smooth, tight curve. Its lines uttered birdlike chirps and whistlings distinct against the heavier voices of the ship and the sea.

Sitting high in the stern at the rudder was his friend from Britany, naked except for a breechcloth. Against the silvery wash he appeared to be exactly the color of the ship's tiller, and the perch upon which he sat, and the salt-stained sail.

Gouvernail was still huddled in his cloak. Tristram made his way aft, creeping between the ill-smelling bales of cargo. Since the wind was favorable only half the crew were at their oars, and the others, wrapped in dirty woolen blankets, lay under their benches asleep.

"Good morning," Tristram said to the steersman. "How do you keep alive in this cold, friend?"

"With work and ale, my lord. What's the trouble in your leg?"

"Nothing that won't mend. I've been wounded twice in half a year, and both times the sea healed me."

"Well, the sea is one kind of physic," the sailor said.

"What news did you hear when you were in Britany last?"

"There were banners out," the sailor said. "An officer from Rome was at the castle on whatever business men in castles do, I suppose. We berthed next to an African unloading brass vessels. And two sailors as black as an Egyptian's behind ambushed a legionary of the officer's guard between the goods sheds and stole his pay." The sailor laughed. "The legionary cried like a calf, and the port reeve came huffing down to the waterside to throw the African out of the harbor. What a noise we had that day!"

"What happened?"

"Nothing. What ever happens in cases like that, my lord? The legionary's pay was spent and the sailors who had ambushed him were safely drunk by the time the reeve had warmed his first 'whereas.' But the nothing was loud while it was going on."

"I must come to Britany again," Tristram said. "In Cornwall we sit with our heels in the weeds and wonder what is moving in the world."

"I supposed you lived in Camelot, my lord."

"You did? Why?"

"I heard it from a lady."

"I don't know any ladies from Camelot."

"A lady in Britany."

"Don't make a riddle of it, man!"

"I heard it from the princess Yseut," the sailor said.

"What on earth was the princess doing with you!"

"She has often spoken with me," the sailor said, peering at Tristram from his shrewd eyes. And he added, "my lord," in a tone of merry malice, as though he recognized their difference as an afterthought.

"Does she send for you?"

"She comes down to the waterside when ships from Cornwall make harbor. On every other trip we carry a cargo of Cornish tin. And the lady Yseut watches for us when we return from Cornwall, and asks for letters and news. Because you knew me, my lord, she asks me whether I have seen you, and if you are well."

Tristram was touched and pleased that little Yseut remembered him still, but rather ashamed, too. He might have written her. Why hadn't he? He recalled how often she had trotted along beside him when he had heard that a ship from Lyonesse was in sight, and how her kind face clouded when he learned the sailors had brought no letters from his father.

"But I never saw you in Cornwall," the man went on. "And the last time I told her I had no word of you, she said you must have gone to Camelot. You planned to go there, she said."

"You must tell her you have seen me, and that I asked after her and sent her my remembrance and my duty. Tell her—" Tristram said, and broke off. Yseut's faithful visits to the harbor troubled him.

"What shall I tell her—my lord?" The sailor had a way of setting out his "my lords" by themselves, with something deliberate in his voice, scorn, perhaps. Yet it was not a resentful scorn, only a hint

151

that all men shared a common lot, though not all men recognized it.

"That I shall write to her," Tristram said. "Tell the princess I am well."

He made his way forward and returned to Gouvernail in the peaked bow. While they were eating what remained of their black loaf, and later during the day, as long as the steersman stood his watch, Tristram felt the man's eyes on him, and felt too the light raillery of his "my lords." He was an impertinent fellow. Some day he would try his wit on a man who would have him whipped.

As the sun grew high the air turned hot and stifling. The reek of the hides seemed enough to destroy human lungs. Tristram lacked ambition to do anything save lie in the small shade of the gunwale and endure the dragging hours. He thought no more of Britany, or of Yseut, or of anything save Isoud. Even of her he did not think rationally, only remembering how poignant her beauty was when she sang, when she ran before him so fleet and slender, when she spoke or laughed or fell silent. He tried to think why it was that this one woman of all the women in the world should have been of the blood of The Marhaus. And why, when he asked of God no gift save a good lord to serve, each lord who met him turned him away. And why honest conduct bred shameful results. And why he had seen Isoud only to lose her. Oh, Isoud! Do you think of me today as I think of you?

"Will you play your harp, Tristram?" Gouvernail asked him.

"Too hot."

"You would please the oarsmen."

"They're used to rowing without harp music."

"If the wind holds we'll be off Cornwall by dawn tomorrow."

"Then what?" Tristram said.

"We ought to know what we're going to do," Gouvernail said. "You spoke last evening of sailing on to Britany."

"Did I? Do you want to sail on to Britany?"

"Tristram," Gouvernail said, "I am your man, and I love you. But sometimes you try even my love."

Tristram sat up. "Forgive me, Gouvernail. I didn't intend to

152

try you. I only meant it doesn't matter to me where we go. Just as you were speaking I was wondering how it would be to land at Lyonesse and serve under my father again."

"Your wits wouldn't drift around this way if you weren't ill."

"I'm not ill."

"Then you are not ill."

"What did you mean when you said I was?"

"Ah, Tristram! I'm going aft."

"No, stay. I'm sorry. Forgive me again. I have a devil in me that wants to quarrel with everybody."

"You can't take it out in quarrels."

"Take what out?"

"You know what I mean, Tristram," Gouvernail said with an impatient sigh. "If you aren't sick in your body, you are at least sick with wanting what you can't have. But you are a knight, and you must serve a lord, and you can't lie here on the sea forever wishing to die."

"Tell them to set us ashore on Tintagel."

"I'll tell them."

"And give me my harp, and I'll harp this stinking tub on her way."

Gouvernail fetched the harp. At the sight of it Tristram felt himself tremble, for he had not played it since the last day he had sat with Isoud under the ash tree. But he was burning with shame to think he had shown his pain so openly for Gouvernail, and everyone else, like enough, to see. He took the harp into his hands and tuned it and tried the strings. He sang a song of King Arthur, how Uther Pendragon, his father, had given him to Merlin to school, and how Arthur was known when he drew the sword from the stone, and how he overcame his enemies, and united Britain. It was a noble song. As Tristram sang it he felt his evil mood fall away. He was thinking, perhaps a man need not call any particular land home. And he was thinking, she said if God is good we shall meet again.

153

Chapter Fifteen

TRISTRAM'S return to Cornwall was proclaimed by his uncle, King Mark, and celebrated with a mass of thanksgiving performed in the castle courtyard. Three days of games were held, and then a feast, and at last a gift of grain was given to the poor. Tristram had become a hero of sorts, in favor with the king, and therefore in favor with influential men interested in pleasing the king. For a month or more he rode from one hall to another, sharing in hunting parties, or watching hawk trials, or participating in exhibitions of the arts of venery and music.

He enjoyed his equality, even his renown, among the men of Cornwall because it gave him a gain to set against the loss of King Anguissh's lordship and his hope to become a member of the Irish household. And the activities it bred filled his hours, too, and stood off the sorrow of remembrance. He could not forget Isoud if he would. He went to sleep thinking of her, and awakened thinking of her, and walked, and rose, and spoke, and listened, with the thought of her always palpable and alive, as though she had become a second mind in him controlling the way his first mind worked. But as time passed he learned to live with this division between his inner and outer self, and to endure his soreness of spirit without sudden rebellions and unmanageable assaults of pain.

Yet there were times when he longed to speak her name, to tell a sympathetic hearer how lovely she was, and how gay. If he saw a girl running he wanted to say, "Isoud runs like a bird flying above the grass." When he played his harp and remembered with what tender grace she bent above its strings, he wished for a friend to whom he could say, "The light glistened over her hair like the light on a polished sword."

In this time when he was a hero in Cornwall Tristram drew near to Dinadan, partly because his friendship was plain and lacked unction, and partly because he seemed to be a man who would comprehend without scorning as unmanly the grief Tristram had borne away from Ireland. Besides, he had a way of deprecating serious things and recommending honest selfishness as the sensiblest means of life. Though he laughed at might, at huge and hopeless courage, at knighthood itself, even at love, he laughed as though he knew something better. When Tristram could free himself from the bustle of court life he sought Dinadan, and listened with delight while the little man scolded folly and gibed at pretension.

One day they were walking together up Tintagel head. The castle stood at the top of the steep just beyond the neck linking Tintagel promontory with the mainland. Above the castle, stretching toward the sea, lay rising headland. It was rough, broken into mounds resembling the graves of exceedingly tall men, and it supported coarse turf and wind-flattened furze. Sheep grazed on this torn upland, but they seemed more like savage beasts than domestic animals, for the wind blew their wool into knots and tangles and taught them a belligerent self-reliance which showed in their thick, short-legged bodies. A spring of sweet water bubbled out here at the very top of the world, and made life for men and sheep alike possible on the great, cubelike shoulder of rock which was Tintagel head.

As Tristram and Dinadan struggled up the pasture against a wind screaming in from the west they could hear the sea bursting on the cliff and booming into the caverns at its foot and seething out again, thickened with foam. They could see squalls of rain far out, and purple streaks on the water alternating with marine blues and greens as the clouds opened or grew dense. The sheep stood with their backs to the wind, their tails between their legs and their heads down, as though their only business was to endure.

"We've been climbing this wind like a ladder," Dinadan complained, "when we might have stayed indoors and weatherproofed ourselves with ale. Why," he asked plaintively, "are we asking to be blown off Tintagel head?"

"Because I've never been out to the end," Tristram said.

"I haven't either," Dinadan said, "and I've lived in Tintagel for fifteen years."

"Then it's time you went, grumbler. If the day clears we might see Ireland."

"Too far."

"How do you know it is too far if you've never been out to the end to look?"

"Because I'm an intelligent man. Besides, if we do see it, what will it be except a smudge on the edge of the world? Do you think you'll recognize your friends waving from the shore?"

"I knew a lady there," Tristram said, "and I wish I might see her waving from the shore."

"I have heard that King Anguissh has a daughter."

"Who told you?"

"I don't know—Andret, perhaps."

"She isn't like other women."

"I suppose not," Dinadan said. "No lady a man remembers is like other women."

"But she really isn't like other women. I taught her to play the harp and sing French songs."

"And did she teach you anything while you were teaching her to play the harp and sing French songs?"

"Oh, yes," Tristram said earnestly. "She told me about the old days in Ireland, and about the voyages of the priests to the western islands."

"What is her name?"

"Isoud." At last he could say it. "Her name is Isoud. It's a French name because her mother is partly of French blood. Only they have turned it into their own tongue, Isoud."

"I see," Dinadan said drily. "Her name is Isoud."

"The Fair," Tristram said. "When there is a state function and the herald calls out her name, he says, 'Isoud the Fair, princess of Ireland.' "

"A fact like that ought to be made plain!"

"I often wished you could see her, Dinadan."

"What! You had time to wish I could see this lady who is different from all other ladies? What were you doing in Ireland!"

The path they were following veered close to the cliff, and the wind leaped on them with fresh violence. Thin rain was in it now, driving horizontally and striking their faces with needle sharpness. A gull had flown up the cliff, and when it reached the top it was snatched by the rushing air and blown before them so close they could see it tilting and tipping, battling to turn seaward again. It flew with its beak open and its legs thrust down stiffly, using all its small force to maintain itself against the storm. They stopped to watch it, fascinated as it beat into the wind and made the cliff edge and disappeared downward.

"Come on," Dinadan said. "Let's get forward and see Ireland."

"I would have stayed in Ireland if I could. But now I am forbidden to go back ever again." Something about the struggling gull had touched Tristram and made his own loneliness more hurtful. He began to speak of Ireland as he had not spoken of it since his return, telling Dinadan about the last day, and how the queen had run into the bathing chamber and struck him with his broken sword, and how King Anguissh had stood in the door and held out the fragment upon which the queen's vengeance was sworn.

"The death of The Marhaus was bound to overtake you," Dinadan said. "It's the habit of princes to believe blood is best paid for with more blood, isn't it?"

"Not King Anguissh. He is different from other princes."

"King Anguissh too!"

Tristram stopped in the path and turned his back against the wind and looked into Dinadan's face. "I can't make you see how it was if you don't know King Anguissh. I've never met a king like him. I wanted to be his man."

"This must be thought of. Let's find ourselves a cranny where

157

we can sit down out of the wind." Dinadan made his way to a low tumulus upon which furze grew. Its lea side offered them some protection.

Tristram drew his cloak around him and sat down under the furze. "What is there to think of? I couldn't deny The Marhaus. They would have killed me in the bathing chamber except I was a guest and King Anguissh forbade it. What can thinking about it do?"

"Nothing to change what is past, I suppose." Dinadan hugged his knees, making himself as small as possible against the foul weather. "I wish I were a fox with a burrow under this mound," he said. "You have to remember Cornwall and Ireland are enemies, Tristram. And what's the good of being enemies if each side can't take an attitude about the other's crimes?"

"But I'm neither of Cornwall nor of Ireland. I was born in Lyonesse, and bred in Britany, and now I am a man of no country. I would have chosen Ireland, but—"

"But you couldn't," Dinadan said. "Something that doesn't ask us picks us up and sets us down, Tristram. So here you are in Cornwall, and the lady Isoud and King Anguissh are in Ireland. And one story has reached its end."

"Sometimes I think I'll go back to Ireland anyway."

"That's a profitless way to use whatever wits you have under all that hair of yours, my friend. You have things enough in Cornwall to think about, haven't you? If I had your reason to think I wouldn't waste my energy on anything but earnest daily meditation."

"What needs so much thought in Cornwall?"

"How to keep dry, for one thing." Dinadan drew himself into an even tighter huddle. "You need to hear some plain talk, man. You've been back in Cornwall how long now, three months? And a good plenty has been going on in Cornwall in three months."

"I know. I've never been in the saddle as much as I've been in the last three months."

"Do you happen to know King Mark's age?"

"Forty," Tristram said. "You and Andret told me when you came to Lyonesse to see my father."

Dinadan nodded. "King Mark is forty years old, more years than many men live."

"He bears himself like a younger man," Tristram said, and thought of the slender, tight-knit figure of his uncle. Mark made the most of his appearance, and took care to dress in a princely way and to carry himself proudly. But in his manners was something shallow and light, a habit of laughing too much when he spoke of serious matters, of gesturing or frowning or spreading his hands. And he came at things subtly from the side.

"He has been king of Cornwall for almost twenty years," Dinadan said, "half his life. And all that time his barons have tried to wring from him a promise that he would marry. You know, Tristram, it takes an agile man to keep a question like that hanging for twenty years."

"Why doesn't he marry?"

"Every man in Cornwall, including me, has a theory," Dinadan said. "The general view is that, as long as he can say he will, and still not do it, he has a control over his barons which would be weakened if he chose a woman one party backed, and others didn't wish to see become queen."

"He can keep all parties thinking he will take their candidate." Tristram smiled. "He's a better politician than he seems."

"But there's a limit to his kind of politics. Your uncle is old enough to set all his barons, whatever faction they favor, to wondering about the succession. And if they hate anything more than they hate each other, it is the thought that one man among them will gain power over the rest."

"So they want the king to marry and get an heir."

"Yes, they want children of Mark's blood."

"He has an heir," Tristram said. "Andret is of the king's blood, his cousin. He expects to be king."

"Andret is the king's cousin, but you are his nephew, Tristram."

"I know. My uncle told me when I was ill that he would make me prince of Cornwall. But I haven't any desire to be king."

159

Dinadan uttered a grunt of laughter. "You can stand in front of the castle and shout out fifty times a day for the next year that you don't want to be king, and not even the village children will believe you."

"Men believe lies with no trouble at all," Tristram said, "but the truth gags them."

"Don't waste your wonder on the obvious, friend. Keep your mind on Andret. He has a party of strong barons to whom he has promised land or something they can't gain from Mark, if he becomes king. How do you think these men feel about your prancing into Cornwall and knocking off champions and getting ahead of Andret with Mark? Do you think *they* believe you don't want to be king? Do you think *they* believe you fought The Marhaus for any other reason in this world than to get your hands on Cornwall?"

"Do you believe I fought to become king, Dinadan?"

"It doesn't make any difference what I believe."

"What do you believe?"

"Well," Dinadan said irritably, "I have an unworldly mind. I am willing to think you were young and crazy. I'm willing to think you wanted nothing except to be made a knight, and mix into a good, rousing hurly-burly, and risk your head for glory, or whatever beefy fellows like you risk their heads for. But," he said, "don't be foolish enough to imagine for one minute that any other man in Cornwall believes what I believe. And I am counting in your uncle, too."

Tristram looked down the slope before them and followed with his eyes the curve where it fell away and formed a close horizon against the sea. The rain had stopped but the wind still raked through the furze above his head and shook drops onto his shoulders. A just cause. It seemed a long time ago that he had fought The Marhaus, a lifetime.

"Politics don't operate like a tournament, Tristram. The barons who have cuddled up to you since you came back from Ireland are showing their wisdom by jumping onto the cart drawn by the biggest horse."

160

"Ugh!" Tristram said, and spat.

"Spit out the taste of it if you like. But," Dinadan said emphatically, "don't think you can spit out Andret. He hasn't any intention of giving up what he almost had his hands on. I'm not trying to scandalize your new friends, Tristram. I'm only trying to warn you that you have trouble ahead. I don't know what, though I've given it some thought. Maybe it'll be crude and final, like an ambush at night. Or maybe it'll have political refinements, something to discredit your loyalty or make you seem to be a downright traitor."

"Once in Ireland," Tristram said, "I saw a man kill a horse because he lost a game. Before I saw him do it, I never knew what men could be."

"It isn't often safe to assume they're more than men."

"But there is a fairness of mind," Tristram said, "that—"

"Our mothers and priests talk to us of fairness of mind," Dinadan said. "And so we can argue it is a dream of women and of men who have renounced the world."

"I knew Andret was jealous," Tristram said after a silence. "I saw it before I went into Ireland."

"He is jealous and clever, a bad combination. I supposed you appreciated your danger, and only your disappointment over the lady Isoud led you not to care what happened. And though I know the stupidity of interfering in another man's concerns, I value that head of yours, Tristram, even though it is too often in the clouds."

Tristram had scrambled to his feet. The wind seized him and blew his cloak out behind him. He stood over Dinadan like some giant bird just alighting in the grass, or like a man who had in all truth flown down from the clouds. "I never spoke of any disappointment," he said. "Until today I never even mentioned the lady Isoud's name, not to you, or to my uncle, or to anyone."

Dinadan rose too. For once his face had lost its usual concealment of derisive mirth and was blank with astonishment. "But you didn't think it wasn't known, did you, Tristram?"

"How could it be known!"

"Why, the news was at the castle half an hour after you were! You were born in one king's house and bred in another, and you

161

certainly realize a king's security depends on his knowing what happens. Your uncle keeps a man whose only business is to question the sailors who land on our coast."

"But why should he ask a spy when he might have asked me?"

"Oh, Tristram, Tristram! He kept in touch with everything you did in Ireland. We knew you called yourself Tramtris of Britany. We knew when you were better. We knew when you were moved from the priest's cell into the hall. We knew when the queen began to doubt you were good for the lady Isoud."

"And you knew I defeated Palamides, the Saracen knight, and was wounded in the leg?"

"The sailors who brought you home brought that news too. And later Mark learned that Palamides escaped into Wales. Haven't you heard?"

"No." Tristram turned against the wind and caught his cloak about him. He felt angry and humiliated to think Isoud's name had been the vulgar gossip of the court, and naked too. The king and the barons who were playing their tug of war around himself and Andret had pawed the precious intimacy of his love as they might have laid their filthy hands on the sacred objects of a religion they couldn't comprehend. He had eaten with them, and sung for them, and gone to their silly games, and listened to the blandishments of their wives, he had been grateful for their companionship, and happy to know them as friends. He had almost felt at home with them, almost believed he could find brothers in Cornwall. And all the while they had been buying the purest secret of his life from hired informers.

He clambered back up to the path and began to walk toward the land's end. Dinadan ran after him and overtook him. "Be watchful, Tristram. I meant it when I said you are in danger."

"I'll be watchful. And thank you for what you have told me."

"Have you a plan?"

"I don't know," Tristram said. "It occurred to me when I was on the sea that I might go back to Britany."

"Or Lyonesse?"

"I'm not looked for in Lyonesse with any glad hope."

162

"You have a gift for making yourself unpopular," Dinadan said with a mournful laugh.

"I've begun to realize I have."

"Well," Dinadan said, "I have an unprofitable liking for unpopular fellows. And I've been meaning to tell you, Tristram, if you go into Britany, or Lyonesse, or some place where your talent for trouble hasn't run ahead of you, even if you stay in Cornwall, I'm your man."

Tristram was moved, and turned to thank him.

"Never mind," Dinadan said, screwing his face into a cynical grimace. "I'm pleasing myself. I like the folly of lost causes."

Chapter Sixteen

THE fact that his life might be in danger acted upon Tristram with something like relief. Besides making plain what had seemed to him farfetched and insincere in his reception at court, peril gave him a center around which to organize his boredom and heaviness. It was one thing to tell himself that, without Isoud, he did not wish to live. It was another to know he moved under the threat of death. He did not propose to die if he could avoid it, and if he could not, he meant to make his last hour as costly for Andret as possible. He was watchful enough to satisfy even Dinadan, and he began to wear his short sword every day.

And, since existence at Tintagel was based on a system of espionage, he repeated to Gouvernail what Dinadan had told him, and instructed him to secure their own lines of information. More, he told King Mark how he had lived in Ireland under the name of Tramtris, and of his dealings with Palamides, and of his discovery and exile. He took a perverse pleasure in appearing open and frank, though he could not bring himself to mention the name of Isoud. Tristram had learned from Dinadan that he had been simple-minded. Now he intended to make his ingenuousness work for him.

In this way he keyed himself to be ready when the time came to protect his life and to defeat Andret if he had to. But days passed, and weeks, and finally months, and he saw nothing, or heard nothing from Gouvernail's sources, to convince him that schemes against him, if there were any, were coming to maturity. He was often with the king, riding in Mark's party on state business and on pleasure. And though his uncle adopted a superior air with him, laughing fondly at his size, at his heathen complexion, at his harping, at the fact that he had been cured by Irish witches of the improbable disease of poison, he was treated as the favorite. He sat next to Mark at meat, and received strangers, and was given an income from a certain number of profitable ferries and toll bridges. Mark included him in government matters, and listened to his advice on problems of garrison and trade and land improvement. And he was made head of the guard at Tintagel. He learned from Dinadan that this could turn out to be a perilous favor, since it put strength into his hands which might be read by Andret as a check to his own ambitions.

Tristram knew Andret grumbled against his pretensions and talked among the barons of the shame of having a foreign prince from a vassal land set over them. Was Andret as clever as Dinadan thought? A clever man would be quiet about his dissatisfactions, wouldn't he? Perhaps Dinadan overestimated the deadliness of this fat little man with the bright eyes. All the same, I shouldn't underestimate him, Tristram told himself.

Andret owned some admirable qualities. He was, and had been for years, held by the king to be the shrewdest and most practical man among the counsel barons. Though Tristram now sat next to the king in counsel, he realized Andret's wisdom was better than his own, and that his advice rightly carried more weight. Whether or not he had lost his influence with the king, Andret was still the largest power in the affairs of Cornwall. And here he had an advantage outweighing even his natural talent for government. His position as Mark's seneschal was granted for life, settled on him at a time when he had extricated Cornwall from an imbroglio with South Wales. His authority was protected by an office from which Tristram could not have dislodged him, even had he wished to.

So these two contenders eyed each other through late autumn, and winter, and spring. Though no one else remembered it, Tristram kept the anniversary of his combat with The Marhaus. Early in the morning he went to the castle church and knelt to say his prayers. Once he had asked God here to make him a good knight and help him prevail in a fair cause. But today he only offered thanks for life and health, and prayed God to protect Isoud's happiness.

A few days after this, when the household were rising from meat, King Mark took him by the arm. "Come with me, Tristram," he said. "I have a matter to discuss with you."

It was evening, and the bronze lamp bowls, hanging on three chains from the ceiling, were lit. Mark's hall was not his whole house as were the halls of Anguissh and Meliodas. It occupied the c nter of the castle, and doors on either side opened into passages offering access to smaller rooms. Though life was mostly lived in the hall chamber where there were lights and a hearth and hangings of linen on the walls, Mark had a little private cell adjoining into which he could withdraw. He led Tristram to this room.

Tristram entered with the wariness become his custom now. A wick was burning in a dish of oil on a standard by the door, and threw a glimmer of flickering light onto the walls. Rushes strawed the floor, and a few stools and a chair with a round back and carved feet were the only furniture. Coming from the warmth of the hall, Tristram shivered and saw his breath in the chill, stale air.

Mark sat down in the round-backed chair and gestured toward a stool. Tristram moved it so he could sit facing the door, another habit he had acquired.

"Andret will be here in a moment," the king said.

State business, Tristram thought. But his uncle spoke of indifferent matters, leaning forward with his hands on his knees, and glancing idly into the shadows moving on the stone walls. He wore a tunic of dark blue wool, and a shawl of the same material folded and draped from one shoulder over a shirt of soft leather. His brooch and breast medallion gleamed in the fitful light. Jewels of amber and amethyst set into the hilt of his short sword burned now and then with sparks of color. In his precise elegance was something kingly, Tristram thought, something confirmed and

166

habitual which, though it lacked force, carried the dignity of rank. And he fell to thinking of the four kings he had known in his lifetime, and how different each was from the other, sharing neither taste nor character nor use, but only the second nature of kingship which, in time, penetrated the clay upon which it fell, and changed it. Was kingship more than a method of meeting the violence and spying and intrigue surrounding it? Yes, he told himself, remembering King Anguissh, it was a strength to strengthen other men. And, as he had done a hundred times since his talk with Dinadan on rainy Tintagel head, he turned back from the thought of his own kingship. It was too strait a destiny, it had no freedom in it to—he could not name the freedom he meant, but he felt it in him like a current. And he thought of Isoud.

Mark was talking of Ireland. Was it, he asked, as rich a land as it was said to be? And did the king support learning and art, and invite accomplished foreigners to his hall? As Tristram returned answers as brief and noncommittal as courtesy allowed, Andret entered.

The seneschal's appearance energized Mark, who sat less carelessly in his chair and emerged from the languor with which he had been speaking. Andret's fat little figure expressed a vitality Tristram felt too. He walked like a man on an errand, moving his short legs purposefully so that his knees nudged his kilts forward and gave his gait an air of emergency. Tristram noted he was not wearing his short sword.

"If I've delayed you, my lord, I'm sorry," he said.

"No, we've just come in. I was asking Tristram about the court in Ireland."

Andret nodded. He had not sat down, and the jumping light afforded Tristram odd perspectives, making him seem at some times taller than he was, and at others shortening him to child's size. "Whatever we can learn of Ireland is a gain."

"For a land made mostly of bogs," the king said, "it lives better than one would think possible."

"Do they build roads?" Andret asked.

"I did not travel much when I was there," Tristram said.

167

"But if as many strangers come to the court as you've told us," the king said, "you must have heard something about the roads from them. I mean, whether they are kept up or neglected, and whether the bridges are regularly repaired."

"You know King Anguissh has garrisoned the south, my lord. And it's a reasonable supposition, I should think, that roads between garrisons anywhere are passable."

Mark laughed in the way he had when he was approaching serious matters. "With eyes at the top of all that length of bone, Tristram, you might have seen more than you saw in Ireland."

"I might have, my lord."

"These garrisons, how are they built?"

"Round towers," Tristram said, "and a camp of foot soldiers near them."

"What strength of foot?"

"I wasn't told."

"Did you need to be told?" Andret asked him. "You had an unparalleled opportunity to bring us back information about an enemy country, Tristram."

"Was I sent into Ireland to spy?" Tristram made his eyes round so as to annoy Andret with a show of innocence. "I was not sent into Ireland at all, was I, Andret? I went there without friends or purveyance or safe-conduct, to seek health."

"But you might have improved the chance you had."

"I supposed Cornwall had men who collect information about roads and garrisons—and whatever else is wanted—for a fee."

"I should have thought any Cornish knight on any foreign soil would have considered it his duty to learn all he could to help his own land."

"Except I am not a Cornish knight," Tristram said.

Andret turned to Mark. "My lord, you have done me the honor of asking my advice in this matter of Ireland."

"Let me hear it," Mark said.

"What is your matter with Ireland, my lord?" Tristram said.

"And my advice is this," Andret said, glad to let Tristram know he had been privately consulted in a state concern. "We need more information than we have, but more important than information, we need time. We should give ourselves two years, for we have to recover from bad harvests, and collect money, and build boats, and train more men than we now have under arms. Though Tristram didn't think of supplying us with facts, he has told us enough to confirm what we already knew, that Ireland will be anything but an easy conquest."

"Conquest!" Tristram said. "Your quarrel with Ireland has been settled, my lord!"

Mark laughed his light, false-merry laughter. "Nothing is ever settled with Ireland, Tristram. We are only a little stronger than we were last year. And last year the tax was demanded of us, and it will be again. So unless we want Anguissh to march against us, we must march against him first, I should think. Isn't it wisdom to jump before we are jumped on?"

"He has no intention of marching against us!"

"You must be offering an opinion, Tristram, since you've certainly made it clear you weren't aware of what Anguissh thinks or doesn't think."

"But I lived in his house," Tristram said, "and he is a good man, a good lord. His word is to be trusted because he is—" Just?

"I've no doubt he is polite enough to sick strangers who aren't very observant," Andret said. "But he has never lived long in peace with us, and he never will. All the same," he went on, "we aren't in any condition to act against him now."

"We shall have to be in condition," Mark said. "If he comes on us before we come on him—" He broke off with a restless sigh.

"There is another way," Andret said. "If we can't subdue him, why shouldn't we make an alliance with him?"

"No," Mark said. "We offered him an alliance eight years ago."

"But the situation is different now." Andret stood before the king with his feet wide apart and his hands on his hips, a habit he had to make himself look large. His hands and feet were small and womanishly soft. In his grey kilts, with his black eyes glinting in the unsteady light, and his black hair lost in the shadows so that his face seemed sometimes to become a mask, he looked like an intelligent elf in men's clothes. "Then we had nothing to offer. Now we have something of value."

"We have nothing I will offer Anguissh," Mark said. "We had our necks in that noose for seven years."

"We have a marriage for his daughter," Andret said.

As Tristram absorbed the sense of Andret's proposal he was overwhelmed with the worst confusion he ever felt. If he could marry Isoud, if Anguissh would listen to it, if the queen could be moved from her sworn vengeance—oh, if Isoud herself were willing! But they would view the marriage with horror as a sin against their blood, even Isoud. Surely Mark understood that! If he offered this union and was refused as he must be, then a trouble would come of it beyond any turmoil they dreamed possible, worse than the old enmity between Cornwall and Ireland. Yet, now it had been suggested, Tristram snatched at it with such hot, such unreasoning hope, that he could not warn them.

"The question isn't whether we hate the Irish and would love to defeat them," Andret said. "It is whether we can survive and live with them. And I am confident, my lord, that a marriage of our blood and theirs would end the wars between us and give us a strong friend."

"It might," Mark said without much enthusiasm.

"I know your reluctance," Andret said, "and I only advise it because I believe, my dear lord, that you put Cornwall's happiness above your own."

Mark spread his hands in a gesture of forlorn amusement. "You've set a snare for me, Andret. I've been too clever for you for a dozen years. But I knew one day you would catch me."

Tristram understood nothing of the king's words. He sat there trying to sort out his confusion, trying to protect his hope, trying to find a thread to unravel the snarl into which Andret's advice had thrown him, and the affairs of his uncle, and Cornwall.

"Tell me about the princess," Mark said. He was looking at Tristram. "You have seen her. Is she as beautiful as they say?"

"She is more beautiful than any woman," Tristram said, "and gentler, and more courteous. And she is wise—and kind—and loving. And if she could heal the troubles between Ireland and Cornwall, she would, my lord. I can speak for her."

"She wishes to heal them?"

"Oh, yes," Tristram said. "She wishes it more than anything in the world."

Mark turned back to Andret. "There is the matter of The Marhaus. How can we compound that?"

"We have law with us," Andret said. "Legally, his death is not attributable to Cornwall. For as Tristram has already reminded us, he is not a Cornish knight."

"His mother's blood was Cornish."

"Then," Andret said with a tight smile, "we shall have to stand on his father's blood."

"You have answers for everything, Andret. Well. I have avoided marriage for twenty years because I thought a sovereign needed the freedom a woman's family is bound to curtail. But I knew this hour must come. And so I accept your advice, my lord seneschal. Do you favor our decision, Tristram?"

"What decision, my lord?" Tristram stammered.

"He has already said he favors it," Andret interposed, "when he spoke for the willingness of the princess."

Tristram rose and stood before them caught as a man might have been caught in the sea at the foot of Tintagel cliff. Isoud, as young and fair as a spring morning, trusting, tender; Isoud who had said a good God must bring them together—she was not to be given to him, but to Mark of Cornwall, to this fop, this fly, this grinning, gesticulating, vain, unbearable, old man! She would refuse. Anguissh would refuse for her. It could never happen. It hadn't happened. It had only been suggested. It would be stopped.

"If we accomplish what we hope, my lord," Andret said, "we need to prepare our embassy with some care. We are fortunate in one respect. Only Cornwall has a sovereign who can offer Ireland what you can offer. Our land is peaceful and well-ordered, and if it is not a rich land, it is sound and comfortable." Andret hesitated, not liking to say in so many words that Mark was the only reasonably young and personable king in Britain who needed a wife, and

171

so would have small competition. "These are points which we must present," he said. "And I suggest we send King Anguissh letters asking for audience and telling him we have a matter of importance to both our lands to propose."

"I leave it to you and Tristram," Mark said.

"Our embassy should arrive a day or two after the letters," Andret went on. "I believe, my lord, we have an ambassador who is especially fitted to lay our case before King Anguissh."

"You're thinking of Tristram?"

"Yes. He knows the king and the princess."

"No," Tristram said. "I will not go into Ireland with this embassy."

"He is forbidden Ireland," the king reminded Andret.

"Yes, but our letters will announce him, and say he comes on a state errand, and promise he will leave when his business is done. We shall ask for safe-conduct for him, and swear he will keep the peace."

"I cannot go," Tristram said.

"No one but Tristram himself can cure our troubles with Ireland," Andret insisted. "The grievance is against him because of his battle with The Marhaus. If we can persuade King Anguissh to receive him in friendship and to offer him Ireland's forgiveness, we shall be removing a cause of present resentment and future conflict. Indeed," Andret told the king earnestly, "if Tristram is not received and forgiven, even your marriage to the princess may fail to heal the enmity between our lands."

Mark rose and beckoned Tristram to him and laid a hand on his shoulder. He was standing near the wicklight, the lower part of his face unshadowed. A black gash seemed to lie above his brows. Tristram looked down on him by the height of a head, and as they confronted each other he saw his uncle with the painful clarity this distorting light and shadow induced. His nose and the flesh near it had coarsened and softened, and carried a faint shine. Around his mouth lay the fine wrinkles made by an habitual overexpressiveness, and gave his face, beheld thus closely, the sad, empty look of a mind which had wavered, through a lifetime, between unwanted choices. These signs went unnoticed when the king kept a distance, but as he moved close to Tristram, standing above the cruel light, he brought with him the secret of his fitful, discontented spirit.

"I have given you all Cornwall has to offer, Tristram," he said. "I have set you before old friends, and provided you with money and rank. For your mother's sake I have looked on you as I might have looked on my own son. You delivered Cornwall once. Now I ask you in your mother's name not to endanger our hope to live in peace with Ireland by refusing to take this embassy and throwing away a chance to make your own accord with King Anguissh."

"I cannot," Tristram said.

"I promise you safety. If your life were in danger I wouldn't allow you to go. This is a duty of your blood, nephew."

Desperate, Tristram thought, Anguissh will refuse. He thought, I need not reach Ireland.

"Will you go, Tristram?"

"I—I must go—if you make it a duty, my lord."

In the silence Andret drew a sigh. When Tristram looked at him he saw the knight had closed his eyes as a man might who was worn with a journey and has reached home.

Chapter Seventeen

THE plan was this, that Tristram and whatever knights he chose to take were to leave Cornwall in the same boat as the emissary carrying letters to King Anguissh. Tristram's party was to be put ashore on a small island opposite South Ireland, lying off the west coast of Wales. They were to wait there until the courier returned and told them whether or not Anguissh had received favorably the request for audience. If he consented, Tristram and his guard of knights would set the courier ashore and sail across the channel and land in the harbor below the king's hall. The courier would ask for a horse in Wales, and return to Tintagel overland.

On Gouvernail's advice Tristram did not select soldiers from his own troop at Tintagel to accompany him. The squire knew that some men among them were in Andret's pay, but not which ones. Since Gouvernail, and Dinadan too, expected treachery on the sea, they thought it wiser to sail without any yeomen than to risk adding to Andret's strength. Partly because the same reasoning applied to the household knights, and partly because he wished to have the utmost freedom and mobility, Tristram chose no companion but Dinadan. Gouvernail worried because they would be a party of three against the knight courier and the boat crew of eight. Tristram comforted him as well as ever Gouvernail could be comforted when doubt oppressed him with the reminder that their intention must be not so much to fight as to escape.

"We want no killing if we can help it," Tristram said. "But if it comes to killing, when have three men of our might fallen before eight, or three times eight, oarsmen?"

"We can be as strong as Goliath," Gouvernail said, "and still be taken in ambush."

"Ambushed on a boat a hundred and sixty hands long? We shall keep together, and one of us will always watch. Come, man! This is sport!"

"What do you plan if they set on us in the boat?"

"It won't be in the boat," Tristram said. "The crew dare not come aboard with arms. And they can't set on us naked. If we are to be attacked it will happen on the island."

"And if we have the luck to stand them off, are we to live on the island for the rest of our lives?"

Tristram laughed. "We can become hermits, and catch birds by running them to death!"

He set their departure on a day when the tide began to ebb an hour before dusk, hoping they would reach the island on the morrow while they still had light enough to assess their situation. Mark and Andret and an escort of household knights rode down to the shore to see them sail. Presents for King Anguissh and the princess were carried aboard, and farewells said. Tristram endured his uncle's emotional parting without much thinking of it, for he was still tense from the moves he had been making in his bloody game with Andret. But as Tintagel head fell away and was lost in the purple twilight, as the silence of the outer sea came over them, and stars began to appear, his nerves and mind relaxed, and he felt his weariness. He sat down under the forward gunwale and leaned against the oak timbers through which he could hear the running sea, and closed his eyes.

He was returning to Ireland, but not as his heart had hoped. He would see Isoud, but at a distance he could never cross. In the time since he had given his promise to Mark he had thought of a hundred extreme shifts to escape this errand, and now he reviewed them slowly and saw their futility. Kill Andret? Without stopping his uncle's marriage he would lose his own life, or become a fugitive with no country, not even a borrowed one, to receive him. Kill Mark? It would be a crime against blood and against sovereignty for which God would reject him forever. Flee, and become a disgraced man? Pretend illness or madness, like a child? Return to Mark and say he would not go? He had promised to go in the name of his mother. Ask for help? Who would help him break a sacred promise given his lord? Kill himself? He had thought of it, but a strength within him refused to die. He went painfully around the circle of these alternates, and returned to the necessity he could not evade. He must go.

Dinadan settled beside him. "What ails you?"

"Nothing. Too much waiting."

"We must keep sharp-set."

"Gouvernail is sharp-set enough for the three of us," Tristram said with a sigh. "He's sitting amidships with his sword all but held between his teeth."

"If any man loved me as Gouvernail loves you, Tristram, I would count myself lucky."

"I know. He was my mother when I was a child, and he is my soul now."

Dinadan leaned close. "Did you see where the food bags and waterskins are stored?"

"No."

"Aft, along the gunwales on each side. And under the bags they've stowed clubs."

"So they mean to take us with clubs, do they?" Tristram was amused at such simplicity. "How did you find out, Dinadan?"

"When I came aboard. I knew I'd have a minute to see things before anybody thought of watching us. I stuck my foot under the bags and felt them."

"Andret doesn't esteem us very highly, does he?"

"If it is to be tonight—"

"Not tonight," Tristram said. "Tomorrow in the island."

"All the same, we must keep our wits about us tonight."

"Yes," Tristram said, "and so we had better sleep while we can. Will you sleep first, or shall I?"

"You. There's no sleep in me."

176

"You and Gouvernail!" Tristram said. "I can't fight when I'm hungry, or when my hands are cold, or when I lack sleep." He stretched out under the gunwale, and loosened his sword in the scabbard, and removed his cloak and spread it over him, so he could throw it off and be unencumbered if he had to rise quickly. "Call me when it's my watch. Now God keep you, Dinadan."

"And you," Dinadan said.

Thinking of Isoud, wanting to pray for her, and finding no words for prayer, only feeling in himself a longing for God, he fell asleep. In his dreams he was conscious of the motion of the boat and the sound of water, and even of Dinadan sitting on the bench above him, his hand resting on the pommel of his sword. Sometimes it seemed to him that gardens grew in the boat, and that Isoud was there, and that they played the harp and sang, and that she kissed him. And at other times he thought he lay in the little ship of oxhide in which he had first sailed to Ireland, and that he was forbidden to land anywhere.

When Dinadan woke him he leaped up, for he had been dreaming Andret climbed over the side, only Andret had become the sailor from Britany and was trying to lift Yseut into the boat.

"Easy!" Dinadan said.

"I thought you were Andret."

"An unhealthy thought, friend! It's your watch."

"Lie down, then," Tristram said. "What is the order with the crew?"

"Two men sleeping at a time under their benches. Things seem normal enough."

"I'll fetch Gouvernail."

The night was without a moon. The black water twinkled with dots and tiny trails of phosphorus where the oars broke it, and close to the boat Tristram could see rushing in and falling away the pale, ghostly collars of the waves. A stream of powdery stars divided the sky, fading into clouds or mist around the horizon. He looked for familiar constellations, and realized the hour was late, near morning.

"Gouvernail's asleep on the other side," Dinadan said. "I persuaded him a while ago because it has been so quiet."

"Good!" Tristram said. "Rest well." The air was cold, and he hugged himself to keep from shivering. Now Ireland and Cornwall alike seemed distant, not only in space but in time as well. The present was vast all around him, one limitless darkness marked with nothing save the rhythm of the oars and the swell and pitch of the sea. Strange that the water ran along the boat with a dry sound, like grain being shaken in a wooden mortar. If you did not feel the spray and hear the gurgle and suck of the oars, you might think you were rocking along through a desert of sand.

He was soothed by the regular dip and rise of the blades. His mind drifted from one shapeless fancy to another as though it were compelled by the pulse of the boat to be vacant. He noticed when a thin shimmer of pearl began to show on the water without knowing he noticed, without remembering it was the first hint of dawn. And though he roused dimly and told himself the stars would be paling out in another half hour, it was as though he rehearsed some large, unrealizable truth, such as that all men die.

Someone was snoring, Gouvernail or Dinadan, or perhaps a sailor asleep under a bench. Tristram was drowsy enough to marvel that so small a sound as a human snore should make itself heard against the greater sound of the sea. He listened for the grunting breath, bent irrationally upon catching each repetition of it. It might be a fox barking, he thought, except the fox is so far away. He struggled with the bad logic of the thought. A fox barking far away. What did he mean by the fox?

Knowledge rushed over him like a hand opening the closed doors of his brain. A fox was barking, its voice floating over the water shrill and faint, but real. Where were they that they could hear a fox bark? Alarm rang through him, hurrying his heart and stretching his nerves. He strained to hear the fox again, and to learn its direction. To the right? Ahead of the ship? It was ahead if he wasn't deceived by its voice echoing over the sounding plain of the sea. He peered into the misty dark, hoping to find a landmark, but, though light was growing, he could see only a few yards of grey water.

If they had sailed close enough to shore to hear a fox bark, how close would it be? A mile? A half mile? The boat should not be within half a mile of shore until tomorrow afternoon when they were preparing to make their island landfall. He tried to read the dissolving stars, and could no longer be sure of them. But as nearly as he could judge, the boat was holding a course straight north. Shouldn't it be northwest? If they had not borne west at all since they left Tintagel they would have sailed right across the great channel between Cornwall and Wales. And if the voice of the fox came from a shore ahead of them they were at this moment making their way toward the south coast of Wales. Why? The island lay off its west coast.

If this was the beginning of Andret's ambush it would be useless to ask the sailors for information, or to order them to change the course. If it were not, if an inexpert navigator had lost the way in the night, dawn would correct them. All the time he was staring into the mist which tossed itself into smoky clouds as the prow of the boat cut through it. And at last he saw a bulk, a darkness, something neither water nor fog.

He dropped onto his knees and crawled to Dinadan. "Wake up, man," he said close to his ear. "We are for it now."

Dinadan sat up, his hand on his sword.

"Be ready," Tristram said. "I'll wake Gouvernail." He crept under the bench and reached the other side of the boat where Gouvernail lay in his cloak. Tristram took him by the shoulder. "Gouvernail! We need you!"

"What is it?"

"I don't know. Something. We're off course and heading ashore." Because the squire roused slowly Tristram caught a handful of his shirt and lifted him and shook him. "Come on, Gouvernail! Come alive!" He helped the man to his feet. "We'll hold the forward bench. Do you hear me, Gouvernail?"

"Yes."

They disposed themselves as Tristram decreed, standing across the ship between the first and second benches, his two friends at right and left of him. He and Dinadan faced aft, able to discern now the bending backs of the oarsmen, and the dim shape of the helmsman in the stern. The boat was at full crew. Gouvernail faced ashore.

"What do you see?" Tristram asked him softly.

"Land, right enough—trees in the midst. There's a cove, I think."

"Men, or boats?"

"Too much fog on the water," Gouvernail said.

"I'm going to hail the steersman," Tristram said, and shouted "Hey!"

"Hey!" his hail came back, not from the helmsman, but landward, from the water ahead of them.

"Who are you?" Tristram called.

Some answer was returned, but it was vague and muffled by the fog.

At Tristram's cry the crewmen shipped oars and began to leap over benches toward the stern. The helmsman cramped the tiller and brought them around broadside to the shore. "Come aft, my lords," he shouted, "come aft! We're set on by pirates!"

"Don't move," Tristram commanded them. "If we're set on by pirates, it is because a meeting was arranged. What do you see, Gouvernail?"

"Curraghs," he said, "three—four—five of them."

"How many men?"

"I can't tell—three to a boat."

"Come aft for your lives!" the helmsman shouted.

"Fix on a boat, Gouvernail," Tristram said. "One curragh, whichever one comes closest to the bow. Never mind the others. Is there a line on our prow?"

"Yes."

Tristram was watching the men around the helmsmen. They seemed to be confused, gesticulating and pointing forward. The knight emissary had flattened himself against the boat's side and pulled his cloak around him. But he had drawn his sword.

"Throw the line to the curragh," Tristram said, "and call it in. Make them think you're chief, make them think you're helping them board us. Put your heart into it, my son!"

"I hear you," Gouvernail said.

"No matter what the others do, that curragh is our boat. We will take it. You and Dinadan are the boarding crew. I'll stand off whatever has to be stood off here. Are they coming in?"

"Where is the knight emissary?" Dinadan said.

"Aft, getting brave to fight pirates," Tristram said. "Are the curraghs coming in, Gouvernail?"

"Deploying. We're to be surrounded."

"Never think of it, man!" Tristram was dancing before his bench in a kind of unbearable joy. "Call your boat in. The clubs will be with us in a minute. Clubs!" he cried, all happiness. "God has given me some jolly boys with clubs to fight!"

Gouvernail climbed onto the head-high gunwale of the tall bow and straddled it, balancing himself with the coiled line in his hand. The fog was boiling everywhere about them, opening onto glimpses of oily water, and shutting down again in turbulent drifts. The sun's rim was above the horizon now, Tristram judged, because the writhing mist was showing casts of gold and rosy light.

"Hey, man!" Gouvernail shouted. "You in the black tunic!" His voice was tremendous with authority. "Come this way, my fellow! We've got your—" and he bellowed two or three unintelligible syllables.

"Who are you?" came to them from the sea.

Tristram had an inspiration. "Tell him you're here to meet the fox, Gouvernail."

"I've come to meet the fox," Gouvernail sang out.

The crewmen were arming themselves with the clubs. They had no room in the narrow boat to form an attack in strength, but must come forward two or three together. They were bawling angrily among themselves, each urging the others to be first, perhaps, or perhaps trying to fix on a new plan.

"Dinadan," Tristram said.

"I know what I'm to do, brother—stand under Gouvernail and

181

knock our friends of the curragh in the head as they come over the side."

"And—"

"Get on, get on!" Dinadan said. "Forget Gouvernail and me!"

Two crewmen were advancing up the boat's aisle, crawling over benches, grasping their clubs. The sail had been left unattended, and now that the boat was brought around, it had slackened, and was flapping with noisy creaks and whistlings. For a moment it hung like some lunatic thing making up its mind, and then, as the second group of attackers reached it, the boom hurled itself at them and skimmed across their heads. Tristram laughed aloud.

Behind him he heard Gouvernail exhorting his man in the curragh to cast in his grapnel hook, and then he heard nothing more. The two crewmen had reached him, holding their clubs by both ends and using them like shields to parry his sword. Tristram knew he could unarm them with two blows, but if he played them they hindered their fellows and offered him some small protection and delay. Now came the moment of blessed calmness and assurance. He was breathing easily, handling his sword exactly as he wished to handle it. He had time to admire the courage of men who walked naked against a blade which could have killed them between one beat of their hearts and the next. To remind them that a sword was to be respected, he struck their hands with the flat side.

Other crewmen were pressing in. Tristram moved lightly along the bench to prevent them from flanking him, wondering whether they would force one of their members onto his blade in order to break his guard. Now he wished he had unarmed the first men to reach him, for he was fighting with all his skill and speed only to keep them off. A little blood was what they needed. He made swift probes for their wrists and fingers, and saw blood spurt, and heard them grunt and curse. Kill one of them? Kill an unarmed churl, and shame his knighthood? Better to give a little ground—only a little, because behind the bench he defended was nothing save the narrowing angle of the prow, a handy trap to be clubbed to death in.

182

He leaped upon the bench, praying they would not think to throw a club against his legs. But they thought of it. The club took him in a crushing blow across his instep. He jumped back into the prow and landed on sickening softness, the body of a man.

"Dinadan!" Tristram shouted.

"Beside you, brother."

"Who lies here?"

"From the curragh."

A crewman sprang onto the bench. Dinadan felled him with a cut across the knees. Dinadan was not dainty about where his blade landed, and when he had hacked another man's foot in two, so that half of it flew clean off, the crew members held on their side of the bench, having no appetite to feel Dinadan's sword in their bellies.

"Where's Gouvernail?" Tristram said, watching the men who were staring back at him, their mouths open, as though to help them gulp into their bodies a new and more effective idea.

"Over the side. Now you go."

"You first, brother."

"There's a line," Dinadan said. "Don't stand here thinking forgiving thoughts after I'm gone."

The helmsman was shouting to the crewmen, who still hung back sullenly on their side of the bench. Tristram and Dinadan moved sideways toward the gunwale. Tristram stepped onto the fingers of a hand and felt them crush.

"Now!" Dinadan said, and caught the rope and pulled himself up to the gunwale and disappeared over the side. Tristram saw that, to free his hands, he must throw his sword into the sea, and then he must turn his back upon the crewmen for one eternal second while he swung himself to the ship's side. But it was the sword with which he had prevailed against The Marhaus.

He drew air into his lungs and shouted with all his strength and sprang onto the bench. Still shouting, he took the sword hilt in both hands and swung the weapon in a half-circle before him. He might have been going to hurl himself into the men huddling before him. They tumbled backward, appalled by his size, by the screaming blade, by the roar with which he seemed about to devour them. Tristram skipped along the bench, vaulted over the side, and fell into the sea, still clutching his sword. When he came to the surface and took breath he was suffocated with laughter.

Chapter Eighteen

DINADAN and Gouvernail pulled him into their stolen boat. The fog offered them some protection. They could hear the men in the remaining curraghs hailing the ship and boarding her. The action in the bow had been so swift and so well concealed that the pirates or hired murderers, whichever they were, had not learned one curragh had fallen into enemy hands.

The tide was almost high, a half hour from turning, and they used the help it gave them to row into the cove and ascend it, putting distance between them and the discovery on shipboard that they had got off. Time and the fog and the smooth functioning of their plan were on their side.

The cove opened into a little basin cupped by a sand beach hardly wider than a man could jump across. Above this narrow shore they could see steeps upon which pine trees grew, good cover.

"We'll land here," Tristram said. "We'll sink our curragh and take to the forest."

They jumped out in shallow water and tipped the curragh until it filled. Only its peaked stern showed above the surface. They had no time to weight it with stones. It was not wholly concealed, but it would be hard to see in moving swells even if the fog lifted. With his usual methodical foresight Gouvernail had saved their cloaks. Tristram hugged the fur around his wet and shivering body as they began to scale the rocky slope.

185

It was a brutal climb, slippery with pine needles and set with boulders and great bony ledges whose tops jutted beyond their foundations. The morning light strengthened, and the fog thinned out to transparent ribbons and finally fell below them, seen now as a tattered blanket through which tree tops were visible, and glimpses of the cove as blue and peaceful as a lagoon.

Gouvernail and Dinadan ascended nimbly, having a sort of sixth sense which found them crannies among the rocks and small stretches of trail opening through impassable barriers. Tristram's injured foot gave him trouble, swelling within his boot until he felt he was dragging himself upward caught in an iron trap. He was bigger than his friends, too, and had to choke his body through passages they wormed into like snakes. The struggle to keep even with them winded him finally, and he stopped to ease his crammed lungs.

"Are you hurt?" Gouvernail asked him.

"No, but I'm carrying half a man more than you and Dinadan, and I'd love dry clothes."

"There's something that looks like a cave above us," Gouvernail said. "Is it safe to take cover yet?"

"Safe or not."

They pushed on to an opening under a deep shelf of rock tilting into the mountain. It was not a cave, no more than a low shelter dropping at the rear until it was only a couple of feet high. Here they sat down to rest and to listen and to form a plan.

They could hear nothing below, neither voices nor the sound of men beating through the trees. The forest near them was still, but at a distance birds were singing morning songs.

"Unless our friends have a camp near the cove," Dinadan said, "where they've been clever enough to bring dogs, they have no way to trace us. Without hounds it'll be a blind game for them."

"They have plenty of mountain to search, anyway," Tristram said with a laugh. "Tell me what happened with you, Gouvernail. I never knew when you went over the side."

"My man in the curragh came in as peacefully as a pigeon,"

186

Gouvernail said. "What was that business about a fox, Tristram? He liked it, whatever it was."

Tristram told them how he had been warned by the bark of a fox, and how it came over him suddenly that it might be a signal agreed on between the crew and the men ashore.

"He tossed up his boarding hook, and I made him fast," the squire said. "And when he was halfway into the ship Dinadan welcomed him. We worked it on his two friends, too—they couldn't see from the water how we were stowing them away."

"It was ninepins," Dinadan said. "They didn't even have time to say good-by."

"Did you kill them?" Tristram asked, remembering the hand he had stepped on.

"I didn't ask. I was satisfied to knock them in the skull with my sword hilt and let conversation wait."

"It was too easy," Tristram said. "If I had been laying an ambush for Andret I'd have had my bullies armed with knives of some sort. To send men with clubs against us—what kind of scheming was that!"

"It had to look like robbery on the sea, remember," Gouvernail said. "If it had succeeded the crew would have blamed it on piracy, and reported it happened on the course to Ireland."

"Andret couldn't write his name all over this attack," Dinadan said. "They meant to beat us to death while we were asleep, and throw our bodies overboard. It was planned to be easy, Tristram."

"So Andret believed we would lie down like slaughter-mutton and be beaten to death. I gave him credit for better brains."

"Let us not reproach him for being stupid," Dinadan said piously. "He has done us a favor. Besides—"

"Besides what?"

Dinadan grunted with amusement. "He counted on you to rush off to Ireland full of high and suffering purpose, friend. He did not count on you to be clever and think un-Christian thoughts about Christian brothers-in-arms."

"You mean he took me for a fool."

"Something like it."

187

"Well," Tristram said, "we have stuffed a lesson down his throat."

"Yes," Dinadan said. "We have. And now what do we do?"

"Get to Ireland."

"Why?" Gouvernail objected. "So we can fight off armed men instead of unhappy fellows in breechclouts?"

"Because we have an errand there," Tristram said, "and are sworn."

"I supposed so," Dinadan said with a sigh. "But before we go to Ireland we have to find food and clothes and money and a boat. Do you think of walking back to Tintagel and asking your uncle to furnish us for another ambush?"

"First—" Gouvernail said.

"This ambush was no part of my uncle's doing," Tristram said. "First, we must find out where we are."

"I have a feeling we're on the coast of South Wales," Tristram told them. "My father has friends in South Wales, he was bred at court here, and if we can get good bearings I can reach a lord who will purvey us."

"We must walk until we can ask," Gouvernail said. "We'll go inland by the sun."

Dinadan got to his feet. "It's no prospect for hungry men. But since we have no choice, come on, then."

As Tristram rose his foot wrung him, and the pain started sweat on his body. He willed it to hold steady under him, but it was numb, and he stumbled. His leg was white and puffed above his boot.

"You're wounded," Gouvernail said.

"I was hit with a club. It'll limber as we walk."

But after they had fumbled forward a hundred yards, Tristram fell and could not rise. They had two alternatives, to make a camp under the ledge and lie in the forest until his leg healed; or one of them could return to the cove and follow it inland in the hope it would lead to aid and shelter. They decided to adopt this second course.

"I'll be off," Dinadan said, when they had carried Tristram once more to the ledge of rock. "I think you might find a spring near, Gouvernail—slopes like this are always wet somewhere. I'll be back when I can get back. If I'm not here by tomorrow noon, it'll mean I'm beyond helping you."

"God go with you," Gouvernail said.

"Dinadan," Tristram said.

"What is it?"

"I don't know," Tristram said, furious with himself. "God go with you, brother, and someday I shall live to thank you."

Dinadan smiled down on him. "Part of having a great destiny, my son, is having great troubles. God keep you. God keep you, Gouvernail."

No hours ever dragged for Tristram as these hours in the forest dragged. He submitted to Gouvernail's care because he couldn't object, and allowed his squire to take off his boot, and spread his kilts on the rock to dry, and wrap him in his cloak. Cursing the weakness in him he sat in the sun while Gouvernail searched for a spring and brought him water to drink in a scoop of green bark. They appreciated the need for silence, and spoke together as little as possible, an agreement suiting them both, since Tristram was moody and depressed, and Gouvernail was trying to foresee dangers and be ready for them if he could.

After a while Tristram gave up wondering what had happened at the ship. The cove was too shallow to receive the large boat, and the men in the curraghs probably had no very hot desire to search half the world at random for armed knights who seemed easier victims in the dark than they did by day. They realized, like enough, that they would be hanged if they were known. He debated whether he would charge Andret with treachery against king's officers, and give the crewmen to justice. But he was too hungry and wretched to think what he would do if he ever reached Cornwall again, or even whether he would try to return to his uncle's land. He was sure of only one thing, that he had vowed to reach Ireland, that he would reach it if he had to crawl through forests and swim whole seas.

He thought of Isoud and, thinking of her, thought as well of the griefs and failures which had plagued his life since the day he landed in Lyonesse. Were men allotted destinies whose nature never changed, some born to succeed and be happy, and some born to meet misfortune on every road? He would not believe it, for to believe it was to lose heart. And as long as Isoud was in the world, as long as she remembered him, and he her, he would never lose heart. Let his evil luck multiply until it was a thousand times as big as it was today. He would still plant his feet on the shore of Ireland and come before her as he had pledged himself in the name of his knighthood to do. Now, though he had not forgotten he was Mark's ambassador, Tristram began to believe he was sworn to attain Isoud for her sake and his own. He could hold two contradictory faiths at the same time, that he was fulfilling Mark's mission, and yet somehow approaching his own desire. His sorrow, his anger and confusion, had grown into one fervid will, to return to the hall of King Anguissh and to say to Isoud, "I am here." When he had gained so much, God would judge between him and King Mark.

Gouvernail sat down beside him and asked him whether he wouldn't try to sleep.

"Not sleepy."

"I've set a green-twig trap for rabbits."

"Are you hungry enough to eat a raw rabbit?"

"I am that."

"What hour do you think it has got to, Gouvernail?"

"Midday, or near it, I should judge. The shadows are round and small." After a silence he went on, "I've been thinking we could return to Britany and put our case against Andret to King Hoël. He would be a friend to you."

"I thought of it too," Tristram said, "but we haven't any case against Andret, only a suspicion. Our boatmen might have been trying to murder us for the sake of the presents and money we were carrying. I've known men murdered for nothing more than a fur cloak."

"We could wring the truth out of the helmsman, couldn't we?"

"If he doesn't flee," Tristram said. "I would flee if I were in his shoes. Besides, I don't want to have him tortured."

"Why don't we go into Britany, Tristram?"

"Because," Tristram said wearily, "we are king's messengers on a mission to Ireland."

"Listen," Gouvernail said.

They bent forward, cocking their heads toward a sound below them, a rustle of moving men.

"We must take cover under the rock," Gouvernail whispered.

"Wait until we hear voices. If it's Dinadan he will hail us."

"I'll help you put on your kilts."

The squire lifted him to his feet and dressed him. They struggled with the boot and managed to force it onto his shapeless foot. Tristram drew his sword. "I'll make a stand here, Gouvernail. I've no taste for being killed under a rock like a badger."

But as it turned out, they had no need to make a stand. In a few minutes they saw Dinadan coming out of the brake below them, and with him a man in religious habit who carried a bundle.

"I never loved any man as much as I love Dinadan," Gouvernail mumbled. He went down to meet them, and took the bundle from the holy man. Trembling, Tristram leaned against the rock and closed his eyes.

"Well, brother," Dinadan said, and laid an arm around his shoulders. "Put up your sword. We've found a friend." And he explained how he had descended to the cove and followed it inland and reached a hermitage where two brothers, once knights at the Welsh court, were ending their lives as penitents.

"I knew your father, my lord," the hermit told Tristram, "when he was a page and squire in the king's hall. I've taken him fowling many a time."

"He will reward you for this," Tristram said.

The old man wagged his head. He was panting from the ascent, his beard streaked with sweat. "I am rewarded in seeing the son of Meliodas. He was much like you when he was young, only perhaps not so big in the shoulders."

They had brought bread and ale and a sling hammock in which they proposed to carry Tristram down the mountain. The hermit had fetched ointment for his foot, and linen to bind it. As the

191

wound was being dressed Tristram questioned him, and learned that they had landed in the forest of Marydon on the north shore of the Welsh channel, and that, to the east, the land opened into a rolling valley lying along the river into which the sea narrowed to meet fresh water. A half-day's ride would bring them to a ford where they could cross and find themselves in the forests and downs of southwestern Britain.

"Our holy man promises us horses," Dinadan said, "by the time you're able to ride."

"Where will you find horses, friend?"

"If I may send in your father's name, my lord," the hermit told him, "I can have them from the king of South Wales."

"Send, and God prosper you," Tristram said.

The hammock was provided with wooden yokes at each end which Dinadan and Gouvernail took over their shoulders. The hermit helped Tristram lie down, and they began to descend. The holy man was a blessing to them here, for he knew trails avoiding the worst steeps and ledges and leading around boulders. Because he had so little chance to exchange news with his kind, he asked them innumerable questions, not waiting for answers, but rushing on into his own memories of other days when he had been a knight and performed big deeds. They learned he had known King Arthur, and had seen Launcelot fight for half a day against Lamorak of Wales in a tournament whose prize was divided between them. He told them the lady Guenivere herself had attended the tournament and that some men said the ribbon Launcelot wore was given him by her.

"And I have sworn to go back to Camelot," the hermit said, "and sit by the king's gate a whole day asking alms. For I do not believe God will hold me guilty of my wish to see great men once more before I die."

"Dinadan is a member of the Round Table," Tristram told him.

The old hermit stared hard into Dinadan's face. "My dear lord, perhaps I knew you too in the days when I rode to Camelot at Pentecost with my brother, and watched the king's games."

"Not me," Dinadan panted under his yoke. "I never fight when

192

I can sit. I leave that to quarrelsome fellows like Tristram who like better than I to have their legs cut out from under them."

"Don't believe him," Tristram said. "He's a terrible fighter. King Arthur won't let him enter the games because he is afraid he would defeat even Launcelot himself."

"You know the king's custom at Pentecost?" the hermit asked them.

"Yes, I know it," Dinadan said. "Pentecost is the anniversary of Arthur's coronation, and on that day he doesn't sit at meat until he has heard all the causes brought before him to judge. And if there isn't a—" Dinadan puffed his annoyance— "if there isn't something outlandish, he doesn't sit at meat at all."

"Outlandish!" cried the hermit. "You do the king an injustice, my lord. He waits for a truly celebrated cause, something needing might, for he holds that, if he hears of some quarrel which can only be settled by the king's justice, God is giving him a sign He supports his rule over Britain."

"These big fellows," Dinadan complained, "who have to be partners with God!"

Scandalized, the hermit crossed himself. "Don't blaspheme, my lord."

"I wonder what will come to King Arthur this Pentecost," Gouvernail said.

"We have heard in Wales of one matter," the hermit said. The path was easier now, and he had dropped back from his position at the head of their little caravan to walk by Tristram. His ancient face was creased, and dirt was ground into the wrinkles so that he seemed pencilled with a map of age and solitude. From the ragged sleeves of his habit his fists hung in great lumps upon which the hair had turned grey. I have never seen a man so old the hair on his hands was grey, Tristram thought. The hermit's body was bony and stooped, yet a memory of strength remained, some youthful power which stirred in Tristram a vision of what he might have been when he was a knight riding out in the mornings with the king's train, the sun dazzling off the sleek flanks of his horse, and his sword belted onto a silver baldric, and the horns blowing, and dogs crying, and all minds on the day's sport. What a way he had come to this forest of Marydon, and his hermit's cell! Tristram had a moment of chilling insight in which he saw men's lives, and how they sped too swiftly and ended in decay and loneliness and loss.

"What is your rumor?" he asked.

"We've had a man in Wales who troubles our peace," the hermit said, "a foreign knight who has lived in the forests for almost a year as a fugitive. And though he is not a Christian he has taken shelter with hermits and priests, only he has worn a blank shield. And when he comes, he is not suspected. He has a rage in him of some bitter nature, and a few times he has gone into the roads and challenged armed travellers, and fought them, and prevailed. But he has escaped."

"A man like that is not good for any land," Gouvernail said. "He attracts malcontents, and then a band of triflers grows up around him, and before justice can be taken against him he's an outlaw, and unsettles the country and destroys the peace."

"That is what our king feared. And so he sent knights to take this man, and they did take him, and brought him to court. But after a few days the king let him go."

"Now we come to your rumor," Dinadan said. "I foresee that this troubler has gone to Camelot to present a cause before Arthur at Pentecost."

The hermit wrung his hands together in excitement. "So we hear, my lord. I was told only a week ago by the king's forester that he means to appeal the king of Ireland before Arthur for treason."

"What!" Tristram tried to put his feet over the hammock's side.

"Lie still, friend," Dinadan said, "if you don't want these yokes to behead us."

"King Anguissh?" Tristram said. "Has he gone to Camelot to appeal King Anguissh for treason?"

"I was told so," the hermit said. "Do you know King Anguissh, my lord?"

"What is this heathen's name?" Tristram said.

"Palamides, my lord. He is a Saracen."

"God's green hills!"

194

"Oh, what foul luck there is in this world!" Dinadan groaned. "Lie still, Tristram! You can't get at Palamides by jumping out of your hammock."

The hermit was dancing beside him in an agony of curiosity. "Who is Palamides? Do you know him too, my lord? What is his cause against the king of Ireland? I shall pray for you every morning if you will tell me the truth of this affair."

"I know him," Tristram said, "but I don't know his cause against King Anguissh. Where is your cell, old man?"

"Above the water, another mile. Have you seen the Saracen with your own eyes?"

"Let us get on," Tristram said. "I begin to need the horses you promised us, father."

Chapter Nineteen

THE hermit's cell was a strange place. It stood in a ragged grove of oaks, young trees growing up from roots upon which forest giants had once flourished. When or why the parent trees had been cut the hermit could not tell them, only that the ground was said to have been sacred long ago, before the Cross of Christ was brought to Britain.

Two great monoliths across whose tops lay a massive lintel stone stood in what must have been the center of a circular clearing, and between them, under the high lintel, crumbling chips of flint and sandstone hinted that an altar might have been tended here once. The hermit brothers had backed their cells, one for each, against the flat sides of the standing monoliths, rooms of clay and wattle barely large enough to shelter them. But because they had the duty of hospitality they had erected a round stone hut a short distance from their own habitation, and in its dark, ill-smelling chamber Tristram and Gouvernail and Dinadan were invited to make themselves comfortable.

The hermits cooked on an outdoor hearth beside which a post stood, a bronze bell hung from an arm at its head. This bell post was a sort of church to them, forming a crude cross. They rang their prayer hours here and knelt before it to say their offices. At intervals in the night Tristram heard the mellow-throated bell, and woke at dawn to its tone.

"Gouvernail!" he said.

Faithful Gouvernail wrenched himself from sleep. "What is it?"

"This place makes me shiver. I couldn't sleep for thinking about those stones."

"Oh," Gouvernail said, too heavy-witted to remember what stones Tristram meant. "Shall I fetch you water to drink?"

"I think I'll go outside."

Gouvernail fumbled free of the blanket the hermits had provided him and helped Tristram rise. Dinadan still slept as though he were curled in clean feathers, as peaceful as a child.

"I can't bear the thought that we have to delay here," Tristram said when they were outside. "Something about this hermitage makes my flesh crawl."

"You're only restless to get on to Camelot." Gouvernail yawned and rubbed his hair. "You think the hermitage makes you uneasy, but it is more likely your wish to know King Anguissh's trouble and stir up a quarrel with Palamides."

"You're a wise man in the mornings," Tristram said, angry. He limped away, and went to the bell post where the brothers were just rising from the prayers they said at the hour of prime. He knelt and thanked God for his escape, and for life, and asked a blessing on Isoud.

"How did you sleep, my lord?" the hermit who had brought them down the mountain asked him when he had finished.

"Well enough, thanks to your courtesy, old father. My foot is healed today, and I would be glad to have you send for horses. We must ride as soon as may be."

"We have already sent." The second hermit offered Tristram a wide and friendly smile. He was round and pink-faced, a cheerful man upon whom the wear of life showed less than upon his brother. "I sent yesterday, my lord, after your companion told us your story. We have to make our needs known when we can." And he told Tristram how a forester of the king rode by the hermitage once every seven days to see to their health and to carry them meal from the king's granary. He had arrived in the afternoon while the party was still on the mountain. "I supposed you would want horses, as my lord Dinadan suggested. And so I asked the forester to request them from the king."

"Thank you, father. I'll live to reward you."

"And," the cheerful brother went on, tucking his hands into his ragged sleeves in a gesture reminding Tristram of Magan, "I asked for clothing and money too, in King Meliodas' name. For your friend told us you had been surprised in the ship and had to come ashore without your goods."

"How could I have fallen into better hands than yours?"

They gave him porridge in a wooden bowl, and warm barley water. The forester had brought them a treat of cheese which they were anxious to share with him, but the piece was small, and Tristram refused. In gratitude, he told them all he could of the news of the world, what he had seen in Ireland, and how affairs ran at Cornwall. He gave them a tremendous account of the action on shipboard, multiplying the dangers, and assigning such deeds of bravery to Dinadan and Gouvernail as made their eyes glisten with joy.

They showed him the small furniture of their lives as hermits, their tiny cells, and the wooden staves upon which they notched the number of their prayers. The cheerful brother had rough talent for wood carving, and had formed spoons and bowls of oak, and cut upon little plaques figures to represent the guests they had entertained. In a similar fashion he kept a calendar, marking the quarters of the moon and the seasons of the sun.

"They say, my lord, that the men who used these stones"—he pointed to the monoliths—"in the old days worshipped the sun and held a great ceremony every midsummer morning and offered a sacrifice under the lintel."

"That is wicked talk," the elder brother said, the lean old man who had been their guide. "He will bring a demon on us with his heathen thoughts." He crossed himself.

The cheerful brother spread his hands. "Men have been in the world a long time, my lord, and it is reasonable to believe they worshipped as their hearts told them, even before the birth of our God's Son, Jesus. And I can hardly hold the idea that our God

198

refused their prayers, though they made them to the sun or the moon. And so I sometimes look up into the sky, and think of the god who lived in the sun, and I remember this was his temple. What harm does it do if I include him in my prayers?"

"As for me," the elder brother said, "I don't hold with these gods of sun and moon. The stones are here. It is none of our concern what misguided men brought them or what they did with them. And it is foolish and dangerous to offer prayers to any god but our own God."

"In Lyonesse church," Tristram said, "we had two altars, one to our God, and one to the old gods. I have seen my father say his prayers at both altars."

They fell to talking about magic, about spells they had heard of, and brews owning the power to change men's natures and derange their minds. The cheerful brother knew considerable lore of this kind and delighted in telling it, as much to ruffle the elder hermit as to amuse himself. Each tried to maneuver Tristram into a support of his views, but Tristram could not bring himself to take sides. Under the shadow of the silent monoliths he could believe in matters which turned him small and helpless and unsure of truths he was willing to defend with his life in better circumstances. Besides, the feeling between the brothers was a little cruel.

He excused himself on the plea that his foot needed exercise, and wandered about the straggling grove, and watched the small animals freeze in their play to stare at him a quivering moment before they fled to safety. He saw a mound of decaying winter leaves and idly poked it with a stick. He unearthed a bone and gazed down on it, the skin on the back of his neck tingling. He dug among the leaves enough to see the skeleton of a lamb, filthy wool still clinging to the rotted carcass. Why should his friends, the hermits, have buried a lamb here so close to the temple of the old gods? He was afraid to wonder. He kicked the leaves back and hobbled away to seek Gouvernail, suffocated with a sickness of mind the lamb's skeleton had worsened.

The day passed as though it were a week, and another night through which the sound of the hermit's bell mingled with Tristram's dreams. In the morning he could not force himself to kneel and say his prayers in this place where the pagan stones stood so tall and grey and ancient. When two yeomen arrived leading the horses the hermit had requested he could hardly summon patience to hear out the messages sent by the king of Wales. Yet he required himself to return his thanks for the service done him, and to reply courteously to an invitation to accept the king's hospitality and protection at court as long as he had need of them.

The hermits begged him to remain at least until morning, but Tristram reminded them of his errand in Camelot, gave them a parting gift, and received their blessing.

"If you meet any knights who may be riding into our country," the cheerful brother said, "recommend us, and ask them to use our hospitality."

"We shall, father. Now God keep you."

"God go with you, my lords all."

The brothers followed a little way and watched until Tristram could no longer see them. At last he drew a free breath, though the heavy presence of the stones seemed to follow him through the darkest paths of the forest, even as far as the valley down which the river flowed to the sea.

"Well," Dinadan said to him, "that was a comfortable pair of old men. We had luck in Marydon."

They reached and crossed the ford and rode into country less thickly wooded than Marydon. As they went eastward the land was gentler, fens and ferny tracts opening onto moors, and at last onto cultivated fields and tamed forests. A few times they passed a walled village around a hall, and saw cattle grazing on common pasture. They met a party of knights from Camelot with whom they paused and asked for news of King Anguissh. But the knights had been travelling too long to have heard Palamides' cause. Nor did they learn anything from a merchant's train of two-wheeled oxcarts and drivers except that the freight was leather wineskins and cowrie shells, on its way to Glastonbury.

By sundown they had reached country familiar to Dinadan who had been bred at the court of Camelot. He led them to a house in which they spent the night, an inn where men and animals sheltered under the same roof. It was run by an old woman who made a living concluding marriages between freeholders and performing the duties of midwife. She had an evil face and a foul tongue, but she was kind and friendly, and joked with Dinadan because he was willing to submit his knighthood to the smells of old straw and sheep urine.

In the morning she provided them with yeomen who would return their horses to the king, and found fresh mounts for their journey to Camelot. When Tristram gave her a coin she put it quickly into her mouth, and he wondered whether, like some ancient squirrel, she made a practice of stowing her earnings there.

"How is your foot?" Dinadan asked him.

"Healed." The foot was hardly healed, being still dark with blood and stiff after yesterday's ride. But Tristram was resentful that injury seemed to be the monotonous price of victory.

"I wonder what our friends in the boat made of our disappearance," Dinadan said.

"Do you believe the knight courier was part of the scheme?"

"He's a stupid fellow," Dinadan said. "I've known him for ten years. I'm of the opinion Andret picked him because he is dullbrained enough to swallow the pirate story. Anyway, he is Andret's man, and will swear what he is told to swear."

"If he won't witness for us we haven't much hope of a judgment against Andret."

"None at all," Dinadan agreed. "Our kettle of mutton won't boil that way. You know, Tristram, if we go back to Cornwall Andret will hate you twice as much as he did before. He'll realize you suspect what he attempted, even if you can't charge him."

"Andret is worry for another day. He seems unimportant to me now."

"What do you expect with your matter in Camelot?"

"To offer King Anguissh my help if he will see me. The custom for justice there is the same as it is in other courts, isn't it?"

"Yes. Anguissh will hear the charge, and be given a chance to defend himself, body for body, on Palamides."

"Do you think he is being held in prison?"

"No," Dinadan said with a laugh. "Kings don't throw one another into dungeons, you know, unless they have a taste for each others' lands. I imagine Anguissh is living in Arthur's hall and being treated handsomely to meat and wine and music after dinner."

"How will it go on the morning of the feast day?"

"On Pentecost? Well, Anguissh will ride to the jousting field and wait in a pavilion. Arthur's herald will read the causes, Anguissh's first, probably, since he is likely to be the biggest fish in the king's net this time. Then Palamides will ride before Arthur and make his accusation of treason, whatever it is, and Anguissh will be summoned and asked whether the charge is true. If he denies it he must fight. Or you must, or whoever he elects to defend his quarrel."

"You can reach Anguissh in Arthur's hall, Dinadan. Will you carry a message for me?"

"Yes, brother. I expected to."

"Tell him I have come in gratitude for his good lordship in Ireland, and that I wish to relieve him."

"What if he is guilty? Don't you want to hear the charge?"

"No," Tristram said.

"But—"

"No. When I fought The Marhaus I thought it was easy to tell a just cause from an unjust one. But I have been educated since my day in the island."

They approached Camelot at the day's end when the sky above the town was stained with gold and rose and lavender. As they neared the gate they could see King Arthur's castle on rising ground. In its great tower the glass windows were burning with sunset lights. They pulled up their horses to stand a moment and look at it.

Here before them lay Britain's heart, a citadel fit to house the king who was the lord of every faithful man's allegiance. Tristram stared at the tower dark against the colored sky, patched with golden windows, its base lost in folded shadows of purple. Within it keeping state sat the king he had never seen but whom he would see tomorrow robed and crowned and speaking the words of justice. Perhaps at this moment he was with his knights at the Round Table, with Launcelot, and Bors, and Bedivere, and Gawaine, and his own son Mordred and all the Hundred and Forty; and the white-haired bishop near, and the lady Guenivere going among the brave men with a jewelled cup of wine. Arthur would be more princely than any man, large and grave and showing the power of spirit and body which had allowed him to draw the sword from the stone and stand revealed as the lord of the future.

Tristram thought of little Lyonesse lying half in the sea, and of its poor fishermen and farmers, and of his father in his yeoman's kilts. He thought of Mark, so fashionable and worldly, and of Cornwall's many-colored cliffs, and of the sea beating this moment upon Tintagel head; and of the smiling peace of Ireland, and of the fields where mulberry trees grew, and of the humpbacked goldsmith who was a slave; and of the forests rising out of the Welsh channel, and of the brother hermits ringing their prayers under the shadow of the monoliths; and of the road he and his companions had just ridden, and of the knights and merchants, and of the old midwife at the inn. These were Arthur's lands. And these were Arthur's people, different from each other in loving and hating, in their habit of talk, in the bread they ate, in the desires they slept on and awakened to. But with all their differences they were a brotherhood because of the king in the tall tower, Arthur, toward whom they turned with faith as to a father.

He is the king I serve, Tristram thought, and his eyes filled with tears.

"Well, there it is," Dinadan said, "Camelot."

Tristram could not answer. He was thinking of King Hoël, and of Isoud, and wishing these two people he loved most in the world could be with him, and see him ride into Camelot to fight before Arthur on Pentecost. For a moment he felt cleansed of all the wretchedness and mischance of his life, free, confident the world offered good causes to fight for. Once he had prayed to God to make him a worthy knight. Now as he sat his horse and looked over Camelot the prayer welled up in him again. He prayed for his knighthood, and for King Anguissh's cause, and for Isoud.

"You've been on your way here a long time, Tristram," Gouvernail said, his voice quiet.

"You too, Gouvernail."

"Ever since I became your man."

"Plenty of nonsense is talked in Camelot," Dinadan said, "but every time I ride up on it this way, and see it looking so—so—I mean," he interrupted himself, "that—that—" and even Dinadan could find no more words.

Chapter Twenty

AS they rode toward the castle Tristram peered into the dusk to see all he might of Arthur's capital. They passed through the center of the town where the king's shops made their own district, and Tristram was delighted with the clean plaster and timber houses and the swept dooryards. Dinadan pointed out the metalsmiths, the toolmakers, the furriers, the weavers, the harness and leather workers, the wood carvers, the furniture and pottery artisans. Granaries and a mill, with the family dwellings of the men who worked in them, occupied their own ground, as did the blacksmithies and the shops of the armorers. But Dinadan explained that he would have to wait until morning to see the stables, the kennels, and the hawk mews, which were nearer the castle, across the earthworks and ditch separating the king's citadel from the town.

Though this was Britain's capital, and looked like Britain, and felt like it as well, the strangers in its streets gave it a foreign cast. Tristram did not need Dinadan to tell him that among the groups of noblemen walking, unarmed, to see the town were knights from other countries, and that the priests of many habits and tonsures came from Italy and Africa and Spain. He saw Moorish merchants in long, belted dresses and high hats of rolled cloth, and king's foresters wearing short axes and cow-horn trumpets in their belts, and messengers in riding capes, and women in cloaks and pleated skirts who looked into the faces of the men as they passed. There were herdsmen and farmers clothed in the everlasting brown linen of the west, and peddlers crying needles and combs and tinder, ringing small bells of bronze. Beggars, their legs and bodies wrapped in rags, called in hoarse voices after every condition of men, beseeching them for God's love to give alms. Children were everywhere, and near each child was a dog or a goat or a few geese or hens.

Yet, though Tristram was excited because this was Camelot and he was here, he did not forget why he had come. When he saw two yeomen in the knee-length colored tunics of Ireland he pointed them out to Dinadan, and told him about the day on which he had first beheld such men. "Should we question them about King Anguissh?"

"I don't think so," Dinadan said. "They are probably freemen who have come to Britain to seek service. Gossip flies in the streets here. They are as likely to tell us King Anguissh has been hanged as to know something we can depend on. Rest easier, brother," he said with a crabbed smile. "I'll find your king for you."

"Let us go to a place where we can learn the truth."

"We can do it at the castle, and wash and eat, too."

"Not I," Tristram said. "I must push on with what I have come to do."

"You can't push on with it until tomorrow," Dinadan reminded him reasonably, "and so you might as well sleep on feathers tonight."

"At least we can inquire where King Anguissh is."

Dinadan sighed. He was tired and hungry, and he had seen Camelot before, and he was of the opinion that kings were better equipped than poor knights on borrowed horses to take care of themselves. But he had argued with Tristram on other days, and lost his breath. He reigned in his horse near the Irish yeomen and asked them what they heard of their master, King Anguissh.

"He is appealed for treason, my lord," the older of the men answered, "and must defend himself in the morning."

"Are you of his party?"

"No. He has no party. He is alone in Camelot."

206

"Where is he?" Dinadan asked.

"They say," the yeoman told them, "he has refused the king's hospitality, and has stayed at the jousting field in the pavilion given for his use."

"I told you, Dinadan," Tristram said, his heart rushing upward in a surge of pride, "King Anguissh is——"

"Yes, I remember," Dinadan said. "He is wonderful." He gave a Welsh coin to the yeoman, and thanked him. "Well. I shall take your message to this Anguissh of yours, but first let us——"

"Let us do nothing first, brother. Where is the jousting field?"

Dinadan bade a mournful farewell to the ale and the hot joint of meat which had been in his mind for the last hour. He led Tristram and Gouvernail up the hill to the castle wall, rode west there, and followed a broad highway for half a mile. Except for the green afterglow in the west, the sky was lost above them, starless. Tristram peered into the thick dusk and could see nothing save a sort of impression of flat land to their right.

"Wait here," Dinadan said. "I'll be back in God's time, and I'll tell you what your king of Ireland answers to your message."

"Tell him," Tristram said, "he was a good lord to me, and I remember."

Dinadan trotted off. They heard his horse's feet after they could no longer see its grey flanks. And then they heard nothing, only silence, and far away behind them the dogs of Camelot, and somewhere a bell ringing the hour of compline.

"Dinadan is a patient man," Gouvernail said.

"He loves nothing enough to be impatient," Tristram said.

"It may be, or it may be his love is cool, and doesn't fly after one thing more than after all things. Some men love the world only because they see its flaws."

"There are right things to love," Tristram said, "and wrong things to hate. And how can you be cool about that?"

Gouvernail recognized in his lord a mood which resisted reason. He was hungry too, but he was schooled to endure hunger, as well as cold, and thirst, and discomfort, and large causes, for Tristram's sake. "We had luck to reach Camelot before dark," he began again temperately. "It is more prosperous than Cornwall. On the other hand," he went on, his voice judicious, "it lacks Cornwall's beauty of coast and the benefit of salt air."

Tristram was silent.

"Don't you think so?" his squire inquired.

"Don't I think what?"

"Don't you think," Gouvernail repeated, "that the country around Camelot is more prosperous than Cornwall, but that it lacks the beauty of sea coasts, and the benefit of salt air?"

"Yes," Tristram said.

"I wonder if the lord Launcelot is in Camelot," Gouvernail tried again.

Silence.

"I have heard," Gouvernail went on, "that he owns a great hall in the north, once he captured in war, and that he changed its name from Dolorous Gard to Joyous Gard. He holds lands in France."

"Perhaps we should ride after Dinadan," Tristram said.

"They say Queen Guenivere is his lady."

"I wonder whether Dinadan lost his bearings in the dark."

Gouvernail fell silent. Weariness was easier to put up with if men could lighten it with a little cheerful intercourse. But if that could not be had, weariness could be borne without it. The squire eased his weight in the saddle, resigning himself to stillness and shadows and the faith that every day sooner or later reached an end.

After what seemed to him a long time he heard Dinadan returning. He hailed him.

"Did you find the king?" Tristram said. "What did he answer?"

Dinadan's horse, better able to choose its way in the dark than its rider, trotted up to its two companions, and shook its head and swung its tail against its flanks as though to tell them matters were in hand.

"I found him," Dinadan said. "There's a flambeau before his pavilion. A squire is with him."

"Dinadan!"

"I gave him your message, Tristram. And he said to tell you

208

he accepts you as his champion, and he thanks you, and he will see you now or in the morning, whichever you wish."

"Ah!"

"And he will purvey you tomorrow when you go against Palamides."

"Did you ask him his cause?" Gouvernail said.

"No, that's between him and Tristram." Dinadan's horse tugged forward, and the knight slapped its neck softly to steady it. "What will you do, Tristram?"

"I'll speak with him in the morning. Did you see him clearly, Dinadan?"

"I saw him clearly enough to know you were right, my son. Your king is a man."

They turned their mounts and went back along the Roman road, beholding Camelot emerge in dots and gleams of light. They felt the influence of the two kings with whose destinies their own future would mingle tomorrow, of Arthur waiting for a cause worthy of his feast at Pentecost, and of Anguissh whose quarrel they did not know. These mighty figures haunted their minds and isolated each man in silence.

In town they found lighted windows and a few guides, or messengers, or men required to be abroad for whatever reason, carrying flambeaux through the dark streets. Smells of wood smoke and hot food reached them and enlivened their hunger. Dinadan led them to an inn, complaining he was behaving like a madman to give up the comfort of the castle for a bed of straw.

After they had bathed and eaten and were warming themselves by the hearth Dinadan found many things to deplore in Camelot. And though he appealed to Gouvernail for confirmation as to a sensible soul, though he asked whoever would listen whether it was not the part of fools to roister about Britain and fight pirates and climb topless mountains and ride cart horses for two days on end, he managed to draw their hearts together, his and Tristram's and Gouvernail's, in something secret, chosen, a brotherhood. When they went to their straw pallets at last, they went as people do for whom victory is prepared.

At daybreak they parted, Dinadan to join his fellows of the Round Table, and Tristram and Gouvernail to ride to the jousting ground. This field lay beyond the town. Against the section of wall overlooking it a row of permanent boxes for spectators was built, roofed, with low towers at each end where ladies might withdraw. Opposite the wall at the far limit of the ground stood the knights' pavilions, cone-shaped wooden structures with flattened tops closed by tent peaks and standards for banners. Laborers were already at work fixing pennants to posts along the field's sides, and carrying out the goods and furnishings the day's business required.

As Tristram approached the pavilions he saw hanging on one of them the shield of the king of Ireland. He dismounted and struck the shield lightly with his sword.

His own sword in hand, King Anguissh came out to him.

"My lord," Tristram said, "you know why I am here."

The sun shone all around Anguissh, on his bright hair, on the shirt of fine chain covering his breast, on the blade of his sword which he raised and pushed into its sheath. He was as tall as Tristram, but twenty years of campaigning, twenty years of living with such luxury as his kingship afforded, had made him heavier. He seemed neither young nor old, only strong, only planted on the earth like a tree in summer.

"Welcome, Tristram," he said, "and take my thanks. I am glad you remember me."

"When I left Ireland I promised you my service."

"I have never needed any man's service until today," the king said. "How do you happen to be in Camelot at the moment when I am without friends?"

"After I have fought with Palamides I shall tell you."

"I never thought to live to be appealed of treason by a Saracen," Anguissh said. "There is no treason against me, either."

"I haven't asked you your cause, my lord."

"No, but you must hear it. Are you still so young, Tristram, that you take the world's mischance as an outrage? You can't abuse your knighthood because some quarrels seem unjust."

"I must decide my own causes."

"Bravely spoken." Anguissh motioned him into the pavilion. "I don't quarrel with your courage, Tristram. But hear my matter with Palamides." And he related how one of his Irish barons had raised his district and attacked a king's garrison and destroyed twenty foot soldiers. Anguissh marched against him and in the course of the battle killed the baron's cousin. When he had subdued the rebel Anguissh exacted from him the full fine for his twenty foot, and for every king's man who had fallen in the battle. The cost was heavy enough to deprive the baron of a third of his lands.

"He was disgruntled," Anguissh said, "and a disgruntled man is always a danger. Palamides got to him somehow, though Palamides was still a fugitive then after that disgraceful killing of the horse. The two of them hatched this scheme. In the name of a blood killing my baron has appealed me for his cousin's death, and I am summoned before Arthur to answer it body for body."

"Palamides is your baron's champion?"

"Yes, and he carried the appeal to Arthur. You can see what a pretty plot it is, worthy of a man who would stab a horse."

"My lord," Tristram said, "I never felt so well able in my life to fight a Saracen as I feel this morning. And if you will allow me, I shall go back to Ireland with you and fight your baron too, and all his cousins, however many cousins he has."

"I can take care of my baron middling well," the king said. "Will you fight under my shield, Tristram?"

"Yes." Such a crowding happiness filled him, such a sense of might that he felt he could fight naked against Palamides.

"I shall squire you," the king said.

He dressed Tristram in his own mail, and set his shield on his shoulder. But when he would have belted his champion with his own baldric and sword Tristram refused. "My sword and I are brothers, my lord, and we fight better when we stay together."

"We have time yet," Anguissh said. "What have you done since I saw you last?"

Tristram spoke a little of Cornwall and of his uncle. He longed to ask about Isoud, yet he could not, for even more than he wished to hear of her he wished to postpone the moment when he must inform the king what his mission was, and how he was going into Ireland.

When they heard the notes of the herald's trumpet, Tristram said, "Dinadan told me your cause would be presented first, my lord. Answer that your champion is ready, and give them my name."

"What reward can I offer you, Tristram?"

"I have never fought for a reward. But if I prevail today, I shall tell you a desire I have."

The king nodded, satisfied. "Now God strengthen you." He took Tristram by the shoulders, and kissed him, and stepped outside.

Tristram drew his sword and thrust its point into the earth floor of the pavilion. He knelt before the cross its hilt formed and said the prayers of a knight going into battle, and asked God's care for King Anguissh and King Arthur and for Isoud. Then he rose and pulled aside the hanging over the entrance of the pavilion and watched what took place on the field.

He could see the royal box, and the tall figure of Arthur himself, but he was too far away to read the king's features. Knights were with him, perhaps even Launcelot. The ladies were seated together, their colored dresses fair against the green turf. Men from Camelot, yeomen and churls making a brotherhood of their common desire to see, had climbed to the wall and sat along its top shoulder to shoulder. The herald and his pages in blue and scarlet were riding a parade the length of the field and back. But because this was a day for justice, not for games, no contending knights accompanied them. The atmosphere lacked the gaiety of a tournament.

The herald returned to the king's box and read the first cause. Tristram could hear his voice though not his words. But he knew this was the appeal against Anguissh, for he saw the king of Ireland enter the field and ride before Arthur and dismount, and he recognized the strong gesture with which Anguissh denied the charge. Palamides had entered too. The black war horse of the Saracen, his gleaming armor, his Scythian trousers of scarlet added foreign

212

splendor to this field of Britons. He was armed with shield and spear and wore his sword. I remember your sword, friend, Tristram thought. Today you shall have a taste of mine.

He stepped outside the pavilion and found Gouvernail there. He was holding a saddled horse, King Anguissh's gift.

"You've been summoned, Tristram."

"I heard them. Put me up."

"Remember, Palamides doesn't fight like an honest man."

But Tristram could not delay for cautions. The feeling had come over him, the cool readiness, the joy that took him when he was riding toward an enemy. He heard his name called, and his lineage recited, and found himself before Arthur without recalling how he had ridden down the field. He looked at Arthur without seeing him (though later he remembered) and heard himself say how he had come to defend King Anguissh in a just cause.

Then he was walking his horse toward Palamides, seeing the angry surprise in the eyes peering out of the leather visor, turning, galloping back, and sweeping around for the charge. Oh, this was the moment! He seated his spear in the saddle, finding in the seconds of the charge time to plan, time to know that in this encounter he would unhorse Palamides with the first blow, and that then they would fight to the uttermost with swords.

They swept together with a crash that drove their horses onto their haunches, a clean hit on both sides. Tristram leaped backward over his mount's croup and landed on his feet, his hand already on his sword. Palamides had fallen. I could have him now, Tristram thought, I could unarm him and kill him before he gets to his knees. He would kill me. But he waited while the Saracen struggled to his feet.

He fought carefully, feeling Palamides press for a quick victory. He was willing to defend himself a while, dancing lightly from right to left as he was tried on each side, giving ground, slowly circling. But after a time the foot which had been crushed by the oarsman's club began to trouble him and slow his power to choose his ground. You must give as well as take, he told himself, and he began to probe the Saracen's guard, making him shift his shield in

213

rapid turns, feinting toward his head, then lunging at his body. He cut him in the shoulder close to the neck, and saw blood run down his chain shirt. He sheered off one leather gauntlet and felt his sword touch bone.

With his hand spurting blood, Palamides still gripped his sword. He was rushing in without caution, wild to bear Tristram down with weight and force while he could still command his weapon. His point stuck Tristram in the chest and knocked the wind clean out of him. Tristram sprang backwards gasping for air, suffocating, seeing black before him, and against the black the spinning lightning of the Saracen's sword. The breath scorched into his lungs like fire. A fair hit, he thought, and felt something he had never felt for Palamides before, something like respect.

The blow had brought water into his eyes, and now he saw Palamides fighting in a rainbow, oddly diminished by the lenslike tears. His bleeding hand, the muscles laid bare, seemed to be a long way distant, yet not so distant but what Tristram knew it for his target. Fighting backwards, defending himself while he sucked reviving air, he watched the hand and its convulsive grip on the sword.

Suddenly Palamides threw away his shield and clutched his sword in both hands. He ran in on Tristram and swept his blade in a whistling blow toward his legs. Tristram caught the edge on his own sword, thrust Palamides' weapon upward, and saw it fly from his hand. He laid two terrible lashes across the Saracen's chest, and Palamides fell.

Tristram ran and seized his sword. "Yield," he said, "or I shall kill you."

"Kill me," Palamides said. He lay on his back staring up at Tristram, his eyes behind his visor gleaming red.

Tristram threw Palamides' sword as far as he could hurl it and raised his own. "Yield, for God's sake, my lord."

"I will never yield."

Tristram lowered his arm. "Then get up and retrieve your sword, and we shall fight here until one of us dies."

Palamides rolled over onto his face and raised himself onto his knees. For a moment he stayed thus, in the attitude of a man in prayer, and then he sighed and fell forward.

Tristram looked down on him with a queer sort of amazement. He had his own courage, this heathen who killed horses in rage and cut at men's legs like a butcher. His hand was hacked so that tendons had parted and curled back on either side of the wound. How had he held his sword so long? And what will in him had made him struggle to rise and take it up again? Blood from the gash in his shoulder ran down and stained the grass. Tristram stared at his own hands, felt his shoulders, moved one leg, then the other. He was whole. He turned away from Palamides, his exaltation tempered by a feeling of kinship with the fallen knight, of admiration too, almost of affection.

Men were running onto the field. They had brought a horse litter for Palamides. As they lifted him Anguissh reached Tristram and took him by the shoulders, and shook him in rough joy. "They say you fight like Launcelot himself, Tristram! I have never seen a sword better handled!" And he flung an arm around Tristram. "Come on, come on! Arthur is waiting to welcome you."

"Let me speak with you first. Go with me to the pavilion."

"I never saw a man more desired than you are this minute, Tristram!"

"Are you cleared, my lord?"

"Yes," Anguissh said, "I was cleared when you drew your sword."

They made their way through the crowd around Palamides and returned to the pavilion. As the king helped him remove his armor Tristram said, "I thank God He gave me this chance to relieve you, my dear lord, for I would rather do you service than any man."

"I would rather have you than any man, Tristram, and not only because of what you have done today. I was deprived of a good knight when you left Ireland." The king's face still showed the hot pride he had felt on the field, and he spoke in the tone of a man who would ask for understanding. "I could not prevent what happaned there."

"I know."

"But now I can mend it. Tell me the desire you have, Tristram."

"My lord," Tristram said, "before I came to Camelot I was sailing into Ireland to seek peace with you. But—" he paused to think whether to tell of Andret's ambush, and decided against it, since it might besmirch his uncle's name—"but I was shipwrecked on the Welsh coast. And in Wales I heard how Palamides had appealed you."

"There is peace between us," the king said. "You left me with honor, and I would never have followed you."

"I have been gone from Ireland a year," Tristram said, "and in that year I have wanted nothing except to return."

"Ah, Tristram!"

"Now," Tristram said, feeling himself tremble, "I ask to return. I ask you in the name of your good lordship to give me the princess Isoud."

Anguissh was holding the chain shirt in his hands. He stood still, clutching it, looking into Tristram's face. "Your reward?"

"If it must be as reward. But I would be glad if you answered me freely without weighing rewards."

"I can't," Anguissh said. "I am sworn to reward you. But if you ask her freely I cannot give her to you."

"Then—"

"I can give you lands, money, ships, anything else. I can make you a great lord. But you know I cannot yield Isoud."

"Does she hate me so much?"

"The queen hates you."

"Beyond forgiveness?"

"Beyond the grave, Tristram. She would raise her kin against me. She would divide my land, and bring war on me, and pursue you wherever you go. She would kill Isoud before she would see her given to you." The king wrung the shirt between his hands, making its links rattle and murmur. "You are young, and you have lived with men. You don't know what women are!"

Tristram felt rising around him a sort of sickness. Anguissh prowled the narrow pavilion, his brows drawn down, his face all creased and seamed with torment. "I hoped for this once, when

216

you were mending in Ireland and coming on like the knight I knew you were to be. But the queen—"

Tristram's clothing borrowed from the king of Wales still lay on the floor. He gathered up the garments and began to dress himself. Beyond the grave. What hope was there in a world where hatred rushed willingly onto death? I will have Isoud at any cost, he told himself, even if I betray King Mark, even if Anguissh and I become enemies, even if the queen kills me. But he knew he would not have her, even at any cost. For His own reason, God had refused him his love when Tristram went into Cornwall to fight The Marhaus. God's reason was cruel, it was brutal, it was unhuman. But above all, it was past overreaching.

"King Mark sent me into Ireland," he said, his voice dull. "It was he who asked me to make my peace with you for the sake of quiet between your land and his. It is my uncle who desires this marriage."

"Mark!"

"Yes."

"He wishes to marry Isoud?"

"That is my message."

"No," Anguissh said.

"It is for his peace and yours," Tristram said.

"No, no, it will not bring peace. I am not blind, my son. I have seen how it is with you. Cornwall is not big enough for this marriage, and you."

"I am the king's ambassador," Tristram said heavily, "and I am chosen to bring the princess to Tintagel. Afterwards," he said, "afterwards, my lord, I—I shall go into—into Britany where I was bred. I shall not trouble Isoud's happiness."

"God has ways to try men," the king said, and sat down and dug his hands into his hair.

"Give me an answer, my lord. I ask this as my reward."

Anguissh groaned. "I am sworn. Take her to Mark."

Part IV

Part IV

Chapter Twenty-one

TRISTRAM attended the high feast of Pentecost at the castle. He was received by Arthur, and talked with Launcelot and his kinsmen, Bors and Bleobaris, and with Gawaine and his brothers, Gareth and Gaheris, and with his own father, and with many brave men of the fellowship of the Round Table. He saw Queen Guenivere and was moved by her beauty. And wretched as he was, he felt himself happy to share the brotherhood he had hoped for since the days when he was a squire in King Hoël's court. But he did not remember clearly his day in Camelot until later, when he had a reason to remember it. For he was consumed with the thought that he was soon to see Isoud at whatever hopeless distance. And he desired so fervently the moment of meeting that all moments before it became time in a dream.

He told Dinadan how he had fulfilled their mission as Mark's ambassadors, and how Anguissh would take him into Ireland and present the king of Cornwall's suit to his barons, and the queen.

"Then what, Tristram?" Dinadan said.

"Then I shall bring the princess to Tintagel."

Dinadan was silent a while, as though he meditated some comfort for Tristram, or some advice, it might be. But at last he drew breath and said, "Well, there's a promise kept, friend. Shall I go with you and Gouvernail and Anguissh?"

"No," Tristram said. "Stay in Camelot, if you want to take part

221

in the holiday games. But come back to Cornwall in time to bid me good-by."

"You plan to return to Biitany?"

"Yes."

Dinadan nodded. "I suppose you must, Tristram." He took him by the shoulders. "God strengthen you. If you want a friend in Britany, I know a man who will go with you."

"I'll not forget, Dinadan."

So they parted. And so Tristram made ready, and left Camelot with King Anguissh and Gouvernail. They rode northwest, across the river, and through the dark forests of Wales, and kept the king's meeting with the boat which had brought him to Britain. In this way, after a year, Tristram sailed once more into the harbor he had seen first from the little ship of oxhide against whose thwarts he had lain and harped a song for the strangers on the shore.

"Now, Tristram," Anguissh said, "we have come home."

"You have come home, my lord."

"Wait in the boat," the king said, "and when I have prepared for you, I'll send clothing and arms and a guard to bring you to the hall fittingly."

"I shall wait."

"You are under my protection, Tristram, at all times, whenever you need me."

"Thank you, my lord. And my might is yours, whenever you need me."

"Tristram."

"My lord?"

"Brother," the king said.

Tristram was silent.

"Stay in Ireland," the king said, "and share it with me."

"That isn't possible. I would disturb your land."

"I will make it possible."

"No," Tristram said, "I shall go into Britany."

"What do you desire that I can give you, Tristram?"

"Nothing, my lord."

"Farewell, then," Anguissh said, "and may God deserve you."

Tristram watched him go up the sloping ground above the harbor. The king's people, the herdsmen and fishers, saw him and ran out of their boat-roofed huts and pressed around him, kneeling, touching his hands. He stood among them, his great head glowing, his body strong and tall, speaking to them and pointing to the ship. As he reached the crest of the hill the priests arrived and greeted him, and with them the dog Pickpocket leaping as high as his breast, crying so joyfully that his voice belled over the water, mellow, half-sad. Pickpocket was too much for Tristram. He turned his back on the sunswept slope and sat down on a bench and dropped his head onto his hands.

Gouvernail regarded him with an anxious frown. It was his desire to do something for his lord, to warm the chill in his heart, to protect him as he did when Tristram was hurt in battle. But this was an extremity beyond his skill. And he thought that, though Tristram was the most reckless of men, running into needless dangers and breaking his body in fights he could have avoided, he was better off, his life was more manageable, when he had conquests to fight, and wounds, even poisoned wounds, to recover from. Perhaps God had ordained some men to wield the sword, and others to think cleverly, to master their spirits, to become the kings and husbands of the world. Perhaps it was true that courage withered a man's wits. What a long, slow, secret, unspectacular process it was to grow wise!

Two hours passed before the king's guard appeared on the shore, two hours in which Tristram had time to suffer a hundred imaginings of Anguissh's talk with his queen, and of Isoud. That the queen would yield to her lord's will he had no doubt, however angrily she did it, since she could not, with justice, push her blood quarrel as far as Mark. Isoud too. But how would Isoud receive the news that she was to be married to a man she had never seen, an old man? Above all, what would she think when she learned Tristram was this man's ambassador, waiting to escort her to him? Would she know herself betrayed, and hate him for his share in her betrayal? Or would she feel a springing joy that she was to

223

see him again, that tomorrow was a century away, that they were possessors of today?

The king had sent a full ceremonial guard, his seneschal and chamberlain, his herald and port reeve, a troup of uniformed yeomen led by the chief of his counsel barons, and his senior priest. Except for the priest who led them they were mounted, their horses in the parade regalia of saddle cloths and enamelled cheek buttons. And they were unarmed, wearing tunics of the king's scarlet, the chains and medallions of their rank, and baldrics and short swords. The yeomen carried the standards of Ireland and Cornwall.

The seneschal and port reeve came aboard to greet Tristram and to give him a gift of clothing, arms, and a gilt medallion and chain. To Gouvernail they presented a tunic and a short sword.

They bore themselves with a courtesy in which he could find no flaw. But he could read in the cold solemnity of their faces the fact that they had submitted to the king's will because their duty required submission. The eager pleasure, the willing, friendly curiosity he had met when he first came to Ireland, were missing. As they conducted Tristram and the squire to horses and led them up the slope, the men and women who lived in the strange, round houses and the narrow, boat-roofed huts near shore came only as far as their dooryards to see the party pass. They stood without cheering, and Tristram realized that news of his return, and of his errand too, like enough, had flown through the harbor district, and was probably at this moment being sped by messengers over all Ireland.

They trotted past the fields where the crops of oats and onions were still showing the tender color of young growth, and entered the courtyard. It had been emptied of the idlers and dogs and geese and children who usually made it a noisy place. The workers in the king's shops came to their doors. Tristram was touched when he saw the humpbacked goldsmith hastening across the cobbles on his thin legs, like some half-lame, ancient bird. Here was one man whose heart remembered him. Tristram pulled up his horse and said, "How are you, smith?"

"I am well, my lord. I am glad to see you again."

"Is the vessel finished?" Tristram said.

"Just finished," the goldsmith said. "I hope you will come to look at it while you are here."

Tristram nodded, wondering whether this gesture of kindness would recoil against the old artist. "God bless your work," he said.

"God bless you, my lord."

They approached the hall. The party dismounted in order. Tristram's heart pressed upward and knocked at his ribs. The king and as many counsel barons as could reach the court on a short summons emerged and conducted him within. Tristram saw them, heard them, made his replies, greeted them in the name of King Mark, since he was a prince and had been bred to discharge his office. But all his soul streamed away from them and ran to Isoud and knelt before her where she stood with the ladies behind the king's chair.

Oh, she was beautiful, straight and slender, her face pale, her hair shimmering in the muted light like new embers! And she was queenly as he had never seen her. Though the year had enriched her fairness and confirmed the grace of her body, though the feelings she had felt, whatever they were, had purged away her soft girlhood and given her the lustre of an ardent woman, he did not see this as a truth of time. He saw nothing except her beauty, and that her eyes, looking right into his, told him he was a stranger.

"Welcome, Lord Tristram," the queen said. Because she was a woman whose emotions flew outward in hot words she was not pale, but flushed, and the sharpness of her quarrel with Anguissh still showed in her set face and the angry tension of her body. She had said all she had been instructed to say but she could not forbear some small show of wrath. "I did not expect to see you in Ireland today, my lord, or ever again."

"We are indebted to you, my lord," Isoud said, "for your relief of King Anguissh at Camelot."

"Yes," the queen said, "we are indebted to you, and we remember that."

The moment had come when he must make the formal recital

225

of his errand. He looked at Isoud, praying to see some sign, some secret of hope between them which would, even now, tell him it was possible to ask mercy in Ireland, to be received in love, to stay. But she would not help him.

"I left Cornwall as the ambassador of my uncle, King Mark," he said, and informed them how he had been shipwrecked in Wales and lost in the sea the gifts Mark had sent, and the letters. And he said how he had met King Anguissh in Camelot, and how they had journeyed, and how they had treated together in the matter of Mark's mission. "And my uncle seeks a marriage with," he said, "with the lady Isoud," he said, "as an honor to himself, and his house, and his land of Cornwall."

"We agree to this marriage," the king said, "if the queen and the lady Isoud and our barons are willing. My lady?" he asked the queen.

"I am willing," she said, her voice strangled.

"My lady?" he asked Isoud.

"I am willing."

"My lords?"

The chief counsel baron spoke. "We are willing, my lord, since Tristram has fought for you and you have sworn."

"In the name of the king of Cornwall," Tristram said, "I thank you."

So his mission was accomplished. He asked to retire, and was led, not to his old place in the hall, but to a priest's cell. And then he was free to do whatever he liked in Ireland so long as what he liked was to remove himself from the sight of the queen and Isoud.

There were days to be got through, since the queen was determined to send her daughter into Cornwall with a magnificence which would shame Mark's court. While the wives of barons and yeomen were summoned to help, while work went on in the hall and the king's shops by daylight and by lamplight, while visits were made by the lords of the south, and gifts received and packed, Tristram walked on the shore with Pickpocket or rode listlessly at dummy shields on the tournament ground. He paid

226

the goldsmith one brief visit and learned from him that the house slave whose freedom he had purchased was living on a small farm north of the harbor. He rode past the man's house and was pleased to see it snug, a well-thatched clay-and-wattle cottage. But he did not dismount and go in.

He made his appearance in the hall at meat as he was expected to do, and was received by the household with the sober courtesy agreed among them. The queen carried the cup to the guests now, he did not know whether because it was a new custom, or whether to defend Isoud against the need to speak with him each day. The queen learned, as the days passed, to bear herself with more civility toward him. And at last he seemed to be at home in the house of King Anguissh. Almost. The difference was that he knew, and everybody else knew too, that he was not at home. He did not belong to them, or they to him.

One evening his isolation overwhelmed him. The servants had carried away the food, and the lamp bowls were lit, and the men were preparing for the talk they shared of hunting and seafaring and the days when they made war. But before they had settled around the hearth a servant entered and informed them that three sailors from a French boat anchored in the harbor had come to the hall and said they were musicians, and asked whether the king would care to hear them perform.

"Yes," Anguissh said. "Give them welcome."

Though the sailors were dressed in the leather breeches and short tunics of their calling they did not seem to have altogether the habit of mariners. Tristram asked them how they happened to be musicians and crewmen at the same time.

"Because, my lord," the leader said, "we are willing the same as other men to eat our meals, and there isn't much nourishment in this." He slapped his harp. "Besides, we see the world. We have sung all the way from Byzantium to Spain, and we can give you songs in any tongue you like."

"Do you know any music of Britany?"

"Yes indeed, my lord." He tuned his harp and they began to sing. Their voices were mediocre and their melodies were common and coarse, but they performed with spirit and drew applause. When they were finished and the king had ordered them paid, Tristram called the harper to him and took the instrument into his hands.

He found his harmony and began to play. He chose a song he had taught Isoud when they had sat in the freckled shade of the ash tree. It was a whimsical song, lightly tender, gaining its effect from a set refrain whose meanings were changed by the changing sense of the verses preceding it. When he was done his hearers were silent, but it was the kind of silence Tristram had evoked before, a sort of willingness among them to believe the unbelievable, inviting more. If she hears it she will remember, he thought, and if she remembers she will speak with me.

The barons stirred from the magic in which he had held them. The king said, "We have not heard such music here since you left Ireland."

Tristram followed the musicians from the hall. "Would you part with your harp, friend?" he asked the leader.

"For what, my lord?"

"For this?" Tristram held out two gold coins.

The harper took them, tried them in his mouth, and spat them into his hand. "For those I would part with my brother, my lord."

"Get yourself another instrument," Tristram said with a smile. "The world can't spare a single harper."

"You make me want to put mine away," the man said. "Are you from Britany?"

"Yes, or from any place you like. Thanks, and God go with you, friend."

"With you."

He returned to the priest's cell but he was restless and could not bear to shut himself into the black smother of its windowless room. After a while he left it and made his way across the dark courtyard and walked in the direction of Isoud's garden. He smelled the fragrance of the hedge of thorns, and found it, and followed it to the ash tree.

"Tristram," Isoud said.

She was so near he could hear her soft breath, and he would have taken her into his arms. But she held him away.

"Don't, Tristram! I've done what I wouldn't do before—deceived the king and queen. Tristram!"

"I have thought of you every day—"

"I was followed," she said. "My woman, Bragwain, followed me." She spoke low, close to his ear. "But if I don't stay she will not tell them."

"I sang for you."

"I know, and I came. I came to tell you—"

"What?"

"I came to tell you," she began in a calmer voice, "that we must sail together into Cornwall, and that you must not sing any more, Tristram."

"You came when I sang." He took her hands. "Isoud—"

But she moved away from him. "I don't know why you chose this mission, or why—"

"I did not choose. I was—"

"—or why you must take me into Cornwall," she went on, "but I know this, Tristram. I am going because my father says you asked it as your reward and I will not see him forsworn. I couldn't if I would. But if you make it hard for me I shall—I shall—"

"Wait," he said, "I would have—"

"I shall drown myself," she said. "Good-by, Tristram. This is the last time."

"Isoud! Kiss me good-by!"

"No." She was running. He stumbled after her, and caught her, and kissed her.

She clung to him but when he let her go she said, "I shall never forgive you, Tristram."

Chapter Twenty-two

THE ship the king gave them had been altered for Isoud's comfort. Aft of the mast two benches had been decked over, and a little pavilion of dressed hides arranged in such a way that its sidepieces could be rolled up in the daytime and dropped at night. By her own choice Isoud took only one woman with her, her lady Bragwain, under whose governance she had been placed when she was a child.

They left Ireland on a day when the tide turned in the morning. The king and queen, the officers of the house, and a crowd of ladies rode down to the harbor. Many children, and all the priests, and the goldsmith hopping and trotting along, and servants who made no attempt to hide their tears gathered to wave them away and call farewells as long as their voices could be heard. Isoud stood at the gunwale, proud and queenly, waving back as the shore of her homeland diminished. Bragwain wept but the princess did not.

The boat came into the wind. Tristram heard over the chant of the oarsmen the bell of the church ringing the hour of tierce. He wondered whether King Anguissh had gone back to the great altar slab to kneel and say prayers for Isoud's happiness. With the bell echoing softly across the water he tried to pray for her and for himself too, and to ask God to shorten their journey and give them a speedy parting. But his prayer was empty of meaning.

Sea gulls followed them, flying along at the height of the mast in the stupid, sedate way of their kind when they police the strange conveyances of human animals. Tristram could see Isoud watching them, even smiling at their deliberate flight or at their expressionless eyes, or perhaps to encourage them. Should he speak with her? She had said he must not trouble her, but surely if they were to spend the days together in anything like endurance they could not behave as though each was alone in the boat. Besides, he longed to stand by her, to see her hair blowing and the sun on her smooth cheek.

"Isoud."

"My lord?"

"Let me be Tristram for a few days more," he said. "Are you afraid to call me Tristram?"

"No."

"Or Tramtris. I was happy when I was Tramtris."

"I wish to go to the pavilion," she said.

"Shall I go with you and roll up the sides?"

"A sailor will do that, my—Tristram."

"Have you ever been to sea before, Isoud?"

"Only in small boats along the coast."

"Let us go to the pavilion, and I'll tell you about the sea."

He would have helped her over the benches, but she moved quickly before him, suiting her body to the quiet progress of the ship. She called a sailor to raise the curtains. Tristram sat on the boards near her. He spoke of the coasts of Britany, and told her of the rocks standing offshore as big as castles, in shapes so strange they filled men's minds with fantasy. And he recounted the stories fisherfolk invented to explain these massive stones, and of the magic and mystery people who dealt with the sea believed in. He described the sailors who came into the ports of Britany, and told her of their black skins and their outlandish manners, and of the forays they made to rob men abroad near the harbor at night, and of their gift for drunkenness. He won smiles from her, and then laughter, and at last talk.

They were burdened with so much they could not speak that indifferent talk eased them. The day passed better than they

231

dreamed it could. When the sun was riding, cut in two, on the western water, and long, moving trails of gold and purple and scarlet lay on the sea, they looked into each other's eyes almost as friends, weary with so much talk but stirred and teased too. After they had eaten they would have begun again, but suddenly they were hollow and cold and full of despair.

At the end of a shivering silence Isoud said, "Tell me about King Mark."

"He is handsome."

"Young?"

"Your father knows him," Tristram said. "He has told you, hasn't he?"

"I want to hear you tell me. Is he young?"

"Isoud!"

"Tell me," she said. "How old is King Mark?"

"I don't know."

"I know," she said. "He is forty-one."

Silence.

"Forty-one is very old," she said. "He is older than my father. Why wouldn't you tell me he was old, Tristram?"

"I don't want to talk of him."

"Why?" she said wonderingly. "He is your uncle, and he is handsome."

Tristram scrambled to his feet. "Good night, Isoud."

"Tristram!"

"What is it?"

"When I am married I shall learn to love King Mark."

He sprang off the deck of the pavilion and went forward. Gouvernail was lying under the gunwale already wrapped in his cloak. I shall play my harp, Tristram thought, and punish her. I will punish her! He sank down, trembling.

In the morning she asked him how he had slept.

"As well as a person ever sleeps on a boat, I suppose."

"I didn't sleep, Tristram. I was sorry I had been cruel, and I wished to tell you so."

"You weren't cruel, Isoud."

232

"I don't know why," she said, "but I feel angry because you slept and I didn't."

"I didn't sleep either. I followed our course by the stars and wondered whether you could read the sky, and I thought I would like to show you, if you couldn't."

She gave him an uncertain smile. "Let us be friends today, Tristram."

But they were restless. The boat confined them, and the presence of Gouvernail and Bragwain robbed them of the dear intimacy which, though they had sworn in a moment of extreme purpose to avoid it, they desired. And now they could not speak together without reminding each other of their wretchedness. All subjects were dangerous, their lives before they met because they lived in ignorance of their meeting, and the time after because the meeting had overtaken them. When the sun passed midday and began to decline they were divided by a silence so full of pain they wished nothing save to escape it. Isoud retired to the pavilion and ordered the curtains closed.

The sea was flat and oily with heat. The sail hung slack. All the oarsmen were at their blades, pulling to a grunted rhythm. They were stripped to the waist, and the sweat ran down their backs and dried on the benches in salty stains. Tristram sought Gouvernail.

"If the wind doesn't freshen we won't reach Tintagel tomorrow," he said.

"It will freshen," Gouvernail told him.

"You know everything," Tristram said. "How can you be sure it will freshen?"

"Look at the west. You can see for yourself."

"I've never been this hot."

"It isn't bad," Gouvernail said reasonably. "The morning was cool, and it will be cool again this evening. It will probably rain by dusk."

"All weather is the same to you, isn't it, Gouvernail?"

The squire returned no answer. He said, "I'm afraid the princess suffers in the closed pavilion."

233

Tristram was already troubled enough by the thought of Isoud under the baking curtains, troubled because she had gone there to escape him and all the nearing unhappiness of Cornwall. She had not eaten the cheese and wine offered her by Bragwain at midday, and light shadows had lain under her eyes. Had the sea given her a sickness to deepen her misery?

He called her. "Isoud."

"What is it, Tristram?"

"Are you ill?"

"Wait," she said, "I'll come out." She pushed aside the curtains and stepped down into the boat. The heat had given her a high, soft color, all roses, like a just-awakened child. "Bragwain is asleep. It is cooler, isn't it?"

"A little. There's a breeze coming up from the west. Gouvernail thinks it will rain."

"Oh," she said, "I don't want it to rain while we are on the sea!"

"Come here, Isoud." They went to the side and leaned on their arms and looked down into the clean water. White crests broke away from the oars, and the blue depths were streaked with broken green and pale gold reflections of sun. They could smell the salt refreshing as dew to their fevered minds. "I love you," Tristram said.

"I know."

"I shall go into Britany."

"My father told me."

"Do you want me to go, Isoud?"

She was silent.

"Tell me what you are thinking."

"I am thinking I am thirsty. Look, Tristram!" And she pointed to a school of porpoises playing off the port side. "Aren't they beautiful, the way they're all the same size and keep the same distance apart?"

"How can anything with such a snout be beautiful!" he said, angry. "Fishermen call them hogfish."

"They're not the least like hogs," Isoud said, as though she had been elected to teach him the nature of porpoises. "They're so fast and clean and such a lovely color. Fishermen only give them that name because they don't care how beautiful anything is, only if it can be eaten."

"You are more interested in hogfish than you are in me."

"If you call them that," she said, her voice furious, "I shall stay in the pavilion until we reach Tintagel."

"What difference does it make whether I call them hogfish or—"

"Tristram!"

"Or porpoises?"

She turned away from him and gazed into the water curling back from the prow in an immaculate ruff of foam. "It looks so cool," she said peacefully. "I wish we were swimming."

"Why did you speak of Tintagel?"

"We must remember it. We are going there."

"Tell me what you want, Isoud."

"I think I want a drink," she said. "Aren't you thirsty, Tristram?"

"All right," he said, knowing he was defeated, "I'll fetch you wine."

"My mother gave Bragwain a little gold flacket of wine the morning we left. Bragwain has kept it hidden in her linens."

"Why?"

"I think it is the best wine from the wine cave, and my mother probably meant it for a help in case I wept. But I don't weep," she said lightly.

They looked into each other's eyes. "Where is the flacket?" Tristram asked her.

"In the oxhide chest, the one bound with bronze."

"Wait for me."

"Be careful," she warned him. "Bragwain may be awake."

He moved toward the pavilion and softly lifted the curtain. The heat within met him in a stifling gust. He could discern Bragwain lying on her couch, her mouth open. Asleep, she looked diminished, pitiful. But Tristram was in no mood to appreciate her discomfort, or the courage with which she was leaving her home and going into a foreign land.

The chest stood at the foot of her couch, its bronze hasps fastened with thongs. He eased his knife from its sheath and cut the leather ties and raised the lid. Pressing the fresh linens he felt the shape of the flacket, and reached among the folded garments, and found it. He rose as quietly as a shade and stepped backwards and pushed clear of the curtains.

The flacket and another object were wrapped in fine linen embroidered with spirals in threads of scarlet and gold. When Tristram laid back the cloth he saw a small vessel, all bright gold, around its narrowing throat two ribbon lacings of enamel, blue and green. A cup matched it, as though the two objects formed a ceremonial pair. They were wrought with the simplicity he had learned to love in Ireland, and as he gazed at them their beauty subdued him, as well as the mysterious sense of significance they owned.

"Did the smith make these?" he asked Isoud.

"I don't know. They belonged to my mother. Give them to me, Tristram."

He put the cup into her hands.

"Did you disturb Bragwain?"

"I don't think so." He still studied the flacket. "I think this must hold something precious, Isoud. Are you sure it is wine?"

"Yes, yes," she said. "Let us hurry, before Bragwain wakes and finds we have taken it." She held out the cup. "Drink first, Tristram."

"If it isn't wine I shall know." He raised the golden vessel and filled the cup, and took it from her, and drank.

"Is it wine?" she demanded.

He did not answer, savoring a flavor so delicate, so pure, yet so heady it seemed to reach his heart and blow upon it, like cool air.

She seized his arm. "Is it wine, Tristram? Give it to me!"

"It is wine, but—"

Isoud drank. "Oh, isn't it fresh and soft!"

236

"Shall I put the things back?"

"No, keep the flacket, and I shall keep the cup. And we shall remember today when we drank together."

The wine, or the fact they had conspired to drink it, restored their spirits and cleansed them of the fitfulness which had made them worry and pry at each other's peace of mind. They smiled together, laughed, dared to touch shoulders and hands as though by some delicious accident. For a little space the shadow of Tintagel cliff was lifted, and they felt only reckless joy.

"Sing for me," Isoud said.

"I'll play the harp, and you sing."

"No," she said, "I want to hear the song about King Arthur, the one you sang for my father."

"Did you know I saw King Arthur, and spoke with him when I was in Camelot at Pentecost?"

"What is he like? Is he strong and young? Is he as serious as men say, and as beautiful?"

"He is strong and serious," Tristram told her, "but he is not young and I do not believe I would call him beautiful."

"You know what I mean by beautiful!"

"I can't guess."

"I mean," she said, looking at him, "is he as tall as you, and is his color fair, and does he wait when he speaks to draw breath and then raise his eyebrows a little, as though he meant to let his words show in his eyes?"

Tristram laughed. "He doesn't do any of that. He just speaks straight out, like a captain."

"Is he tall?"

"Tall and thick," Tristram said, remembering the king now as clearly as if he had seen him an hour before, and the Round Table brotherhood, and all the glory of Camelot. As it came back to him he told her of the day he had spent, and how he fought Palamides for the second time and wounded him, and how he had stood before Arthur, and how Arthur had risen and said, "Well done, Tristram," and how he rode to the castle and saw the knights go each to his chair upon whose back his name was carved in gilded letters. He told her of the bishop who said the grace before meat, and of the knights rising to relate what they had done in the year past, and of how he had seen his own father, King Meliodas.

"Was King Meliodas proud that you had won against Palamides?" she asked.

"I don't know."

"What did he say?"

"He said, 'Well Tristram,' and I said, 'My lord,' and he said, 'I hear you have become a champion,' and I said—I had to say something, you know—I said, 'I have done what I could, my lord,' and he said—"

"If I had been your father," Isoud said, "I would have taken you by the shoulders the way my father does a man he is proud of, and I would have cried before them all, 'This is my son.' "

"King Meliodas and I are strangers," Tristram said. "When we saw each other I was surprised—he was too—to realize we are of one blood."

"Do you think of him?"

"Sometimes. Not often."

"Let us not talk of him," Isoud said. "Bring your harp and sing me the song about King Arthur."

"Look, Isoud." Tristram pointed to the west. "Gouvernail was wrong. This will be a clear evening."

"Is it our last?"

"Yes."

"Sing now, Tristram."

Tristram took his harp and tightened the strings and sang the song Isoud had asked. The sun was low, its light lying almost level on the western sea, falling upon Isoud in warm gold. The last evening. But it could not be the last for them unless it were also the last evening of the world. If it could be that! If this twilight would never dim into night, if the ship might ride the long swells forever! Tristram changed the chords at the end of the song toward the harmony of the melody he had taught her under the ash tree. He saw her hear, turn her head, look at him, lips parted.

238

And then behind her he saw the curtains of the pavilion thrust aside, and Bragwain appear, all disordered, her cheek still creased with the marks of sleep.

"Isoud!" she cried. "My lady!"

Isoud sprang up. "What ails you, Bragwain?"

"The flacket is gone!"

"I know. I took it."

The woman clutched her by the elbows. "Did you drink?"

Isoud pulled herself free. "Don't make such a noise, Bragwain. I drank it. What of it?"

"I took it," Tristram said. "We drank the wine together. You will not be blamed, Bragwain. The flacket and cup are safe."

"They are nothing! The flacket and cup are nothing!" The woman moaned and hugged her body. "It was the wine!"

"What about the wine?" Tristram said.

"The queen will have me disgraced!" Bragwain was grey with fright. "She will make me an exile! She trusted the wine to me, and now—"

"What is this wine?" Tristram rose and took her gently by the shoulders. "Come, Bragwain, we won't let you be made an exile. Tell us."

"Oh, my lord, the wine was a philtre!"

"A philtre! Poisoned?"

"No, no, not poisoned. The queen medicined it with her own hands. She made it for Isoud to drink with King Mark on their wedding night."

"A love philtre!"

"Tristram," Isoud said.

"Don't let it frighten you, Isoud. Bragwain only repeats what the queen told her. But these old things, these spells, they aren't —we needn't—"

"You don't believe it?"

A will to believe rushed through him. If the wine truly owned some unnatural power beyond resistance it would free him, free them both, from the suffocating prison of their consciences. He stood before her remembering what he had sworn to do, remem-

239

bering as well that though he loved her more than any trifling philtre could enforce she had never said she loved him. He must choose.

"Do you believe?" she said.

"We offend God with such things."

A felicity had taken her clearer than the westering light glowing upon her beauty. She was all one radiance, one grace, one high, assenting faith. "I believe," she said.

Bragwain covered her face with her scarf and wept.

"Do you believe this philtre is God's will, Isoud?" Tristram said.

"I believe it is too late to wonder what it is."

"It is too late," Bragwain sobbed.

"Do you love me, Isoud?"

"Yes."

"Before today?"

"Since the first day in Ireland."

Bragwain rose and, blind with tears, staggered toward the pavilion. "God help them!" she was crying. "God pity them!"

Chapter Twenty-three

THE night did not clear as Tristram thought it might. A warm, wet wind carried mist which was too thin to settle on the water as fog. But it muffled the starlight and created a dark as dense and oppressive as a cave. Tristram lay under the gunwale and listened to the sail straining at its lines and to the regular thrust of the oars driving the ship into Cornwall. Because the wind was favorable only four crewmen were rowing, and if the breeze strengthened even they would be allowed to sleep. As he harkened to the ship speeding through the heavy night he thought of the oarsmen and how they were moving him and Isoud upon a future to which they were indifferent. They wielded their blades for pay, and it was all the same to them whether their freight was dead things or whether it lived and suffered confusion enough to founder the boat, if human feelings could be assessed, like grain or earthenware, on balance and scale.

But whatever thoughts he started, his mind returned to the golden flacket and the wine Bragwain believed, and Isoud too, was a spell to tie him and the princess of Ireland together forever. The queen had given it a fatality beyond evasion or revoke, or they were convinced she had. And like the sailors, the potion was the indifferent instrument of whatever will had the affairs of men in its hand. God's will? Tristram did not believe the drugged wine was God's will. But perhaps God's will was in it. For hadn't Isoud admitted—free to say her heart by reason of the release

241

the potion gave her silence—that she had loved him since the day his little ship floated into the harbor? Hadn't God intended that they love each other? Or was God Himself, like the sailors and the wine, indifferent?

Tristram was haunted by much he had heard and seen of magic, by the possibility that he had himself once been poisoned with an enchantment, by the shadowy forces in his own mother's death, by the stories he had listened to sailors and farmers tell, by the lamb he had unearthed under the great stones in Wales. He remembered the seahorse in the church at Lyonesse and the crossroad shrines with their offerings of fruit and barley. And it came over him that he should have known by now what he believed of these things, and how truth was to be separated from the fears and false hopes which made lies.

He should know, but he didn't. He should be able to think wisely, but he wasn't. For potion or no potion Isoud loved and desired him as he loved and desired her. And that was a miracle, a true miracle, a beautiful one, and it carried with it, like a wave sweeping in unbroken from the sea, such a force it did not matter where the force had gathered itself or upon what desert headland it would be spent. This force flooded him with wild happiness. He could no longer lie still and sift his thoughts like so much arid sand.

He rose and crept along the boat's side.

"Wait, Tristram." Gouvernail spoke close to his ear.

"What is it, man?"

"Where are you going?"

"For a walk," Tristram said. "Where would I be going on a boat in the middle of the sea?"

"Can I do anything for you?"

Tristram was ashamed of his surly answer. "Thanks, but I'm only tired of the water and darkness."

"It is hard to sleep after what Bragwain told us," the squire said. "And I have prayed this heathen business of the philtre wouldn't weigh with you, Tristram."

"Bragwain thinks it is too late for prayers."

242

"Bragwain is a lady who does not have to decide what must be done," Gouvernail said, polite even in the dark, whispering. "But it is not so easy for you to say too late. I supposed you were awake making a plan. What will you do?"

"Take the princess into Britany with me if she will go."

"And ask King Hoël to receive you?"

"Who else?" Tristram said. "I am welcome with King Hoël."

"Yes, he would receive you," Gouvernail said slowly.

"He would receive me. But what? You have a 'but' in your thoughts, Gouvernail."

"Nothing that hasn't already been in your thoughts, Tristram."

"You believe my uncle will follow us and make war against Hoël."

"King Anguissh will follow you as well."

"I believe it too," Tristram said. "I know I can't ask Hoël to receive us unless I am willing to raise a war against him. And I cannot take Isoud into Lyonesse, even if I were welcome there, for the same reason. I cannot send her back to Ireland without shaming her, and shaming Mark, and shaming my own knighthood." He clenched his hands and pressed the knuckles together. "I know. But in the dark I gave myself a little ease imagining some land in the world would trust us and take us in."

"Ah, Tristram!"

"Unless we die on the sea," he said, "it must be fought out somewhere. And so it had better be fought out in Cornwall."

"How can it be fought out?" said Gouvernail, grief-stricken. "Will you battle single-handed against the armies of two kings?"

"I don't know what I shall do. Tell me what you would do if you were Tristram."

"I suppose I would do less than Tristram," Gouvernail said. "I suppose I would take the princess to King Mark and then go to Britany alone."

"The princess does not love you."

"That is true, Tristram, and if she did I would be a different man. I know it is easier for me to see reason than you. But you have only one life, my dear lord, and you can lose it between dark and daylight. And then it won't matter that a princess loves you."

Tristram was silent, touching for one terribly clear moment the coldness of death.

Gouvernail let the silence run on as they stood together in the smothering dark and felt the strengthening wind pull at their clothes and heard the sea hiss away in a high wake as the senseless prow cut forward. The boat seemed a frail, small thing to him, and himself small and frail, and Tristram too, in the mighty swing of the sky and the water and the wind and all things of earth and air moving around and past them. At last he said, "You have risked your life in just causes before now, Tristram. Perhaps there's a glory when you can risk your life. But sometimes a man may have to be humble enough to serve justice with less than his life."

"Justice is words," Tristram said. "It is something to give lustre to a quarrel. Justice is the dress one side wears to fight the dress the other side wears."

"Perhaps," Gouvernail said. It occurred to him to tell Tristram justice was not the putting on of a fancy costume, like a mummer, or even the truth of opposing sides of a cause, rather it was patience and a way of living. But he understood that his lord was, at least for the present, beyond appeal. Could he be blamed, standing only a few short strides away from a lady as young and fair as the princess? The time for reason might come. It had not come tonight. "I think I'll go back and lie down again," he said. "God keep you, Tristram."

"And you, brother." Tristram pu a hand on his shoulder and held him a moment, wishing to say a healing word, but he could not.

He was moved by his squire's entreaty. He thought of death, trying to accept the fact that it could be the payment of his love for Isoud. But because he had met death boldly and escaped it he was not able to believe it could take him. He might make new enemies to add to his old ones, yet what enemy could be more ferocious than The Marhaus, or more passionate than Palamides, or more hidden and crafty than Andret? Let his enemies multiply. He would deal with them joyfully.

As for justice—well—he had not said to Gouvernail all there was to be said of justice. It might be that justice was only words. Nothing was clear, even now, in his fight with The Marhaus. And like enough Palamides thought of Tristram as the most unjust of men, and Andret too. Justice could not be weighed in this dispute or that like so many ounces of salt. All the same, it moved inside a man, and knew whether it had been served or denied. In the end justice was not how he answered others but how he answered himself. He was pledged as a true knight to bring Isoud to Cornwall, to yield her to Mark, and to go into Britany. He had two simple choices: to keep his word, or to break it. How was he to answer himself on these?

Needing God's help he tried to pray, even drew his dagger and held its hilt as he might cling to the Cross. God, I desire to be a good knight and uphold my sworn promise, but—

Oh, God, I love Isoud and she loves me, and we have not schemed to lie to King Auguissh and to cheat King Mark, but—

Could You not give us our happiness? If You can't, if You will not, then strengthen me, but—

He pressed the dagger hilt to his forehead and felt its cold metal like a wound.

If I may speak with her once more alone tonight, then tomorrow I shall bring her to Cornwall, and find a ship to Britany.

The resolve taken, he put his dagger away. He became aware that the wind had increased and that the boat was running swiftly, pitching a little in the swells. Spray was blowing, torn from the crests of waves he could not see. As he stood by the ship's side waiting for Isoud, half-convinced she would rise and come straight to him now his bargain had been made, he felt a change in the rhythm of their progress and realized the diminished crew had shipped its oars. That meant the wind was heavy enough in the sail to carry them, and that the sailors would roll themselves in their blankets and snatch what sleep they could under their benches. The course would be left to the helmsman.

245

Perhaps this wind was an answer to his prayer to see Isoud once more alone.

He waited, giving the oarsmen time to fall asleep. He knew the black night would conceal him from the helmsman. He stole aft, slipping over the benches with a cat's caution so as not to step on a sleeping man's hand and rouse him, and start gossip which would cast an ugly slur upon Isoud. He reached the pavilion and crawled along the wooden deck and knelt by the curtain behind which he knew Isoud's couch to lie.

Call her? He listened, hoping to hear a sound which would tell him she was awake. The thought of her so near, so soft with sleep, thickened the breath in his throat. He whispered her name. "Isoud!"

He waited in a silence made heavy by the loud drum of his heart. She had not heard. Or she had heard and not answered, willing him to go away.

He felt her touch the curtain. He pressed his hand to hers. "Isoud! Come out!"

She withdrew her hand. If God was on their side she was rising, moving in the dark as still as a shadow's shadow, assuring herself Bragwain slept. He felt the curtain stir and part.

"Where are you?" she whispered.

He caught her hand and drew her down onto the deck. "I was afraid you wouldn't come to me, Isoud."

"Why were you afraid?"

"Because of tomorrow."

"This is tonight."

"We have only tonight." He took her into his arm. "I've been praying," he said, his lips against her cheek, "to be strong enough to leave you tomorrow."

"You must never leave me," she said.

"I am sworn."

"That is past." She folded her hands around his and lifted it to her mouth and whispered against it as he had whispered against her cheek. "Nothing we have sworn is as strong as the wine we drank."

246

"I did not need the wine."

"I did not need it either. But we drank it. And now it has sworn us to each other as long as we live."

Her hair, unbound, fell over his hand, its light curls slipping between his fingers. "Even when I can't see you, you are beautiful."

"You are beautiful too, Tristram."

"It is foolish to say a man is beautiful."

"When I said how King Arthur looked, I meant you."

"Oh, I love you!"

"Love me now."

"I do love you now."

"I mean," she said, "I am yours. Now."

"Here?"

She kissed him. He could feel the pulse in her throat, all her sweetness close, fervid, so warm, so fresh! "I have never kissed anyone before, Tristram."

"Never kiss anyone but me."

"I shall never love anyone but you."

"Tomorrow—"

"But it is tonight." She spoke with her soft mouth upon his. "We must ask God to marry us tonight."

"How can we ask God to marry us?"

"I shall ask Him." She moved away from him. "Take my hand, Tristram. God," she whispered into the blowing air, "look on us, Tristram and Isoud, and bless our marriage. Amen. Now we are married, Tristram."

In this way their faith was made by whatever God held them in His care, the One Isoud prayed to, or the one her mother invoked when she brewed the potion. Their wedding bed was the bare deck, their cover the wind hastening them to Cornwall. When they had loved and slept a little and turned to each other with proud joy, when they had kissed again and whispered promises and vowed never to leave each other as long as life lasted, Tristram said, "It will be morning soon."

"How can you be wise enough in this blackness," she said, "to know when it will be morning?"

247

"I can smell morning air in the wind. I must leave you before the oarsmen waken."

"Wait," she said.

"Isoud," he said, "come with me into Britany."

"I can't."

"Why?"

"You know why—because it will make a war."

"There is no land where we can go without war. But we must go to some land."

"Cornwall," she said.

"No. What can we do?"

"Only what we have done."

"I will not give you to Mark."

"Hush," she said, "my Tristram. I have never seen Mark, and I shall never love him. But we must keep peace between our two countries. My dear lord," she said, "if we could have done anything in the world but this, we would have. It must be this or it must be nothing. And I could not live if it were nothing." She put her head on his breast and stretched her arm across his body.

Tristram lay beside her knowing that in another moment he must leave her, knowing too that she was right, that nowhere in the world was a hall, a cottage even, a cave in the forest, which would shelter them deeply enough to protect them. His spirit had already beat itself senseless against this knowledge, not only now in the ship, but for a year past, ever since the queen had run upon him with his sword. He thought one last hopeless time of Britany, wringing his brain to see a shift he had overlooked, some frail, final chance that they could claim Hoël's friendship without destroying him. Not Britany, not anywhere.

"When we feel we can't bear our lives," Isoud said, "we must remember each other, Tristram. Promise me you will remember."

"Forever," he said.

"Kiss me good-by."

"Good-by, my lovely Isoud."

"It is only for a little while," she comforted him.

He waited until she was safely within the pavilion, then he returned to the forward part of the ship as he had come down it, creeping with the silence of an animal. He could not guess whether Gouvernail slept or whether he had seen or surmised his absence. But he could not think of Gouvernail or of anything except Isoud, and that she was his, even desperately and with peril.

Chapter Twenty-four

THEY sailed into the shallow harbor below Tintagel head about noon. Because they were not expected no party had come down to welcome them. Tristram sent a sailor up the cliff road to inform the king of their arrival and to ask for horses and a guard of knights to bring Isoud to the hall. As they waited he sat in the opened pavilion with her, and so did Gouvernail and Bragwain, the four of them clinging together as though they might somehow protect the secret of the wine more closely if they did not separate.

He played the harp and sang so as to relieve them of the need to fill the dragging time with talk. Isoud was self-possessed, leaning back in a quiet pose, her hands in her lap. It seemed to Tristram that between twilight and morning her fairness had grown and opened as a fresh flower opens, and he wondered whether Gouvernail and Bragwain discerned upon her this new beauty of love. He could not read Gouvernail who had the gift of hiding his thoughts. But Bragwain was an easy lesson. Her face was haggard and swollen with tears, and her thoughts were still so turned upon yesterday's deed that she could hardly answer when she was spoken to. She could have served them better—herself too—with some small show of fortitude. For what did regret accomplish now?

The time for regret was past even as the time for turning back was past. We have done what we could, Isoud said, it must be this or nothing, she said. Mixed with his unrepentant joy in the love they had loved Tristram felt a sombre relief. He had lived in doubt and grief for a year, cleaving to his knighthood and at the same time desiring what would soil it. It was soiled. And he was hardly surprised to discover, as he played his harp and waited for the king's messengers, how little it mattered. This morning at last we are what we are, Isoud and I, he thought, each the other's. And for that truth room must be made.

Yet this new firmness of soul which had risen within him almost unsummoned faltered when he came before the king. It had been possible when he was fighting pirates and pushing through forests and trading blows with Palamides, when he had been holding, against obstacles, to his purpose as his uncle's ambassador, to forget Mark's dark elegance and his power in Cornwall over his life and Isoud's. But face to face with the king Tristram's jealousy swelled in fierce anger. What was to prevent him from putting his hands about the throat of this little, spry, grinning, talking man and squeezing out his foolish life?

One thing prevented him, which was that he had been trained by King Hoël and by the two years passed since he left Hoël's house to command himself. He said, "My lord, I was delayed on my journey into Ireland."

"I heard of the piracy when your ship returned," Mark said, "and we have sent crews to look for the men who attacked you. A half dozen of my knights are still in Wales searching for you."

"But I reached Ireland," Tristram said, "though I might have been prevented."

"I thank God you are safe, Tristram." Mark rose and took him affectionately by the arms. "I must learn to stop worrying about your safety, nephew. You own a gift for making bad fortune work for you."

"I have," Tristram said, swallowing the thickness in his throat, "I have brought the Princess Isoud into Cornwall, my lord."

"Your runner told me. I could wish we had had more time to prepare for her."

"Will you receive the princess now?"

"I shall wait on her wish."

251

"She is in the church," Tristram said. "She expects you."

"Lead the way, Tristram."

"Her woman, the lady Bragwain, is with her. They desired to give thanks for a safe voyage. It would be fitting for you to go alone and welcome her to Cornwall."

"As you think best." Mark uttered his light, self-conscious laugh. "You know the princess, and I do not. You think she would rather I came alone?"

"I am sure of it," Tristram said fervently.

"I owe you my thanks, Tristram. When the time comes you must tell me what reward you will take for the dangers you've suffered on this mission."

"When the time comes. My lord."

"Yes?"

"Where is Andret?"

"He is with the knights searching for you. He was concerned for your life, Tristram. The sailors could tell us nothing about you except how you had jumped into the sea. We feared you were drowned."

Tristram could not resist a thrust at the seneschal. "Is Andret swimming in the waters of Wales looking for me?"

The king took it as a joke and laughed and swore he would tell Andret what Tristram had said. He went off still chuckling and grimacing, and Tristram wondered whether he had not been more moved by a foolish jest than by the fact that the loveliest woman in the world waited for him.

He had no desire to see Isoud's return from the church. He called a servant and ordered his horse saddled, and rode south until he reached the yellow sand beach from which he had sailed to fight The Marhaus. There he bathed in the sea, and afterwards lay under the shadow of a rock and watched the tide come in, and thought of what his life must be.

He must learn to foresee danger to himself and Isoud before danger became a reality. And that meant he must remember Andret as he would remember a brother, for Andret, having conspired once, would conspire again. And he would seek the weak place, the unguarded place, in Tristram's situation at court. Tris-tram knew he was vulnerable as he had not been before Isoud's coming. I must send for Dinadan, he thought. And I must get into this unhandsome game of politics, and know more, if I can, than anybody else knows.

Yet under this cool assessment lay something headlong which did not wish to be ruled by wisdom. Whatever was necessary to shield Isoud, more urgent than anything was their need to meet, to restore their love against the separation and the rebellion and the pain Isoud's marriage must bring. Tristram dug his hands into the sand as he realized how their high faith would become a thing of snatched moments, of hideous deceits and concealments, of long schemings and frustrations. No! It was intolerable to sub-mit their joy to what was mean, vulgar, deformed! Isoud's sov-ereign fairness, his own knighthood, these precious essences which sustained them in the vast, indifferent void of the world, must not be nibbled away through a hundred humiliating lies!

They must meet, but truthfully, even if their truth was only a secret between them. He would find a place of meeting and a means which would not smirch and belittle them. He wondered whether he could build a pavilion in the woods so well hidden the king's foresters would not find it. He could not, he knew it well enough. Make a friend who would protect them in his hall? That was impossible in a court pulling this way and that for gain, one side against the other. Bribe a farmer or herdsman? No, for even if he could find a man brave enough to risk treachery against the king, Isoud would be open to the gossip of the cottage women, even the heedless chatter of children. No plan was large enough for another person in it.

Tristram sat up and stared at the moving sea. To the north and south the cliffs rose above the tiny beach, and against them the water flung itself, incoming breakers hurling into foam-streaked masses beating back from the rocks and crevasses upon which they had shattered. Great jets exploded upward and fell like waterfalls. But beyond the tumult of the shore the purple surface stretched away to the west, a quiet plain above which gulls wheeled, silver

253

when the sun took them, black when they flew against it. Could a man somehow make head against the crashing surf and reach the blue, and ride it like the peaceful gulls? Or was the blue an illusion, perhaps the illusion of death that followed life? It was only yesterday that he and Isoud had been cradled on the sea's breast, half ready to believe they need reach no destination beyond its limitless stillness. And then they had drunk the wine and learned the pause that lulled them between one shore and another was only the moment in which the future gathers itself. The cup they shared had put an end to all drifting, to all pause, to all lingering between headland and headland upon whose sides the surf broke in thunder. The cup was as wide as the sea, it was the sea, its peace a dream, its horizon the very name of peril.

He rose and mounted his horse and rode landward. As he approached Tintagel he could not prevent his thoughts from returning to Isoud's encounter with King Mark. She would be grave, courteous, her strength of soul beyond any show of dislike or surprise. But her heart would clench itself within her breast and draw from her face the warm tints of rose and scarlet. He had seen her pale this way twice, the first time at the door of the bathing chamber, and again when he stood before her as King Mark's ambassador. Oh, he knew! She would walk beside the king lightly, so straight and slender, her small feet carrying her with grace, the sun on her hair, everything about her luminous, defined, tenderly beautiful, so that no one who saw her would guess the leaden grief she carried. She was the queen of all queens, Isoud of Ireland, the nobler, the more royal the more she was beleaguered. But Mark would not understand this. His wit was too frivolous to read the first letter of her truth. His hungry stare would see only that she was a woman, a young one, well-made, promising—

Tristram struck his horse and felt it leap forward. I cannot endure what I must endure, he thought. I will not stay in Cornwall and see Isoud married to King Mark. As his mind ran this way and that hunting for escape he thought of Dinadan. He would ride to Camelot himself, and tell Dinadan the outcome of his journey into Ireland. They would delay their return to Tintagel until the days of preparation were over, and the marriage, and the month of feasting and games. Isoud must wish it even as he.

Yet he must be sure Isoud wished it, for his only reason for life was to serve her. If she was frightened and lonely, if she felt herself without friends, if she asked him to stay, he would stay. He would find a way this very day to learn her desire.

He did not turn into the road that led across the causeway to Tintagel head. His purpose led him north for a little way, through the forest along the cliff which thinned out, to the left, in a strip of wind-worried gorse and fern. He avoided this half-open ground, keeping among the trees, hearing the sea now as a heavy murmur, sometimes even as a breathless silence when the inrushing waves were gathering themselves before they broke. He let his horse pick its own way through brush and fallen timber, only guiding it.

Presently the cliff curved in and lost height. Tristram watched for landmarks, making sure he knew the point at which he wished to turn away from the sea. He brought the horse down a slope so steep he dismounted and walked beside it, starting a rock now and then and watching it bound before him and bury itself in the leaves of years forming a springy cover over the ground. They were descending into a pinched glen through which a stream was flowing, its edges green with hart's-tongue ferns and the broad-leaved plants thriving on dampness. The cool freshness here seemed uninfluenced by sea mist and salt air, having the mossy smell of sweet water.

Tristram followed the stream, riding sometimes, sometimes walking. The trees were below the wind and seemed to stand in stillness as in the element they were meant to inhabit. They were thick enough to allow only gleams and flickers of sun, now and then pressing him so close his horse could only move forward in the stream itself. But after a while the ravine opened and became flatter, and the brook broadened, though it still ran swiftly. Tristram could hear the sound of a waterfall.

He had come out just where he wished to be. He dismounted and tied his horse and scrambled down the precipice over which the stream fell. Yes, he remembered. He had found this waterfall one day when he had outrun the members of the king's hunt, and now he was glad his delight in its great, pouring slide, all mottled with sun, and its backlash foaming almost as high as his head had prompted him to keep it a secret. Trees met above it, and the moss on the rocks sparkled with the mist flung upon them by the backlash. But today he had no mind to think of its beauty, or of the speckled sun which jewelled it, or of the dripping ferns, or of the pulseless roar of its fall. He was forcing his way through the undergrowth right into the edge of the down-slipping water. It was as he thought. Behind the fall a narrow path could be followed. And the path led into a cave.

He stepped within. A pale, watery glow lit the interior so that he could see it was clothed in moss, even a few yellowish ferns. Light entered not alone through the waterfall, but from a narrow hole near its top. He thrust his head and shoulders into the hole and saw it was a sort of natural tunnel opening into the underbrush of fern and bracken. He turned back to the cave, edged along the path, and emerged into the forest. He had found a little, perfect room, its air sweet, its floor a velvet of moss. And it was hidden as though by the merciful hand of God Himself. Isoud could come here and be safe. Not only safe. She would be attended by the forest's friendliness, the tall, screening trees, the clean ferns and kind moss. Birds would make her music, and her jewels would be the small flowers of pink and blue, and the splendid butterflies.

He stood by the waterfall a moment dreaming of her, the queen of this new kingdom. Something pure and silent in the forest, a breath that seemed to come from a better place than earth, comforted him. For his love and Isoud's he desired what was fair, what was spotless. And in the cave behind the waterfall he felt he had found it.

Chapter Twenty-five

WHEN Tristram returned to Tintagel he learned from Gouvernail that the king had sent for him.

"Why?" he asked his squire.

"I don't know," Gouvernail said. "He doesn't take me into his confidence, Tristram. But I think it has to do with his plans for the marriage."

"Let him make the plans."

"Do you mean to quarrel with him?"

"No," Tristram said, too weary to object to Gouvernail's good sense. "I don't mean to quarrel with him. But we've had hard shift for the last month on land and on sea, and I have no mind to talk—with Mark or anyone else."

Gouvernail was silent.

"You want to know where we're going," Tristram went on. "I have given up the idea of Britany. In the morning I shall start for Camelot to find Dinadan and bring him home. I'm better out of Cornwall while the feast days are held." After a pause he added, "Where is the princess?"

"In the women's quarters."

"Has she asked for me?"

"Not that I know."

"Do something for me, Gouvernail. Speak with Bragwain and learn whether Isoud wishes me to stay in Tintagel for—while —when—"

"For the marriage?"

"Yes."

The squire nodded without words. "The king expects you, Tristram. He is in the chamber by the hall."

"I am going." He wondered a little why Gouvernail had raised no question over his abandonment of his promise to King Anguissh to go into Britany. Perhaps Gouvernail believed in the magic of the wine too, or perhaps, Tristram thought, he knows I can't keep the promise and has given up hoping I shall. His exhausted spirit recoiled from any more consideration of it. Gouvernail was right to be silent. The decision was made, and talk was only a means with which to plague and torment each other.

He found the king in the small counsel chamber. The dusk was heavy here, and the oil-dish lamp was lit. He realized Mark had adorned himself beyond his usual habit, wearing gilt bracelets as well as his Roman medallion and rings of gold in his ears. Besides, he had rubbed some unguent into his skin, something smelling of musk or sweet herbs.

"Where have you been, Tristram?" he said. "I've been waiting for an hour or more to speak with you."

"I went down to bathe in the sea."

Even in the wicklight Tristram could see that his uncle was excited. His eyes were gleaming and hot color lay along his cheekbones. "Never mind," he said, "now you are here. I have been thinking about my marriage, nephew. And it seems to me best to go ahead with it in the morning at mass."

"In the morning!"

"Why not? It isn't fitting, it shows less than respect to King Anguissh, to ask the princess to remain long in the castle unmarried. This is her home and she should assume her state at once."

"But," Tristram said, his heart beating like a sledge in his head, "you can't assemble your barons. Your seneschal is still in Wales. You have no time to send word to King Arthur or King Meliodas."

"We shall have feast days enough for everybody," Mark said, grinning with a sort of nervous haste. "And games. We won't do without ceremony, but it can come as lawfully and properly after the marriage as before. I am determined, Tristram."

"Have you informed the princess?"

"Yes, yes, she is willing."

"Are you sure?" Tristram said stupidly.

"What do you mean? I asked her and she said she was willing. How can I be surer than that?" Mark drew breath. "Do you question me, Tristram?"

"No, my lord. But the princess has had a journey and is only a few days from her home. And she is a stranger in Cornwall."

"All the more reason," Mark said. "After she is married she will be its queen."

"What do you desire of me?"

"To tell you," the king answered, "and to secure your presence at mass."

"I shall be present."

Yet Mark wished more. He was burning with a need to talk of Isoud, to boast of her beauty and the fact that she was to be his. He went on rapidly, interrupting himself to ask Tristram whether he had seen the gifts sent by King Anguissh, and if in Ireland they used such gold cups and jewelled chains and enamelled horse-gear, such daggers and drinking horns, such fine colored linen, as a matter of daily living. He did not pause for answers. He spoke of Isoud's youth and royal bearing, of her voice, her manners, her modesty. He recalled the years through which he had avoided marriage so as to be free of its claims. "And doesn't the lady Isoud prove I was right?" he said, laughing all the while as was his habit, only louder and less elegantly. "What if I had been urged into marrying some dark-faced Cornish woman who walked like a plough horse!"

Tristram racked his stumbling brain for words. "The princess brings Cornwall much honor, my lord."

"I am satisfied with her, and with you too, Tristram. You served me well when you made this alliance."

"Andret made the alliance."

259

"Andret did what he is practiced at doing," Mark said, panting with laughter. "He stayed at home and talked while someone else bearded the dragon."

Tristram was glad to seize a chance to reprove his uncle, even if it meant defending the fat knight who had ambushed him. "Your seneschal is a brave man and deserves your grateful regard, my lord. No one but you could question his courage."

"Yes, of course," Mark said, hardly hearing. "Now we must go to meat, Tristram, but first, wish me well."

"I wish every happiness for Cornwall."

"Cornwall," Mark said, "and me too. Wish *me* well, Tristram."

It was a small point, a form, but Tristram had to cudgel his willingness. "I wish you well, uncle."

"Tomorrow this time," the king cried, gaily seizing Tristram's arm and leading him from the chamber, "I shall have a wife."

Isoud did not appear in the hall, a fact Mark explained as the natural result of her discretion and good breeding. He was merry and drank late and demanded music of Tristram, harping and singing. The household barons took their mood from him, and when they arose finally many men were drunk. Mark himself was drunk, or as drunk as he ever became. He was by temperament moderate, disliking the sensation that something larger than himself, if it were only the influence of ale, had invaded his unroomy soul.

Tristram beckoned to Gouvernail and moved toward the door.

"Where are you going?" Mark asked.

"To the church."

"To the church! Who but Tristram would think of going to the church to say his matins at midnight!" Mark flung an arm around him. "You'll have to say prayers enough for us all, nephew. For me too. Say mine for me."

Tristram shook himself free of Mark's clutch and began to walk away. But the king ran after him and caught him by the arm. "You shall be Prince of Cornwall, nephew, I say it before them all. You have done more for me than any man."

Motioning Gouvernail to follow, Tristram escaped into the warm night. He strode across the lawns, feeling the grass dewy and thick under his feet. The evening fragrance of flowers mingled with the odor of salt and wet stone, pleasantly clean after the hot stuffiness of the hall. He did not take the direction to the church but found the cliff path and followed it a little distance past the rocks which had been his mother's and Magan's chairs.

"Where are you bound for?" Gouvernail asked him.

"Nowhere—just walking."

"I have enough ale between my ears to float my head like a tub," Gouvernail said, "but all the same, I don't care to walk over the edge of the cliff."

"I know the way. I only wanted to escape from the king. Have you had a chance to speak with Bragwain?"

"Yes, I gave her your message. And she said the princess asks you to be present in the morning."

"Why did she consent to be hurried so?"

"I didn't inquire. But why not, Tristram? It seems to me the best way. Once it is over we can all draw breath and begin to get used to it. Perhaps she thinks so too."

"Gouvernail, I must see her!"

"You'll see her in the morning."

"Tonight," Tristram said. "I must see her now."

"It is too dangerous. If you are caught—"

"I won't be caught. I'll speak with her at the window. You must stand watch for me."

"Bragwain will raise an outcry," Gouvernail said.

"Bragwain can't raise an outcry. She is too afraid of being punished herself to say a word."

"At least let us go back to the church. We may have been followed, and if we were we must find out."

They returned through the black, windless air, and reached the church before whose altar Tristram had taken the oath of his knighthood. He waited by the threshold stone while Gouvernail entered and satisfied himself that no one was hidden there to spy on them. They stole across the gardens and crept along the castle wall, around the end, until they found the window they were seeking.

261

The opening in the wall was recessed so that it was wider outside than within. Tristram pulled himself up and crouched in the embrasure and peered into the room. He could see nothing. "Bragwain!" he whispered.

He heard a squeak of alarm. "Who's there!"

"Tristram. Be quiet! Come to the window."

There was whispering, then silence, then a rustle of steps moving lightly across the floor reeds. His face was taken between two warm hands. "I have been praying you would come," Isoud told him.

They kissed, straining toward each other through the narrow aperture. It was too small to admit him, even to allow Isoud to slip out. They had to be content with murmurs, with eager assurances, with new vows hastily sworn. Did he love her? Oh, more than life! And she? Until she died. They would belong to each other as long as the world lasted.

"The king told me you have agreed to be married in the morning, Isoud."

"It must be tomorrow or some other morning, Tristram. When it happens doesn't make any difference."

"Bragwain says you want me to come to mass."

"If you come I shall feel less alone."

"Then I'll come for your sake. But afterwards—"

"I know," she said, "afterwards we must not look at each other and think what has happened. Afterwards you must ride to Camelot."

Here, when she was so close, when he could touch her soft cheek and her soft mouth, his desire to go away died. "If I ride into Camelot we'll be separated a long time."

"Not long—hardly a month."

"That is forever," he said. "It will seem like a year."

"I shall miss you as though it were a year. But it is better if you go. Only, when you come back, you must never leave me again."

"Why must I go at all?"

"Because," she said, "we shall need a month to teach ourselves how difficult and how beautiful our lives will be."

262

"Will you think of me?"

"Every minute, my dear lord. Now kiss me good night."

"Isoud! Promise me you won't love him."

"I shall never love any man but you, Tristram. Don't think of anything except that I am yours."

They went on saying good-by until they were trembling, until they felt they could pass through the stone of Tintagel castle and meet and cling, inseparable. But they parted at last, and when they had gone to their beds they slept, because they were young and had endured much, and because promises, even impossible promises, comforted them.

In the morning Tristram stood by the church with the household barons. The news had flown through the countryside that the king was taking a wife, and every soul who could reach the hall had come to see what was to be seen and to share in the royal gifts. Beggars, peddlers, farmers, holy men, sailors, herdsmen, king's foresters, fowlers and huntsmen, village women and children, all thronged the greens and stood in the early light staring over each other's heads, telling what they had heard of the fairness of the Irish princess. The priest of Tintagel led the king from the hall, and took him into the church. He returned, and met Isoud, and accompanied her from the castle. The crowd murmured as they saw her, for though they had expected much they expected less than they saw. She wore a robe of fine white wool, full, gathered around her narrow waist with a girdle of gold. This white gown, simple as only the genius of Ireland could make simple things, freed her beauty of all distraction and let it shine, so warm, so tender, so young, that the people staring at her felt their hearts cleansed for a moment of every dark greed, of misery and sorrow and disappointment, like souls delivered from a prison.

She entered the church, and when she had made her confession, and Mark his, the king's barons followed and saw them married. Isoud did not look at Tristram or speak with him, but he knew she was aware of him and that, with whatever pain, he had served her.

He did not think how this was the end of a year and more of

263

high, passionate hope. He did not remember how Isoud sat under the ash tree with him, or how he taught her to play the harp, or how he fought Palamides for her sake, or how they had sailed together into Cornwall and drunk the wine and loved and sworn to love while breath was in their bodies. For now that the thing had happened he would have died to prevent, his will loosened, his purpose too, even his life, as though the substance which was Tristram had been untied in a hundred places, and had grown all slack and slipping and heavy and shapeless. He stood at the church door trembling, not with anger, not with loss, but with the dull sickness of defeat.

He asked leave of his uncle to depart and ride into Camelot to seek Dinadan.

"We need you for the feast and games, Tristram," Mark said. "delay a while."

"I cannot delay, my lord. I gave my word to Dinadan to return as soon as I could."

"The princess—the queen I should say—will feel you do her a discourtesy."

"He does me a courtesy to keep a promise given," Isoud said. "And I am glad I have a knight so true and faithful." She offered him a grave smile. "Go to Camelot, my lord. And when you return you will be welcome."

"My lady," he said, "I shall ask God to let me deserve you."

And so they parted, happy for a moment because under the king's very eyes they had renewed their pledge each to the other.

Tristram rode alone, for he wished Gouvernail to remain near Isoud, to watch and protect her, and to strengthen her with the knowledge that she had a friend. He was glad to have no company but his own. As he left the high coastal forests behind him, as he kept along steadily over bleak moors where the wind beat upon him and whistled and wailed through the bracken, as he passed strange, isolated peaks having the look of giant fists thrusting up under the sod, he seemed for a while to be free of himself, as void and desolate as the land. This was peace of a sort, the peace born of the vast elements of the earth and sky when they are old and barren and silent. As he jogged forward by day and stopped at night with a hermit or a friendly freeholder, his exhausted will was mending, and his spirit was refreshed enough to conquer the sorest and most bitter thoughts Isoud's marriage inspired. He could bedevil himself with the memory of her beauty and the knowledge that it must be revealed to Mark and become his possession. He could lie awake in torment at the thought of the king's marriage bed. But these sufferings were relieved by the long, still miles he covered, and by his solitude.

On the third day he rode into the country near Camelot. He had passed through farm land and entered a well-kept forest. After the hot sun of midmorning he was grateful for the shade, and began to look for a spring where he could dismount and bathe his head and give his horse water and rest. He was walking his horse, moving along easily as he glanced into the woods on either side of the path he followed, listening for sounds which could mean other riders were near.

He heard something, a moan or a cry, perhaps the complaint of an animal caught in a snare. The sound was human, and it was uttered in distress or pain. Tristram turned his horse into the trees and rode toward it.

He reached a clearing and saw a spring there, and a black horse, and a man lying on the ground, his shield and sword and helm beside him. He lay on his back, his arm folded over his eyes. He mumbled to himself, sometimes loudly, sometimes with groans. Tristram recognized the black war horse, and the man too, and with recognition all his suspended life rushed back and poured into his heart like strong ale. The disordered knight was Palamides.

Tristram dismounted and drew his sword. As he approached the Saracen he stared at his hand and saw the great, brown, half-healed wound, and remembered how the blood had sprung from this same wound, and how the tendons had parted.

"Palamides!"

The Saracen sat up. His face was bloated and streaked with dirt and tears. His eyes were red-rimmed, but the passion had gone out of them and left them the look of blind eyes. Dully he gazed at Tristram. "Who are you?"

"You have reason to remember me, my lord. I am Tristram of Lyonesse, son of King Meliodas."

"I remember you, Tristram. But I am unarmed."

"What ails you, my lord?"

"Why do you draw your sword against an unarmed knight?"

"Because I feel friendlier to you with a sword in my hand. Arm yourself and fight. Or yield to me now. Choose."

"Do whatever you will," Palamides said, and dropped his head into his hands. "Offer me a kindness and kill me."

Tristram stood watching him, uncertain what course to follow. It would be a proud thing to ride into Camelot with this unruly heathen his prisoner, but he could not make a conquest of a man who refused to defend himself. Besides, though he never expected to pity Palamides, he pitied him now. His shining black hair was rusty and dishevelled and his moustaches drooped like wilted leaves. "I shall help you if you need help," Tristram said.

"I need nothing from you."

"Then get to your feet and take your sword."

Palamides rose. He found his sword and gripped it with his wounded hand and put himself on guard.

"Your shield and helm," Tristram said.

"I'll fight without my shield and helm." And, as though he summoned himself suddenly from some waste place, he ran upon Tristram and struck a fierce blow which Tristram had hardly time to take on his blade. He lashed out twice more, strong and cunning, and cut a billet from Tristram's shield. Then he leaped backward and flung his weapon away and dropped onto his knees. He rocked back and forth, moaning.

Tristram stuck his own sword's point into the ground and hung his shield and helm over its hilt. He knelt by Palamides and took him by the shoulders. "Let me help you, my lord."

"You can't help me."

"Then let me take you to a hermit to whom you can confess and be eased."

266

"You Christians don't know what it is to suffer for a woman," Palamides told him. "You have hearts that think only of bread and fighting. And if you don't gain what you want you'll take something else, like a dog willing to eat a cabbage if it can't eat a hare. I despise you," Palamides said.

"Christians perform less than they hope sometimes," Tristram said. "That is certainly true. As for the pain a woman can give, it may be Christians and Saracens suffer equally, but in different ways."

"She would have been mine except for you."

"Do you mean the Princess Isoud would have been yours?"

"I would have won her at the games."

Tristram sat back on his heels looking helplessly into the Saracen's distorted face. It seemed more than he could accomplish to make the weeping man understand that, whatever poets and singers said of them, women were not won, like bracelets and medallions, because one knight knocked another knight from the saddle. He did not understand this love which was so noisy and violent, which seemed as extreme as death, and yet which grasped so little the gift a heart made of itself. But he knew well the wretchedness he saw, and he was moved by it to a surprising tenderness.

"The lady Isoud was married three days ago to the king of Cornwall," he said.

"I learned in Camelot she was to be married, and that is why I am here. If I had won her I wouldn't have given her away like an unvalued slave." Palamides sprang up. "I must fight you, Tristram. Take your sword."

In this way they fought for the third time. Without squires or judges, life against life, they traced back and forth by the spring, striking blows which echoed under the branches. And because Palamides was too angry, too feverishly bent on victory, Tristram unarmed him and forced him to his knees. They were both bleeding and overspent.

They knelt together at the spring and bathed each other's wounds. And when they parted, Tristram to go into Camelot,

Palamides to seek, it might be, a deeper part of the forest, they embraced.

"Some day we shall fight until I kill you," Palamides said. "Until then, farewell, Tristram."

"Farewell, brother," Tristram said.

Chapter Twenty-six

TRISTRAM arrived at Arthur's capital in need of medicining. He was cut on the breast and thigh, and he had lost enough blood to make his legs unsteady.

"Where have you been selling your head this time?" Dinadan asked him.

Tristram told him of his encounter with the Saracen knight. Palamides' story led into a relation of Isoud's marriage, and he recounted as briefly as he could the events of his journey into Ireland. But he did not speak of the flacket of wine, contenting himself with saying that, as he brought the princess home to Cornwall, they had tried to discover some escape from their situation which would not bring ruin and death upon their friends or families.

"Are you on your way to Britany now, Tristram?"

"No," Tristram said. "Except for me, Isoud is friendless. I cannot leave her."

Dinadan sat through a considerable silence. Then he drew a slow breath. "Well, my son, the time for talk is past. So let us enjoy ourselves in Camelot, and when we return to Cornwall, keep our wits about us. Can you ride a little way?"

"Not with pleasure," Tristram said. "How far?"

"Only as far as the castle. An inn is no place for a wounded man—no place for a sensible man who loves comfort, either.

269

Besides, you won the big fellows the day you whacked Palamides out of the saddle. They want to know you better."

"What big fellows?"

"Oh—Launcelot. Gawaine. The ones who love a quarrel. And the ladies are curious about you too."

"When I was a squire," Tristram said, "I used to tell Yseut—she was King Hoël's daughter—I'd sit at the Round Table some day. She remembered it, but I've almost forgotten."

"Have you?" Dinadan said dryly.

"You doubt it?"

Dinadan only laughed. "Come on, get up and try your legs. Can you make it?"

They rode up the street of shops, past the granary and mill, across the bridge, and into the great courtyard of Arthur's castle. Part of the court was paved with flagstones, and part was in grass and gardens. Its wall was garrisoned with towers, the foot soldiers who manned them having their barracks within the wall.

"They say this was a Roman camp once," Dinadan told him with a sweeping gesture taking in the courtyard and the wall, "and that King Arthur's grandfather, Constantine, beat the Romans here and destroyed their citadel, and that it lay in ruins until Arthur rebuilt it to make Camelot."

"A song I know about Arthur says Merlin built Camelot."

"Whoever built it," Dinadan said, "it's the place to live well. Let us go in."

Grooms in kilts of the king's purple dismounted them. They went under a square gate topped with a single massive lintel stone, across a small inner court, and into the tower whose glass windows on the evening when Tristram first saw Camelot had been glowing with a gold and scarlet sunset. This was not the place of the Round Table. It occupied a room of its own older than the tower, built, like the hall of King Anguissh, without partitions, to serve the common life of kings whose names in Arthur's time were forgotten. The tower room was smaller, round, lighter by reason of the windows than Tristram imagined any space enclosed by walls could be. Its curving surface was hung with war banners and

270

colored linens from many quarters of Britain. Tristram recognized rich, soft colors from Ireland and printed patterns from Cornwall. Among the hangings shields were suspended by leather thongs, round, with bosses of gilt or bronze, many of them carrying escutcheons.

The room was furnished with chairs, barrel-backed, their legs carved to resemble the feet of wild animals. At a table men were playing a game with small pieces they shook in a cup of horn and tossed onto a board marked with squares of white and black. These were household knights. Dinadan led Tristram to the table and told them his name and lineage, and repeated theirs.

Tristram learned that the king was absent on a routine visit to the country south of the Humber River. Some members of the Round Table who had come to Camelot for the meeting at Pentecost had ridden with him, but others remained, waiting for new weapons ordered from the shops of the armorers, or delaying until a cause or quarrel demanded them, or stopping while wounds healed. The queen was at Camelot and so was Launcelot.

The days passed more pleasantly for Tristram than he had imagined time would ever pass again. The blows Palamides gave him mended quickly and his strength returned as he spent hours in talk with Dinadan's friends, Gawaine and his brothers, or rode in the mornings with the hunters. It was not that he did not long for Isoud, did not think how he would love to show her every beautiful thing at Camelot, see her flower in this new comfort and luxury, be proud she was fairer than the fairest ladies at court, even the queen. It was only that now he knew these dreams were dreams beyond the possibility of fulfillment. The tense readiness hope had given him to fight, to make desire come true, was gone. He could never bring Isoud to Camelot. But he could linger here a little while remembering her, living for a day a dear myth in which they explored the city together and retired afterwards to cool themselves in the shadows of the flowering trees.

One afternoon Queen Guenivere sent for him. He found her in the garden sitting under a cloth of linen stretched on poles to make a shade. The queen was fair, grey-eyed, still almost as slender as Isoud, only curved more fully, her skin glowing, not as Isoud's glowed from some inner light, but warmly, as it might when sun touched her. Tristram could appreciate her beauty though he was unmoved by it.

"You do not come to talk with me, Tristram," she said. "That is unfriendly of you."

"I didn't know you expected me, my lady."

She smiled. "When do splendid young knights like you wait to be expected? You bear your own welcome with you, my lord."

Tristram did not wish to pursue a conversation of this sort even with Queen Guenivere. He said, "Shall I send for a harp and sing for you? I know a song of King Arthur."

"King Arthur, yes," she said. "You must sing in the hall after meat one evening, Tristram. Now I would rather hear you talk."

"Shall I tell you about Lyonesse? Or Britany?"

"About yourself," she said, "and about the new queen of Cornwall. Is she as beautiful as men say, Tristram? Did you know the Saracen knight you fought for the sake of King Anguissh is mad in the forest because of her beauty?"

"She is fair," Tristram said.

"How young is she?"

"Nineteen."

"And you, Tristram, how young are you?"

"I am twenty, my lady."

"Twenty," she said. "Nineteen," she said, and smiled. "Do you know the lord Launcelot?" she said.

"I have seen him and spoken with him."

"And will you believe me when I tell you he was twenty once?"

"All men are twenty at one time in their lives," Tristram said gravely. "That doesn't mean they are children, my lady."

"I see it doesn't. I am rebuked."

Tristram was silent.

"I sent for you to tell you something my lord Launcelot and I were speaking of this morning," she said.

"What is it, my lady?"

"If you need a friend, he will be your friend. And you are to remember Joyous Gard."

Confused, Tristram understood that in some way beyond his comprehension the queen had discerned his love and sympathized with it. Her kindness and Launcelot's did what the cruel accidents of destiny had not been able to do: penetrate the secrecy, the wary loneliness which had been his shield. "If I can ever serve you," he said, "if you need my arms—"

"Will you take a message to the queen of Cornwall from me?"

"Willingly."

"Tell her—" Guenivere paused. "Give her my greetings, Tristram."

"I shall tell her."

After this conversation with Arthur's queen he looked for a chance to speak with Launcelot. But Launcelot seldom came to the tower room and never rode with the hunters. In the mornings he went out alone, a tall, strong figure on his grey horse, always armed, moving as though a circle were drawn around him which could not be crossed. Though he was courteous he was not an easy person to approach. And one day it came over Tristram that this was what he might be when he was Launcelot's age, a closed man, a man worn fine by enduring in isolation what others could admit before the world, a man without fellows among men. Perhaps Launcelot had offered him Joyous Gard not only as a haven if trouble overwhelmed him—perhaps it was also because this grey and lonely knight desired to call one man brother.

He made an occasion to speak to Dinadan of Launcelot. It was on a morning when they had gone to the hawk mews to watch a fowler teaching a half-trained goshawk to feed from his hand. They knew their duty to stand still, to avoid sudden gestures, and to talk, if they talked at all, in low, monotonous voices. For the bird was still being schooled to strangers, and if it were frightened or made angry its education would be set back days, even weeks, depending on the wildness of its temperament. They took up their positions a little distance from the fowler, under a tree whose branches half screened them. The goshawk, a long line fastened to its jesses, sat on a perch at the end of a grassy course. The fowler stood at the other end holding out a dead pigeon. Years of training had given the man skill to remain motionless, his arm extended, for twenty minutes, for an hour, for three hours if need be, controlling the trembling boredom which would have afflicted a less dedicated soul. "A hawk knows if you are cursing him," he explained to Tristram and Dinadan, "even if you smile and speak softly. And so you must never be tempted to curse him. You must love him."

There he stood in the sun, moveless, his arm outstretched, loving his pupil. The bird shifted restlessly on the perch, raising a murderous claw now and then and clenching it on air, its beak half-open and its round yellow eye staring with a savagery rejecting all love, all kindness, all coaxing. Its flat head and the scimitar curve of its beak were deadly in poise, exactly formed for the hawk's work, which was to kill.

"No hawk prepares you for any other," Dinadan murmured. "They have souls, I think, like men, each different."

"No," Tristram said, "their manners are different, but their souls are all the same. Men get over fury and resentment, but hawks can't, any more than they can get over their shape or their color."

"Who told you men get over fury and resentment, my son?"

"You can read it if you look," Tristram said. "You yourself know men who have racked the anger out of their hearts. Launcelot, for one. Name me a person Launcelot hates."

"He chastises a good plenty of men," Dinadan said with a smile.

"That's a different matter. He might hate what men do. But not the man himself."

"It is easy to be calm and charitable and wise if you happen to be Launcelot. I could be a tremendous fellow on a quarter of his gifts."

"I don't believe it was easy for him to learn to be calm and charitable. Wise either. He doubts still that he is wise."

Dinadan gave him a surprised look. "How do you know so much about Launcelot?"

"I have seen him. What makes him sad, Dinadan?"

"A lady."

"The queen?"

"You've seen her too," Dinadan said. "Is it your opinion she could make a man sad?"

Suddenly the hawk hurled itself from its perch. It came level along the course, its powerful wings ferrying it with vicious speed. It aimed itself at the fowler, and as it rushed forward its size seemed to increase. It did not alight on its master's arm, but his shoulder, and Tristram winced, feeling the hooked talons in his own flesh. The fowler stood perfectly still, his hand unshaken before him holding the bait.

"That drew blood," Tristram said. They watched as the hawk perched, uncertain whether it would fly, or attack, or fling itself headlong with a scream. The fowler murmured to it softly as to a fretful child. In a moment it began to walk down his arm, clutching its feet into the stuff of his sleeve as though it took a pleasure in every brutal embrace of its claws. It ate the pigeon in a few convulsive gulps, feathers, bones, and all.

"Ah!" said Dinadan.

"Well done!" Tristram said. "That was beautiful."

"I can feel my arm hanging in strings," Dinadan said. "Have you seen enough for today?"

They congratulated the fowler, still speaking softly from a distance, and moved away. The display of the bird of prey put Dinadan in a moral mood, and he commented that, in this life, a man must choose whether he was to be a hawk or the helpless bait of hawks.

"You deal in such vast blacks and whites today, Dinadan," Tristram said. "It isn't like you to find lessons wherever you look."

The little knight uttered an embarrassed laugh. "The fact is, Tristram, I'm trying to screw up my courage to give you some advice."

"When have you needed courage to give me advice?"

"Only now."

"And why now?"

"Perhaps because you've outgrown advice. Perhaps because, since you left Camelot with King Anguissh, you've made up your mind what world you're living in."

"Get on," Tristram said. "What wisdom have you for me?"

"A while ago we were speaking of Launcelot. And it occurs to me Launcelot's story might offer you one of these lessons you complain of."

"There's a lesson I'm willing to hear."

"You know what they say of Launcelot and the queen."

"I never heard anyone say it."

"That's the point I'm making. No one does say it, but everyone knows. Everyone has known for almost as many years as you've been alive. And the reason it isn't cried into a scandal and a war is that Launcelot has had the grace to take account of two things."

Here comes the lesson, Tristram thought, but I don't want to hear it after all. I can't let any man, even Dinadan, talk to me of Isoud, however much he talks in riddles. All the same, he listened.

"First and least forgettable," Dinadan went on, "he knows where his duty is sworn. He remembers he is Arthur's knight, and if he is not that, he is nothing."

"He has a lord to hold to."

"That may be," Dinadan agreed. "I admit Arthur is easy to love. Nevertheless, Launcelot loves his duty more. Not even Arthur doubts it."

"Go on."

"The other thing," Dinadan said quietly, "is that Launcelot knows he has no rights."

"No rights!"

"None at all," Dinadan said. "Men honor and respect him and many men love him. But these are gifts on tenure, not enforceable, and Launcelot never draws on them. He makes nobody his partisan or his defender."

276

"He is alone," Tristram said, "even among men of his blood."

"Even," Dinadan said, "with the queen."

"Not with the queen!"

"What if, some morning, the queen said to him, 'I never want to see you again, my lord Launcelot'? He would have no answer because he has no rights. Whatever he and the lady may have felt and shared, it doesn't entitle him to anything, not even a protest."

Tristram walked along in silence. He was trying to apply to himself what Dinadan had told him, trying to see himself wear his allegiance to King Mark like a prize, to put it first, above his own pride, above Isoud. Mark! Weak and trivial, vain, pompous, absurd, how could Mark be put above Isoud! It was as much beyond possibility to compare Mark with King Arthur as it was to compare Isoud with Guenivere. For though the queen of Camelot might be fitful enough to despoil her love and Launcelot's, Isoud's truth was not cut off that bolt of cloth. Isoud would love him until she died. She had promised.

"Once," Dinadan said, "a jealous man went to Arthur and told him he had a matter to discuss touching the queen and Launcelot. And Arthur had this man banished. Arthur isn't exactly a child, you know, Tristram. He understands well enough that Launcelot appreciates his limits. But if Launcelot made claims and forgot his duty and drew the court into parties, then Arthur might listen to the tales plenty of disgruntled toads are aching to tell him. Toads," Dinadan said, "of the same cast of features as our Andret."

"Do you mean Arthur knows and tolerates—?"

"I mean he has lived some years in this world," Dinadan said. "Perhaps when they were younger than they are now, the three of them, they were more turbulent and tragic. Perhaps then they thought their situation had some awful uniqueness, something secret and peculiar to themselves. But now I expect they appreciate that everything, even lawlessness, settles into a way of life. And ways of life have rules. They keep the rules."

Dinadan believes love is like fighting or sailing for cargo or copying books, Tristram was thinking, something a man does because he is skilled or trained to do it or because he must live. Tristram knew it was not like that, he knew it was a force no rule could contain, a glory like the light of the sun, and incapable, like light, of being caught and bottled up and kept its shining self by rules. It was free. Even when it was beset with the utmost secrecy and peril, it was free.

"I am grateful for your lesson, brother," he said.

"You are grateful, but—"

"Why do you say 'but—'?"

"Because," Dinadan said, "our king is not the only man who has lived some years in this world."

Chapter Twenty-seven

WHEN Tristram returned to Tintagel he discovered that Andret had come back from Wales. The seneschal received him with courtesy, even with a moderate show of interest and gratitude. If he had had a hand in the attack off the Welsh coast he had taught himself to speak of it openly, expressing regret. He said frankly he was surprised when he learned Tristram had reached Ireland and accomplished the king's mission.

"And promptly too," he said. "Who could have dreamed the king's marriage would occur so soon?"

"Your concern for my safety made you miss the ceremony, my lord," Tristram said. "I am sorry to have robbed you of a pleasure."

"How could you rob me of a pleasure when you have given Cornwall such an excellent queen? As a Cornish knight I am in your debt, Tristram."

A debt you have your own plans for settling, Tristram thought. In a way he was glad to have Andret to keep him sharpset. For his days were burdensome enough, lustreless and restive except in the rare times when he could be alone with Isoud. As Andret had taught him once before, life gained point when it held a threat.

After his month's absence he found Isoud at home in Mark's house, or seeming to be at home. She had been bred for sovereign duties, and her pride led her to discharge her office well in all its small and large details. Her presence in the hall added a grace which influenced everyone. As she went about the table with the cup, knights who were used to brawling and drunkenness bore themselves with new decorum. All things seemed fresher, kindlier, more fitting. It was as though a young spirit of loyalty had been born, the allegiance she won from the household growing from the center she gave it and attaching the barons to each other with revived respect and brotherhood. Tristram did not need to be told that every man in Tintagel had become Isoud's subject, Mark more than any.

When he saw Mark the jealousy which had chafed him less painfully in Camelot opened again like a galled wound. The king looked sleek and jovial, the pouting discontent of his face smoothed into a sort of unctuous comfort. Perhaps to prove his youth he stirred from the mild laziness characteristic of him, and stamped about the castle and court, leaped from his horse, talked loudly, affected big gestures. Yet these exertions made him appear a good deal less young. They did not suit his neatness and elegance, and robbed him of the dignity he had spent a lifetime cultivating.

This exuberance was curbed somewhat when he was with Isoud. For she bore herself with a cool poise not less invulnerable for being gentle. She did not rebuke his boisterousness. It simply could not survive in her presence. As Tristram watched them in the hall, Isoud's firm self-possession reassured him a little, and he gave God thanks that Mark had been unable to hurt and humiliate her spirit. But it was not enough to know she had triumphed at least in one way over the outrage of her situation. That was too small a blessing if they could not meet, if they could not hearten each other, if they could not hold together and promise again and again how they would never forget their love.

They contrived an hour alone now and then. The continuation of Isoud's lessons on the harp furnished them one useful reason for solitude. They could sit in the garden or they could linger awhile in the chamber the queen used as a withdrawing room, and as Tristram played they could speak the burden of their hearts. They could meet as if by accident at the church door and walk for a few precious minutes in the courtyard. And, rarely, when Mark was absent on state business, Tristram could take his uncle's place at the head of the hunt and ride beside Isoud and hear her say softly how she thought of him always, and how she longed for the moment she was sure God would send them when they could be truly together.

But these encounters, treasured as they were, offered them little ease, defining only the huge and hopeless terms of their separation. As the summer ran forward, as the court settled down to the regime under its new queen, as Mark's excited enthusiasm as a husband began to take on the color of habit, they dared more and bolder meetings. If Tristram lacked the excuse of a music lesson to spend time in Isoud's chamber he spent time there for no reason. He invented small errands for Bragwain so that they might hasten into each other's arms and kiss and swear that soon they would share whole hours together, whole nights.

"Come away from the castle for a day," Tristram urged her.

"How can I?"

"When the king is absent."

"Someone is always watching me," she said. "If I walk even as far as the cliff my ladies follow me."

"Andret spies on us, I think. I am watched too. But we must be cleverer than Andret."

"Tell me how we can be cleverer. Oh, my Tristram," she said, "I lie awake in the dark and think of you, and I know you are awake thinking of me, and it seems some strong and beautiful thing will make us both rise and come to each other, no matter who sees us, no matter if they take us and kill us."

"I too," Tristram said. "When I wake I think we belong to each other, and it is a wickedness to be apart, and all the good in the world will help and shelter us if we say before everybody that I am yours and you are mine. But then I see my uncle in the dark and I know he would imprison you and kill you. And I do not rise."

"We are trees without flowers," Isoud said, and tears gathered in her eyes. Tristram had never seen her weep. He remembered

281

how when they were in the boat, before they had drunk the wine, she said, "I do not weep." Now he was broken with her tears, driven desperate, seeing her courage racked. He had wasted her hope trying to keep her safe. They did not dare to be safe. They must risk everything or they would have nothing.

"Listen, Isoud, I know a place." And he told her about the cave, and how he remembered it and searched it out again the first day they were in Cornwall together. "A little way to the north the coast bends to the east. Have you seen the place?"

"Yes."

"And as you ride away from the sea you find a ravine with a stream."

"I know, I know."

"Tomorrow I shall say I am going to—oh—to a hermitage to keep a fast day with prayers. I'll stay in the forest all night. And the day after tomorrow in the morning you will ride with Bragwain to the ravine where the stream flows down. Tell them—let me think—"

"I'll tell them it is the season to gather a certain healing herb."

"Yes, tell them that. Gouvernail will meet you at the ravine and bring you to the cave. And he will stand watch for us."

"And they won't suspect us because you will have been gone all night."

"They may suspect us. This is full of danger, my only Isoud."

"Then we shall be all the happier," she said. "I love the danger for your sake, Tristram."

"Little flowers grow around the cave the color of your eyes, Isoud."

"You are smiling, Tristram. You must be grave and sad or they will guess how light our hearts are. Do you know you are always sad now, and stern, and have great hollows in your cheeks?"

"When you are sad it makes you more beautiful."

"If I am beautiful it is because you are looking at me."

The next day Tristram told the king his intention to ride into the forest and seek a hermitage and keep a fast. With Gouvernail he departed, holding his way south for a few hours in order to be sure they were not followed and to lend the hue of truth to his story. He went so far as to find a hermitage and to dismount there and to spend what remained of the day with the old man who had chosen to live his last years in penance. When he heard his host singing his midnight service of matins, he roused Gouvernail.

"What is it?" Gouvernail mumbled, and sat up.

"We must saddle our horses."

"Again? Where are we going in this blackness?"

"I'll tell you in a little while."

They left as quietly as they could, for Tristram hoped to avoid the hermit's questions. Because the darkness under the trees was impenetrable they rode inland and emerged onto the wild waste of a moor. Wind skirled over the uneven ground, rubbing the ferns together with a tearing sound and rattling the furze. A half-moon gave them a little light.

"The world reaches its end on this moor," Gouvernail said. "Even in daylight it is a black place. Why must we ride these infernal hills in the middle of the night, Tristram?"

"For a lady," Tristram said.

"The queen?"

"Isoud." And he told Gouvernail of the cave and the meeting they had planned.

The squire received this news in silence.

"Are you thinking of the danger?" Tristram asked.

Surprisingly Gouvernail laughed. "If I were not thinking of danger I wouldn't be with you, Tristram. I live on danger. With any other food I should grow as lean as a crow."

Robbed of Gouvernail's objections Tristram felt ruffled. "I thought the diet disagreed with you."

"They say horses that escape and turn wild live on thistles and poison vines," Gouvernail said, "and grow fat, too. I knew we would fare on thistles soon. We've lived too comfortably too long."

"You think I court danger for danger's sake."

"Never mind what I think, Tristram."

"Tell me what you think," Tristram said angrily.

283

"I think I am your man," Gouvernail said, "and if you ride on the moors to meet a lady, I ride too."

"You put me off."

"Well, then, I think you need occupation, Tristram. You hardly stir from the castle. The king rides more than you do."

Tristram felt the shamed blood rush into his face. "I lack a good lord to serve, Gouvernail."

"That is true," Gouvernail said quietly.

His agreement put an end to their conversation. Tristram rode along defending himself. Gouvernail could not understand his situation, no man could understand it who was not loved and needed by Isoud. She was more important than a good lord, a king like Anguissh, her father, or like Arthur. Or Hoël. If he could have taken her into Britany! If they could have married, if he could have returned to King Hoël's house as a son might, if he could have assumed there a place entitling him to respect and honor and freedom before the world, all things done openly as he longed to do them, true with truthful men, then Gouvernail would not have to complain that he lacked occupation. For the first time since he returned to Cornwall Tristram realized what he had lost. But it was not Isoud's fault. Long ago before he ever saw Isoud he had learned that justice is hard to serve and that a man does not gain a good lord merely because he wishes one.

No, nothing was Isoud's fault. From her came all the good life had to offer. However men shifted and changed, seeming to be one thing and proving to be another, Isoud was as firm as God's truth. And I will be her knight if I am never anything else in this world, Tristram told himself. Let Gouvernail despise him for an idler, and Dinadan too, and every man. They did not know that to be Isoud's knight was to be exalted above other men.

They reached the cave before the sun was high enough to cast its spotted patterns on the waterfall. They could see long, pale beams gilding the very tops of the trees, but at the foot of the ledge over which the stream fell they still moved in a pearly twilight. The air was deliciously fresh and cool, scented with moss and wet rock and the mouldering leaves which made the forest's floor. Birds were singing everywhere, darting down boldly to the stream's edge and flinging crystal drops as they bathed.

Tristram told Gouvernail how to climb the ravine and follow the stream and reach the place where he was to meet Isoud. Then when he had washed he stretched out on a ledge by the brook to watch the morning come and to wait for the queen. As he lay in the still peace with the ferns brushing his arms and the waterfall drumming tuneless music and butterflies winking in and out of the dappled sun, he made a song. In the song he called all things, birds and beasts and serpents, to come to Isoud's brook, to lay down their stings and poisons, to sing for her who could, and who could not, to be clean and pretty for her. And in that way they would gain souls and live forever. He was whistling a melody for the song, trying high notes and low, when Isoud came.

This was the first time they had ever been alone, truly by themselves beyond the reach of any voice or summons. In the beginning they could not trust their fortune but clung together whispering, startling at the cries of birds, peering at the wind shaking the trees. As the sun reached them and coaxed the flowers open and threw gleams of silver onto the waterfall, they realized their freedom with a sudden, welling joy. And all they had never dared to do, to laugh aloud, to run, to play like children, they did on that fresh first morning, but because they were not children, to pause too, to turn to each other with kisses, to touch hands and bodies, to lose themselves in the expectation of love. Then they searched out the narrow path behind the waterfall and crept under its glinting curtain and came into their cave. Isoud! Oh, my Tristram! I have longed for you! You are my king!

The cave was lightened only a little by the soft dusk the waterfall let through. Its air was drowsy with the scent of moss and fern. When they had loved they were lulled by this warm and fragrant twilight and by the murmur of the waterfall. They slept, and wakened to the wonder of being together.

"We must never leave this lovely place," Isoud said.

"We shall never leave it. We'll live in the forest, and I shall hunt, and make you a robe of fur."

285

"The sun will turn me brown, Tristram, but it will turn you red."

"I shall be known as the Red Knight."

"Were you here last night, Tristram?"

"No, I stayed at a hermitage, in case Andret had a will to inquire whether a moody fellow with his mind on prayers had been by."

"I told them about gathering herbs. I said I had to rise at daybreak and pick the plants while the dew was still on them. And as a special favor I gave my ladies leave to remain at home and sleep."

"Did they try to come with you anyway?"

"No," she said. "I only told them after meat when we had retired from the hall. They had no time to speak with Andret or to think I might be deceiving them."

He drew her close and kissed her. "You are the bravest of all brave queens, Isoud. Were you frightened?"

"A little, but I liked being frightened. Sometimes I dream I am running before some dangerous thing, and in the dream I always run right into your arms. And then I have come home."

"Yes," he said, "I know. When I was a young knight in Lyonesse I used to think of coming home too. Only no place I ever reached was home. Now," he said, leaning on his elbow and laying a hand over her heart, "I am at home here."

"We are a castle by ourselves, Tristram, just our two bodies and our two souls."

They were silent for a moment, enchanted as they thought of their loneliness and their strength.

"Only," Isoud said, "we can't always tell them we are praying and gathering herbs. What shall we say the next time?"

"When is the next time?"

"Soon. Seven days from now."

"That isn't soon."

"It must be seven days, Tristram. What shall we tell them?"

"My beautiful Isoud," he said, "I am too happy to think what we shall tell them. But I'll provide us a means."

"Let me get up, Tristram."

"No, stay."

"I am the most blessed among women."

"I know."

"But ask me why I am blessed."

"Why, Isoud?"

"Because you are happy when you are with me," she said.

They rose and left the cave, surprised to find the sun still shining and all things by the waterfall as they had been in the morning. Gouvernail and Bragwain sat together a little way down the stream, the basket between them which the woman had filled with medicinal plants. Tristram beckoned to them.

"You and the queen will return to Tintagel first," he said to Bragwain. "You will arrive easily before the hour of vesper."

"What shall we say if we are questioned?"

"Nothing," Tristram told her. "Nobody can question the queen."

"Don't be afraid," Isoud comforted the woman, whose face was set in a sort of desperate calm. "I'll protect us. When will you come, Tristram?"

"Late," he said. "Good-by for a little while, Isoud."

"Good-by, my dear lord."

"Ride with them as far as the cliff, Gouvernail, and wait for me there."

He listened until he could no longer hear them in the forest. He was drugged with warm peace, with the joy of the only day he had ever spent with Isoud. Yet the triumph of their success did not lull him into the belief that they could always meet so easily. And later as he rode to keep his rendezvous with Gouvernail he thought of their future, and of what new inventions he must devise. He remembered how his squire had rebuked his idleness, and he realized how men laughed at a brother who was woman-bound, and he understood that his very dawdling about the court, even if he never spoke with the queen, would bring upon him mirthful gossip which at any moment could harden into suspicion. He resolved to join the hunt again, recognizing in it a freedom of movement which could help his plans and Isoud's.

Every hunt saw one or another knight belated and separated from his party. Tristram smiled to think how bold he would be in the pursuit of game, how he would outrun his fellows, how he would circle away like a swift fox and come home to the cave behind the waterfall.

It was a good plan. A week after their first meeting he used it, and found the queen waiting for him as they had appointed. Even a second time this scheme succeeded for them. But in the hall on the evening after the hunt Tristram was rallied humorously by Andret for losing his way. "Perhaps you ride to game you do not care to disclose to us, my lord," he said.

So Tristram was put to new shifts. And as time passed, as the precarious joy of the cave increased their longing one for the other, he and Isoud had no choice but to grow rash. The summer cooled, and storms blew in from the west over Tintagel head, and the forest trees dropped their leaves and stood bare, the concealment they had offered stripped away. Now the lovers could not endure the nagging anxiety of long plans, of burdensome contrivances built a little at a time through days and weeks. They began to snatch at dangerous chances, to fly to the cave whenever opportunity gave them a hazardous two hours, an hour clear. With winter even these stolen meetings became impossible.

Driven, their wits grew sharp beyond any cleverness the cave had demanded of them. For now they had only one place to meet, the hall itself. Yet they met. They fled sometimes before escapes so close and perilous that they seemed almost tangible, almost a presence clutching at them with a hand like the bare and knuckled hand of death.

Part V

Chapter Twenty-eight

A FEW days after the feast of Christmas King Mark entered Isoud's chamber and found Tristram there. By luck Bragwain was present, and other ladies of the queen's household. Among them they were working a hanging, sitting around a frame upon which heavy linen was stretched, each with a skein of colored thread in her hands.

Isoud rose. "Welcome, my lord. You see us occupied."

"So I do, my lady." Mark was not smiling as he so often smiled in these days. Above his neat beard his mouth was set in a sullen line. "And you, Tristram, are you helping with this needlework too?"

"My lord," Tristram said, "I can't give you an answer to your question here. But if you like, we can walk into the hall, and there I shall be glad to tell you whether or not I have been engaged on this hanging." And he laid his hand on the hilt of his short sword. In Isoud's eyes he could read a warning so guarded and brief it was not apparent to anyone but himself.

The king confronted him, his face slowly reddening with wrathful blood. He seemed old. As Tristram looked down on him he could discern between the strands of his hair gleams of yellow scalp. Though his cheeks were lean, his flesh sagged at the jawbone and pulled itself into a corded hollow under his chin. His eyelids had fattened a little, and were shiny, almost translucent, giving the impression that lymph had swollen them. It was as though between last night and this morning the sum of a hundred minute changes, none of them noticeable by itself, had merged into one large change and become manifest on the person of the king.

"I was joking," Mark said. "A champion of your powers can be rallied, can't he, when he is found among ladies?"

"Ladies are improved by the society of champions, my lord," Isoud said. "And now we are twice lucky to have you with us. Let me show you our work."

"I'll see it another time. Today I've come to speak to Tristram on a state matter."

"Shall we leave you?" Isoud asked.

"No, it isn't secret. I have to go on a journey which will take me three days. The seneschal will accompany me. And you, Tristram, must keep the affairs of Tintagel in order."

"What is your business?" Tristram said, annoyed that Andret had pushed ahead of him in something confidential.

Mark hesitated, as though he wished Tristram to realize he was concealing his true errand. "A port inspection. We shall ride as far as the border of Lyonesse."

Tristram nodded. But he was not indifferent. He was standing before his uncle thinking of lies and ambush and violence and murder. He had lived, fretting, inactive, under the threat of all these. And now, like a sea upon cliffs, his mind rushed up, and broke, and turned back from the vision of himself as the conspirator, not the conspired against. He could waylay this little king who was planted between his heart and Isoud's, pull him off his horse and strangle him without so much as drawing his sword. Why didn't he? He could not answer his own wonder. He knew only that within his soul the will to murder like a hired cutthroat could not be born.

"Now, Tristram," Mark said, "keep state fittingly, and see to the protection of the queen. I shall hold you responsible."

"You have no reason to doubt me," Tristram said.

"I shall return," the king said, "the third evening from today." Isoud said, "Let me go with you, my lord."

"Go with me!"

She smiled. "Is it unreasonable? It would make me happy to be near you. Besides, the wind and bad weather have kept us prisoners a month and more, and I miss the taste of outdoor air, even if it is stormy. In Ireland I often rode with my father in the rain."

Mark looked into her face, trying to read more than she had spoken. Under the spell of her pleading smile his frown relaxed. "I believe you truly would put up with the rain and mud for my sake, Isoud. But this will be a rough journey. Wait until spring, and then you may go whenever I go."

"Is your departure set?" she asked him.

"Yes, in an hour."

Isoud turned to her ladies. "Leave us, please. And you too, my lord," she said to Tristram.

Tristram went off, half torn with jealousy, half marvelling at Isoud's courage and cunning. She had mended his own rashness with this request to accompany Mark. But what if he had agreed to take her? Had she counted on a refusal, or did she really wish to leave Tintagel behind her for a while? Perhaps she, like himself, suffered a sudden revulsion against the life they led, its fear and constriction and deceit. And against him, too, Tristram?

He flung himself once more upon the unyielding rock of their situation. And once more he understood that every escape was blocked. They had love, but they had no peace. Their hours, being stolen, could only be spent in panic fervor, never idly, never in the ease of talk or silence. They were enforced to love. And though love was precious, the more so when every meeting must be lived as though it were their last, it became a sort of tyranny from which there was no appeal, dear and desired, but inexorable. Perhaps Isoud had moments when, womanlike, she longed for less than love.

In this mood of rebellious doubt Tristram idled away an hour, waiting until the king and Andret and the two knights accompanying them had ridden from the courtyard. Then he returned to Isoud. She was pale.

"It is a trap," she said. "We must not meet while the king is absent."

"How do you know? What did he tell you?"

"He didn't tell me anything, and I don't know it with proof. We can't guess what they may have learned about us, Tristram. Only I am sure this journey is a pretense to try us. And you must go away too."

"He put Tintagel in my charge. Besides, I won't leave you, Isoud."

She clung to him, pressing her body close as though she would conceal herself in his strength. "Oh, my Tristram, our time is short! I am afraid!"

"Why do you suspect him now when you haven't before?"

"I saw it in his face. He has begun to hate you."

"If he hates me I am glad. I've wanted to fight him and Andret too. If the time has come to fight—"

"No, no, don't talk of fighting, Tristram."

"I must fight, or I must take you away."

She moved free of him, summoning from some last desperate source endurance for one more day. "I am sorry I was weak, my dear lord. Remember, we bear what we must to keep peace between Ireland and Cornwall."

"But we must put an end—"

"Do you love me, Tristram?"

"With all my life, but—"

"Then be patient."

"Patient!" he said. "I have been patient until I am rotted with patience. We live in prison, Isoud."

"But we live in prison together."

"Let me take you away tonight."

"No, you must not even come to me tonight. Not at all while the king is absent."

"I should have sent a man after him to return and warn us."

"Any man you sent would have been his man."

Tristram knew she was right. He could not trust even his own guard at Tintagel. "I am too restless to stay indoors, Isoud, if we

294

are not to spend our time together. I think I'll have my horse saddled and go visit granaries. If I take Gouvernail and some yeomen you could come with me."

But she shook her head. "This time we must be more careful than we have ever been. Visit the granaries, Tristram. Take yeomen, but leave Gouvernail with me. I shall feel happier."

He chose to ride alone. It was a day of raw wind and fitful squalls of rain. He could hear the sea rumbling on Tintagel head, not in bursts of thunder, but monotonously, like an engine gnawing away the foundations of the earth. As he fought the wild weather the sickness of his mind found some relief. Thinking of Isoud's cave he rode north, but followed the cliff past the slope where they had so often turned landward into the forest. Presently he saw what he was seeking, a stone church planted so close to the cliff that its outer wall was only a continuation of the sheer rock dropping below it to the sea.

This was an abandoned church, and nobody at Tintagel knew why it had been built, or when. It interested Tristram because it bore a resemblance to the church in King Anguissh's courtyard. Like it this one was round, constructed of flat stones trued up without mortar, pierced by a low door and one window behind the altar stone on the side toward the sea. The altar had long since been removed, though the marks of its massive slab still showed on the packed earth of the floor.

As he had often done, he dismounted and entered under the lintel of the door. The threshold stone had crumbled so that its traceries were hardly discernible, but some faint spirals blackened by a growth of moss were still visible. These delicate coils too reminded him of Ireland.

The church smelled of wet stone and the dry, unfertile ground of its floor. Its interior was almost dark, so that he saw its window as an oblong of light, even on this gloomy day. He thrust his shoulders through the embrasure, and leaning on his arms, looked right down into the sea. It heaved below him, cold grey, streaked with yellowish foam. Sometimes it rose swiftly against the cliff, unbroken, then gathered itself and toppled over in a vast fall.

And at other times it splintered on the rock, and hurled itself upward in points and arcs, rattling like dry gravel. He stared down, fascinated by the turbulence, imagining himself leaping from the window and beating his way through the convulsed water and gaining the quiet deeps beyond. Before today he had thought this same thought, standing at this same window. And it soothed him, like a vision of peace.

He turned away from the window presently and knelt before the marks of the altar. But he could not pray, either to ask help or blessing. He wondered whether at times God grew sick of the world He had made and left it for a while, and whether it was then that a man's prayers would not rise in his heart; or whether God was indifferent altogether, and only seemed to listen when prayers came freely. Perhaps God had abandoned him because he had sinned. Have I sinned? No. I have given my faith once in my life, and I have served my faith with all I have of service. God could not reject that as a sin. But if He did reject it?

Tristram returned to the castle in the early dusk, seeing its bulk against the sky as he crossed the neck of Tintagel head, and thinking of Isoud within, and feeling descend on him the weight of grief and anger from which for a little while he had been free. Why would not Isoud let him take her away? They could go to nothing more oppressive than their lives in Tintagel. As for the peace between Ireland and Cornwall, why was it their responsibility? Why could not Mark and Anguissh be forced to compound their own jealousies and tie their lands together with something stronger than the cords of Isoud's loyal heart? Like a pair of cannibals they sacrificed her to their own lust for war. And me too, Tristram thought, though if it were not for Isoud I would answer the sacrifice they make of me.

He did not see the queen until they met in the hall at meat. She was dressed in green and wore her jewels, as though she made herself lovely to inspirit the household in their lord's absence. And she did inspirit them, encouraging their mirth, yet keeping it within bounds, drawing from this man or that tales of bravery, courteously praising the valor of Cornwall. Yet Tristram

296

could see under her beauty something tense, something with-drawn, as though she listened for a sound audible only to herself. This look haunted him. And later, when the lamp bowls had been extinguished and the household gone to bed, he could not forget it.

He lay awake remembering how pale she was, how, when she passed among them with the cup, her hands had seemed almost transparent. When had she grown pale, she in whose cheek the tints of rose always bloomed? A fear came over him that she was ill, that her tender woman's body could not sustain the burden of her life, that she would die. She must let him take her away. If she would not yield he must take her anyway, carry her to some safe spot if it were only their cave behind the waterfall, and there tend and serve her, and restore her strength, and be her protection, and give her back the proud joy, the unspoiled freedom of life she had known before she came into Cornwall. It must be tonight, he told himself. I will take her to—to—where! To Britany. There was no other land. They must trust King Hoël, because they could not trust anyone else, to make their peace with King Anguissh.

He forced himself to lie still until he was sure the household were asleep. Then he rose and dressed and girded himself with his battle sword. Moving as quietly as the mist blowing in from the sea he left the hall and flattened himself against the wall of the corridor to learn whether he had been followed. He could hear nothing but his own heart. After he had waited long enough to know himself clear, he stole along the corridor and reached the door of the queen's quarters. He slipped within. Bragwain slept in an antechamber behind which was the room of Isoud and King Mark. He heard Bragwain breathing slow breaths. He fol-lowed the wall and gained Isoud's door and opened it and entered.

A wicklight was burning on a standard beyond her bed. Against its light he could see her. A wool shawl about her, she was sitting in the bed, her hair unbound over her shoulders.

"Tristram," she said in a kind of despair.

"I had to come to you."

"I have been praying God not to let me want you."

"You must leave Tintagel with me, Isoud."

"No, Tristram, never." She rose from the bed and extinguished the wicklight and came into his arms. "We have so little time! We must make this moment the most beautiful in all our lives." Swiftly she felt for the buckle of his baldric and unclasped it. His sword slipped to the floor. When he would have prevented her, she drew his head down and kissed his mouth. Tristram's purpose floundered helplessly and was lost.

In the king's bed Tristram remembered that never before had they lain together on soft linen and wool. Their love had been deprived of all kindness and comfort, made keen by cold earth, made poignant by excited fear. Now the fresh and fragrant cover enchanted them like some new magic, and when they had loved they yielded themselves to the warm ease of their first bed. Between sleeping and waking Tristram knew he should arise and leave her, since sharing this bed in love, they shared it also in the expectation of death. But he could not bear to move from her whose hair lay upon his naked breast, whose breathing he could hear as light as the sigh of a bird's wing. Yet he knew her bright beauty was not his to hold save as he held it now. In a little while, he told himself, in a quarter of an hour I shall go. But as the quarter hour passed the care of the kind of love which must run always before discovery fell away from him, and a blest peace took him, and he slept as Isoud slept, in peace, these two like a wife and husband who lie dreamless as bells chime away the night and the moon sets.

He was awakened by hands which seized him and dragged him to the floor. He was too stupefied to know what had happened, yet he snatched at his sword and felt himself naked.

"Clothe him," Mark said.

Grey light showed him the shape of the window. He struggled against the hands imprisoning him but he could not wrench himself free. Each of his wrists was bound with thongs to the hands of other men. A third man roughly dressed him. A woman was sob-

298

bing. As his wits came back to him, as sight was restored to his sleep-drugged eyes, he saw Andret standing by the bed with the king. Isoud lay as still as death under the cover, but she was not dead. Even in the gloom of the early light her eyes were wide and calm, looking into his. Bragwain huddled beside her. It was Bragwain who wept.

"The queen is guiltless," Tristram said. "I am here against her will."

"That is a treacherous lie," Andret said.

"I will prove its truth on you, body for body, cousin," Tristram said, "if you dare abide the proof."

"Take him away," Mark said. "The time for talk is past."

"Stop," Tristram said. "Justice gives me a chance to clear the queen. I will prove her innocence on Andret, or on you, uncle, or on any man, or on all the barons of this court, one by one."

"Take him away," Mark said.

"What will you do with the queen?" Tristram fought crazily against his bonds, pulling the men to whom he was tied forward and back as he tried to loose his hands. Mark clutched him, and so did Andret, and they and his captors dragged him from the room. In the corridor a troop of foot soldiers fell upon him so that he was hauled along with six men clinging to his arms like dogs around a trapped wild boar.

"Take him to the church," Andret said.

He was to be judged and sentenced at daybreak, then. When the king gave summary justice, he did it this way, at the church, in the first hour after lauds. And he would be hanged, like enough, as common thieves were hanged, from a stake driven into the earth before the cross. Such a rage was boiling in Tristram as almost burst his heart, but he was able to think, even to plan.

What would Mark do with Isoud? Not hang her, since she was not being dragged to the church. Give her body to the fire? If he intended that, she would have some hours of life yet, perhaps a day. They had a little time. He said to the captain of the foot soldiers, "Do me one last kindness in this world, brother."

"I am ordered to take you to the church, my lord."

299

"As you hope for God in your last hour, friend, give me one kindness."

"What is your need?" This captain was a member of Tristram's own guard, and he suffered some sense of shame. He kept himself beyond Tristram's reach, standing aside and refusing to meet his eyes.

"Only this. Send a man to the king to ask him to judge me, not here, but in the deserted church to the north on the cliff."

The captain's delay brought a pause among the soldiers. They stood irresolute, looking from their captive to their leader. Between Tristram's wrists and those of the men to whom he was bound the thongs hung slack. Tristram sprang back with a great leap. The two men hurtled forward and crashed together. While they were still staggering, blinded by the impact with which their skulls had struck, he wrenched the short sword from the hand of one of them and thrust it upward against the thongs.

The troop, used to obeying orders and now having none to obey, stood for a moment too paralyzed to move. Tristram cut his other hand free. And then he ran, his long legs carrying him like an athlete across the courtyard. He gained the stables thirty lengths ahead of the soldiers, cut the line tying the first horse he saw, and catching its mane, vaulted onto its back. Hugging its bare sides with his legs, his hand clutching its mane, he brought it around, struck its haunch with the flat of the short sword, and galloped it right through the soldiers. He raced for the gate, turned the horse down the road over the neck, and felt it skid on the broken rubble of slate. "Steady, my soul!" he entreated it.

The soldiers would have to use time to saddle horses before they pursued him. He brought his beast across the neck onto the mainland. There he headed north along the cliff. When he reached the church he had not yet heard any cry behind him. He turned his horse loose and went in and looked for something with which to block the door. There was nothing in the bare building, nothing outside it, either. Never mind, he was not in need of a stronghold, only walls around him, and a narrow entrance he could de-

300

fend. You will have to serve me today, he said to the short sword, but if I could pray another four hands of length onto your blade, I would. He ran to the place of the altar, thrust the sword into the earth, and knelt before it. God, give me wits and strength to save Isoud, he said. Send me Andret, he said, if You care for the cleanliness of this world, Lord God.

Then he rose and went to the window and studied the cliff and the sea. The tide lacked only a little time of being full, and the sea stood high on the cliff, its roar muted by its fullness, its fury calmed. Tristram leaned out, looking north and south, marking what ledges and footholes he could discern at the water line. If you are to be my grave, he said, take me swiftly. But I shall dispute my death if I can.

He returned to the door and stood by it, sword in hand. He had not long to wait. He heard the horses before he saw them, and he grinned with fierce joy to think he had brought his men where he wanted them to be.

When the troop rode into the clearing before the church he saw that not only had knights of the household joined them, but King Mark and Andret as well. And Dinadan, as God loves me! "Welcome, my lords," Tristram called. "I sent for you."

The king stared down on him heavily. "This is useless, Tristram. You are taken."

"I may be taken in time," Tristram said, "but now I stand here free in this door which is wide enough only for me. Whoever takes me must encounter with me first."

"I shall order you taken in force if I have to," Mark said. "You have been a traitor to me, Tristram."

"Whoever says so, let him prove it on me. I have done some service to Cornwall, uncle. I met The Marhaus when no knight of yours would go against him. I was promised a reward for that, and I was promised a reward when I brought the queen from Ireland. And neither reward has been given me."

"Don't treat with him, my lord," Andret said. "He has shamed you."

"You are shamed if you deny me the reward you have sworn

to give me," Tristram said. "I ask it now. I ask to be allowed to prove the charge against me on whoever makes it."

"Tristram is right, my lord," Dinadan said. "You have sworn to reward him."

Oh, valiant little man, Tristram thought! Now you have ruined yourself for me.

"Besides," Dinadan was going on, "he is a king's son, and every lord in Britain will raise a cry if he is judged like a felon without trial."

"Even a king's son has no rights if he is a traitor," Mark said. "I will not stand here and talk. I order you to take this traitor and return him to Tintagel."

"Then," Dinadan said, "I yield you the lands I hold from you, Mark, and I am no longer your man. I shall fight with Tristram." And he struck his horse and leaped from it right into the door. He unsheathed his battle sword and put it in Tristram's hand, receiving the short sword.

Mark turned upon Andret. "Are you a traitor too? I have ordered Tristram taken."

"Take me, Andret!" Tristram cried happily.

"My shield," Dinadan said, and hung it on Tristram's shoulder.

The knights dismounted and, led by Andret, moved upon the church. But the door was narrow and they could not storm it in force. All the same they crowded together, none among them having any very urgent wish to encounter Tristram alone. Tristram drew a long breath, feeling the steady joy come over him he knew so well. Yet it was not easy to defend the door. He could not fight with his feet planted, like a tree. He must move from side to side, leaving himself open to be flanked. But the knights hindered each other, striking ill-aimed blows, or blows without strategy. They must fight singly, or they must form in close order and overwhelm him by sheer weight. And nobody seemed to wish to stand first to be pushed upon his blade.

They were willing enough, though, to keep behind Andret and let him fight first. And after a few moments Tristram found himself face to face with the seneschal of Cornwall. Andret was fighting with desperate courage, wielding his sword rapidly and with skill. But Tristram reached over and under his guard, drawing him in, playing him, waiting for the moment when he would unguard himself. It came quickly. Andret lunged and flung up his shield, and Tristram's point took him cleanly in the heart.

When Andret fell, blood bursting from his mouth, the knights dropped back. Men stood near the seneschal staring down on him, absorbing the fact that Tristram had killed him.

"Is he dead?" Mark said.

"Yes. His breast is cut in two."

"This is an unequal fight, my lord," a knight said. "You can keep Tristram a prisoner in the church, or you can treat with him. But if he is taken, he will kill us first. Is your cause worth all our lives?"

Mark sat still, his head bowed as he gazed on the body of his seneschal. In the twenty-four hours since he left Tintagel on the false errand whose results had destroyed the peace of Cornwall he had lost all the spring of his second youth and become a hollow, worn, old man. His black eyes, always so bright, were dull and purplish in his sallow face, sunk into grey pits. His beard and hair were dishevelled, and even his clothes sagged upon him, his medallion hanging awry under his arm. His was not a soul able to show grief or righteous anger, only this sudden, sad decay.

"Tristram must be taken," he said.

The knights drew together, murmuring. They stood shoulder to shoulder, their shields before them, and pressed toward the church. Tristram defended the door with all his strength, but though he killed two knights, and wounded others, they were twelve against him, and he was thrust back until he was fighting against the window.

He leaped into the embrasure. "Save yourself, Dinadan," he said, and threw the sword from him, and, with a prayer, sprang wide into the sea.

Chapter Twenty-nine

F ROM the water he saw the cliff cruelly high and sheer. And now the breakers which had seemed lulled by the tide when he stood above them were swells capable of hiding the sky. But the wicked currents, the crashings of incoming waves upon outgoing, the tortured spouts and falls, were smoothed away by the very moment of high tide. The sea lay still, or as still as it ever lay on the rocks of Cornish coasts, neither ebbing nor flowing. And as Tristram rode the crests and troughs he began to hope he would not be broken against the wall of slate upon whose top he could see the church and even the window black against grey stone.

He could make headway swimming, at least enough to keep his body clear of ragged points offering no foothold. He was not able to guess whether he was watched from above or, if he were, whether he was visible. He labored toward the outer sea, trusting that when he was beyond the shadow of the cliff the dazzle of sun on the silvery wash would conceal his head or confuse it with gulls riding the surf. Birds waiting for ebb tide perched in hundreds on every cranny of the cliff large enough to take them, and at times many would rise together and wheel and float above the waves. They offered him a little cover because they were distracting and presented visual patterns between himself and whoever might be leaning from the window trying to follow his progress.

Slowly fighting his way toward the south he hoped to discover a ledge he might reach without destroying himself. They were too high or too narrow or lying over recesses into which the current scoured with too wild a swirl. When time had passed, he could not estimate how much, half an hour, an hour perhaps, his legs were numb with cold and he could see his hands white and bloodless. He asked himself whether he could stay alive long enough to swim to the beach below Tintagel head, or to the island where he had fought The Marhaus. He knew he could not. He must come ashore soon or he would not come ashore at all.

As he was beating his way seaward after a wave had pushed him perilously close to the cliff, he was aware for a second of something dark and immense above him, and before he could realize it was the round shoulder of a breaker he was caught and tossed upward and smothered in the water's black breast. He felt himself roll and tumble like a pebble, then shoot forward and strike rock and skid along it and be halted by some violent embrace around his body. The wave churned away, and he sucked air into his bursting lungs, unable to think why he was not rushing back with the force of water draining off the slate walls around him as though through sluices. Then he became aware that his arms were flung above his head and that he was clutching the rim of a cup-shaped depression worn into the cliff. He had been washed into a narrow crevasse and wedged there like driftwood. And now he was hugged between the two slate sides. As he moved his feet cautiously, feeling for a solid ledge, he had time to wonder that Providence had dropped him into this very spot where he had no choice but to land arms upward, hands grasped over the supporting rim.

He found a foothold, tried it distrustfully, rested upon it. He was too beset by the walls to be able to look down and see what held him. Each moment he expected a fresh wave to roar into the cranny and mangle him or sweep him back into the sea, but as the minutes passed and none came, he guessed that the breaker which had driven him there was the last and greatest effort of the tide. He could hear waves shatter horribly close, even feel water tug at his feet and knees. Yet no second giant roller followed the first. And he dared to tell himself he was safe.

305

Safe, but pinned into a slit from which he could imagine no means of escape. He drew himself in as small as possible and rocked his body gently, loosening it from the pinching walls. When he slid free a pain caught him in the chest. But if he was injured, if his ribs were broken or his lungs crushed, it was a small price to pay for the blessed fact that he was alive. He could not climb up. He could emerge from this precarious crevasse only by edging along it toward its opening in the cliff. Bracing himself with a hand on each wall he moved as delicately as a serpent along the tiny ledge and reached the outer cliff and looked dizzily into the water boiling almost level with him.

I'm this far, he thought. Now what? Praying for balance he turned slowly and looked up the face of the cliff. He could see just above his head a rim of stone, and beyond it nothing but sky. That must mean a wide offset in the slate wall. He clamped his hands over the offset and, urging his body to make one final effort, pulled himself up as, when he was a child, he had chinned himself on a branch. The pain knifed him and brought tears into his throat, but he raised himself head high, then shoulder high. Pushing himself with his feet, clutching at any unevenness big enough to get a hand over, he toppled onto the ledge and lay on his face, panting, half-blind with the agony in his chest, but free.

I'll turn over in a minute, he thought. I'll see how many steps of this sort I have to climb before I walk on grass again. But he lay still. After a little while he thought, I could thankfully live on this ledge a lifetime, but if there is a warmer, roomier place to live I would be glad to find it. And he planned how, when the tide had receded and the sea was less ravenously close, he would move, sit up, rise, find footholds, reach the top. But first he would rest. Only a minute. No more than five minutes. Certainly no longer than he needed to feel living warmth again.

He thought he was asleep, and that in his sleep a voice hailed him. It was not near but it was strong and urgent. "Tristram!" called the voice. "Look up!"

He pushed himself onto his hands. The pain moved in his chest like a stone falling. But he looked up and saw the cliff rising

306

straight, cut off in a black line against blue sky. On this near
horizon two men stood, and Tristram's heart recognized Gouvernail and Dinadan.

"Are you alive?" Gouvernail shouted.

He pulled himself to his feet, but when he tried to answer he
could not.

They called unintelligible directions, but better than that, they
threw down a line whose end was knotted into a loop. He passed
the loop under his arms and felt it tighten and jerk him heavily
against the cliff. He wished to tell them to wait, but he was being
dragged upward, his body slowly turning in the loop, grating upon
the stone. He held himself off with his feet as well as he was able.
When he reached the top he was torn and bleeding, incapable even
of whispering his thanks.

"Ah, Tristram!" Gouvernail said, and put an arm around him.
"This time I thought we had said good-by for good!"

"Can you walk, Tristram?" Dinadan asked him.

He nodded, yes. But he could not walk, only stumble between
them, his arms over their shoulders. And as they were lifting him
onto a horse he coughed a foam of blood, and strangled, and saw
his life fleeing before him, diminishing as an animal diminishes
running down a grey road.

When sense returned to him he was lying on a straw pallet in
an evil-smelling room into which a little light filtered through a
door blocked with branches. A man crouched beside him. "Gouvernail," he mumbled.

"It's Dinadan, brother. Do you know me?"

"Yes."

"Gouvernail will be here soon."

"Where is here?"

"We're in a swineherd's camp in the forest," Dinadan said, "a
deserted one, by luck. We must wait for darkness to move."

"Is Gouvernail—"

"Don't talk, Tristram. This is what happened. The king watched
you from the chapel until you were lost. Everybody thought you
were drowned. I did too. On the theory you were done for, Mark

307

didn't charge me with treason, but he exiled me with a handsome ·
gesture then and there, and said I must leave Cornwall before the
day was out."

"Gouvernail—"

"I'm coming to Gouvernail, my son." And Dinadan told him
how he had ridden alone toward Tintagel, hoping to hear word of
the queen, and how he met Gouvernail searching for Tristram,
and how the squire refused to believe his lord was dead, and
how they had sought him along the cliffs, and seen him lying on
the ledge. "And we took you into the forest hoping to hide you,
and had God's guidance to this herdsman's hut. We have waited
until dusk, and now Gouvernail has returned to Tintagel, because
he has friends in the hall who will conceal him and get him a word
with Bragwain. And when he knows what the situation is he'll
come back to us, and we'll make plans."

"Mark will put her to the fire," Tristram said, and tried to rise.

"No, no." Dinadan gently thrust him back onto the straw pallet.
"Mark thinks you are dead. He won't put Isoud to the fire."

Tristram turned his head and closed his eyes. What had he
intended when he leaped into the sea? He could not remember.
He had not meant to jump from the window, he had meant to
defend the chapel, and kill Andret, and make a bargain with the
king. Hadn't he killed Andret? He wasn't sure. Yes, he had. Then
he must have made his bargain with Mark, and the bargain was—
his mind hurried anxiously this way and that, trying to tell him
what the bargain was. He knew. The bargain was that, if the king
swore before his barons to let Isoud go unpunished, he, Tristram,
would sail into Britany and remain there, an exile.

So they had reached their separation at last, this time beyond
appeal. Why had not Mark permitted him the charity of a farewell to her as Anguissh had when they learned he was not Tramtris, but Tristram? Because he had leaped into the sea? The cycle
began again as he asked himself once more why he had hurled
himself from the high window. And his confused thoughts were
mingled with memories of Isoud, of her dear and splendid beauty,

308

of the love they had loved, of her eyes looking so steadfast and absolute into his in the bedchamber.

He knew when Gouvernail returned, knew he was being bathed and given bread and water to drink. And they talked to him, but he could not follow their talk. Finally they lifted him, and helped him onto a horse, and one of them rode with him, holding an arm around his body. They took him somewhere through darkness, and lifted him down, and carried him in their arms, and put him on a hard bed, and covered him with furs. But he could not fix his mind on any of this, he could not hold it as present truth. For he was tormented all the while with the fear that Isoud was being led from the castle and chained to a stake, and that the fire took her bright body and her clear eyes.

Then he dreamed of The Marhaus, and of his wound, and of sailing into Ireland in the little ship of oxhide. Many days passed before he realized he was wounded, only this time by the sea which had crushed him, and that he had sailed in a boat, not to Ireland, but to Britany. When he was able to see what he looked at, to ask questions and receive answers rationally, he learned he was lying in the hall of King Hoël. Yseut's face told him he had been near death.

She was sitting beside him, and he grew aware she was holding his hand in hers. "I never wrote you the letter I promised," he said, hoping he was smiling.

She raised his hand and laid it lightly against her cheek. "It doesn't matter now, Tristram. You have come home to us."

"Home?"

"Oh, Tristram, I have made you weep! Don't weep, Tristram!"

He was angry because her word, home, had stripped him so, because his weakness had started tears for Yseut to see. "I'm not weeping. How long have I lain here, Yseut?"

"You've had a terrible fever," she said. "They carried you from the ship on a horse litter, and you have been sick for nine days. My mother and I have nursed you."

"You've grown up," he said.

"Did you think I wouldn't?"

He nodded. "It seems strange to see you changed. Where is Gouvernail, Yseut?"

"Poor .Gouvernail, let him rest. He sits by your bed all night long."

"Is he sleeping?"

"Tell me what you need. I'll fetch it for you."

Tristram could not tell her his need. He had returned to life thinking of Isoud, racked with the fear that she was put to the fire, that she was dead. He tried to assort his memories, to learn from his own recollection whether he had saved her. Oh, where was she! What had Mark done with her! He tried to lift himself from the bed.

"Poor Tristram," Yseut said. "You have had such bad dreams. Now you'll forget them, won't you?"

"Yseut. Tell me what happened in—in Cornwall."

"That is all past now," she said, "isn't it, Tristram?"

"Tell me!"

"Nothing happened. They were cruel to you in Cornwall—all of them—and Gouvernail and Dinadan brought you home. That's all. And you will be strong soon, and happy again the way we were happy before." She leaned above him and smoothed his brow, possessive of him as a whole person is of a sick one. "Don't you remember how happy we were, Tristram?"

"I must speak to Gouvernail, Yseut. If you'll only call him I'll remember anything you ask me to."

She drew away from him and let go his hand. He could see she felt rebuffed, but he was too weary and excited to care. "I have prayed God," she said, "to let me be with you when you waked from the fever, Tristram. I have waited through so many hours, so many days, for you."

Her dark eyes bent on his affected him like a dream of his illness, like something inescapable. He turned his head fretfully.

"I'll call Gouvernail," she said.

I can't have them hanging over me, he thought, prating of home, and staring into my soul. Home. Why had Yseut's insistence on the word cut him so? Home meant nothing, not in Britany, not

310

anywhere. Isoud was his home, and when they were separated they were exiles on the earth, no matter what welcome they received from strangers, even from friends. Oh, my only Isoud! Unless God brings me to you again I would better have died in the sea.

"Tristram," Gouvernail said.

"I'm alive again, brother."

"It was close this time, Tristram."

"Tell me what you know of Isoud."

The squire sat down in the chair Yseut had left. His face was puffy with sleep, worn by the long nights of his vigil too. As the princess had done, he bent above the bed, possessive of the sick one. But Tristram bore him better because his eyes lacked the hungry tenderness of Yseut's. "Your illness has deafened you," he said. "You have asked me fifty times, and I have told you fifty times. Isoud was not punished. Do you remember her letter?"

"Did she send me a letter?"

Gouvernail rehearsed again what had happened after they drew Tristram up the cliff. He had ridden back to Tintagel secretly and bribed a friendly servant to summon Bragwain to the garden. When evening covered her coming she met him, and told him of Mark's return to the castle and how he entered Isoud's chamber and informed her Tristram was drowned. Isoud said, "I am guilty, my lord, and I ask to die." And they had stood looking into each other's faces until the king turned and left her. He went into the hall and called his barons together and decreed three days of mourning for the seneschal and the two knights slain by the cliff. Then he said, "Tristram's death establishes the queen's innocence, and let it never be spoken of again." And he went to the church and forbade any man to follow him. He was still in the church when Bragwain and Gouvernail met.

"I told Bragwain you were not drowned," Gouvernail said, "and that Dinadan and I needed a boat to take you away. She asked me to wait. She returned to the castle, and after an hour she came back to me, and she brought the letter from the queen, and money, and word that a ship would take us off a cove north

311

of the church. I don't know how the queen secured the ship, Tristram, only that she did secure it."

"Let me see the letter."

"I have kept it with me," Gouvernail said, and he drew a folded parchment from the pouch hanging at his belt.

Tristram took Isoud's letter, feeling himself tremble. "My Tristram," she had written, "I am all one joy because you are alive when I thought you dead. I would have died too. Because we have been near death, think only how precious it is that we are alive in the same world, and do not grieve because we are separated. We must not meet again, my dear lord, for the king will never trust you. But as long as we live our love lives. I am yours."

Isoud, Isoud, I am yours too, and I will return to Cornwall and take you away! The memory of her shook him and blinded him to everything except the memory. Mark wasn't strong enough to keep them apart, nothing was strong enough, not even God's will.

"Bragwain told me," Gouvernail said, "that the queen sent you a warning. She said you must never forget that, when the king learns you are alive, he will kill you."

"He will threaten me, anyway," Tristram said, "but—"

"And I have a warning for you too, Tristram," Gouvernail said quietly. "The queen's innocence rests on the king's belief in your death. If you return to Cornwall, she will stand in peril of the fire."

Tristram lay back in the bed. For the first time since he was dragged from Isoud's chamber his mind was clear of the need for action, of the pressure of danger, of the vague timelessness of illness. And for the first time he was overwhelmed with the mortal realization that he had lost Isoud.

Chapter Thirty

TRISTRAM'S broken body mended under the care of Yseut and the queen of Britany. When spring returned, and flowers opened, and new green plumed the trees, he was well enough to ride down to the port and bid Dinadan good-by. The little knight, sure Tristram would soon be whole, was returning to Britain to offer King Arthur his service.

He made a joke of it. "Now I'm for it," he said. "Now I shall have to live up to Gawaine and Launcelot. For a peaceable man like me Camelot is a sentence."

"You should stay in Britany, Dinadan, as Hoël wants you to."

Dinadan shook his head. "For better or worse I'm a Briton, and Britons are always restless on strange ground."

"Will you go on the Grail quest?"

"No, that's too big an enterprise for a man whose morals are kept busy enough getting him through each day as it comes. I haven't much desire to whore after vast truths, you know."

"I always thought of the Grail quest as a kind of dream," Tristram said. "I don't understand why we hear so much of it all at once."

"Perhaps it's only traveller's gossip, Tristram. Things have a way of enlarging when they cross seas."

"If you learn anything of Cornwall, send me word."

"I'll do that. Now God keep you, my son."

"God keep you, brother."

313

He was lonely after Dinadan left. For he found that the life he had lived since his days as a squire in Hoël's court, his journeys into Ireland, and his position as a prince in Cornwall, had altered him, or altered his memory of the household in Britany. He recalled how Lyonesse seemed to have grown small when he returned to it, and understood that Hoël's house had undergone the same process of change. Yet he was touched with a homesick sense of youth as he came upon one remembered detail after another, and he half wished it was possible for a man to retreat to the time when his heart was free and careless, and his desire was all for the great trifles of childhood: to fly his first hawk, to bring down his first game, to ride on his first armed action. After a while nothing could be first, nothing careless, either.

He required himself to enter King Hoël's service with the will to do well, hoping by the practice of his knighthood to find knighthood worth bearing. Yet his duty returned him no joy. He fought when he had to fight, offered hospitality when hospitality was expected, discharged every office when it was given him to discharge. But his goings and comings seemed to him an empty box around his life, meaningless. Even his prayers were meaningless. Always like a subsill under his days and nights lay the knowledge that Isoud was lost to him. He did not need to remember it. He did not need to think of her, though he thought of her. Her loss was not thoughts, not memories, not words. It was the fibre of his body, the whole fullness of his soul.

He learned from Gouvernail that he had talked of her in his illness, and he was aware Hoël knew the truth of his love and his exile. But the king did not speak of it, or the queen either, and Tristram was grateful for their forbearance. They accepted him affectionately as they might have accepted a son. And it came over Tristram that, when he had so many times longed to live in Britany again, when he had dreamed of his adopted land as of a haven, he should experience a filial thankfulness to be here at last. But he could not draw from his withered heart any feeling at all, and only his mind told him he was a returning son thankful for welcome.

He was ashamed of his apathy for he knew the family of King Hoël exerted themselves to encourage and restore him. Hoël sent him on missions to the Rhine valley and to Rome, praising his skill in diplomacy, and drawing him out with questions touching the white city of the south. The queen spurred him gently into the society of the court, making opportunities for him to visit the halls of the chief barons, and to show his skill in music, and to pass time with ladies. He tried to earn their trust, giving himself willingly to their loving conspiracies for his soul's health. Yet he knew he did not deceive them, for now and again he would look up to see the king studying him with a thoughtful frown, or he would hear the queen sigh.

It was Yseut who tended him most faithfully. In the beginning when he was too feeble to endure so much persistent sympathy her kindness depressed, even annoyed him. He had been ill only once before, in Ireland, and there, though he had been watched and cared for, no woman had brooded over him, none had been at the same time a humble and a wilful servant. But as his strength gave him the means to be more wholly himself he found her less trying. And by the time he could walk, and ride a horse, and tease her for her tyranny, he had forgotten her clutch upon his illness, and could see how pleasant she was, what an even disposition she had, and how amusing was her gift of pretty small talk. Besides, she was charming to look at. She was still a little thing, though no longer in the childish mold of fifteen. Now her body had taken on dainty curves, and the dusky complexion of her girlhood had paled into creamy tints over which the sun of Britany had painted soft lights of gold.

After a struggle to maintain the ascendancy her power as nurse gave her, she seemed to have made up her mind to accept the change his restoration brought. Once she had gulped down the fact that he hated the well-meant espionage his sickness had opened him to, she accepted him as a whole and happy man. And always she had a diversion to propose. She walked with him to the harbor to see the trading ships come in, or she showed him trails along the low cliffs against which the summer sea murmured its music,

315

or she led him over pebbly beaches to talk to the men raking sea-weed into long, squared-off ricks. One day she would order a picnic of bread and wine and take him to visit fields where rows of ancient monoliths stood like some unearthly crop sowed by the hands of giants; another they would go to a legendary battle-ground whose contending armies had once been separated by a massive stone flung down from heaven by the gods.

All the while she bubbled along gaily as though talk were the only delight in the world. Did Tristram know a sunken city lay off the coast of her father's land? And in a church there a priest celebrated mass every day while fish swam in and out of the windows? The priests in Britany were clever men. Once each year —so farmers said, at least—the priests summoned the devil from under the foundations of their churches, and made him show his claws.

"Now why would a priest want to see the devil's claws?" Tristram asked her.

"So as to make sure the devil hasn't hidden the souls of the dead under his fingernails."

"Oh, Yseut!" Tristram laughed at her. He had never known a woman well in his life except Isoud of Ireland, she whose temperament was all fire, and he was surprised and diverted by this little, cheerful, talking, helpful Yseut.

"And they have to use awfully strong spells to call the devil," she told him wisely. "The poor priests are panting and bleeding from the nose when they have finished."

"That's the oddest reason for getting a bloody nose I ever heard."

"You should remember," she said, "that many odd things happen in Britany."

He smiled his answer.

"What did you remember of Britany when you were away, Tristram?"

"Oh—the sun pouring down on everything, and the smell of harvest, and bonfires on the hills of summer evenings. Cornwall

316

is windy and stormy. Nobody in Cornwall would light a bonfire at night just to see it blaze."

"They don't light them here just to see them blaze, either. Young married couples make fires on Midsummer Eve and jump over them so as to take the strength of the smoke into their bodies and have healthy children."

"How did you get your head crammed with all this nonsense, Yseut?"

"Is it nonsense?" She gave him a sidelong look.

"Isn't it?"

"I've been telling you these old things to make you laugh. You *are* laughing," she said with glee.

"And why is it important when I laugh?"

"Because," she said, "you were sad when you came home, Tristram. And if you laugh I know you are not sad now. Are you sad now?" And she gave him a pleading glance.

"No."

She sighed. "Sometimes you are. I keep hoping you will tell me why."

But he could not bear to speak to her of the sorrow which had brought him to Britany. For one reason, the secret was his. For another, Yseut seemed to him to have the wild innocence of a bird, her spirit so simple, so clear, so removed from darkness and grief that it would be cruelty to tell her the world was not everywhere the sunny place she found it in Britany. As he looked at her smooth cheek, at her childishly long eyelashes, at her rosy mouth, he was moved by her innocence, seeing in it a new meaning of the word. Hers was the innocence of the nestling cuckoo before it had learned of the hawk.

"If you will not tell me why you are sad," she said, "at least tell me what else you remembered of Britany while you were in Cornwall."

"I don't know—chestnut trees in bloom."

"And?"

"And what?"

"What other thing?"

317

"Roman officers coming to see your father."

"Did you think sometimes of how we used to go together to the docks to watch for ships from Lyonesse?"

"That reminds me," Tristram said. "Did a sailor on a merchantman ever give you a message from me?"

"No."

"I knew he was a lying pirate, that fellow," Tristram said. "I should wait for him and have him flogged."

"He told me."

"But you said—"

"I said he didn't because your message made me angry."

Tristram laughed. "I don't believe you were ever angry with anyone in your life, Yseut."

"I was angry with you."

"Why on earth! It was a friendly message, wasn't it?"

"You sent me your duty," she said.

"Of course I did."

"If," she said, "if I had been you, and you me, I would have sent you my love."

He did not wish to follow where this conversation led, even in jest. "Duty and love are the same thing. Let us not quarrel about the message, Yseut. I dislike quarrelling."

"Always?"

"Always with ladies," he said firmly.

When the summer had passed, and the oak trees showed their bronze, and the beeches began to drop the mast which would take the swineherds into winter camp in the forest, Hoël sent for Tristram. They went from the hall into the queen's chamber where they found her alone. Because the day was low and brumous, logs were burning in the fireplace, and the room was fragrant with hearth odors. It was a cheerful room, its walls warmed with hangings, and lamp dishes of tallow set about it to lighten it in the evenings for the handwork the queen did so expertly.

She rose and greeted them with a serious smile. "Welcome, my two lords. I've been expecting you." She gave them chairs, and

318

hot spiced wine to drink, and seated herself near the king. And there was a silence.

"I think you have something to tell me, my lady," Tristram said. The king nodded. "So we have, Tristram."

Looking into their grave faces he felt his heart contract, he felt as though he had returned to a crossroad in his life at whose junction he had many times suffered defeat. They would send him away. He was to be forbidden Britany as he had been forbidden Ireland and Cornwall, even Lyonesse. Facing this new exile, his heart told him he had been happy here however heavy the burden under which he labored. Between one breath and the next he saw his happiness shattered, and the warmth and welcome which had revived him lost.

"If I have done anything to hurt Britany—" he began.

"No, no," the king said, "you misunderstand us. Britany is fortunate to have such a knight as you."

"Tell him quickly you are only going to send him on a mission," the queen said.

"That's what it is," Hoël said. "I have a mission for you."

"My poor Tristram," the queen said, " you look as though we meant to hang you!"

"My errand will occupy you from now through most of the winter," Hoël told him. "For a year and more I have meant to survey my garrisons and re-form my camps. But I have put it off because the times are stable, and because there never seems to be enough leisure to do something not crying to be done. Your being here is good fortune for me, Tristram. This is a work I don't want to trust to my barons."

"I should like nothing better than to do it, my lord," Tristram said. "I have ideas about garrisoning I've never been able to put into practice."

"I'll give you a party of mounted yeomen, say twenty men, and two knights courier. And I want you to stay at each camp a week, or as long as you need to read its effectiveness and estimate its position as a member of our whole defense. And when you return in the spring you'll report to me, and together we shall devise such plans as you think we need."

They fell to talking military details, fortifications, roads, heavy weapons, even strategy in battle. And Tristram spoke of the garrisons of King Anguissh, and how he left his heights undefended, but of how in Cornwall each cape and headland had its own tower, its runners and foot soldiers. "The way the land lies is everything," he said happily, "and the best captain is the man who makes the land fight with him."

"I can see my garrisons will be in good hands," Hoël said. "When you were a squire, Tristram, I was sure you had a future in military campaigns."

"But a knight must have his own country, and a good lord, and a settled future, to learn to campaign," Tristram said. "If he wanders, as I have, his skill is spent in combat."

"True," Hoël said, "and you bring me to the second thing I wish to say to you."

Now a sense of joy took Tristram such as he had not felt in long months, for he understood the king might offer to make him prince of Britany. And though he had been taught in Cornwall that a foreigner who comes into a kingdom and supercedes its barons is not loved, he knew affairs at King Hoël's court were better run than at Mark's, subject to a stronger, less wavering control. Besides, Hoël had no heir, not even a cousin. In Britany no Andret would connive against him.

"You were bred with us," the king said.

"I remember, my lord."

"You lived with us nine years, and in those nine years we learned to hope you would remain in Britany, and that our court would become your home."

"But we thought it fair that your father, King Meliodas, should knight you," the queen said, "and only for that reason we let you go."

"I was knighted in Cornwall, my lady, before I fought The Marhaus."

"Yes," Hoël said, "we have followed you, Tristram. Each year since you left us we have had news of you. And we hoped your fortune would be better than it turned out."

"Dinadan told me once I have the gift of making myself unpopular," Tristram said, "but—"

"There is some truth in what he says, Tristram. But you were young and without strong friends, and your judgment was still forming. It is not a bad thing," he went on quietly, "for a young knight to try the world alone and make his mistakes and even suffer for them. All these things shape and educate him. A time comes, though, when he leaves unprofitable roving behind."

"We know you have had misfortunes," the queen said, "perhaps heavier than many men have. I used to say of you when you were young," she told him with a smile, "that you did things more intensely than my other pages, Tristram. And so we rather expected you would meet difficulties. But they are in the past now, and need not be spoken of."

"Yes, the past is spent," Hoël said.

Tristram did not understand them. For he hardly viewed his past as a series of errors only. To himself he seemed a man who had done what courage required, and what faith required, not always brilliantly, but some of the time with honor.

"The past is spent," Hoël repeated, "and now we think of the present."

"And of the future," the queen said.

"Yes, of the future, Tristram. And this is what we propose. Spend the winter refreshing your knowledge of Britany and overseeing the garrisons and preparing your report. And when you return to us in the spring we shall hope to make you prince of our land."

"My dear lord," Tristram said, "if I deserve that of you, you shall have my best service as long as I have strength to give it."

"Well said, Tristram. And now our chiefest hope is that the season in camp will clear you of—of—" he said, and looked to the queen for help.

"Of your sorrow," she said gently. "We know it, Tristram. It will lessen. You will free yourself. And when you return you will see that Yseut has never forgotten you."

"Don't answer us now, Tristram. Give yourself the time in camp. Only remember that, since you and Yseut were children, we have hoped for your marriage."

Now he understood. Now his mind flew open, and he realized how King Hoël and the queen considered his love for Isoud a weakness and a calamity, an illness of the mind, a shame from which he must himself wish to recover. But they did not know Isoud, they had never seen her shining beauty, they did not begin to comprehend how his faith had been pledged, how his life was nothing but his faith. And he understood more, that he was to be made prince of Britany for Yseut's sake. Yseut. The thought of her invaded his mind slowly and with pain. She was dear to him, all kindness and gentle ways, so pretty, so generous. But no, not Yseut, not any woman save Isoud.

"My lord—" he said.

"Wait," Hoël interrupted him. "Wait, Tristram. Give yourself until spring."

"Give yourself until spring," the queen said, "but don't forget us, Tristram. Remember, we have loved you, all of us, almost as long as you have been in this world."

Chapter Thirty-one

IF Yseut knew of her parents' conversation with Tristram she did not let her knowledge show as self-consciousness when she bade him farewell and wished him God's protection through the winter. Though she would miss him, she said, she would think how he was in his homeland of Britany again, and how the fogs and winds from the northeast would soon be over, and how they would all be together in the spring, a reunited family. And she gave him a bronze medal engraved with a cross to keep him safe.

He left the court with the premonition he had felt before in his life, that he was leaving a place to which he would never return. Yet, though a part of his spirit was leaden and numbed with regret, a part was alert, almost happy. He was riding at the head of his first military command, charged with a duty he was anxious to perform. And he could not help take pleasure in his troop of mounted yeomen carrying the king's standard, and the horses, and the new shield with his own blazon, and Gouvernail beside him wearing his own colors. Perhaps it was better not to look into the future, not to think of spring, and whether or how he would return to Hoël's house. It was better to do knightly and well the work assigned to his hand. And as time passed God might give him wisdom and shape his course.

Hoël's garrisons were spaced around the coasts and along the eastern borders of Britany. Tristram turned southeast and led his party slowly along shores indented with bays and coves and deep, narrow river valleys up which the tides rushed twice each day, bringing with them flocks of gulls as well as the coastal boats of fishermen coming home with their catch. There were times when the sea still seemed empurpled with summer weather, when in port towns the scent of salt and seaweed and barnacle-encrusted timbers mingled with flowery odors and the fragrance of fresh earth. For winter was late and languid along this island-bejewelled south edge of Hoël's country. As Tristram and his men moved from one port town to the next, sometimes passing along sunken roads above which trees almost met, sometimes through beech forests or glades of chestnut or redolent groves of pine, they came now and then upon a farm where oat stubble still lay dry in the fields, and heaps of turnips and parsnips were being mounded in for cattle food. And there were days when, riding back from the sea to a ford or bridge, they crossed undulating stretches of moor where thorn broom or whin owned the land. He loved the moors for their changing color under skies of grey or blue or tarnished pearl.

He talked the king's business with port reeves and captains, and visited castle barons whose obligation it was to know the condition of the coast and what men came, on what errands. When he reached fortified camps he stayed in the rude field barracks of the soldiers, inspecting earthworks and round towers, and estimating the utility of roads tying one garrison to another or to some common center. Among the soldiers he found many men who claimed the blood of Britons, men who could still sing songs in which the flight of their forefathers was remembered, they who had fled from Britain across the sea before the invading heathens in white helms. But these men seemed like strangers because their speech had altered through the generations of their exile, and because they lived under a warmer, more glowing sun than any sun Britain knew.

He visited slate mines and marshes where salt pans were standing on wooden trestles, and as he turned north again, passed through the wide lowland where ferriers smelted out iron ore. And he thought how Britany, which seemed like one vast forest washed by the sea, opened, when you were close to its soil, into a little self-sufficient world needing nothing for survival it could not draw from its own breast. This was a fortunate country. Its king had a good life among people not rich, not great, but given their moderate requirements by Providence, and living in peace and the fear of God. A man could be content as prince of Britany, he could be content only to live here without state dignities, seeing honor enough in a useful life and a home among friends. I could live in Britany, Tristram thought, if I could forget Isoud. But I can't forget her. I have no will to forget her. If I forgot her I would be as empty as a ruin whose time and function are beyond the knowledge of men.

Though he did not forget her, though he remembered her beauty and her mirth and her love, she had receded beyond new and poignant recall as a person who has died recedes. He could remember how, when she smiled, a tiny dimple lay in her upper lip, how a strand of her hair sprang into a curl around his finger, how she spoke his name. But sometimes he could not summon her whole image clearly, seeing it blurred as through a mist. And because he had so little besides their love to remember he grew weary at times remembering only love. Absent, she exacted more of him than he could give, a high, impassioned zeal for remembrance which he could hardly sustain without the help of the thousand little memories less demanding than the one overwhelming memory of love.

Yet when he reached the north coast and stood on the cliff looking out on the Narrow Seas and thought how Cornwall lay beyond, and Tintagel, and Mark's castle, all that time had dimmed and softened started awake. Now he saw her plain. Now he recalled not only her fairness but every moment of her fairness he had known. And a will to return to her took him with such violence that he thought how he would ride down to the port and find a boat, and leave his party to get back to Hoël's castle the best way they could. Like a sick man he had been dreaming a dream of death when he believed he could live content away from Isoud.

"Here in the north," Gouvernail said to him, "we may learn news of Cornwall, Tristram."

"I was thinking the same thing."

"Do you want me to ask whether any Cornish sailors are in harbor?"

"No," Tristram said, "but there is something I want you to do for me, Gouvernail."

"What is it?"

"Go into Cornwall yourself. See Bragwain and the queen if you can. And meet me again fourteen days from today." Tristram named a port to the west whose garrison he was to inspect. "I shall wait for you there."

"What do you hope from this, Tristram? Since you can't go back to Cornwall, wouldn't it be wiser not to trouble yourself with a half-return?"

"I must know whether she needs me."

They were standing on a headland forming the western curve of a little bay. Beyond them the rocks ran down into the sea, flat sheets of slate resting almost on their edges, and pressed against each other like leaves. Together they formed one ragged spine of grey and yellow, bare, cold under the northern light, ruffled with rattling surf. In the harbor fishing curraghs waited for ebbing water, and on the beach boats which, in summer, sailed along the coast with meal and onions and cabbages, were turned over like faded beetles to wait out the dead season. Something was going on at the harbor, a religious procession or a ceremony of petition to the sea, and from their height Tristram and Gouvernail could see people walking, and hear the faint echo of their song.

"Look." The squire pointed down. "These Bretons live with God as though He were a local reeve."

"God has been good to them."

"I know," Gouvernail said. "Many times I've thought so these past weeks when we've been riding from valley to valley. This is a blest place. I wish you could make up your mind to stay, Tristram."

"If I stay I must marry the lady Yseut."

"Yes. But that has been expected since you were a squire at the court. Would it be such a difficult thing?"

326

"What do you mean, it has been expected? It was never mentioned to me until a few days before we began our inspection."

"Tristram," Gouvernail said, "everybody at the court but you knows the lady Yseut has refused to marry at all unless she marries you. Don't you remember when she was a child how she followed you?"

Tristram shook his head, not so much to deny what Gouvernail said as to put it from him. He was not so innocent as to mistake Yseut's feelings. But he had no wish to understand them, he did not want to hear her love spoken.

"She is beyond the age when women marry," Gouvernail said, "because she has waited for your return."

"She is a child," Tristram said.

"She is twenty-one."

"I can't marry anyone, Gouvernail."

"What shall we do, then," the squire said, "when we leave Britany?"

Tristram struck his horse and brought it around, prancing. "Will you take the trip to Cornwall for me, Gouvernail? Will you ride down to the port today and find out whether a boat is leaving?"

"I'll go wherever you send me," Gouvernail said with a sigh.

As Tristram led his troop westward he was haunted by this conversation he had had with Gouvernail on the high cape above the harbor. He saw again and again the dark sea, and the yellow-grey backbone of rock, and the priests and townsfolk winding along the waterside making their prayers for deliverance, or abundance, or whatever it was they prayed for that day. And he thought how the sea and the cliff and all the things of earth were indifferent to the prayers men made, his own and the parading votaries' alike. But these meditations did not help him outride what Gouvernail had told him. And he thought of Yseut, so small and pretty, so kind, so sure that love, like prayer, would be answered, and he felt as though he had betrayed her simple soul.

In this way, racked between guilt and his longing for Isoud, he reached the port garrison where Gouvernail's return from Cornwall was appointed. He spent the days of waiting doing the work he had to do, but for once he could not keep his mind on his duties. He had been separated from Isoud for more than a year, and in the year he had heard nothing of her save Hoël's routine reports from Cornwall. She had sent him no letters, no messenger. And now that he was to receive her own word to him he labored under an excitement dulling him to everything else. He rode with the captains and civil officers, was given counts of soldiers and supplies, learned what repairs were needed. And because he had been trained to perform all things faithfully he preserved this information for the king. But he did not think of it, or of Yseut, or of how the princess of Britany had waited for him, or of how her woman's destiny lay in his hands.

Each day he rode to the harbor to watch for Gouvernail's ship. And when it came, and the squire was ashore, Tristram took him by the shoulders. "Did you see her?"

"Yes."

"Did she—is she as—as—"

"She is well, Tristram. We can walk on the beach, and I'll tell you what I know."

It was high tide, and the sand was narrowed to strips and little shining islands. Behind the beach lay a slope covered with thin yellow sedge. They mounted this slope and walked along its crest, hearing quiet surf below them, and the wind rustling through the winter grass.

"I spoke with Bragwain," Gouvernail said, "and Bragwain told me the king has been courteous with the queen. He has aged, and his temper is short with his barons, and he has no favorites. But he treats Isoud with kindness."

"But Isoud—"

"I spoke with her," Gouvernail said. "Bragwain smuggled me into the spinning room, and I spoke with her there."

Tristram's heart pressed upward into his throat. "Did she remember me?"

"She said I was to tell you she would never forget you while she lived, Tristram. But she said you must never come back to

328

Cornwall. Mark has a watch kept for you at every port and at his borders with Britain. And he keeps a watch over her too. She says you must understand he lives only to hate you, and to kill you if you return."

"But—"

"And as soon as he hears you have set one foot ashore, he will imprison the queen. Or kill her."

"I must go back," Tristram said.

"Never," Gouvernail said, "if you care for her life and her happiness."

Then Tristram asked him a hundred questions. Was Isoud's beauty unspoiled? Was she pale? What words had she said? He must know every one. Had she wept? Was she frightened? Had Gouvernail surely told her he thought of her, and prayed for her, and would deliver her if she would let him? Gouvernail repeated again and again his small store of information. When Tristram had grown a little calm he said, "I learned something in Cornwall that will surprise you."

"Tell me."

"Palamides is living at the court."

"What!"

Gouvernail nodded. "I know how you feel. I could hardly believe it. Our Saracen is a baron of King Mark's, sworn to him. And," the squire said, smiling incredulously, "he has been baptized and received Our Lord."

"If he is at Mark's court he is there for an evil reason. He will do the queen harm."

"I don't think so, Tristram. I think he has somehow managed to subdue himself. He is as passionate as ever, and sighs and weeps and laments his bad luck, but he is there in peace."

"Did you see him?"

"No, Bragwain told me."

"I should like to go back if only to teach him Cornwall has no room for him. I shall fight him someday to the uttermost," Tristram said. "I was a fool to spare him."

"He dreams of fighting you too. Bragwain says he speaks of

fighting you, sometimes with hatred, and sometimes with a kind of brotherly desire. Bragwain thinks he is a madman."

"Did Isoud mention him?"

"She is proud that he has become a Christian. But she pities him."

Tristram's angry jealousy would not let go the thought of Palamides. He had done what Tristram could not do, be near Isoud, see her each day, speak with her, receive her smile and her pity. And though all this could be a cross to a man who loved her—even brutishly and with monstrous conceit, as Palamides did—it was better than the crawling absence and grey silence to which Tristram was sentenced. What could have moved Isoud to receive the Saracen knight, and turn him into a Christian, and endure his noisy, violent presence? Had some sisterly interest in him persisted since the days when he had been her father's man? Tristram would not believe it. He told himself nothing in Isoud's clean spirit could feel a sympathy for this murderous heathen. She could not even pity him. Especially she could not pity him.

Through the last weeks of his errand for King Hoël Tristram dragged himself unwillingly, sometimes depressed because Isoud had not cried for his return to Cornwall, sometimes brooding over Palamides. He had good days when he could free himself of this double burden, for the weather was softening, and mild airs coaxed buds onto the trees. The small first flowers of spring stood in the grass, blue and white. Yet nothing sprang alive in him, glad and full of hope, as his heart had sprung alive in other years when the flowers winked bravely on the slopes and the cuckoos sang their nesting songs. And he began to believe his youth was past, and his power to feel the poignant joy of springtime gone.

On the day he rode into the courtyard of Hoël's house he did not remember the premonition with which he left it. He did not even see the courtyard as he might have beheld a new thing, for its old familiarity slipped over him without wonder, receiving him as a known room receives a man returning home at the end of a day. He dismounted, ordered food and ale for his troop, and followed the yeomen who had emerged to take him to the king.

330

"Welcome, Tristram," Hoël said. "We've been expecting you any time these seven days past." The king took him by the shoulders. "Your journey has agreed with you, my lord."

Hoël had never addressed him this way before. Now as he gave him the term of respect, Tristram experienced a warm, refreshing pride.

"Britany has agreed with me," he said.

"I have had your messages from your knights courier, and I can see your work has been well done. Will you rest, or shall we talk?"

"I don't need rest," Tristram said. And he sat down with his sovereign and told him what he had seen, and what he had learned, and how Britany's garrisons might be strengthened and put into closer touch with each other. He spoke of the barons he met, and of the sheriffs and reeves and captains, and described the little things, the mirth and mishaps, which made his journey memorable.

"You have performed your duty honorably," Hoël said. "Have you been as successful with your own trouble, Tristram?"

Tristram did not answer at once, seeing within himself Isoud's pure loveliness, all that was queenly in her, all that he would remember, unfading, until he died. She was not a trouble of his mind with which he must struggle more or less successfully. The king's question had no reply.

But she was lost. She was in a prison whose guardian was death. She was beyond his hope in this world, keeping state in a forbidden land with an old, embittered, revengeful king, her loyal subject a heathen with his will bent on murder.

"I have no trouble, my lord," Tristram said.

"Well done," the king said. "The princess is waiting for you."

He found Yseut in the queen's chamber alone. She ran to him and took his hand between hers, her face bright with welcome. "I felt sure you would come home today," she said.

Tristram did not notice the word she used, home. Now that he was home he had no reason to think how only wanderers and strangers without walls to return to heard the word with surprise or, it might be, with pain.

Chapter Thirty-two

TRISTRAM and Yseut were married in the castle church on the first day of summer. And because in Britany many men believed couples married on the same day as the sovereign would prosper and have healthy children, betrothed youths and girls attached to the court and the villages nearby shared the wedding mass, pressing around Tristram and Yseut afterwards to touch them for good fortune. Food, fuel, and linen were given to the poor, and troops of musicians performed in the courtyard, and tumblers and wrestlers as well. In the month following Hoël summoned his knights to a grand tournament, and the chief barons of Britany ordained hunts and exhibitions of venery.

Because messages and gifts arrived from Hoël's brother kings, among them, from Arthur and Meliodas and Anguissh of Ireland, Tristram knew word of his marriage had reached Cornwall. But when he thought of Isoud, even when he lay awake asking himself whether his marriage had cut her heart, he thought of her through a distance he could not shorten. She moved always in his mind, yet not near him, rather like the dreams which, in sleep, soothe and mend the rough confusions of life and flee when day begins. Now she was an evocation, strong and real because memory was strong and real, but beyond presence.

He entered into his marriage with a resolve to be mindful of Yseut's happiness. Hers was not a temperament to excite fervor or to inspire the spirit, but it was loyal and good-natured, and there was no question about its devotion. And she was charming. She had the gift of making serious, even pompous matters seem gay, like games. She added a sort of prettiness to every duty she performed, an air of delighted surprise that the obligations of wifehood were hers to fulfill. It was her way of showing her joy, and because it rose from a truthful soul it infected others. Always about her was a sense of pert and dainty bustle, and always about her were people who smiled, or who sighed, it might be, remembering not so much their own youth as all youth, and how brief it was.

She did not cling to Tristram. Perhaps she was wise enough to know she secured him the more surely by freeing him. When he left her to join the hunt, or to go on a journey, or only because he was weary of the castle and wished to ride along the harbor cliffs, she assured him she would not be lonely.

"I have things to do too," she would say.

"What are these things you have to do?" he asked her, seeing she waited to be asked.

"I am working a cloth. And I have to visit the smith's wife to see the new baby. And if that isn't enough, my lord, I have to improve the manners of my page."

"And if you do not do these things, the world will tremble."

"Will the world tremble if you miss the hunt? Let me tell you," Yseut said, "that men's business and women's business are different matters, but women's business is as large to women as yours is to you." She mimicked the air of a scold as she informed him of this truth, amused to play a forbidding role.

This distinction she drew between men's and women's concerns, or her will to busy herself with the warm details of life, or the fact that she had nothing hidden to reveal, set the tone of their marriage, and in a matter of weeks built around them the feeling of familiar usage. One day ran on like another. And though Tristram was dull now and then he was moved by her pleasure, and sought to suit himself to her light humors and her enthusiasm for ordinary things. When he was absent he remembered her small, eager face, and her welcome waiting him, and

333

he would tell himself that existence with her seemed monotonous because he did not make a sufficient effort to enliven it. He would buy gifts to carry home to her, jewels, or fine cloth, or a singing bird, once even a monkey purchased from Moorish sailors. And, at home, he would exert himself to interest her. If she demanded that he tell her about the world he had seen he would spend hours describing Rome to her, and the courts of the north and south. Since she seemed to desire knowledge, he established a travelled holy man in the house to be her instructor and to teach her foreign languages. But this did not work out well, for Yseut always had a dozen distracting things to do, and never found time for her lessons. All the same she liked the priest, and petted him with comforts and made him fat and lazy.

Tristram felt the days going over them, the weeks and months too, one after another, unvaried, like time in a halted season. Whether he rode on state business, or journeyed to foreign capitals on the king's behalf, or hunted, or inspected herds of cattle and horses, or visited fisheries and slate works, whether he sat with the counsel barons to discuss taxation, or shipping, or the king's justice, he moved with a sense that time was suspended, that life had paused, as though by enchantment, on one sunny afternoon of a day without morning and without evening. He was neither unhappy nor happy. He was simply going from one place to another through the mild, friendly, uninvigorating climate of consent.

One day shortly after the feast of the New Year a cold wind blew over the coast from the northwest. It carried the smell of grey sea and grey rock, of wild water breaking in thunder on a rugged shore. And Tristram felt it on his face with a pang of remembrance. He thought of Tintagel head, and how the tides crashed upon its colored cliffs and roared into its caves. He thought how the gales shrieked around the castle walls, and how the furze on the headland shook and rattled, and how the branches of the yew trees streamed all eastward, and how the sheep planted their feet and hung their heads, enduring the weather which was their element. Oh, Cornwall! It was Isoud's land, and it was forbidden him! For a moment he longed to forget Isoud. But if he forgot her, what would remain of his life? His service to the queen of Cornwall was in him like prayer, like the love of God. And circumstance could not move it any more than circumstance could move God's love, even if circumstance were absence and marriage and a position of state in Britany.

He was restless, and went to the church hoping to find there some medicine for the throb of recollection which had roused him from the contented stupor of his existence. Hoël's church was a low stone building altogether unlike the churches Tristram knew best, Mark's and that of the Irish priests. It was roofed with high, steep slopes of thatch ending in heavy eaves. And as Tristram approached it he looked at it with dislike, thinking it was foreign and strange and without grace.

Nevertheless he went in. The interior was dim, but not so dim he failed to see Yseut. She was kneeling before the altar, and she was weeping.

"What are you doing here?" he said.

"Oh, Tristram!" She rose hastily and clutched her cloak around her. "You shouldn't have stolen on me without warning."

"I didn't mean to frighten you, Yseut. Tell me what is wrong."

"Nothing. I was saying prayers."

"Come outside."

"I hate the wind," Yseut said.

Tristram took her hand. "My dear lady, if you have a trouble, you should tell me."

The tears brimmed again into her eyes. "I don't know, Tristram. Sometimes I think I don't—don't make you glad you came back to Britany."

"Now that is a foolish worry." He put a finger under her chin and raised her face. "The weather has depressed you. You're cold too. Even your chin is cold. We'll go home, and I'll send for warm wine to drink."

"Are you sure you're glad you came back?"

"Of course." He took her by the hand and led her over the winter grass.

"I'll be wiser, Tristram. I'll study with my priest and learn all the things you know."

"You please me the way you are. I don't want you to do anything you'd rather not."

She clung to him, hard to reassure. Afterwards Tristram wondered what he had done to hurt her. And he tried to be especially tender with her, hoping to soothe a grief whose reason he did not understand. This required him to subdue his temperament somewhat, for he was not suited to deal with melancholy or with vague emotional fevers. Yseut's charm lay in even spirits and the cheerful rattle with which she surrounded her duties. And when she sighed, when she demanded whether he was sure he loved her, he felt at first helpless, and next impatient, and finally short-tempered. Then he must escape from her and from the overheated atmosphere which he hated to think might be cleared by a quarrel.

Yet Yseut did not persist in her mood, whatever caused it. She was restored in time. But something between them had changed. It was as though she had made up her mind to transform herself and meet some conception of Yseut she believed, or hoped, he held. She made new efforts with the priest, trying to interest herself in history and music, and to shape her soft mouth around the syllables of the languages she wished to master. She reported her progress earnestly to her husband, asking him whether he was not pleased to see her learn so much. She was attentive to visitors at court, and pressed them with questions, and talked wisely of war and politics. She paid particular attention to her appearance, wearing rich stuffs and heavy jewels not quite becoming to her slight figure and her fresh, girlish manners. And in love she strove for a new warmth. In these ways she who had been a simple lady endeavored to become a woman of the world.

But for all her attempts the princess of Britany remained a person whose character was set in its own unique mold. Her artless innocence was her genius. And when she reached for the powers wisdom and seduction might yield, she obscured her natural gifts without attaining new ones. By the time she had been married a year the outward signs of her life were changed. And

336

what was inward, what rose from her guileless spirit, looked from her eyes doubtfully, as though she asked to be forgiven for flaws she herself did not understand.

In the second summer of their marriage an accident of government separated Tristram and Yseut for a month. Before dawn one morning harbor guards roused the castle with the cry of pirates. A fleet of fast small boats was attacking a ship from Britain whose cargo was woolen cloth. Tristram armed and rode down to the waterside with Hoël, and took command of a vessel which they hoped was light and maneuverable enough to overtake the marauders and return them to the shore for justice. But the pirates had an hour's start, and were sailing craft exactly designed to scud before pursuit. And although Tristram chased them north across the Narrow Seas as far as the coast of Lyonesse, he lost them at dusk and knew they were beyond capture. He ordered his own boat into harbor to wait for morning and fresh purveyance from the port of Lyonesse.

Daylight showed him shores he had never forgotten, marsh grass rippling in the breeze, and birds flying, and low uplands where the smoke of peat fires was rising. The sight of laborers in brown kilts, bare to the waist and bronzed with sun, stung him with homesickness. He called the helmsman, put the ship in his charge, gave him messages for Hoël and the princess, and went ashore. He secured a horse and began to ride north to his father's house, slowly experiencing again the colors and odors of his own land.

He hardly intended to linger in Lyonesse, but one warm day passed into another, and he did not leave. Something about the shabby court, and the stooped figure of Meliodas, and the dogs, and the rude existence of the barons charmed and held him. Besides, Cornwall was near, only a short few days to the north. And in Cornwall Isoud lived and thought of him, perhaps, as he thought of her. He asked Meliodas' priest what was the news of Cornwall, and learned that Mark's knights were discontented, divided among themselves into quarrelling parties, some of them almost openly rebellious. And the queen, how was she?

"They say," the priest told him, "that the queen holds all together still. They say it is for love of her that the barons do not rise."

"Is her beauty untouched?"

"Always they speak of her beauty, my lord, and so it must be untouched."

"And how are matters with the king?"

The priest shook his head. "He keeps to the castle. He does not seem to care that his country is loosely ruled and in turmoil. They say he does not hunt any more, or maintain his forts, or mend his shipping. They say he does not even give the king's justice unless causes are brought to him at Tintagel. Travellers who come to us from Cornwall say openly that Mark is a bad king, indifferent to everything except his wife."

"Ah!" Tristram said.

"Women can destroy us when they are beautiful," the priest said with a sigh.

Tristram delayed in Lyonesse because he could not make up his mind to return to Britany without seeing Isoud. And as he thought of one means after another to reach her he received a message from King Hoël. "If you are well and able to travel," the king wrote, "you are needed at home."

It was a summons he must answer one way or another, a reminder no less firm for being courteous that he was not free to wander rootless about the country of his past. Did he want his freedom? Freedom was meaningless without Isoud. And Isoud was now, as she had been, beyond attaining.

He took ship and sailed back to Britany. Hoël welcomed him gravely. "We were concerned for you," he said.

"I have not visited my father since I was a squire," Tristram told him a little defensively.

"Is he well?"

"Older," Tristram said.

"Yes," Hoël answered, "that must happen. Did Meliodas ask you to remain? Was your delay the result of your having to make a decision, Tristram?"

Tristram felt invaded by the question, seeing beyond it a fear Hoël might have suffered that he was still moved by Isoud. "I delayed because Lyonesse was pleasant and I felt at home," he said.

"You have friends in Britany who hope your home is here."

"I know, my lord. I am sorry if my absence troubled you."

"It troubled the princess."

"I will see her," Tristram said.

He found Yseut worn and pale as though she had been ill. "I thought you would never come back," she said.

"I sent messages. Didn't you receive them?"

"The sailors said you were in Lyonesse."

"So I was," he told her. "The pirates escaped us, and since I had gone so far I had a notion to see my own land again, and my father."

"What did you do in Lyonesse, Tristram?"

"Nothing important—looked at it, and thought about an old tutor I had when I was a child, and found that few people remembered me."

Because she was thin her dark eyes were enormous in her face. "A month is a long time," she said slowly, "to spend doing nothing."

"Doing nothing takes longer than anything else," he said, making a joke of it. "Don't you realize that?"

"You might have ridden into Cornwall, mightn't you?"

"I might have."

"Did you?"

He was angry. "No."

"You must not leave me so strangely again, Tristram. It is not fitting that the court should wonder where my husband is, and why he goes from me."

Tristram was silent. Her reference to Cornwall had cut so close to his own thoughts that he felt almost as though she had looked within him and read him. But nothing in his marriage required him to think only Yseut's thoughts, did it? His own held no treachery to her. How did he fail her if he remembered Cornwall, and the castle there, and Isoud standing on the cliff in a green gown, the wind blowing her hair?

On other days Yseut spoke of his journey, and of Lyonesse. She asked him to tell her about Lyonesse, and about what he had seen there, and about what he remembered of it from his childhood. He found these questions difficult to answer, even to endure patiently. And he replied to them briefly or not at all. He fell into the habit of silence, not only about Lyonesse, but about many matters upon which she queried him. For he had a sense that her curiosity was aimed at something different and deeper than the subjects she touched, as though she might enter his mind and see what lay there beyond telling.

Yet he could not live with her in churlish muteness. He wished to serve her if he could, and to assure for her at least as much content as it was possible to wring from life. He tried to inspire her old gaiety, to lead her once more into the simple joy which was the best part of her spirit. Sometimes as he wandered along the waterside with a hunting dog for a companion he would find himself thinking beyond her of women as a special race. And he would ask himself whether their view, being limited by their duties, was the more intense for its narrow horizon; and whether their happiness, feeding on trifles, was the more delicate and rarefied for this diet. He had reached the condition of experience as a husband which allowed him to generalize the nature of all women from the nature of his wife. All women save Isoud, she who was incomparable.

As time passed Yseut grew less tolerant of his silences. On some evenings when they had gone together to their chamber, when she sat under the wicklight embroidering with colored threads and he stared into the fire or into nothingness, she would ask him what he thought of.

"You are not here, my lord," she said. "You leave me when you turn moody and morose."

"I'm not morose, Yseut."

"But you have pulled your mouth down in a great frown. Why do you frown, Tristram?"

340

"Was I frowning? It is only that my eyes are tired of the fire."

"You were thinking of something you do not wish to tell me."

"I was thinking we shall need more horses for the mounted soldiers in the spring. And I was wondering what farms I would see about them."

"And why should horses make you frown?"

"Believe me," he said, "I was not frowning."

She was silent a little while. "Tell me about Ireland," she said.

"I have told you many times about Ireland."

"No," she said, "when I ask about it, you tell of ships, or priests, or birds flying from cliffs."

"Those things are Ireland."

"You never tell me about the people," she said.

"Irish people are friendly and pleasant."

"Friendlier and more pleasant than our Bretons?"

"Perhaps in a different way."

"Tell me about some special person, one person you remember more than others."

"I have forgotten the people I knew in Ireland."

"Even the king?"

"Yes."

"I do not believe, Tristram," Yseut said, "that you have forgotten the king of Ireland, or anyone else you knew there, either."

"What is this thirst for Ireland? Why must we always speak of Ireland? Let me tell you about Camelot."

"Very well, my lord," she said. "Tell me about Camelot."

Tristram described the walled city, and its street of shops, and Arthur's tower standing on the hill, and said how the sun gilded its windows with gold and scarlet in the late afternoon. "I saw Camelot first at sundown," he said, "when the windows were burning with evening fire."

"Did you see the Round Table?"

"Yes. And I thought of you when I saw it. I remembered how I told you when I was a squire I would sit at the Round Table someday and be Arthur's man."

Yseut was silent. She was silent so long that presently Tristram became aware of the stillness in the room, and looked through the flickering firelight at her, and saw she was sitting with her head bowed, her work dropped. He heard the soft lipping of the flames, and the silvery tinkle of the embers, small sounds to emerge so loudly in the silence between them.

"What is it, Yseut?"

"You do not love me, Tristram." Her voice had lost its bright insistence. She spoke with a kind of heavy quiet.

"I have given you my faith."

"You are kind," she said, "and you are true. And you have been my husband for a year and a half." She leaned forward and covered her face with her hands. "Oh," she said, "I am tired."

"My dear lady—"

"I have hoped and hoped," she said. "I have prayed and prayed. I have held up my spirits for you, and let you go free. But now I know you will never love me, and I am tired."

"Yseut, Yseut!"

"I even know you would like to love me. And that is why I have hoped so long."

"What can I do for you I haven't done? Tell me what you want of me."

"What she has," Yseut said. "What Isoud of Ireland has."

The name fell between them like a sword. Tristram had never spoken it to her or to anyone in Britany save Gouvernail. And Yseut had never spoken it. Yet it had lain under their lives as the earth itself lay under them, horizon wide and deep beyond measuring. As Tristram heard it, Isoud of Ireland, he knew the summer peace he had shared with Yseut was a dream.

"What is she," Yseut said, "that you can't forget her?"

"I can't talk of her."

"Is she so beautiful? Is she taller than I, or more slender? Is she fair? How is she different from me, Tristram?"

He rose. "I am your husband, Yseut. Let us speak of other things."

"Is her love more than mine? Does she care for your happiness beyond my care?"

342

"I must leave you."

"Wait, Tristram!" She sprang up and caught him by the arms. "I have asked myself these questions until I am blind. You must tell me what Isoud of Ireland is, how she is different from me."

"I can't tell you."

"One thing! Tell me only one thing. One little thing. Tell me what you remember."

Trembling, he put her hands from him and left her. The trance of content in which he had lived in Britany was shattered, and every protective web of his cocoon torn away. As he fled through the house he could hear Yseut's voice in his ears saying again and again, "Tell me!" And he saw her suffering, how her gaiety and her pertness and her proud babble of work to be done had covered a grief whose soreness he had not even glimpsed. He had been cruel to her, he was the first person from whom she had ever taken cruelty, and now it made no difference that he had thought of her happiness and wished to shield it.

Nothing made any difference, not even her suffering or his. He was bound to Isoud. Isoud was Tristram, and Tristram Isoud. The tie was beyond appeal. I must see her, he thought, if I die for it. I will see her, and I will willingly die.

Chapter Thirty-three

At daybreak Tristram left the castle and spent the day riding alone. He tried to make a plan by which he could tell Hoël of his decision to return to Britain. He knew well enough that no plan could make his departure plausible or acceptable. He was retreating from honors the king had given him, and from a life of peace and stability. And Hoël would find him less than he had hoped, wilful at best, at worst treacherous to his word and to Yseut. Well. If honorable conduct was possible in dishonor, he could only say to Hoël that he was going. And whatever consequences that had, he must take them.

But as it happened he did not have cause to uncover for the king of Britany the breach between himself and Yseut, and the decision come of it. For when he returned to the castle in the chilly dusk he found messengers waiting for him. They were two barons he knew, and they came from Cornwall.

"Before you see them," Hoël told him, "let me speak with you." And he led Tristram into the withdrawing room of the queen. The queen was absent, but her work stood on its frame, and a fire of peat bricks was burning on the hearth.

"When did they arrive?" Tristram asked.

"On the flood tide. They have been waiting for you since about the hour of nones."

"Is it a plot? Are they sent to take me?"

"Two Cornish barons?" Hoël spread his hands. "It may be a

plot, but they are not simple enough to think they can take you from this court like a felon."

"I should be glad to have them try," Tristram said.

"They have talked freely to me, Tristram. Their errand is no secret. You are sent for by King Mark to relieve him. His country has risen, and there is civil war."

"King Mark!"

"I was as surprised as you are. But he sends you offers of accord and safe-conduct. They say he made oath in the church before his loyal barons that he would receive you in friendship, and that your life would be held sacred."

"God's green hills!" Tristram breathed. "My uncle must be in trouble over his ears and eyes if he sends for me!"

"That," Hoël said, "or the barons are suborned."

"You think it is treachery?"

Hoël was silent a minute. Then he said, "I don't believe it matters whether or not it is treachery, Tristram. If you return to Cornwall you take the better part of Britany with you. And you know without my asking whether you will return to us."

"I am sworn as a knight to give help when help is asked, my lord."

"Yes," Hoël answered him slowly, "you are sworn. Unless it is treachery."

Tristram knew the king was asking him to weigh his duty in Britany against his duty in Cornwall. But he could not think of his duty now, for within him was a joy beyond duty, beyond gratitude, beyond the faith he owed to the man who had bred him and honored him and made him a prince. He could return to Isoud. Past the hope of his return he could see nothing.

"I shall speak to the barons," he said.

"Yes, you must. If it is treachery you are clear. If it is not treachery," Hoël said, "you must decide, as God gives you strength to decide, what faith claims you most."

They looked into each other's faces a moment, and it came over Tristram that he could tell Hoël how he had tried to subdue himself for the sake of Britany, and Hoël's own lordship, and

Yseut, and how he had failed. But he knew this was an illusion. He knew well enough that, though Hoël loved him, he loved his land more, and beyond his land, his child, Yseut. Tristram's honors had been given for Yseut's sake. He had understood that in the beginning when he was sent on his mission to the garrisons. Nothing had changed since then—nothing except that now he could return to Isoud. He could not plead his case with Hoël unless he added hypocrisy to broken faith. For he knew, even if the king did not, that even before the messengers arrived he had determined to go back to Cornwall.

"Will you come with me and question the barons?" he asked.

"No, Tristram. Here is a matter you must decide yourself."

Feeling he had said farewell to friend already lost, Tristram went into the hall.

"Welcome, my lords," he said. "We have not met since we parted at the church on the cliffs."

"We must accept your reminder, my lord," a baron named Bruel said, "since our king has need of you."

"Tell me his need."

"Four of his barons have revolted and raised the country toward the south against him. He is beleaguered in Tintagel and requires a champion. He asks us to tell you you have a duty of blood to relieve him."

Tristram questioned them closely about what barons had risen, and with how many men, and where they had fought, and how prevailed. As he drew from them the details, pressing them for actual figures of fighting strength, he began to doubt that Mark was as sorely beset as they reported. The rising appeared to be genuine enough, but it seemed small, easily put down by a resolute show of strength from Tintagel. The king's forces were neglected, but not in a condition unfitting them to fight. Treachery? It began to wear the color of treachery.

"Do you doubt us, my lord?" Bruel asked him.

"I have reason not to believe you too soon, my lords."

"The queen has sent you a message," Bruel said. And he handed Tristram a parchment, folded and sealed.

Tristram moved away from them and, turning his back, opened Isoud's letter. Nothing was written on the parchment. Within was a stamp of wax fastening to the sheet the two ends of a thread. And from the thread hung the little gold ring Tristram had given her in Ireland. If you need me, he had told her, send me the ring, and I shall come to you. He detached the golden circlet, remembering as he touched the filigree how the goldsmith had said, "It will live like a glowworm under the sod," and remembering more, remembering how he had kissed Isoud under the ash tree and how she said, "If God is good we shall meet again."

He put the ring into the pouch at his belt, and folding the parchment, turned back to Mark's emissaries. "The queen informs me that she saw the king take oath to be accorded with me. She says you bring me safe-conduct. Let me see it, my lords."

The barons produced a second parchment, this one bearing the signature and seal of King Mark. It was a safe-conduct, and testified to the king's oath. The document was in order, yet Tristram knew it was only as trustworthy as Mark's mind when he made it.

"When do you return to Cornwall?" he asked Bruel.

"At high tide, my lord, three hours after midnight."

"I shall sail with you."

He received their thanks, and ordered hospitality for them, and left them, and returned to King Hoël. He told Hoël how he had questioned the messengers, and showed him the safe-conduct. "I think my uncle could put down this revolt himself," he said, "except that he has lost his will to defend himself. He has sent for me in the name of our common blood."

"And you will go?"

"I shall go, my lord."

Hoël was a man who recognized when the time for talk was past. He heard Tristram's decision in silence. "God go with you, Tristram," he said.

Tristram had no words either. He went to his own quarters to tell Yseut what had happened. He had not been with her for twenty-four hours, not since she had questioned him about Isoud.

347

He could see that she had wept, but now her tears were spent, and she was calm.

"You know messengers are here from Cornwall, Yseut?"

"Yes?"

"And that I am sent for to deliver my uncle?"

"I have heard it, Tristram."

"We sail on the high tide."

"I have done this," she said, "haven't I?"

"War is my business, Yseut. And this war is my duty as well."

"But you were going," she said, "before the barons brought King Mark's message."

"Let us forget what is past, my dear lady."

She rose and took his hands. "Forget it if you can, Tristram. I shall never forget you."

"You speak as though I—would—never—" but he could not bring himself to promise, even by indirection, that he would return. "No one knows the fortunes of war, Yseut. I can't say—I don't know—what will happen."

"Will you kiss me good-by, Tristram?"

He kissed her. When he left her he was trembling with shame and sorrow, remembering how she had deserved nothing but good from him, how she had driven herself to please him, how she loved him. As he loved Isoud? As much as she could, at least, and beyond the whole of love, love could not be measured. His mind floundered in the trap which had caught her and him too, longing to ease her pain, and knowing it could not be eased.

He could hardly endure the dragging hours before flood tide, and only got through them because they could be spent in preparation for his journey. Though Hoël offered him soldiers he refused. He was required to accept arms, since he had come into Britany naked of even a sword. But save for arms he departed as he had come, with nothing.

In the boat he and Gouvernail kept to themselves, apart from Mark's couriers. The squire was a silent companion. At last Tristram said, "Are you doubtful of this enterprise, Gouvernail?"

"No more than of any enterprise."

"I have jumped ahead of death nimbly enough, haven't I?" Tristram asked him. "We've come through some narrow passes in our day."

Gouvernail made no answer.

"My friends have never been so willing to sing my dirge as now," Tristram said, angry.

"Perhaps," Gouvernail said, "that is because we have never had friends until now."

"Britany—" Tristram said, and broke off. For a moment he was swamped under the multiplying confusions of life, the high intentions which bred ill, the betrayals not meant to betray, the joys whose fruit was sorrow. Knighthood. Was it a name to cover guilt and shame?

In the dark Tristram heard Gouvernail draw a slow breath. "We do what we must," he said. "I spoke like a churl, Tristram."

"The queen sent for me."

"I'll tell you something. I liked Britany. I hoped we would remain, and live out our lives there. But if the queen had sent for me I would be sitting where you are sitting now. I am a squire," Gouvernail said in a low voice, "but I have seen the queen too. And remembered her."

"She is unforgettable."

"Yes," Gouvernail murmured, "when you have drunk the wine."

The brotherhood between them was restored. Presently they wrapped themselves in their cloaks and slept. And when their journey was over, when they came ashore on the sand beach below Tintagel head, they were men who dared no longer torment themselves with the griefs of the past, because their present was danger, and danger was the profession they were bred to.

"I appointed men to meet us here with horses," Bruel said, walking back and forth on the empty sand to stretch his legs.

"Horsemen are coming through the trees," Tristram said. "At least one horseman is."

They stared into the woods covering the slope above the beach. They could see only a single rider. As he emerged and the sun fell upon the black flanks of his mount, Tristram flung his shield onto his shoulder and unsheathed his sword. He knew the black horse, and the man who rode it, though the rider no longer wore the scarlet war trousers of the Scythians. Palamides was dressed in kilts of Mark's color, but he carried his own shield.

"It is the Saracen," Bruel said. "He is our baron now. Don't draw your sword against Palamides, my lord."

Palamides trotted his horse to the edge of the sand and dismounted. He dressed his shield and pulled his blade from its scabbard. "Guard yourself, Tristram," he said. "I have been waiting for you. And today we must fight to the uttermost."

"He is under a safe-conduct," Gouvernail said. "You break the king's peace."

But Palamides was advancing, his red mouth drawn tight against his teeth. With a lifting sense of joy Tristram recognized the light of war in his eyes, burning hot, and his great moustaches gleaming like dagger points. Calmly he assessed the ground upon which they would battle, learning where the sand was hard and would help him and where it would sink and shift. "Come on, my lord," he called. "I am ready for you."

He was aware that Bruel and his companion were running back to the boat. But he did not watch them or think of them, for Palamides had begun to try him, right and left, probing his guard. I know you, brother, Tristram told himself, you press too soon and too fast. Come on, come forward! You make me happy! And when you think you have me, I shall have you.

Palamides did not fight as Tristram had learned to expect. Usually he liked to drive his man back, make him defend himself going away, but today he began with feints, with half-strokes meant to draw Tristram in. Now they were doing something they had never done before, circling each other warily, waiting for their chance for counter blows. "The baptismal water has made you stiff," Tristram cried to him. "You fight like a priest, my lord."

Oh, it was good to have an enemy at the end of his sword! Tristram could feel his life awake within him as though from a long and torpid sleep. He saw the sun on the yellow sand, and heard the sea rumbling on the cliff to the north of them, and

350

knew the gulls were floating in silvery circles over the blue. Everything had become new, everything had become shining and fresh for this hour. He was fighting like a genius, observing his own skill with delight, applauding every subtle turn of his sword. I have missed you, Palamides, he thought. I needed you in Britany.

Palamides was sweating, and Tristram saw, fascinated, a drop form on the point of his moustache and fall. The Saracen fought with grunts and cries—that was familiar too. Now he had become angry. Now he began to press. Now I shall take you, Tristram thought, but his lunge missed, and Palamides leaped back with a laugh. *"You* fight like a Frenchman," he said. And with rapid thrusts he pushed Tristram into the soft sand.

Tristram moved deeper into the sand drawing Palamides after him. If he must flounder to escape the bad ground, Palamides must too. Because they had lost good footing they must strike and endure heavier blows. Tristram saw blood on his sword, high, close to his hand. He realized it was not Palamides' blood but his own. He did not feel the wound, could not tell where he had been hit. But he saw the Saracen's grin of wicked joy, and knew he had seen the blood too.

"Turn, Tristram!" Gouvernail shouted. "To your right!"

Tristram labored through the sand to his right. The muscles in his legs were taut and trembling from the effort he had made on shifting ground. Fighting more carefully he forced the turn and worked up the beach and felt hard earth under him. Sweat ran into his own eyes, and he was blowing for breath. But so was the Saracen.

Now neither wished to give ground. Each forced the other to take the heaviest blows he could deliver on his sword or shield, or on his body. Tristram could feel his breath hiss from his lungs with the strokes Palamides laid to his chest and sides. He was fighting in a rainbow mist. He was bloody, and the Saracen was bloody, and he did not know whose flesh had been opened.

As he moved slowly, trying to keep Palamides on the left, he became aware that the sun was lying right on the horizon between the sea and the sky. Why? What caused the sun to set in mid-

351

afternoon? It was setting. The beach was orange in the late light, and his shadow and Palamides' moved long on the sand. When Tristram thought of the sun next, his body cast no shadow at all, and a grey veil seemed to hang over the shore.

"Truce," Palamides said.

"Hold your sword first."

Palamides lowered his blade. "Ugh! I am blown. We have fought the sun under, Tristram."

"Do you yield, brother?"

"Do you? If you have a will to fight in the dark, why, let us fight."

"How long have we fought?"

"Two hours," Palamides said.

"Set the day and the place," Tristram said, "and I shall meet you and finish what we have begun."

Palamides flung his sword from him and sat down on a stone. He was panting like a spent animal. He propped his elbows on his knees and held his face in his hands. "I shall never encounter with you again, Tristram."

"Then yield now."

"Come here and I shall tell you something."

Tristram approached him, still gripping his sword.

"I am forsworn," Palamides said. "I have broken the king's peace, and I have broken my promise to the lady Isoud. But I do not yield. Finish the fight and kill me."

"You ask to be killed," Tristram said, "to the point of monotony. If I had meant to kill you unarmed I would have done it long ago."

Tears began to fall from the Saracen's eyes. "I have lost what I desire most in the world. I have lost the friendship of the lady Isoud, and I have lost my fellowship with you, Lord Tristram."

"What ails you?"

"Isoud sent me here to meet and protect you."

"Protect me! Me?"

"You would have been ambushed," Palamides said.

"Oh! So my uncle was dealing in treachery after all!"

352

"Not when he sent Bruel to Britany with the safe-conduct. He was frightened then because a baron had tried to kill him. But now he has strengthened Tintagel, and he feels secure, and he sent two men to murder you as you came up the trail."

"Isoud knew this?"

Palamides nodded, yes. Exhausted, he stretched out his legs and dropped his arms. In the failing light he looked diminished, beaten. "She learned it, and she sent me to protect you."

"Where are these fellows now?"

"Dead," Palamides said. "I ended their mission."

"I owe you thanks, brother."

"I would have killed you if I could, Tristram. Isoud is waiting for you, and I would have killed you."

"Well," Tristram said, "it was a worthy intention, but it failed. Now rise and arm yourself, and between us we shall think of a way to pull the king out of Tintagel and ask him a few questions."

"He is guarded with eight troops of foot, and five troops of mounted yeomen. We shall not pull him out of Tintagel tonight."

"I admit, that makes it difficult. What did you mean when you said the queen was waiting for me?"

"She has fled from the king, and she is in the church on the cliff."

Tristram pulled him up from the stone. "Fled! How? Does Mark know? Why didn't you tell me this two hours ago!"

"The foot soldiers helped her. Any man in Tintagel would help her. They passed her through their guard. And I myself took her to the church."

"Mark—"

"Mark is drunk," Palamides said.

"Gouvernail!" Tristram cried. "We must have horses."

"There are horses in the forest," Palamides said, "tied at the head of the trail."

"Who planned this?"

"Isoud planned it when she learned you were to be ambushed. And I executed it. Only," the Saracen said, wrenching himself from Tristram's hands, "I meant to kill you. And now I have lost

353

the queen's trust, and I have lost my honor with you, and I wish nothing except to die."

"Come with me to the queen and I'll speak for you."

But Palamides would not. He searched about on the dark sand and found his sword and sheathed it, and, groaning with fatigue and the smart of his wounds, mounted his horse. "Farewell, Tristram. We shall never meet again in this world."

"Where will you go, brother?"

The Saracen knight gave him no answer. He turned his horse and rode into the woods. For a moment they heard him on the trail, and then they heard nothing but the heavy voice of the sea. As Tristram watched him go his heart moved strangely, and tears stung his eyes. The Saracen owned a sort of greatness, something a man must finally love.

"He would have killed you," Gouvernail said, "but—"

"Yes," Tristram said, "but—" And they were silent.

At last Tristram said, "Where are Bruel and his fellow, Gouvernail?"

"In the boat, I suppose."

"Let us get off before they come ashore."

"You are wounded, Tristram."

"My shoulder is cut, but it is slight. Come on, man! We must hurry."

They clambered up the ascending trail. Here night had shut down, and they could see only a little distance before them. But they knew this path, and in a few minutes they had reached the top. They found horses, as Palamides promised.

Tristram was winded and his legs were shaking under him. But his fatigue was nothing, and his wound was nothing, and the possibility that a new ambush might have been laid was nothing. He did not fear Mark and all his troops of foot and yeomen, or Bruel, or the bodiless things haunting the night. Isoud was waiting for him, she whose beauty healed his broken body and strengthened his imperfect soul until he could prevail against all the threats of Cornwall, and all the evil of the world.

354

Chapter Thirty-four

AT the church Tristram said, "Wait for me, Gouvernail. I wish to go in alone."

"I shall wait, Tristram."

He dismounted and moved into the black door. He would have spoken her name, but he could not. She came into his arms. They held each other in silence, tears on their lips as they kissed.

"I sent you the ring," she whispered, "and afterwards I was afraid it called you home to your death."

"I was coming before you sent the ring."

"Tristram!"

"I love you."

"Often," she murmured, "we stood on our shores looking across the sea into each other's hearts."

"Every day."

"Did you think we would meet?"

"Yes," he said.

"So did I. I love you, my dear lord."

"You must come with me."

"Wherever you take me."

"It is a long way."

"You told me once we would live in the forest, and you would make me a fur cloak."

"Do you remember the cave, Isoud?"

"I remember it."

355

"Someday," he said, "when we are old, we shall come back to the cave. Only you will never be old, Isoud."

"You will never be old either, Tristram."

"Are you frightened?"

"I am trembling," she said. "I trembled when we said we would never be old."

"We must leave here," he said. "This is a cold place." He drew her cloak around her and led her outside. "Gouvernail is with me. We have horses."

"Where are we going, Tristram?"

"Into Britain. First to Camelot, and then into the north. Once Launcelot offered me haven in Joyous Gard. We are going to Joyous Gard."

"I must speak to Gouvernail."

"I am here, my lady," the squire said.

In the dark Isoud found his hand. "You have been our friend, Gouvernail. I give you my loving thanks."

"I am glad," the squire stammered, feeling his hand in the queen's, "I am glad if I could serve you, my lady."

Tristram mounted her before him on his own horse. "We have a rough ride ahead, Isoud, and we cannot stop until we have crossed the border into Britain."

"I know."

"We'll find fresh horses when we can."

"And if we can't find horses," she said, "we shall walk to Camelot."

They followed the cliff north, having the light of a starry sky to guide them. Tristram had the need of seeking landmarks, remembering that above Tintagel Cornwall narrowed into a long finger of land lying between the sea and Britain, and that when he reached this finger he must turn east. If they pushed on steadily, if the horse endured its double burden, if he found the point he hoped for, they would be in Britain by daybreak, or so near it they could begin to feel safe. Safe? Mark would follow them. And he had a cause against them which would stretch beyond the boundaries of Cornwall. It was a crime for any man to steal any woman. But it was a capital crime to steal the wife of a king, a crime for which they could be pursued and brought home for justice. Yet Tristram did not believe Mark would overtake them. They were together. And together they were strong enough to influence fortune and bend it to protect them.

He told their progress by the constellations. They reached their eastward turn in good time, and rode for a while through the forest, slower here because he had to find gaps in the trees above which he could see the heavens. Then they were on moorland, riding against a wind rushing upon them from many directions, blowing the gorse and whistling over the crest of low hills. Moor or forest, hills or streams, all of nature was their friend on this night when they had returned to each other, even the owls speaking ghostly to them, even the foxes running like shadows and turning to bark from a safe distance.

At sunrise they rode into a wide valley where sheep were grazing. They learned from the shepherd that a farm was near, and from the farmer they asked food and rest. At midmorning they rose, and bargained for fresh horses, and rode on toward Camelot. In this way, riding both day and night, resting when they could, they reached Arthur's city. Here they took shelter in an inn, and lingered a day and a night. And here Tristram and Isoud turned to each other in love, and pledged their faith new, swearing each to the other that nothing would part them as long as life was in their hearts.

Tristram sent a message to Dinadan saying where he was, and asking Dinadan, if he was in Camelot, to come to him. In an hour the little knight was at the inn.

"I was never so glad to see any man as I am you, Tristram. Why didn't you ride to the castle?"

"I don't wish it known that I'm here."

"Why? Are you playing another of your wild games, my son?"

"I haven't much time, but I'll tell you," Tristram said. And he described to Dinadan what had passed in Britany, and how he had come back to Cornwall, and how he had fought Palamides and learned of the ambush of the king. "Isoud is with me," he finished, "and I am taking her to Joyous Gard."

"Ah, Tristram! You will die for this lady of yours."

"If I die," Tristram said, "I shall have been alive first. I have learned something, Dinadan. I have learned that death is an empty word if, before you die, you have lived all of life that is given to live—even for one short hour."

"It sounds like poetry," Dinadan said.

"You may laugh," Tristram said, "but unless you can tell me you do not envy me, brother, I shall not believe your laughter."

Dinadan shrugged, opened his mouth as if to speak, and was silent.

"Find me a man," Tristram said, "as fortunate as I."

"You are too big for me," Dinadan said. "I may live on a smaller scale than you, but I am a comfortable fellow. Comfort is my wife and my lady."

"Do something for me, brother."

"If I can without finding myself hanged."

Tristram laughed and put an arm around him. "This will not catch your head in a noose. Send a runner to Launcelot at Joyous Gard and tell him I am coming, and that I am bringing Isoud with me."

"You *are* a fortunate fellow," Dinadan said with an envious sigh. "Who but you could walk under Launcelot's shield? Mark can drag you out of any court in Britain, but not even Arthur would drag you out of Launcelot's hall."

"Come with me to Joyous Gard."

"No," Dinadan said, "this enterprise is not for me. I'm not against you, Tristram, but I am not on your side, either. You know well enough it is rash beyond all rashness to do what you are doing."

"Then," Tristram asked him, "are we to say farewell?"

"Yes." Dinadan reached up and laid his hands affectionately on Tristram's shoulders. "I cannot follow you to the end of your destiny, brother, except with love."

Tristram stood under Dinadan's hold feeling the grief of their parting. It would be the first of many, he realized, for he had chosen Isoud against the world. Only no other parting would hurt like this.

"You should know," Dinadan went on, "that Launcelot will soon leave Joyous Gard to undertake the quest of the Grail."

"Who goes on the quest?"

Dinadan gestured toward the castle. "All these fine fellows. They leave from Camelot after the feast of Pentecost."

"And you?"

Dinadan shook his head. "Like you, brother, that quest is too big for me."

"Good-by, Dinadan. God keep you."

"Good-by, Tristram. I shall never know a man of your cut in this world."

Tristram stood before the inn and watched Dinadan ride up the street of shops, and saw him turn and wave, and pass out of sight. And it came over him that, in one way, the life he lived with men was finished. In Palamides he had lost a noble enemy. And in Dinadan he had lost a faithful friend. The lords he had served were lost too, Hoël, and Anguissh of Ireland. Yet Isoud waited for him, she whose love transmitted all loss into gain. But still looking up the empty street Tristram sighed.

They secured good horses from the innkeeper, and bread and ale to carry with them. Their rest at Camelot had refreshed them a little, but more than rest restored them. For among them, Tristram and Isoud and Gouvernail, was stretched a fine sense of victory. They knew themselves invincible. And as they rode under the cool sun of Britain they rode through the winelike air of the first freedom they ever shared. Now the need to talk awakened in them, the desire to tell each other all that had passed since the day Tristram leaped from the church window into the sea. And now it seemed to them that the sorrow of their years apart had owned splendors of faith and courage, that a glory had attended them because always they had known they were moving toward their return. For unless they had been separated, how could they have felt the high, undefiled joy of this meeting? Unless their love had been interrupted, how could it renew itself with such pure fervor? Oh, they were fortunate, they were blessed! Now they marvelled to think how the accidents, the error and malice and suffering of life, had been their friends, and how all things had united for their happiness.

Their ride into the north was long, covering almost the whole span of Arthur's Britain. And as they passed through leagues of winter forests, through valleys where sheep and cattle foraged, and over hills and streams, Tristram told Isoud of the wars of the king, and how he had defeated Britain's enemies and made one land for its people. He sang the songs poets had made of Arthur's birth, and of his knighthood, and of his kingship. He made a new song in which he told how the wild animals of the forest taught Arthur cunning, badgers and foxes, and how hawks taught him sudden valor, and how he learned patience and the skill to read the souls of men from serpents, and how dogs and horses taught him faith. "The earth bred Arthur to be its true son," Tristram sang to Isoud, "so that he might rule the hearts of men with love and justice."

They took shelter at night with farmers or herdsmen, sometimes sharing a rude bed, sometimes lying under their cloaks on clean straw. There were nights when they loved and slept without dreams. And on other nights they turned to each other and whispered mirthfully of old things, past things, of Ireland, and of the dog Pickpocket, and of how they played the harp under the ash tree. Now their memories told them that all they had done together had been gay and beautiful, yet not so gay and beautiful as this ride into the north toward Joyous Gard.

At last they were travelling through rugged country, finding a slow way along narrow glens whose sides ascended so steeply they shut out the sky. Their horses labored forward breathing great clouds of steam into the icy air of the heights, their hooves ringing on the frozen ground as though on stone. On the tenth day after they left Camelot they came down from the frost-locked hills and reached a river winding to the north and east.

"We shall follow this river to the sea," Tristram told Isoud, "and when we have found the sea we shall be at Joyous Gard."

"I have been thinking," Isoud said, "that at Joyous Gard we shall see the spring return."

"Dinadan says Launcelot lives in more splendor even than King Arthur."

"Perhaps Queen Guenivere will come to Joyous Gard in the spring," Isoud said. "Perhaps we shall see her and speak with her, Tristram. Did you know Queen Guenivere wrote me a letter once, and sent it to me secretly, and that I still have it?"

"Did she! What did she say?"

"It was a secret," Isoud said primly, like a nun.

"Tell me what she wrote!"

"She wrote that she had seen you at Camelot, my lord, and that you were very large, and that your hair was red."

"Wonderful! She is an observant lady."

"She wrote me this," Isoud said, a slow smile curving her mouth. " 'There are only four lovers in Britain.' "

Tristram returned Isoud's proud smile, but he was silent. He was thinking of Launcelot, the tall, grey man who rode out in the morning alone, and returned alone at night. And of Guenivere who was still a queen. Four lovers in Britain? Why had not Guenivere dared what Isoud dared?

The river broadened as they rode east, sometimes opening into valley land, sometimes banked by rocky slopes. In the morning of the next day they began to smell the salt, and by noon they saw gulls wheeling, and a clean emptiness in the east which they knew meant they had reached the sea.

A grey stone wall enclosed Joyous Gard as well as its village and garrison. The house was grey too, strong and steep, as though it had grown from the earth's stone.

"We are met," Tristram said. "Dinadan's runner has been before us."

Six mounted yeomen in white and black kilts led them through the gate and dismounted them. Launcelot was a king in his own right, though not in Britain. His father held sovereignty in France, and most men knew, even if they did not say it, that Launcelot had given up his kingship for the sake of the lady Guenivere. Yet his blood allowed him to live in the north with kingly state. He maintained officers whose rank was royal in everything but name. And now his seneschal and chamberlain emerged from the castle to greet Tristram, and to bring the travellers to their lord.

"Welcome, Tristram," Launcelot said, "and you, my lady. I expected you."

"Before you receive us, my lord," Tristram said, "you must know we are fugitives. The lady Isoud is with me unlawfully."

"We are rustics here," Launcelot said with a smile, "and questions of law do not often reach us from the world. Baths are prepared for you, and when you have rested we shall meet in the hall." He moved to Isoud, and took her hand and kissed it, and stood looking down into her face. "I am your servant, my lady," he said.

Isoud gave him back his look, gravely sweet and courteous. But when she was alone with Tristram she came into his arms and pressed her head against his breast and wept.

"What is it, Isoud?"

"I did not know he would be so—" she sought for words—"so alone. You did not tell me truly what he is, Tristram."

"I told you he was noble and that all men loved him."

"He is like a wounded man," she said. "He is like a wounded knight who hides his wound."

"He seems to me strong and whole. He is older than we, Isoud."

"He has received us," she said, "because he has stopped believing in happiness and he wants to believe again."

Whatever was Launcelot's reason for offering them his protection, he was a good host to them. Through the first few days he remained at Joyous Gard, showing them the castle and telling them its history, leading them himself to see his horses and hawks, opening his armory, and introducing them to his priest who was a learned man and an artist. He gave them clothing, and presented a sword to Tristram, and to Isoud a carved jewel. And though he

362

talked with them, delighting them with his wit and charm, he asked them nothing of their story, and told them nothing of himself. He was content to make a seemly present for them almost as though his condition was that they should admit no past and anticipate no future. At Joyous Gard Launcelot had mastered the delicate art of today.

When a week had passed he left them to themselves. Sometimes at dawn Tristram would see him riding out of the courtyard, armed and alone. He might return in the evening, or he might be absent for several days together, coming home finally without explanation. But because of the miracle of his own peace with Isoud, because they were not haunted with danger and oppressed by fears, he could not think of Launcelot save now and then with gratitude, as a man who has no need to pray might remember God.

They lived at Joyous Gard with a happiness subdued from the tense fervor they had shared in Cornwall. This was in part because they had no need to run before discovery, but mostly it was because the north was here, cool, silvery, slow to fly its colors. Their world was brown and grey, touched sometimes by the sun and clear air into bronze or gold, but always muted. The spring did not return with great masses of flowers, with warm scents drifting on the air, with heavy sun and white moonlight. It came in small single blossoms pushing through dead leaves, in a slow green spreading from lawn to lawn, in high clouds floating seaward and melting into purple mist. They numbered its quiet signs, marvelling how it increased a little and a little until, one sudden morning, it set the fruit trees with blossoms, and roused the bees, and filled the woods with bird song.

"This is the first spring of the world," Isoud said.

"Yes—until next spring."

"I wish we could stop the world now, Tristram. I wish we did not wonder whether spring will come again next year."

"I don't wonder."

"I don't either," she told him. They were lying on the grass under a flowering tree, and now she moved and put her head in his lap, and her hair fell softly about her face. "I only said so to make this weather hurt us gently, so that we shall know how happy we are."

"Do you need to know?"

"Sometimes," she said, "I think we have been given all God can give His friends, Tristram. Sometimes I wonder what is left for us to have next week, and next year, and when we are old."

"That is a greedy thought, my dear lady."

"But a true one, isn't it?"

"If you say so."

"What are you thinking of?"

"Oh," he said, "of Pentecost. Launcelot begins his journey to Camelot tomorrow."

"Would you like to be riding on the Grail quest, Tristram?"

"No," he said slowly, "not exactly."

"What does 'not exactly' mean?"

"I don't understand the Grail quest," he said. "I do not know why men ride after something more than life. Life fills us, doesn't it?"

"But you think of the quest."

"I think of the knights gathering in Camelot."

Isoud was silent. Each knew well enough Tristram could not join his brothers at the Round Table, or ride on any quest. Yet they must not regret it. Here in Joyous Gard they had attained what they had hoped for since the day Tristram sailed into the harbor below King Anguissh's hall. And if it had a price they had known it must have a price, and they must hold their right to pay it a privilege. Isoud sat up and kissed him lightly. "Not a single shadow must fall on us, Tristram. Let us move into the sun."

As they were walking toward the sea they heard Launcelot call Tristram's name. He was running toward them, beckoning.

"What is it, my lord?" Tristram said.

"Messengers have come for you, Tristram." He drew even with them, and his face was set, stern, grey. His blue eyes looked at them, from Tristram to Isoud, compassionate, quiet.

"From Cornwall?"

"From Cornwall."

"I am not armed," Tristram said.

"The messengers are not armed," he said, and took Isoud by the hand and led her a little way aside. "I must speak to Tristram alone, my lady. Wait for us."

"Is it bad, Launcelot?" Tristram said. "Tell me quickly."

"It is King Mark himself."

"With soldiers?"

"No, only his squire. He has come to ask you to return to Cornwall and he swears your safety. The queen's too."

"He swore my safety once before, and ambushed me. I will not trust him."

"You must not trust him," Launcelot said with force. "But you must speak with him."

"Let us go, then."

Launcelot took him by the shoulders. "Remember, Tristram, a man has only one chance to prove whether he is to be trusted. And if he betrays his first chance he is never a safe friend. Remember!"

"I'll remember."

"He asks to speak with Isoud," Launcelot said. "And though you may not wish it, he will speak with her sooner or later. It had better be now."

"Let me tell her." Tristram went to Isoud and took her hands in his.

"I know," she said softly. "Mark is here."

"Did you hear us?"

"I see it in your face, Tristram. I am ready. Nothing can part us but death, my dear lord."

"Nothing, Isoud."

With Launcelot they passed over the green lawns and entered the castle of Joyous Gard. Tristram expected to see Mark old, worn, even ill. But he could not take into himself the figure standing before him. Mark was more than old. He was ruined, a man whose hands shook, and whose mouth trembled, and whose reddened eyelids sagged away from his eyes which were thickened and dead with tears. As he stood he supported himself on the arm of his squire.

"I have come in peace, Tristram," he said. "I am in great need. And I am lonely."

"My lord," Tristram stammered.

"The ambush on the shore was none of my doing," he said. "I agreed to it without understanding it. It was a move of the barons hostile to me."

"Tristram," Isoud said.

"But even if I had done it willingly," Mark said, and raised a fluttering hand to his face as though to steady his speech, "I have had the time to regret it. I have purged my soul before God. And I have travelled, ill as I am, to ask you myself to return to Cornwall, and to be my prince, and to take my affairs into your hand. I have come myself as an earnest of my faith."

"I dare not trust you," Tristram said.

Mark turned to Isoud. "My lady, I have only just learned of the wine you drank with Tristram. And I reproach you because you did not tell me. You have had enough courtesy from me to know I was not beyond comprehending your trouble."

"I am Tristram's," Isoud said.

"I know that now. Return with him to Cornwall. You shall be free. The two of you. I will not burden you."

They were silent. Launcelot stood aside watching Mark, watching Tristram too, his eyes beyond reading.

Mark fumbled at his belt and drew his short sword. Raising it, he kissed its hilt which was made in the shape of a cross. "I swear before you, Tristram, and before you, Launcelot, and before God who sees all our hearts, that I have come in peace and truth, and that no evil shall be done you in Cornwall." Again he solemnly kissed the hilt, and made before his breast the sign of Christ's cross. And he wept. "I need you," he said. "I am friendless."

"Ah!" Tristram's heart swelled with such a pity for this tottering, sunken old man that he could hardly rule himself. For years he had hated and feared Mark, knowing only that he was a treacherous enemy. Until this moment he had never seen him as a shattered victim of the love between himself and Isoud, he had never felt a sympathy for his pain. Now he beheld in Mark a man he had destroyed by his own youth, by his will to have what he must have. Now he remembered how he had sworn to bring Isoud into Cornwall for Mark's sake, and how he had failed his own promise, knightly given.

"My lord," he said, "if you will swear the queen's safety as you have sworn mine, if you will vow before Launcelot to yield your lands and your kingship to your barons forever if any evil comes to her, I shall return with you to Cornwall."

"Tristram," Launcelot said. "Remember."

"But he has purged his soul," Tristram said. "And he is my blood."

"Let him go, my lord," Isoud said to Launcelot. "It is time." For a moment they looked into each other's eyes, the fair young queen of Cornwall, and Launcelot, the grey knight whose goings and comings were solitude. "You leave on your quest tomorrow," Isoud said, "with all the knights of the Round Table. To quest is a knight's life. I am satisfied," she said, speaking to Launcelot as though no one were present but themselves. "We have God's whole blessing." And she moved to Launcelot and laid her hands on his breast. "Kiss me good-by, my lord."

Launcelot kissed her. "God shield you," he said, "since He made you brave."

In this way, because Tristram saw the destruction he had worked on the mind and body of King Mark, he returned to Cornwall, and with him Isoud. And in that high land of cliffs and sea they lived a little while in love and peace.

A little while. On a summer day Tristram and Isoud were sitting in the garden. Above them over the cliff edge they saw the gulls flying, and they heard the sea moving and speaking against the many-hued slates. It was a day when white clouds were riding on a warm west wind, when shadows ran silently over the gardens at Tintagel, and darkened for a moment the ancient yew trees, and then yielded their twisted branches again to the sun. It was a day when the scent of ripening fruit blew past them in fragrant drifts, when the smell of mowed grain and drying clover added a sense of harvest to the soft air. It was a day of peace and fulfillment.

"Are you content, Isoud?" Tristram said.

"Yes, my dear lord. Only I would be more content if you would sing to me."

Tristram's harp was leaning against the hedge of yew trees before which they were sitting. He picked it up, and kneeling by Isoud, he began to sing the song he had taught her in Ireland.

Something, his schooled sense of danger, told him his death had come, but it told him too late. The yews were thrust aside, and Mark stood above him with his short sword raised between his hands. Not seeing the king, Tristram leaped up. The sword took him fair between the shoulders, straight, deep.

"I love you," Tristram said, and fell forward upon his harp.

With a cry Isoud flung herself onto her knees and turned his body, and saw that his life was spent. And the knights who had run from the castle in pursuit of the king told among themselves, and to all the world afterwards, how she had stooped and kissed Tristram's mouth, and how, because she was an Irish lady, she had lamented him, and how, then, she had stretched herself beside him and died as he died, since her heart could not live after his. The knights told this story weeping, because Isoud was the most beautiful of all ladies, and because Tristram was the fairest and strongest knight of the world, save only Launcelot, who was seeking the Grail.

(1)